The Glebe Field

– a novel set in Cornwall

By
George Macpherson

*This is partly Hilary's work! Best wishes,
George Macpher—
Oct 2012*

*Cover picture - detail of a watercolour
by Joan Macpherson*

The Glebe Field

First Published as a Kindle e-book in 2012
Copyright © George Macpherson 2012

ISBN **978-1479180448**

Prepared for this publication by
Just Do It Publications © 2012

Prologue

The Glebe Field is tranquil enough now, basking in calm sun, It is almost silent; the lush Cornish grass barely moves in a warm breeze from the bay. The only inhabitants, a donkey and a plump Shetland pony, hardly interrupt their grazing at the squeak of the gate.

It was on such a day that Emily found the ring; so different from the stormy night two centuries ago when a distraught young woman hurled it from the wall of the adjacent cemetery. The rain had been sweeping horizontally across the headland, swept by the tempest as it hissed and sizzled off the Atlantic, stinging her cheeks and washing away salt tears as she pulled her soaking cloak more tightly around her shoulders. She no longer wanted to live and the freezing rain was too much to bear.

The District Council planning committee members file through into the soft sward. They gather around their chairman Mrs Nancy Libby as she spells out the choices on which they have to decide.

"The application is for half of this field to be sold as a car-park and toilets; a small kiosk for teas and ice-cream – and the other half for the construction of a three-bedroom 'Cornish cottage' of traditional design."

She detaches the first sheet from her clipboard and slips it behind the remaining papers.

"It's submitted by the Lantrelland Parish Council and its vicar. I understand they badly need money to repair the church roof." She pointed beyond the lichen-covered wall. "As you can see, the tower too, needs re-pointing."

"'Tis true. We can't get any more grants and there's still a terrible lot of work to save it," adds Councillor Trevor Philp, churchwarden of St Gluvias, which has stood there for nearly a thousand years, resisting everything the elements and mankind can throw at it. Mr Philp clears his throat to continue but is talked down abruptly by Nancy Libby, who knows just how much to raise her voice without it being rude.

"And it is opposed by various organisations, chief amongst which is the Campaign to Protect Rural England, which I understand is employing a barrister to press its case," she continues.

Emily's mother, Rose Yi Johnson, newly elected and attending her first site visit as a member of the committee, looks around the disparate group of her companions. While some, like Mrs Libby and Mr Philp, are from ancient Cornish families, others, like her, are of incomer families from up-country.

Well, not *quite* like her because she looks different, with her light gold skin, long black hair and upward tilted, single-lidded eyes. Being half Chinese has not prevented her from being voted in: she finds this reassuring.

Since she first came from East Africa to visit her grandparents in Polperris as a child, everyone has called her Rosie. Her 'unexplained' daughter Emily, now nearing her twenty-second birthday, has been a hit with the locals from the moment Rose brought her, newborn from London one summer – to stay.

Rose looked at the meadow, taking in its tranquillity; its solitude. How could they sacrifice all this to repair the battered old building, precious though it may be but so rarely used? As a new-girl on the committee she wondered how much clout she could wield and how she might devise a discrete strategy to save the meadow from violation. Her thoughts were interrupted by her smartphone. She wished she had not chosen such a raunchy clip of heavy metal as a ring tone and blushed as she plunged into her velvet handbag, trying one inside pocket after another trying to silence the wretched thing. All eyes turned on her as she fled to the back of the group, out of earshot.

"Hello?"

"Mum?"

"Yes – darling! Where are you?"

"At work. Can you pick me up at Liskeard at about three next Thursday, please?"

"Course I can – lovely! I'll be there."

"You out for a walk?"

"No, I'm in a planning committee meeting."

"Outdoors? That's what it sounds like?"

"We're in the Glebe field by the church at Lantrelland. They want to make it into a tourist attraction and car park.'

"Oh NO! That would be awful!"

"I can't stop now, darling – I'll tell you about it when you get here. Perhaps you'll be able to help do something about it. Must go!"

"OK Mum – love you so much!"

"Me too – bye!"

In London Emily put down the phone. As she sat back, enjoying the thought of a few days off, her left hand traced the scrolls and central flower of the ring she wore on the third finger of her other hand. She was sure it had always brought her luck.

THE GLEBE FIELD

CHAPTER 1

Rose looked at her watch. The London train was due any minute. Why was it that her daughter always chose a train that meant trailing up to Liskeard in the middle of the afternoon? No time for even a short siesta. It seemed that other people's families were more accommodating because the car park was deserted and the platform empty: not even station staff. Rosie hoped she had the right time. It was quite possible she had muddled Emily's call. Since the site visit her head was spinning with public enquiries, appeals and the intricacies of 'planning advice' that arrived almost daily in the post.

"I'll be positive," Rosie told herself out loud. "I've got the time right: it's a lovely day; I'm warm, nothing hurts and I'm not hungry, just addled. Be calm, Rosie: sit on that comfortable bench and take some deep breaths; relax!"

She took her own advice and sat down, remembering to sit well back, not perch on the edge; not to cross her legs but to consciously allow her body to release the urgency that had made her so alert as she steered through the deep-cut lanes between the wooded hills and valleys of East Cornwall between Polperris and Liskeard. She could have let Emily catch the little branch-line connection to Looe but the picture of her pretty daughter waiting on a deserted platform on the edge of a once sleepy market town, worried her. What happened if she were accosted: or disappeared? In any case, the time driving back from the station was always so special: absence made the heart less irritable and the celebration of reunited affection between single mother and precious daughter after months of only chatting on the phone or quipping on Facebook allowed exchange of confidences that

1

were not as easy after a day or two together. By then, having had to ask the thoughtless girl to turn down her blaring radio and make some effort to tidy her room took the edge off easy communication.

The trip home from the station was always a pleasure: the opposite of taking her back at the end of a weekend break or summer vacation when both of them had that hollow feeling of knowing that the nearest they would come to a comforting embrace would be 'hello Mum,' on a crackly line; or a hasty text message so easily misunderstood.

The sun and silence, drifting Rosie into reverie, was interrupted by a faint metallic echo from the rails heralding a distant train. Looking up, she could just see its engine emerge from a far cutting. It was one of those long-distance expresses that tied Penzance to Paddington and the rest of the world. At least Emily had not had to change in Plymouth and might arrive more rested, ready to take up village life with her usual gusto. Rosie wouldn't see all that much of the girl during the next couple of weeks because she'd be out most of the time with any friends who had not left East Cornwall in search of a career.

Emily heaved her knapsack down on to the platform and slammed the carriage door. No one else left the long train, dutifully waiting for the scheduled departure time before revving its diesel to shriek level and imperceptibly resuming movement westwards, gathering momentum and speed. Emily's happy voice soon broke the new silence as she called to the lone figure waiting for her:

"Hey Mum, congratulations on getting elected! You didn't expect to, did you?" She gave her mother an extra long hug before they broke apart from the joyous embrace that always marked her arrival.

"I'm so proud of you! How did you do it?"

"It *was* a surprise but I did put in a lot of legwork, knocking on doors and making a nuisance of myself. I think Radio Cornwall dreaded me phoning up trying to get on chat shows but I managed it at least once a week. I've got lots to say! And it seems that enough people agree with me to put a cross against my name."

2

"Wasn't it awful, chatting up people who won't vote anyway?"

"No – funnily enough it wasn't. I loved it! I met so many people in the villages and out on the farms who I never knew existed and it's been fascinating to hear what they have to say. Apart from a few, they were glad to get the chance to air their views. No one seems to ask their opinion and I discovered all kinds of things. Practically all of them seemed to be fed up because they felt so helpless. All they heard on the news was that the world was falling apart and here they were, unable to do anything about very much! Some of them were really angry and others, quite depressed. My only problem was getting away – they all had so much to tell me. I don't think some of them have anyone else to talk to!"

"I expect they were hoping you might 'do something about it all'?"

"I think they did: I feel I've collected quite a burden of responsibility and I'm wondering what to do: as if little-old me can make a difference in the world!"

"Margaret Thatcher did!"

"Thank you very much – but no thank you! Emily, are you trying to wind me up?"

Emily laughed: "Well only a bit! But she did make a difference, even if you didn't agree with her. I'm just saying don't give up, Mum. You stood for election – you must have thought it was worth a try?"

"You're right! I've been feeling desperate. Every day something or another sets all my alarm bells ringing as the human race blindly pursues money, sex and rock and roll as if there's no tomorrow."

"There probably isn't – if we go on at this rate!"

"Don't tell me you feel the same, Emily – at your age you should be full of optimism."

"Well I hope I am: but like all those people out in their cottages, I don't see what we can do to persuade our government to be brave enough to take decisions that won't be popular. They're so worried about not getting re-elected they go around kissing everyone's bottom and giving them tax cuts. Then they go out to lunch with all the lobbyists and get chatted up about allowing more oil exploration in National Parks; or selling a few more tanks to some fat-cat dictator in the Middle East!"

"You sound like me! Where did you get it from? You weren't even interested when you went off to college?"

"I suppose I've been meeting lots of emotional people who get me fired up – well I did at art school anyway. These days I tend to meet more of the people who have made their little pile and don't know what to spend it on. To hear them talk you would never believe that millions of people are having to find somewhere else to live because their country is disappearing below the waves. Sometimes it makes my blood boil and I have to concentrate on selling them some crappy picture they think might be more valuable in a year or two."

"You *are* fired up! There's politics in the family on your Chinese side; perhaps you've got an angry gene, like me. My grandfather was quite important locally, in the revolution of 1949. You ought to ask Granny about it – but I'm glad I can count on your support. Let's hope we can get something going!"

They stopped chatting as Rose negotiated her way down the lane that spiralled downwards from the last few houses in Liskeard, back into 'the bottoms' on the way home. Paint marks from scraped cars on corner stones showed that full concentration was needed if expensive mistakes were to be avoided. Now Emily was safely aboard, Rosie's sense of pressure had gone. Stopping at one end of a narrow bridge for a tractor and trailer coming the other way she glanced across at her daughter. What a beautiful young woman Emily had become. There was a new strength about her, somehow. Rose was excited by her daughter's positive response to her own feeling of mission. Emily was now seeing the same scenario that she could. Her daughter had emerged from the pink fog of pretty girlhood into full awareness and was now a clear-thinking and formidable woman. She had always been single-minded when she wanted something and in the past, mother and daughter had had some epic struggles but they had been about things like the length of Emily's skirt or the colour she wanted to dye her hair.

No wonder she was now being so successful at the gallery, once her good looks, charm and intellect were focused upon selling a picture.

At graduation, a couple of years ago, she had been such a child but since starting at the Hanover Gallery she had taken on the dress and demeanour of a sophisticated businesswoman. She was certainly no-one's pushover now. What a relief! Rose snatched another proud glance at her offspring as they came to a wider piece of road.

"I do like your hair like that," she commented.

"I've given up wishing it wasn't so Chinese;" said Emily, checking the hairpins in her bun before folding her hands again on her lap. "I used to hate it being so straight, so heavy and black, always growing like fury. Now I'm grateful it's so easy to manage. I just keep it like this most of the time. It makes me look a bit older and more knowledgeable."

"Mine's going grey! Already! It's not fair: Granny's is still jet black and she's not far off retirement! There must be grey hair in my English half. Let's hope you haven't inherited *that* too."

"Well there's still hope. I've got her flat eye-lids and people used to call me Chinky at school but I've decided it's an advantage now, instead of wishing I was the same as everyone else. I'm 'exotic' and 'full of Eastern Promise'."

"Not too much, I hope!" They both laughed.

"Anyway, it helps me sell stuff – especially to Oriental visitors. They think they'll get preferential deals. But you were saying – about people on the doorsteps. What else were they telling you?"

"Well, about The Glebe at Lantrelland, for a start."

"I was going to ask you about that. I hope I haven't made you come away from any more site meetings?" A fond image of the tranquil meadow came into Emily's mind and she touched her gold ring. It confirmed that she hadn't lost it or left it anywhere. It felt important ever since its shine had caught her eye ten years ago during a picnic. Her imagination had created a host of myths about how it got there. After leaving it at the local police station for the required time she had claimed it and shown it to the

5

museum in Plymouth which had confirmed its antiquity. Somehow she felt a connection with its previous owner, whoever that might be.

"No meeting this afternoon: a bit late to ask, but you haven't. We had one this morning and then lunch at the pub. I *was* going to write up my notes and have a zizz but I'd much rather come and meet you. I always miss you when you're not here." Rosie took one hand off the wheel and patted Emily's knee. It was so good to have someone to touch. Perhaps there *was* something to be said for having a husband or a least a lover around but her lack of success in making relationships last had always put paid to that. She had loads of friends locally and welcoming so many visitors to the studio and gallery was stimulating and rewarding – even if not financially – but when Emily was at home, despite the noise and muddle, Rosie felt more alive, more complete. Being able to swear, knowing that someone was going to ask 'what's the matter?' allowing you to express frustration over a tin that wouldn't open or having pinched your finger – relieved the moment. Equally, having a vibrant young thing suddenly throwing her arms around you just because she felt like it – was so good; as was kissing Emily's cheek with its cool, perfect complexion. Her physical presence, affection, exchanging remarks, hearing movement about the house – it all made one come to life.

Rose could recall other chapters of her life during which she had felt this vivacity. They contrasted with periods of painful solitude, such as when leaving her parents to return to boarding school. Charles Johnson, her father, easy-going and immersed in his rural development work with the UN, had not been able to dissuade her mother from insisting on such drastic separation. Zhang Li was convinced that rigorous education was the only way to give a girl eventual freedom. That was what had saved herself from an intolerable situation when her father died, back in Shenyang. Achieving an internationally recognised doctorate in anthropology had taken her from the family problems and political turmoil at home to Tanganyika to assist in the planning of the Tanzam railway, back in the sixties. That's where she had met – and instantly disliked – Charles, when he was an agriculturist working as a volunteer. Only his persistence, devotion and resistance to all her animosity had finally won her love and released the passion she had so long controlled.

Rosie had always feared she wasn't really necessary to Charles and Zhang Li, who made each other so complete. Being sent away from them, from her Tanzanian primary school friends and from the children of other expatriates at the research station was like being banished out of the real world. It was only the half terms and holidays with her parents there, near Lake Victoria and their later UNESCO postings in other countries that had enabled her to survive the years of exile at school, the art foundation course in Wiltshire and finally the chaos of Camberwell Art School.

Rosie's other oases of 'real life' had been vacations spent at Polperris with Charles' parents – artists both – at their studio and gallery on the quayside by the harbour between terraced cottages and gardens, steep streets and slate cliffs. She grew up with the smell of oil paints, tar and fishing boats; listening to her grandparents and their summer students enthusing about shapes and colours. There was never any doubt about what she wanted to do when she left school.

Zhang Li had never encouraged her to visit the Chinese side of the family and Rose had not yet discovered why, except that there had been some unresolved enmity between Zhang Li, her brother and other relatives. Some day, Rose felt, when her mother had mellowed, she would investigate the full story. It was so tantalising, not knowing more about that side of her background, especially now that China was becoming a major player in world events.

It was during a vacuum of loneliness after completing her art degree that Rose's hunger for warmth and closeness had taken her to bed one night with a law student after an end-of-term party. It wasn't just his looks that had attracted her – as had those of a teenage Sukuma youth during a school holiday some years ago at the research station in Africa. He too had been charming, funny and so good-looking with his silky black skin and wide shoulders. He had finally won her by producing a fresh packet of condoms the night she allowed him to take her virginity – which he did with great consideration and skill, giving her a delightful experience.

From the age when her body had begun to become interesting to herself and boys her parents had inculcated her with the risks of HIV and other perils of sexual delight. During her teenage years, caution and contraception featured frequently in conversation at mealtimes around the Johnson/Yi dinner table, in a mixture of English and Swahili. That was before Zhang Li had decided to learn English despite it being the language of 'imperialist running dogs of the Americans'. Zhang Li had always said that, after Mandarin, Swahili was the language she needed for her work – why learn the vile tongue of capitalism?

It had been the tri-lingual Rose who had finally persuaded her mother that English was useful too, much to Charles' relief when it came to seeking new contracts within the UN in different countries. Rose spoke English, Sukuma – the home-language of her school-mates – and Swahili, the language of East Africa. Speaking to adults in Swahili didn't seem at all strange, unless the 'wrong' person used an unaccustomed language, which always jarred and even when she was quite small she used to rebuke her mother for trying to speak to her in English. "Talk properly, Mummy," she would say in Swahili.

Years later in London, Emily had been conceived one evening in a milieu of English. Homesick but elated, Rose and the law student had been enjoying a few glasses of wine. Both had received excellent exam results and their mood was of release and freedom. Add to this the overwhelming desire for love – to hold, be held, embrace and caress; to release so much pent-up lust – and it became an explosive situation when they found themselves alone together. On just this one occasion, despite her rules, it all happened in the absence of any birth control or protection. The result, nine months later, was Emily, without the law student even being aware of the consequence of the wonderful one-night stand.

"Can we go and take a look at The Glebe on the way home," asked Emily.

"There's no hurry. Why not?"

"I love it there! I can just remember our times there with Great-Granny. I used to make daisy chains and catch grasshoppers while you were both sketching."

"I've still got some of those pictures and drawings of the church there and even a couple of you, playing in The Glebe."

"You're not selling them are you?"

"No of course not! Not the ones with you in them; but there are several that my granny painted just for sale – she knew she had to keep pictures on the wall to pay their bills. So did Grandpa. He was painting the day he had his heart attack. Granny worked on for another couple of years even after losing him."

"Was that why you came to live down here: to look after her?"

"Well partly: but you were the main reason. I was lucky to have somewhere to go and something to do despite having you in my womb! It wasn't so easy in those days! It was Granny Johnson's own idea – she was very broad-minded and backed me up in wanting to go ahead and have you. My mother was horrified at me getting pregnant and Daddy didn't have much say in the matter."

Emily always enjoyed hearing the story of her birth: it made her feel loved and wanted. She knew how much Zhang Li now doted over her and was so proud of her successes at school and work. Ever since she was small her mother had answered Emily's questions about 'not having a father' and reassured her that after her birth, from the moment they saw her, her grandparents had fallen in love with her and accepted her as part of the family. It made her feel special – even now when she was in her twenties.

Rose had not, however, told Emily the whole story. She never talked of Zhang Li's rage at her 'folly' of becoming pregnant and of her mother's pressure for her to have an abortion, which had been hard to resist. That was better forgotten. Rose understood why Zhang Li had reacted in that way after her own upbringing in a strict communist household in the north of China. During a period of struggle and hardship

9

there had been no room for girls just 'getting pregnant' but only dedication to The Party, one's education, chores and making a living. Rose had had to stand very firm to defend her embryo but when Rose introduced the beautiful baby Emily to Zhang Li it was instant acceptance. Zhang Li doted over the child and made sure that she and Charles always spent a large part of their leave with their daughter and grand-daughter. Those had been joyous times for them all in the house on the quay in Polperris.

As a child Emily had made visits to stay with them in distant countries, travelling in the care of attentive air-hostesses. It was these visits that had made her aware of the reality of deserts, starvation, poverty and environmental degradation. She had soaked up Zhang Li and Charles' missionary zeal for their work with the UN – seeking ways to alleviate the lot of those who had to live in such circumstances.

Emily also loved to hear Rose relate how welcome her new baby's arrival had been to the old Mrs Johnson. As they drove through the winding lanes it set the tone for a good atmosphere over the next few days.

"Granny Johnson was wonderful. She made me so welcome here in Cornwall, and respected my decision to go ahead with the pregnancy. She said you were a 'Godsend' because she was all alone now that Grandpa had died; she needed another artist to help supply the gallery with paintings to sell and run the summer courses. It would be wonderful to have a child around the house again. That's when I came to stay here permanently – carrying you – and living happily ever after!"

"Except when she was so ill and you had to look after her, me *and* all the work," said Emily.

"You were a happy little soul and she was no trouble. We had daily visits by the district nurse and then at the end in the nursing home, she just faded away and died one night in her sleep. I'd only just popped in to see her and we'd had such a lovely few minutes together. I've always been glad it worked out like that – being able to say goodbye."

"Don't forget to turn right at the next crossing, Mum!"

"No I won't. Sorry, I was getting carried away." Rose wiped a tear away as she took the side road westwards towards Lantrelland. She cried easily, like Zhang Li – such a let-down when it came to a confrontation.

"And when Great-Granny died it was just you and me!"

"Yes it was; and we were fine, weren't we? You didn't seem to miss not having a father."

"I don't think I did, really. I've had grandpa all this time – at least when they are home on leave. But we did have one or two 'Dads' on trial, didn't we?"

"I suppose you could put it like that: there must have been four or five, over the years!" Rose laughed. "A pity I couldn't get any of them to stick!"

"A good job too, with some of them," said Emily. "One of them was really creepy with me – do you remember? He kept wanting to pat my bottom!"

"He didn't last long after that," said Rose. "It's a good job you told me about it!"

"But you're still young, Mum. You never know, you might meet someone really nice on one of your summer courses? Maybe even on The Council!"

"Some hopes! I'm forty-three and my skirts are getting tighter. I spend most of my time sitting in the gallery hoping for people to come in to spend money and the rest of my time teaching or out sketching in the summer. Then in winter, I'm in the studio getting ready for next season. Social life in Polperris is church, chapel or pub and I'm not keen on any of those. And I certainly don't fit amongst the other 'artists' in the village. So many of them are nothing but posers, churning out pot-boilers. "

"There *are* one or two you like – otherwise you wouldn't sell their pictures, Mum."

"That's true but they're either happily married, lesbian or gay – hence I'm still on my own – and I've met no one interesting yet in my political life! But what about you? I haven't heard you talk about anyone lately."

"There hasn't *been* anyone. I'm feeling a bit 'on the shelf'. It's all work and not much play these days. The boss expects me to make all the arrangements for new exhibitions – although he has all the fun chatting up the artists and visiting their studios. I have to produce all the brochures and posters; and do all the mail shots while he enjoys hanging the pictures and placing the sculptures – becoming big friends with the artists. There's no sign of him when I'm sitting for days at the desk being charming to lots of people who are unlikely to buy anything. I even have to vacuum and dust every morning. I feel like a real skivvy, sometimes!"

"I must say I do too! What a pair we are! Never mind, we make a living and we do get around the world now an again, thanks to my parents. Have they asked you out again?"

"They have – but I'm not sure I'm very keen to go to Albania. They say it's 'very basic' and for them, that means something else."

"It will be a chance for you to see some contrasts. They're not going to be there much longer; their contract ends soon, doesn't it?"

They turned right again, away from the winding river, climbing up between wooded hills, until the road emerged once more into open country and undulating fields. The change between the shaded valley and the open sky illuminating bright green pastures was dazzling. Far to the left, the sea, with its perfectly straight horizon, completed the picture. They would have to join the main road for a while before turning off for Lantrelland. Rose groaned as she waited at the next junction to find a gap in the creeping convoys of cars arriving from London and the Midlands.

"The traffic is as bad as ever," she said. "Almost nose to tail. Look at them all!" She put on the hand brake. "Although I don't mind as long as it's the *right people* coming to the village: the ones who will buy my paintings and not behave badly!"

"Mum, do you think they really *will* let those people ruin the Glebe Field? I think it would be awful. It's such a special place."

"I'm afraid they will, if we can't get some sort of campaign going. To most of the local people it's not such a special place – they've grown up with it *and* the old church next to it, which is in danger of falling down despite being such an architectural treasure. That tower has always been a landmark for sailors coming up the Channel and its bells are hundreds of years old – all the visiting ringers want to come and try them; but for most of the time Lantrelland is deserted – except for old Miss Weeks' donkey and the pony."

"What are you doing about it?"

"There's not much I can do – I've only just joined the committee but I've written off to a group in London, asking for advice," said Rose. "We'll see what happens."

CHAPTER 2

"You're Cornish, aren't you, Sebastian? With a name like Trenleven?"

"'Yes, I suppose I am, genetically, although I've never lived there; why?"

"There's a case for you here – public enquiry."

"Who's the client?"

"The CPRE."

"What's that?"

"A bunch of greenies – you know, beards and sandals. You must have heard of them; they make a fuss about new motorways and airports – change in general."

"Why me?" Sebastian sounded defensive.

"Because you're Cornish and your name will give you weight. And because you are the newest in the chambers – that's why! Best of all, it's because your Dad says so! We tend to do what the senior partner wants."

"He seems to do mostly what *you* suggest," complains the younger Trenleven.

"Not at all, I'm just the bloody clerk – I just do as I'm asked."

"I believe you've got a little wand, like the other Harry Potter."

"Leave it off, Seb, I've heard all those jokes before. My mum and dad had never heard of him when I was born: it was during the rationing."

"I think J K Rowling called him that after hearing about you and your spells!"

"I've heard that one too – so just get your head round this lot and let me chase up some of the others."

He plonked a bundle of correspondence tied in a red ribbon on Sebastian's desk and returned to his own table, deep in similar bundles. He threw one last remark as Sebastian settled down to study his new task:

"Actually I had nothing to do with it. Your father met someone at a dinner and told her you were always nagging him to change light bulbs and buy an electric car. I think they were comparing notes about their sons. It turned out she was a volunteer at CPRE. When she heard your father was a barrister she said something about shortage of funds when it came to fighting planning cases – and he more or less volunteered you on special offer! He must have found her attractive!"

"Thanks Dad! I wish he'd keep his love life separate from work."

Harry didn't reply: he would have liked to say something about it being about time that Peter Trenleven met someone nice again. Poor chap; it was nearly four years since Françoise had died. Now *there* was a lovely lady. Harry remembered the waft of her perfume as she called in to the office to pick up Peter for lunch: always so charming; her French accent captivating everyone in the chambers. Her short illness and early death had shocked everyone.

Peter had been distraught and but for the support of the others in the chambers – including Harry himself – might have stayed deep in depression. Peter was only now beginning to regain the old sparkle and sharp interest in everything and everybody that had helped persuade so many judges and juries that his logic left only one conclusion. Many innocents had regained freedom due to his diligence and clear argument: perhaps a few guilty crooks too, when the Crown Prosecution had left gaps in theirs. Harry looked across at Sebastian. The boy wasn't really resentful of being given such a brief: it was right up his street. He wasn't interested in crime or detectives, even though he was so much like his father in other ways. He was, like Harry's own children, a product of the BBC's Blue Peter era – racing home from school to watch heroic young men and women scrabble around in muddy ponds after newts or rescuing wounded hedgehogs. Harry remembered the celebrations when Sebastian had been awarded

15

his Blue Peter Green Badge for organising a bunch of his friends to plant birch trees on the roundabout at the end of their road in Putney.

Receiving his award at the studios had been a highlight of his eleventh year. Since then his interests had been more directed towards sport and girls. He hadn't ever 'set his mind' on becoming a lawyer but drifted into it. As an only child he was used to joining in his parents' conversations at mealtimes – in English or French because each parent spoke to him in their own language and he had grown up bilingual. He had become fascinated by the gruesome cases they talked about. He knew he must not talk about them outside the house but Françoise felt it would do him no harm to know of what his fellow humans were capable in their pursuit of gratification and prosperity.

§

The headed paper announced itself as from CPRE – Campaign To Protect Rural England: standing up for your countryside.

From Lady Henrietta Merchant Wednesday

Dear Mr Trenleven,

You may remember we met at a Guild Hall dinner recently and that we discussed the ambitions and interests of our various offspring, and how much these differed from those of our own.

My children couldn't seem to care less about the way we are destroying the planet on which we depend for a living; you said your son shuns your own passion for the fair application of criminal law while my own brood is more concerned with 'marketing'. I interpret that as 'alerting others to a need they

16

didn't know they had, for something of which they had never heard'. Their aims seem to ignore any consequences of production, promotion, sale and use of such objects or services, whether they pollute the air we breathe (with ever more coughing) or the water we drink, (laced with residues of hormone from the female pill from which, admittedly, we all benefit by being able to enjoy the pleasures of procreation without it actually happening.) Sorry, I digress.

At the Campaign, where I escape during the day to assuage my post-retirement zeal to save the more valuable and beautiful aspects of the British countryside, we are always seeking those who are prepared to help shoulder our burden without the usual high fees that they deserve. You mentioned that your son might consider fighting the occasional Public Enquiry on our behalf. Perhaps you could show him the following paragraph or two, to win his approval? It is abstracted from the CPRE's website. This extract sums up what we are trying to achieve. I should explain (although I'm sure you do not need it) that an 'SSSI' is a 'Site of special scientific interest' and that if an area of land is designated as such, it should receive the protection of British law and it is the duty of various authorities to respect and guard that protection.

'It is essential to preserve our remaining natural heritage for future generations. Wildlife and geological features are under pressure from development, pollution, climate change and unsustainable land management. SSSIs are important as they support plants and animals that find it more difficult to survive in the wider countryside. Protecting and managing SSSIs is a shared responsibility, and an investment for the benefit of future generations.'

The very next day after our fortuitous meeting we received a letter from a newly elected member of Caradon District Council in Cornwall. The lady had an unusual name – Miss Rose Yi Johnson and she expressed the kind of outrage that always fuels my righteous indignation and desire to take up cudgels. Apparently it is proposed that an ancient glebe meadow adjoining, and belonging to an even more ancient Cornish church, is threatened with becoming a car park with snack bar

17

and bungalow. The plants and grasses in the meadow are of great interest to botanists and the lichens on the mediaeval wall enclosing it are apparently most unusual, due to the pureness of the air coming off the Atlantic. You can imagine the effect of a busy car park on these!

In our opinion this is a case similar to that of the coastline near Newquay in North Cornwall, which has been desecrated by hideous estates of bungalows, 'holiday units' and car-parks due to the mindless ineptitude of planning authorities there – a national scandal that you will no doubt remember. I have visited the area and it really is frightful!

A colleague of mine remarked that if such an outrage were not to be repeated on the less spoiled South East Cornwall coastline, the CPRE should get involved with as high-powered legal representation as was possibly available. We both bewailed the fact that the CPRE simply does not have the necessary financial reserves to pay the going rate for such representation. Then I remembered the conversation that you and I enjoyed (well, I did) the previous evening and I resolved to contact you, using the visiting card that you kindly gave me. This, in the hope that you might be able to persuade you son to consider this opportunity to save such a treasured example of Cornish heritage, associated with names such as your own.

I do apologise for this wordy letter. It was my attempt at trying to make the concept of begging less offensive and I would be delighted if you were able to reply offering some degree of encouragement for our cause.

I remain, Sir,

Your brief but amicable acquaintance,

Henrietta Merchant

§

"Dad, what are you letting me in for?" Sebastian asked, over a coffee later that morning. "This lot sound a bit wacky! Are they serious?"

"Lady Merchant is actually very funny – and clever. We got on very well and had a tremendous evening. I haven't laughed so much for ages – but I got the impression that far from being eccentric and weird, the CPRE sound very reasonable and determined, too. If the rest of them are like her they aren't a bit stuffy. I've read a few of their publications and I think you would agree with all their aims."

"But would you want me to go and represent them for no fee?"

"Well, I think I might!"

"Dad! Was she *that* attractive?"

"She was very attractive yes – but Sebastian, she's a bit old for me! She must be at least sixty, if not more."

"Well so are you! It sounds perfect!"

"Wait until *you* are sixty one, Sebastian. I am more interested in 'the younger woman'."

"Oh Dad! You're not going to be one of those old pervs are you?"

"I hope not." Peter looked hurt.

Although he had a close relationship with his son, especially since their mutual loss, the boy could say quite wounding things.

"Well you know what I mean," Sebastian had overstepped the mark and was backing off. "These chaps who go and marry young models and then come to grief. I know you wouldn't be so daft! Sorry Dad!"

"Well I should hope not – you rat! But for that impertinence you can bloody well take the brief and no fee. It will teach you to be more respectful to your elders and betters." He was mollified by Sebastian's apology. "At least we've had a good couple of years, the chambers can afford it. Perhaps it will save us some tax, too; and surely you'll agree it's a good cause?"

"It certainly sounds like it." Sebastian's interest had been sparked. "It will make a change from sports fields in Hounslow.

I've never been to Cornwall. Will you write to her ladyship, or shall I?"

"I will, of course!" She's a charming connection, worth cultivating," said Peter. "You had better get her title correct. She's 'Lady Henrietta Merchant' – her father was an earl so call her 'Lady Henrietta and not Lady Merchant'. You'll have to go round to their office to get yourself fully informed."

"And you'll look after the social side."

"Indeed I shall, you cheeky brat!"

From where he was sitting Harry Potter didn't catch all the conversation but was much encouraged by what he did gather. There was life in the old dog yet – and the young dog sounded enthusiastic.

"How's your diary?" Peter opened his own.

"Pretty busy for a day or two and then I've got some time."

"Once you know what's going on you'd better book yourself in to go down there for a few days. You can meet the intriguing Mrs Rose Yi Johnson and get the whole picture."

On reflection, Sebastian Trenleven noted his father's lighter spirits. What a relief, after all this time of such sadness. The loss of his beloved Françoise had knocked the stuffing out of his father and Sebastian himself had been devastated. Their little trio had been so close: they shared jokes; went to the theatre and dined out together; they discussed everything and everybody; and the three of them made a very tight unit, self sufficient and emotionally so secure.

Sebastian had been on the point of moving out to a flat of his own when his mother had first been diagnosed. Instead, he had stayed and the two men pottered on with the help of a woman who came in daily to do the cleaning and ironing. They rarely saw her but left notes – as did she – when necessary. For the grieving duo, life was mostly work. Sebastian welcomed the prospect of doing something different and began making preparations for a trip to Cornwall.

CHAPTER 3

For the last mile before emerging into the undulating fields on the top of the cliffs around Lantrelland Church the road became narrow and was cut deeper into the land. The passage of boots, horses, carts and wagons had worn through the topsoil, then the slate shale rock beneath, making ruts, widening it, over the centuries, into a lane that was almost a tunnel. Hazel and blackthorn overhanging from the hedges above shaded out the sky. Only the occasional gateway gave a glimpse of green field or isolated cottage. Rose drove out into the open area surrounding the church gate.

"It's not deserted today: there's someone else here already!" Emily was disappointed.

"Posh car, too!" said her mother, parking away from an immaculate Bentley.

"Never mind, they're probably looking around the church; although I think I recognise that car. We can go through into the Glebe and keep out of their way."

Rose turned away from the roofed lychgate and started towards the meadow.

"I want to remember it as I've always known it. I can't bear the thought of it disappearing," she said. "You go on ahead. These shoes are slowing me down! I didn't know we'd be 'off the pavement'."

The field entrance, wide enough for a tractor, was chained and padlocked and Emily waited for her mother to negotiate her way through the adjacent kissing gate. Entering the Glebe was like resuming a peaceful existence. They strolled into the deep grass and flowers. It was warm, with hints of scent from blossom, animals and the sea. On a stormy day you could hear the waves beating against the cliffs two fields away but on a calm day like this it made not a sound: only its bright reflection of the sun on smooth water catching the eye. The view was perfect, unchanging; the stone church, raised above the surrounding land, centred in the graveyard with its stubby square tower and arched entrance; the irregular gravestones showing their age – leaning, some fallen or propped against the turf-topped slate wall that separated them from the Glebe field. The meadow itself, large enough for a football pitch, narrowed into the valley leading down to Lantrelland beach, out of sight below the cliff. Beyond, topping off the valley nearly to the sky, was the blue sparkling sea, its horizon ruled across the view.

Emily sat down, patting the springy turf next to her for Rose to join her.

"It's not damp. Isn't this a perfect place!" She spread her arms with enthusiasm.

"I can't count the number of times I've brought you here, ever since you were a baby: especially when Mummy was alive," said Rose. "We used to love painting the views and the church – from every angle and direction. I think I know every stone of that church and the shape of all the windows and the dips in the roof. I could almost draw it from memory. I remember every bend in that footpath down to the sea, too. And all these flowers! We've never managed to identify all of them?"

"The animals seem to know which ones they like!"

Emily was looking towards the other side of the field where the chubby pony and its donkey companion raised their heads to assess the newcomers. The two animals were standing nose to tail, benefiting from the swishing of their tails to keep off the flies. Normally, Emily would have gone over to them, knowing she would be greeted by nuzzling noses seeking a peppermint or biscuit but this afternoon she dismissed such an idea because she heard men's voices.

"Oh no – they 're coming out here," she said.

"So what? We're not trespassing. Nor are they," said Rose.

"I know but I wanted the Glebe all to myself – to us!"

"That's the thing about it – this field is for everyone and that's why we've got to protect it from being gobbled up by people who want to squeeze out every possible drop of cash. Imagine it being closed to the public whenever they felt like it; and being asked not to walk on the grass or 'please use the litter bins'. The only creatures with exclusive use at present are Miss Weeks' donkey and her pony because she pays the church for the grazing."

"Is she still going strong?" Asked Emily.

"She's marvellous but a bit like those animals, fully retired. That pony must be old as the hills! He's definitely retired. I remember when she used him to pull a pony-trap down to Polperris, shopping. There was a special place reserved for her in the car park. The iron ring is still in the wall there to tie the reins – but she uses her bike now, despite her age. Let's just watch to see what those people are up to."

Three men took their turns through the kissing gate. First was a slim man wearing a crisp dark blue suit; his full head of dark hair perfectly combed back, kept in place by enough mousse to give it that extra shine. He looked as though he was arriving at a board meeting and was gesticulating towards the far side of the Glebe. Neither he nor his companions noticed the two women in jeans and sweaters, sitting watching them, their arms clasped around their knees.

"That's Hugh Olver-Blythe," whispered Rose. "I thought I recognised his car out there. I wonder what he wants?"

"He looks as though he owns the place!"

"Well he owns just about everything else around here," said Rose, "at least in that direction". She pointed west, towards Fowey.

"Like what, apart from Carnhill?"

"He's been buying land all the way to Polruan; getting bigger all the time. He sells off the farm buildings – after doing them up as holiday cottages or luxury houses; and adds the fields to his estate. Goodness knows where he gets the money, the farms aren't very special. I wonder if it's he who's got his eye on The Glebe? I wouldn't put it past him. The application for development was actually made by a local farmer, Eddie Rouse. He's the taller man in the middle. If he's got Hugh Olver-Blythe supporting him, we're really up against it! He's a very smooth operator and quite ruthless. And come to think of it, I recognise

23

the other man too; the large, untidy one: he is Brian Rogersson and he's bad news."

Rose leaned over to make sure she wouldn't be heard.

"Rogersson is the developer who bought an old mill up near Liskeard and turned it into a shopping mall – without any planning permission. He simply walked all over the council planners and did what he liked. It was always in the papers; and from what I gather, the council wouldn't do much about it because of the cost of taking him on in court. Eddie Rouse's farm is over there," she pointed with her chin; "the one with over-grown hedges and great patches of nettles and thistles. He's got a reputation as a failed farmer. Not long ago he was up in front of the magistrates for neglecting his livestock."

Hugh Olver-Blythe had finished what he was saying, and as he turned, saw the two women. His two companions followed his attention and realised they were being observed. Emily had picked a stem of sweet vernal grass and was enjoying the hay-taste. Raising his voice so that the two women could hear, Hugh Olver-Blythe said:

"Oh I say, we have company! How charming!" Noticing their shapely good looks he began walking towards them. Once within polite greeting distance he stopped and almost imperceptibly bowed.

"Good morning, ladies. How delightful on such a lovely morning. Welcome to Lantrelland! May I ask, are you overseas visitors?"

"Good morning, Mr Olver-Blythe. We're not, actually. We're local: I live in Polperris and we *have* met before: I'm Rose Yi Johnson and this is my daughter, Emily; and yes, it's a beautiful day."

"Of course we have. I *do* apologise – I didn't recognise you – this bright sun, you know."

Truth to tell he had thought these oriental visions were tourists and might be beguiled into brightening his life somewhat. He hid his disappointment.

"I think I have to congratulate you on your recent election, don't I?"

24

"I'm not sure that you do, being from the Other Party – but it would be churlish of me not to thank you. Yes you do!"

"But I'm sure I haven't met your lovely daughter before. I thought you might be sisters - how do you do?"

"Fine thank you." Emily smiled but made no move to offer a hand or enquire further as to his health. Rose then spoke:

"I know Mr Rouse, and Mr Rogersson too, by sight – and of course I've read about him in the Cornish Times!"

"Nothing bad, I hope?" Brian Rogersson didn't raise his hat as he addressed her.

"As I recollect it has usually been about planning regulations," said Rosie, sweetly.

"Oh, that nonsense!"

"Better be careful, Brian. Miss Johnson is now on the Planning Committee. Isn't that so, Miss Johnson – or may I call you Rose?"

"I think perhaps, on this occasion, we might stick to Councillor Johnson," said Rose, once more offering a disarming smile. "Since there is currently a query about this important local beauty spot."

"Oh really?" Said Hugh Olver-Blythe. "I was not aware of that?"

"I thought you were on the parochial church council?"

"Not any more, Councillor Johnson. I felt I had been on it for far too long and stood down last summer. Perhaps you can tell me about the 'query'?"

"I think you will find that it has been in the Cornish Times recently," said Rose. "There is an application for this meadow to be commercialised and the planners are opposing it. The Planning Committee has been asked to examine all aspects of the application."

"Indeed? Doubtless we shall be able to read about it in next week's edition."

"No doubt you *will* be able to," said Rose. "A reporter is usually at the Council meetings. And you gentlemen: are you like us, just enjoying this unique place on such a beautiful day?"

"Well – that too – but in fact Mr Rouse here is just showing us around his farm and we popped in here because there's such a good view of all his land from here. Isn't that so, Mr Rouse?"

"Yes, 'tis." Eddie Rouse' answer was terse and Rose detected a slight uneasiness about the way he shifted his feet. "You can see most of it from 'ere, yes." He cleared his throat.

"Well gentlemen," said Hugh Olver-Blythe, "let's not disturb the peace of these charming ladies any longer. Shall we go on our way? Where do you suggest next, Eddie?"

"Er – perhaps down to the beach?"

"What a good idea? Let's get moving then." The three men turned to leave. "I do hope I shall have the pleasure of your company again before long, Councillor Johnson – and Miss Johnson? When you are 'off duty', perhaps? I can look you up in the phone book, can't I?"

"Yes of course. Goodbye for the moment. Enjoy your ramble!"

"Mum, you weren't encouraging him, were you?" Emily waited until they heard the car doors shut.

"Well, I wasn't putting him off!" Rose laughed. "I want to find out what's going on and he's got quite a reputation with the ladies. He was obviously taken with us – and I hope he was thinking that I looked young, rather than you looking as old as me! Men can be so tactless, can't they? Sisters indeed!"

"You *do* look young, though, Mum! And we've got the same hair – and eyes. People ask me if I'm Japanese or Malaysian."

"But you haven't got grey hair!"

"And you've only got a couple – they couldn't possibly have seen them. And you're not *that* old anyway. Forty-three's nothing these days – it's hardly even middle age."

"Thank you very much! You wait until you are forty: it's a disturbing mile-post, especially when you are still single."

"Oh Mum, don't start that again! You're not on the shelf yet. Someone could turn up at any moment. You haven't got fat or anything – I can still borrow your clothes!"

"Well whoever turns up it's unlikely to be Hugh Olver-Blythe – although being married doesn't seem to deter him. I don't know how his wife puts up with it. Surely she must know what he's like? Although from what I hear, she very much leads her own life – playing golf and going to the races."

"I wonder what they were really doing here", said Emily.

"Exactly! I want to find out. That Eddie Rouse looked definitely shifty. And why was Brian Rogersson with them? Talk about an unholy alliance! I wouldn't be a bit surprised if all three of them were involved in this application to ruin this lovely old meadow. I'm glad I wrote away for advice about it. I feel so ignorant and I couldn't think of what else to do. Looking at the application you can see it has a lot of weight behind it; it's been put together by real professionals, not some local farmer; and the planning staff told me they suspected there was big money behind it. They were the ones who suggested the CPRE , the countryside campaign people."

"Have you had a reply?" Asked Emily.

"Yes I have, actually. I was quite surprised when I had a phone call from a Lady Merchant. I thought at first it must be someone ringing up to book a place on the water-colour course but she explained she worked for the CPRE and wanted an informal chat. She was very pleasant and said sometimes it was better to talk rather than write letters because one could be more open about things."

"What did you tell her?"

"Well, I said that the Glebe at Lantrelland was special and why it was important for all kinds of reasons. I told her it is *supposed* to have all kinds of legal environmental protection because of its rare plants and the ancient church and wonderful setting; and that part of the success of Polperris as a holiday destination is that the countryside around here is so unspoiled. I said we get all sorts of visitors who want to enjoy the peace and beauty of the place; the ancient churches and walks through the woods and cliff paths; and it really was an area of outstanding natural beauty."

"You wouldn't get so many artists and people coming if it was all ice-cream parlours and car-parks! Who wants to paint rows of coaches and piskie shops?"

"Quite! We've already got enough of them down in the village. I put that in my letter; and I reminded her of what had happened up on the north coast. She said she didn't need reminding, it had been a disaster for the countryside. She said she would try to set things in motion for the CPRE to come and help us. There was one thing she said that worried me: it was that despite some places being designated as 'green belt' or 'sites of special scientific interest' and even 'of outstanding natural beauty' people have been getting round the regulations by throwing money about – lobbying and suchlike. Unless you have the legal resources to resist them you could be on to a lost cause and she said she *might* be able to find a sympathetic lawyer, willing to waive some of his fees."

"Well done, Mum!"

"Something else I learned when I was going around all those houses canvassing was that practically everyone down here depends on tourism – and not just the mass market. The hotels, bed and breakfasts, shops and restaurants are all fairly up-market and the recession of the last few years has really hit them. If things go down-market, many of the existing businesses will lose their more discerning customers. I promised that if I were elected I would fight to protect the character of the East Cornwall coast."

"I hope that doesn't mean you have become a NIMBY, Mum! We've all got to make huge changes if we're going to avoid making the earth impossible to live on."

"I hope I'm not against change but 'change' does not mean dumbing down and destroying things of value and beauty. There's simply no need to start selling ice-cream and brass piskies on a place like this! It should be kept as it has been for hundreds of years."

"But you can see why the church council needs money. That roof is giving notice: look at those broken slates," said Emily, pointing.

"That's another thing. We shouldn't expect half a dozen church people to raise all the money for repairing ancient monuments like this. They try their best but it's impossible. You can't just repair ancient churches the way you would an ordinary house. The listed building regulations mean you have to use the best oak, thick lead and stone tiles: all that kind of thing. If the general public want churches like this to be preserved they will have to contribute out of their taxes: and that's something else I've been campaigning for."

"And you still got elected?"

"Well, people understand if you explain it properly."

"Except people like your Mr Olver-Blythe! I bet he wouldn't vote for you. He'd do anything to avoid tax – and if he were to stand for the council he would go around promising tax cuts for everyone."

"I bet he would. How else could he stay rich?" Rose stood up and brushed the odd leaf from her jeans.

"But what if I wanted to put up some wind turbines around here – or some kind of generator using wave power? Do you think people would understand that? Would *you?* Would you oppose them?"

"Emily – I know you are always going on about things like that and I realise that we have to find new kinds of energy but yes, I would oppose them if you wanted to plant them in the Glebe!"

"What about over there?" Emily pointed to some higher ground a few fields away.

"I wouldn't want them there, either. I think we have to preserve this coastline as an economic asset. We were discussing it at the planning meeting only last week. We all agreed that we must have more wind energy but there are other parts of the county were they would not be so obtrusive – and of course there's off-shore."

"Well they are bound to be 'obtrusive' to someone, somewhere, aren't they? Even up on Bodmin Moor it took years for people to get permission but now they've almost become quite a feature! Personally I think they are beautiful," said Emily. "OK – you *can* hear them: but you have always been able to hear all the old wooden windmills in Holland. Do you remember we went to visit a whole line of them in West Friesland when I was little? It was a great experience, going inside while they were working. It was like being in something alive, shaking moving and creaking. No one complains about *them*. We all think they're beautiful and you even gave me a model windmill for Christmas that year."

"You're right!" Said Rose. "If we grow up with things we don't seem to notice them – at least until someone wants to knock them down. Mind you, I don't think anyone minded when all those tall factory chimneys stopped belching black smoke and were knocked down; and I would be glad to see the back of most of those pylons that march across so many of our beauty spots. Hey – come on: I want a cup of tea. Let me pull you up."

They might have been sisters as they strolled back to the car and completed their journey to one of the much-coveted lock-up garages near the harbour in Polperris. Driving home to the door was not an option and the two shared the weight of Emily's bag, holding one handle each, as they walked the last few hundreds yards home.

§

"I can't believe they'd ever allow it here," said Hugh Olver-Blythe. He and his two companions were looking down on Lantrelland bay.

"You'd be surprised," said Brian Rogersson. "If you made it look attractive enough to the politicians – lots of jobs for local people; loads of holiday business and all the services you need to go with something like this – boat-builders, chandlers and security people. Then all the bars, cafés and shops: the council would raise a lot of money out of rates and parking alone, let alone all the income for places like Polperris, Polruan and Looe. It would be hard for them to turn down something like this – even if you had to take it to the House of Lords!"

"What about all the countryside designations along here? It's not like your bit of remote woodland – there would be a terrible fuss if you tried to break the rules here." Hugh looked at Brian.

"Of course! You'd have to be ready for quite a heavy legal outlay, getting the permission: all the appeals and suchlike."

"Won't they say it ought to go somewhere else – another bay nearer a town; somewhere with better road access?" Hugh asked.

"Like where? This is about the last privately owned bay all along this part of the coast and you own it, Hugh. The National Trust has all the rest, except the existing harbours; and if you buy Eddie's farm it will connect you up nicely with the main road back there. Perfect! Put in a decent road; build breakwaters; it could be like another Mousehole or Mevagissey without the fishing boats and we could get at least a hundred moorings in the harbour. At fifteen hundred a year each – it could be quite interesting! Then sell some properties and add the rent from the shops, houses and parking: "

"I must say 'Lantrelland Village and Marina' sounds good, doesn't it? And we could offer all kinds of facilities they haven't got in Fowey or Looe." Hugh found himself rubbing his hands. "We must definitely look into it a bit further, don't you think? This beach would more or less disappear, though, wouldn't it?"

"As I see it, that's no great loss. It's not very special; hardly any sand and just a few rocks. We could widen and deepen it; link the breakwater to the shore; then all this could be built up with commercial property and residential moorings along there," he indicated the east side of the bay."

"God! Not those frightful brick flats and boxes we see on 'A place in the sun'?" said Hugh.

"Of course not! We could do it all in local slate – make it look as though it had been here longer than Polperris – all except the pontoons for the moorings – and the yachts themselves would be modern, wouldn't they? But what's different about that? All the Cornish harbours have modern boats moored in them, don't they? What do you think, Eddie?"

Eddie Rouse's vision had not kept up with the conversation.

"What about?"

"If we built a harbour here, with 'traditional fishermen's houses' – you'd buy one, wouldn't you? Just right for your retirement! You'll be able to afford it now you're selling up. In fact you could buy a couple more to rent out!"

"I'd have to think about it. See what the missus said," Eddie replied. "When the sale goes through, if I can buy the Glebe and get a little business going I'll probably build a bungalow in there – keep an eye on things. Anyway 'tis time I got on home. We've got people coming, if you don't mind." He didn't want to tell them that most of the money he would receive from selling his farm would go to paying debts. He'd be lucky if he had enough to build a bungalow and café in The Glebe.

"Certainly, Eddie. I'll drop you off straight away." Hugh Olver-Blythe took his car keys out of his pocket.

Eddie wondered if Mr Olver-Blythe could remember the way to the rather scruffy Rouse farmhouse. He had only been there twice, as far as Eddie knew. He was sure the owner of Carnhill Estate would never even have known of his existence before starting negotiations to buy the farm. It was a matter of minutes, however, before Hugh dropped Eddie at his front gate. The Bentley then headed towards Carnhill.

"I don't think he'll ever get permission for developing the Glebe, do you?" Brian sounded confident as they drove away.

"No I don't but it should take attention away from our plans – and I'm paying him enough for his farm. He should be able to afford a decent lawyer. I think we should back him; or at least encourage him a bit."

"Good thinking," said Brian.

"What are you going to do next?" Emily asked her mother as they sipped a glass of sherry. It had been a toss-up as to whether to have tea or something alcoholic and the latter had won, as both women decided it was a bit of a celebration.

"About the Glebe? Well, first I'm going to get in touch with Lady Merchant again to see whether she has been successful in finding someone to defend our corner. Then I'm going to ask around to see if I can find out what Mr Brian Rogersson has got to do with all this. I'm wondering whether he wants to open up some monstrous supermarket or fairground at Lantrelland! You know what he's like!"

"I don't, really, except that he's defied everyone with his trading estate out in the woods near Liskeard," said Emily. "And from what I heard, people flock to spend their money at his place; and half the people in Polperris work there, either as shop assistants or security men!"

"That's about it; and that's what's worrying me. If Hugh Olver-Blythe and Rogersson are working together you could expect just about anything."

"So where will you start your sleuthing?"

"I think I'll go to see dear old Miss Weeks. She lives nearest to the church and she goes to the Glebe every day to see her animals. She might have heard something."

"Can I come too?"

"Of course you can, my darling girl. I'm sure she will be delighted to see you. We'll go sometime in the next day or two."

CHAPTER 4

Rose was taken by surprise when a Mr Harry Potter telephoned asking if she could spare some time to brief Sebastian Trenleven, a barrister from the Trenleven Chambers in London, about The Glebe Field planning application. When she heard the caller's name, she thought it might be a hoax call but Harry reassured her that it was through the CPRE.

"I never thought it would all happen so soon," she said.

"I think you can put the promptness down to our senior partner, Mr Peter Trenleven, QC; and the fact that Sebastian Trenleven, another partner, has been able to fit this into his schedule. Are you able to recommend any particular hotel in Polperris, Councillor Johnson? He'd like to visit as soon as possible."

"He can stay here with us," said Rose. "It would save a lot of to-ing and fro-ing and we would have more time to talk – if he doesn't mind fairly Spartan conditions. My house and studio are a converted fisherman's cottage and net store by the harbour so it's not luxury accommodation. It would also reduce the expenses. When had you in mind?"

"On Thursday: he could arrive in the late afternoon by train."

"That will be fine, Mr Potter. My daughter and I will be home by then. We have a long-standing invitation for lunch with friends that day but it will fit in perfectly. Are you sure he won't mind staying with us?"

"It sounds most satisfactory, Miss Johnson."

"Sorry, Sir, I'm afraid you will have to walk the last bit. I can come with you to help with your bag if you like. The road's too narrow from here on but it's only a couple of hundred yards."

The taxi had stopped by Polperris harbour, before the fish-market. The driver indicated a narrow humped bridge then a right turn. "I think that's the building you want – the tall one on the quay, across the water there. I quite often bring people for there in the summer. When I pick them up again I have to go round and help them carry all the pictures they've painted. It's some kind of art school. Can you manage?"

"Yes I'll be fine thanks – my bag's got wheels!"

"Ah but there's cobbles along The Warren"

"That's a good name for it! All those houses piled on top of each other!"

"Oh yes! They didn't want to live far from their boats when they built those cottages."

No wonder he had seen so many pictures of this place. As he climbed out of the taxi he took in a whole escarpment of houses rising from the other side of a glistening, narrow harbour. Pastel coloured dwellings, some in their natural slate-grey stone, others whitewashed and garnished by a patch of garden filled his vision, almost to the sky.

Sebastian breathed in a warm scent of seaweed, tar and fish. There was a general feeling of bustle against a background of gulls calling and the bangs of empty fish boxes being stacked. It was as if life started again, having been suspended when he left Paddingdon.

London to Plymouth had seemed to go quickly but from there on, having waited for his connection, it had taken *for ever*. Stopping at every station, the double-unit diesel sprinter seemed determined not to spill a drop of anyone's coffee as it crawled away from each deserted platform to trundle on to the next stop. At Liskeard everyone except him had dissolved into the car park, leaving him to wait for the little train to come from Looe to carry him through yet more of Cornwall's wooded and steep valleys, running alongside a river, which widened into the tidal estuary.

From the station, the taxi had brought him across the ancient bridge linking East and West Looe. The bridge also separated the countryside from the town. Towards the station, perched just above the high water mark, were lagoons, mudflats and green banks. On the seaward side it was more built-up and anything but tranquil. The hills on each side of the river were a wall of houses, starting with tightly packed old dwellings next to the water, gradually getting more modern and larger, further up the hill. Sebastian thought it must be a planner's nightmare. Perhaps there was room for his expertise here in this delightful part of the world: a thought!

As they left the station yard Sebastian was surprised to see, across the lagoon, half a dozen pure white birds with long necks and fine, pointed beaks. They looked like the egrets he'd seen so often in TV programmes on the Serengeti and Maasai Mara game parks.

"Am I seeing things? He asked the taxi driver. "Or do I spot some egrets down there by the water?"

"That's what they are – getting all over the place these days in Cornwall," he was told. "It's only recent, mind; I don't know where they came from but they've made themselves at home. Just up river they've started nesting in the trees – but it's only in the last ten or fifteen years."

He said he and his wife had watched one of these egrets fishing.

"He'd got blue legs," he said. "And was shuffling along in the shallow water, jerking his legs forward and stirring up the bottom, making little fish and waterlife move about – and then he'd stab them with that sharp beak! We were amazed! I believe they come from Africa but it must have taken them some time!"

From the bridge down towards the sea the river became a harbour for fishing boats, dinghies and yachts. Roads ran along both banks – doubling as quays and car parks – passing net stores, boatyards and workshops, many of which had been converted to cafés and other tourist temptations. The driver explained that was comparatively recent, too.

"Pilchards were the big thing here up to the nineteen fifties," he said. "In the old days they used to buy them in from Polperris and other villages, as well as from the boats here in Looe; then pack them into barrels and sell them all over England. Later they canned them in those little tins – the ones that used to cut your fingers; but now there's just a few boats bringing them in and they call them sprats and sell them fresh, up-country."

After crossing the bridge the road climbed away from sea level into wooded slopes, emerging amongst rolling grassland and cornfields for a mile or two before winding its down to Crumplehorn and along the swift River Pol into Polperris. Sebastian learned a lot about the farming and tourism from his driver and had taken a note of the man's phone number, ready for his journey back. Arriving at his destination the world stopped moving past him. He got out, stretched, paid the taxi driver and began bumping his suitcase along The Warren. His whole body seemed to slow down: to become more supple and even his face relaxed. The pressure was off: what a change from London! No traffic: just herring gulls coming, going and calling from above his head. Looking up he was surprised at just how big they were, looking down on him as they perched on stone chimneys and cemented slate roofs.

As instructed he looked for a sign on a green door in the wall on the right hand side saying 'The Studio'. He rang the bell.

"Mrs Johnson?"

"Miss, actually – but you must be Mr Trenleven?"

Rose opened the door wide and ushered Sebastian into a long, wide and bright room, three walls of which were covered by pictures. At one end a doorway led to the rest of the house; next to it, a desk with telephone and a pile of catalogues marked the reception area. At the other, several easels and a large table covered with tubes of paint, bottles of turps and pots of brushes indicated where the work was done. A series of French windows opened on to the quay outside.

"This is the gallery and studio. It used to be a net store, although my parents put in all the windows and the wooden floor when they bought it, back in the sixties. The quay outside is private. It's the nearest we get to a garden and we sit out there but in here is where I make my living – painting and selling these: she waved towards the pictures. We also run short courses but there isn't one on at the moment and we've been out to lunch. Do come in!"

She led him through into a big kitchen with more views of the harbour.

"We tend to eat in here – there's so much room and our classes are usually small. It's very convenient for coffee and tea breaks too. Then upstairs is the sitting room; and above that, there are bedrooms and the bathroom. I'll get Emily – she's my daughter. She can show you your room as soon as we've had a cuppa. The loo is just through there." She pointed down the hallway. "I've switched on the doormat bell so we can hear if anyone comes into the gallery and one of us can nip out and look after them. You'll have to excuse us if that happens – it's beginning to get into my busy time when I hope to sell some paintings." She escorted him up to the sitting room.

"So you see, I feel we have to put up a fight to save this natural treasure that has been looked after for hundreds of years in its present state," said Rosie. "That's why I wrote to the CPRE. I thought it might get their support because it's such a special meadow. If we lost it to commerce I think it would take the neighbouring farm with it too. The man there is trying to sell up, possibly to some local developers, and he's leaving quite a mess. He's never been able to get things together and although I'm not local by birth, the people here tell stories about his long record of failure. What it boils down to is that he's good at spending money but not work. He's not well respected and it's a shame, the way he's let that farm run down. Its buildings are mediaeval; they're listed and he's always on the brink of being issued with a compulsory order to get them repaired. If he sells, he'll move off to Newquay or somewhere and I've no doubt his future neighbours there, too, will have cause to regret it!"

"What's this man called? I ought to start making a full set of notes," said Sebastian, reaching into his briefcase for his foolscap notebook.

"He's called Eddie Rouse. His family's from over towards Plymouth where they survived mostly by selling land for building. His fields are a mess and his livestock always looks mucky and thin. His wife has a hard time keeping him clothed and fed."

"What about the possible buyers for the meadow? Do you know who they are?"

"Not for sure; they are being represented by one of the local land agents."

"So the church is definite about selling, is it?"

"Well, it's the Parochial Church Council. They're desperate for funds to repair the church roof and tower. Hardly anyone *goes* to church – the vicar is really dozy. He's been there for decades and I don't think they know how to get rid of him and the PCC seems to do what it likes. The chairman, who is one of my pet hates, has just stood down. I hope you don't mind me being so frank with you?"

"Not at all, Miss Johnson. I think it's important I understand the whole story."

"Oh do call me Rosie: everyone else does. I'm actually Rose Yi – because my mother's Chinese and my father's English. This was my grandparents' house – they were artists too and started up in Polperris in the sixties when they came down from London. I came to live with them when Emily was on the way – twenty-odd years ago and we've been here ever since – except that she now lives in London. She still comes down whenever she can and helps with the summer courses; she's here this week. It's always been her home. She's going back on Saturday; perhaps you could travel back together? She's in the art world too – works in a gallery in the West End."

"Otherwise you run all this single-handed?" This was Sebastian's tactful way of asking whether Emily's father was still around.

"More or less! There's just Emily – when she's here – and me. My parents work abroad for the UN: they come to stay when they are on leave.

"OK, Rosie – and please call me Sebastian – it looks as though we're going to have to work together for quite some time, if what I hear about public enquiries is typical. Do you mind if we start straight away? I'd like to ask a few questions."

"Fire away! I'm listening – even if I ought to be making the tea."

"Well just before you go I'd like to know who we're up against. Is it only a limp vicar and a few parish councillors? I was wondering why the CPRE felt it needed a barrister to fight their case. I would have thought it was fairly cut and dried – what with The Glebe being a Site of Special Scientific Interest in an Area of Outstanding National Beauty?"

"Well exactly! It should be! That's the scandal of the whole thing. The people here are treating it as though it's a foregone conclusion because the big local landowner always gets his way. His family always has! It's he who used to be chairman of the church council – effectively the owners of the Glebe – but he still has most of them in his pocket and he's mixed up in it."

"He's not Merlin is he?"

"No! I'm sure Merlin was more benign. This man is the owner of the Carnhill Estate. He's called Hugh Olver-Blythe and he's the nearest thing to a great white shark in a dark blue suit that you'll ever come across! Now if you'll excuse me just for a minute I'll call Emily."

§

Truth to tell, Rose and Emily had only just returned home when Sebastian rang the door-bell. The lunch had started late and gone on longer than expected. They had had to excuse themselves immediately after coffee.

"You put the kettle on, Emily, and I'll answer the door: I bet it's Mr Trenleven. At least he'll find us in all our finery after our posh lunch, rather than slopping around. You look good in that!"

Emily was wearing a skirt for the first time since her arrival; and a maroon velvet jacket that fitted her shapely figure. Her grandmother had brought the jacket the previous summer after a rare visit to Shenyang. Today, Emily had left it unbuttoned from the high collar down low enough to show her cleavage and decided to leave it like that in case the expected guest proved to take her fancy. It wasn't something she usually did in London but being back in Polperris, away from the formality of Bond Street and Hanover Square, always made her feel relaxed and flirtatious.

Sebastian Trenleven certainly did take Emily's fancy: so much so that she almost caught her elbow on the door as she carried the tea tray into the sitting room. He was so little like what she had imagined. Instead of a dry middle-aged lawyer, here was a handsome man of about thirty with a head of dark hair, smiling dark eyes, patrician nose and sensuous mouth. He stood up and offered to take the tray – almost took it from her hands.

"Let me, please!"

"It's quite all right," said Emily, completely losing her train of thought. Her legs felt quite weak, making her wonder whether it might be something she'd eaten. She managed to put the tray down on the coffee table in front of the sofa and took the hand that Sebastian offered, trying to regain her composure. Sebastian, too, was caught by surprise – for the second time in a matter of minutes. This wasn't at all what he had expected: yet another ravishing Oriental beauty – a younger version of the lady who had opened the door and welcomed him. This one had even fairer skin and just a hint of brown in her long shining black hair. Unusually for him, he found it hard to say anything:

"How do you do?" He managed.

"How do you do?" She replied; and backed away, looking down. She felt suddenly bashful and exposed. His eyes had almost taken her breath away: the way they seemed to read exactly what she was thinking, while showing instant admiration.

He was taller than she had expected; and much broader across the shoulders – more like an athlete than a barrister.

Rose, following Emily back into the room, noticed with amusement the frisson that had passed between the two young people and came to the rescue.

"Sebastian, this is my daughter Emily; and this is Sebastian Trenleven, the barrister who's going to help us fight for the Glebe. Do you think you could get those chocolate biscuits from the cupboard in the kitchen? I forgot to put them out."

"OK," said Emily, still covered in confusion and glad to find a reason for leaving long enough to do up one more button in her jacket. Sebastian had, however, taken in what he had seen and been duly impressed. Not only was this vision beautiful, she appeared sexy – yet demure. He felt his spirits rising.

Rose continued explaining the outline of the planning application.

"Our problem is that this government seems to have taken all the sting out of laws that protect the countryside – if someone wants to take it over to make money," she said. "This land is supposed to be safe from development because of its various designations and yet anyone putting enough pressure on the district council, or has enough money to keep appealing, can side-step all the rules and do what they like! The 'Big Society' is put across as giving power back to local people but it's more like 'The Big *Money* Society!'"

"I have to confess this is my first brief of quite this kind," said Sebastian. "I'm out of my comfort zone – away from the city streets but I have to agree with you. Even around London I can see luxury flats being built in the Green Belt; and you are right about the big money; chief executive officers have been awarding themselves massive rises in salary – can you believe it – forty percent on average between 2010 and 2011 and goodness knows what it will be this year! But I always thought that rural Cornwall was the place to go for peace and quiet. Have 'the suits' arrived here, too, looking for crisp pound notes?"

"They certainly have! Cornwall used to be an escape from the rat-race for some people," said Rose. "My grandparents were a good example. They came down fifty years ago, buying this house and doing it up. It was one of the few places they could afford to live and the old fishermen used to tell them tales of terrible poverty here in the village at the beginning of the last Century. People sometimes lived on pilchards and bread, if they could afford it; and in winter when the weather was too bad to go to sea, they had to go to the fields at the top of the hill and set baited fish-hooks to catch wild birds for 'birdie-pie'. It *was* peaceful for a few wealthy families who lived like kings but Polperris children often went without shoes, even in winter."

"I thought the two world wars had levelled things up, even in these distant corners of the Empire, but you say it's still poor around here?"

"It's true, Labour governments got the landed gentry to pay huge inheritance taxes and there were others like my grandparents who brought some money with them when they came but this is still officially a deprived area, so we can expect more EU grants for roads and tourism."

"And less resistance to preserving the natural beauty that makes the place so attractive?" Added Sebastian.

"Exactly! That's how North Cornwall was laid waste by developers – it's not much more than a suburb of London now, with surfing beaches attached. Every weekend the young of London race down with their wind-surf boards lashed to the roof of their flash cars."

"Not here on the south coast?"

"No, not yet, thank goodness," said Rose. "We don't have so many Atlantic rollers coming in on sandy beaches. Here in Polperris we are more 'Channel coast' and it's only further down west that you get those enormous waves. It's very different down by Lands End – and every year trippers get washed off the rocks. It's much safer around here."

"I've never been here before," said Sebastian; "or further west, I'm afraid. My parents, although claiming to be Cornish by descent, always took me to France."

"Well we can remedy some of that straight away. It's lovely weather and once you have taken that tie off, I'm sure Emily could take you for a bit of sight-seeing, couldn't you, darling?" Emily was once again taken by surprise; this time by her mother's suggestion. She hadn't mentioned it earlier. "You could go along the cliff path towards Lantrelland and point out the church tower from there. Mr Trenleven could get some idea of the setting."

"Oh! OK," said Emily, still somewhat nonplussed. She would normally have joined in conversation with a visitor like Sebastian but had found herself content simply to watch him and enjoy his soft-spoken voice and cultured speech.

On his part, Sebastian Trenleven could hardly believe his eyes. When the door in the wall had been opened by this smartly dressed and beautiful woman his expectation of a tweedy country lady had been blown away. Then when a younger and even more ravishing version had appeared with the tea tray he had experienced a tightening across his chest and a rush of adrenalin that brought him to his feet effortlessly. Now he was being invited to go walking with this glorious creature who looked as though she was straight from the West End.

"I'd better get out of these clothes," said Emily. "We're just back from a lunch, so if you don't mind hanging on a moment, I'll change. I can show you your room on the way up."

"Well I'm glad you didn't dress up just for me!" Sebastian laughed. "I thought it was all a bit formal!"

"Oh yes, don't worry! We usually scruff around in smocks or trousers covered in paint. We're not unduly impressed by city gents! Some of Mum's students arrive looking like bank managers but it's surprising how soon they thaw out once they have some charcoal or a paint brush in the hand."

Emily picked up Sebastian's case and moved into the narrow passage leading to the stairs.

"This way – it's up two flights. Whatever have you brought in this suitcase? It weighs a tonne." She puts it down.

"Let me! It's my laptop and camera and some books on planning. I've been swotting on the train." Sebastian reached down for the case and bending over to do so, found himself very close to her and her clean floral scent. Emily too, breathed in the fresh maleness of Sebastian's suit and its hint of expensive aftershave. She decided this was very pleasing and stood back against the wall, automatically putting her hands up to push her long hair back over her shoulders. Sebastian was very conscious of her shapely body, as he passed towards the staircase. He had always liked Far Eastern beauty and was already enchanted, enjoying being so close to her. Conservation of East Cornwall suddenly became even more compelling.

"This is my room," said Emily, as they came to a landing. "And we've put you up one more flight, second door on the right. I think you'll find it's all ready but shout if you want anything. I'll nip in here and change." She sought refuge in familiar surroundings, giving the teddy bear that had been her bedmate for more than two decades, a big hug, before undoing those jacket buttons once more.

§

"I know it's nothing to do with me but isn't it a bit odd, you coming all this way to take on a case of this kind?" Emily asked, as she and Sebastian started walking down the Warren towards the harbour.

"It must seem like that but there are two good reasons," said Sebastian. "The first is that I'm always nagging my father about the environment. I've been in Greenpeace ever since I can remember – my mother was a big supporter – they were my heroes. When I was young I was always trying to save the whales and protect seals in Canada; I can even remember when the French secret service sank the Rainbow Warrior in 1985, killing a photographer. I was only about three but my mother was so outraged when we saw it on TV news I've never forgotten it! I couldn't bear to see her upset. She had bought one of their big Rainbow Warrior posters. We've still got it, framed and hanging in the passage upstairs at home."

"Is she still involved?"

"No, she died in 2002."

"I'm sorry – that must have been terrible."

"It was. I don't think Dad and I have ever got over it. She was French – I'm 'half and half'. Are you, too? Hope you don't mind my asking?"

"Everyone does, sooner or later and I don't mind but I think I'm less 'half and half' than 'one-third to two-thirds', although it's hard to tell without a DNA test and that's really expensive for women. My mother is as near half and half as you can get – half Chinese, half English. Her parents met when they were working in Tanzania. They got married and still work abroad. I have no idea about my grandparents on my father's side because I'm not even sure who *he* is! My mother says it was a 'short but passionate relationship' and she didn't realise she was carrying me until later, by which time she had lost touch with him; but as you can see, I'm very much like her to look at – definitely 'Chinesey' and at school they used to call me all the usual racist names. I didn't mind if it was my friends but I used to bash up anyone else who said it!"

"You must have been a terror!" Sebastian took a long glance across at Emily's face, half hidden by her thick wall of hair. She sensed it and looked back: they both smiled, amused and sympathetic.

"I was – am, when roused; although in my present job I have to be the essence of coolness – smart and aloof, that's me. Can't you imagine it?

"Not really!"

"The only time I've got into fights was here in Polperris, when I was a kid but in London my sole aim is to relieve people of cheques or get their credit card into my little machine so I'm always very calm and calculating."

"I wasn't sure whether you might be part Japanese – or perhaps Malaysian – but neither you nor your mother have that usual 'pinkness' from the English side."

"Now you're getting a bit technical!"

"I'm sorry – I don't mean to be. It's just that I admire your complexion: sort of light gold. I don't mean to be pushy but – well – you've kind of taken me by storm."

"I'm not sure if that's a compliment but I think we'd better change the subject," said Emily – although her legs had started to disobey her, becoming reluctant to stride out. "You were saying about Greenpeace."

"Oh yes – and my mother. She had been at school with an Indian girl from Bhopal whose parents worked for Union Carbide. Both of them died one night just before the end of Christmas term, back in the eighties, when poisonous gas escaped from the pesticide plant. I'm sure you know about it."

"I do. I remember people had to wait decades for compensation. There are still court cases going on about it."

"Yes. It was only in June two years ago that seven ex-Union Carbide employees, were convicted of 'causing death by negligence'. They got two years imprisonment and a fine of about $2,000 each."

"Thousands of people died, didn't they?"

"More than two thousand died immediately and a total of nearly four thousand deaths are directly attributed to the disaster; but more than half a million people suffered injuries or illness because of it – and many are still suffering."

"It seems so unjust! These big companies just seem to get away with it. My blood boils when I think how big money tramples over everyone and everything."

"Can I pop into that newspaper shop a minute?" Said Sebastian.

"Sure: I'll wait here." Emily stood casually turning the rack of glossy postcards. They reminded her what a colourful and exotic village this was and how lucky she was to have a family base here. She was glad of the pause but still felt slightly off balance being in Sebastian's company. She couldn't wait to talk to him some more: she wanted to know *all* about him.

"Did you get what you wanted?"

"Oh yes, thanks. Just a lottery ticket. Don't laugh – it gives me a cheap thrill every week. Between now and the next time I buy one I know I'm in with a chance of becoming a Euro-millionaire! I can day-dream about how I'd spend it!"

"Some hopes!" Emily laughed as they resumed their walk.

Her legs had regained their strength as they made their way towards the steps up to the cliff path. Sebastian fell in behind her, nearly tripping on an uneven stone step because he wasn't looking where he was going. He was hypnotised by Emily's perfect shape and mobility. Her skin-hugging jeans presented a vision of such sculptured roundness, and every step made each side move with an independence that shimmered with energy. He noted too that her hair almost reached her waist as it flowed and swayed, shining, down her back.

"I'd still like to hear the other reason as to why you wanted to take on this case, so far from London," Emily turned to ask him.

"I didn't *want* to. My father *told* me to; and that brings me to the second reason. He met a very attractive lady at a dinner who works part-time for CPRE and I think he rather fancied her – but please don't let on that I said so if you meet him."

Emily's amusement and peel of laughter stopped her so suddenly that Sebastian had to put his hands up to stop himself bumping into her. He held her hips just for a moment as they stood on the same step and he felt her shaking with mirth. It was hardly wide enough for two as they laughed at the thought of a dignified senior barrister being beguiled by a middle-aged lady.

"Come on, or it'll be dark," said Emily, taking the lead up the last few steps. They reached the cliff path as it skirted the outer harbour and headed westwards past the fisherman's shelter, winding between overgrown bushes and rocky outcrops.

"I think, to be fair to my father, he wants me to work on a wide variety of briefs so that I can find out where I'd like to specialise. He's a criminal barrister but our chambers cover most things."

"It sounds bad, 'criminal barrister' – as though he's a crook, too!"

"He often says he spends more time with criminals than he does with good honest folk and I think he's become a bit cynical.

He sees himself as a technician, hired to see the law take its proper course, in favour of his client."

"I would have thought that you could win cases better if you felt strongly about something," said Emily, striding ahead.

"Or at least appear to!"

"But *you* wouldn't want to take on our case if you didn't feel it was worthwhile, would you? You won't get paid much!"

"I must say I did like the idea; and the thought of coming down here to Cornwall; and now I've met you I'm actively looking forward to taking the job very seriously."

"But I'm not here most of the time," said Emily, laughing.

"No, but you will be in London and I'm sure I'll have to organise several appointments to update myself on Polperris news, won't I?"

"I'm terribly busy at work, you know."

"Oh – that's sad; but I shall speak with your secretary."

"That's me, too!"

"Well in that case, you will have to work it out with yourself! Just check the diary. This scenery is stunning!" Sebastian stopped for a moment to take in the wide expanse of water and sky as he looked out from the leafy cliff edge. The sea had an oily gloss and made hardly a sound as it lapped against the rocks at the bottom of the sheer drop next to the path. This far from the village even the sea gulls were quiet.

The path climbed steadily upwards. Only when they reached the brow of the hill did the next vista come into sight. It was spectacular.

"That's Lantrelland Bay," said Emily. "Let's sit down a minute." She pointed to a National Trust bench above the path, angled so that walkers could face the scenery ahead. The sun, low above the horizon, was deep red in the darkening sky.

"Isn't that fantastic?"

"It is," said Sebastian. "But you can see the air pollution – the sun should never be that red unless a volcano has filled the air with dust. Look – you can see how mucky the atmosphere is." He pointed towards the horizon. "That's because we in an area of high pressure at the moment – all that muck is just circulating round Western Europe. The darkness and red sun are because of particulates from diesel fuel, rubber dust from car tyres and fumes from power plants. I bet you'll see them announcing poor air quality on the TV news tonight. It's been getting worse over the past few days."

"You can *feel* the difference when the wind goes west again," said Emily. "I think the rain washes the air; it smells so fresh after travelling three thousand miles over the Atlantic. It's lovely having good weather for a bit and I've enjoyed the sun but sometimes you can feel it on your chest, can't you? My mother says when she was a child the sky was much bluer, especially overhead. She says it's always pale now because there's so much 'stuff' floating about above us. But look – Lantrelland church tower is over there – and the Glebe is just next to it. We'll drive over tomorrow so you can take some photos."

"That's what I was hoping," said Sebastian.

"There's just one more place I'd like to show you, now we've walked this far. There's an amazing cave just down below here." Emily pointed to a narrow track leading off the main cliff path. "Not many people know about it."

She let him go ahead, down the steeply winding trail, stepping down from rock to rock until they reached the high-tide mark. Almost at once Sebastian found himself at the opening of a great cleft in the slate cliff. There was even a tiny beach of grey stones sloping into the crystal clear water of the narrow inlet. Inside the cave it was almost dark, only the beach being bathed in red sunlight.

They crunched their way inside and turned to take in a scene that contained no evidence of human existence: just rocks, sea and sky. Away from the shore some gannets were patrolling for pilchards.

For a few moments they stood at the entrance, listening and looking. It was such a perfect setting: quiet, calm and deserted. As if prompted by instinct they turned to each other. Sebastian, unable to restrain himself, took Emily in his arms and kissed her fully on the mouth, pulling her tight to himself. He knew it was risky and beyond the behaviour one could expect from such a new acquaintance but it had taken even him by surprise. It was the look he had seen in Emily's eyes that had been the final key to his boldness. In those dark eyes he could see the pupils, wide open as if taking in as much vision of him as possible.

He was half-expecting to be repulsed. This girl was a feisty creature with a mind of her own yet she yielded, allowing herself to be held, relaxing against him, letting him take some of her weight. He felt her mouth open just slightly, the tip of her tongue just meeting his.

Emily was caught unawares, too, though she knew it was what she wanted almost from the moment she had set eyes on him. She had felt a crazy urge to consume him, ravish and conquer him to make him hers for ever. As she revelled in his strength and firm hold, the memory of nearly dropping the tray at the sight of him made her laugh with pleasure, breaking the magic of the moment. They ended the kiss and he raised his head, looking down at her joyful face.

"Share the joke!"

"We are mad!" She said, and told him – to his instant relief – of the near accident, and he joined her mood of celebration. "Come on: this won't do – but now I feel I've really met you!"

"I must apologise. I'm not usually like this, I promise you! I'm supposed to be a gentleman!" Sebastian's sense of decorum overcame his fast breathing and took his attention away from the stirrings in his trousers.

"It must be the Cornish air – and the cave's probably haunted by all the others who have done the same; but come on, we'll be be-nighted if we don't make our way back."

"I wonder whether it's warm enough for a swim," said Sebastian.

"I expect it is but I don't have my bikini and I don't expect you have yours and it would be daft to go skinny dipping within an hour of meeting!" Emily extricated herself from his embrace and started back up the rocky track.

CHAPTER 5

Emily's mobile starts chirruping.

"I wonder who *that* is? I didn't think it worked out here," she said, digging into her pocket as they neared the fisherman's lookout shelter, on the way home.

"Hello? Mum!" She stopped; and waited in silence for a few seconds.

"OK! See you in a minute! Bye."

"My mother wants us to buy fish and chips on the way through the village. That all right with you? I expect you are starving?"

"That would suit me perfectly: yes I am peckish."

Sebastian was also very happy. He had not felt like this for a very long time.

It was now almost dusk and from the high path they looked down on the village. This was Polperris at its very best: early evening in mid-summer, the houses clean and freshly painted; in the harbour, orderly rows of a colourful mixture of fishing boats and sailing dinghies gently rocking at high tide.

What he couldn't see, on this his first visit, was the advance of small crabs and fish that came in with the sea, twice a day, to begin their work of retrieving tiny pieces of food, dead leaf, insects and anything edible that may have come down in Polperris' fast-flowing stream from under the bridge. At high tide like this there was no muddled seaweed or stony streamlets in view; boats no longer tilted over on their keel, tethered by long ropes draped with green algae, waiting for the fresh salty tide to refloat them. The clear water, fresh from ocean currents passing the harbour entrance now hid the untidy harbour bottom to give polished reflections of the quaint and jumbled village that rose around them.

That was one of the pleasures to come when he and Emily worked on the family dinghy in months to come, cleaning and painting at low tide, then watching the creatures following the wavelets as they advanced almost imperceptibly, refreshing the harbour once again.

"How about a nightcap?" Rose asked their guest as they finished clearing away the polystyrene chip boxes and paper napkins. "Can you manage a whisky? We always keep a stock in case my parents turn up. It's my father's tipple."

"That would be great, thanks," said Sebastian. "And perhaps we could talk a little business; otherwise I shall feel guilty of wasting the chamber's resources."

"I'm sure you are allowed a certain amount of time off," said Emily. "If you ignore the 'work to life balance' you know what will happen – as it did to Jack!"

"Become a dull boy? You're not far wrong. I think I already have! The past couple of years have been a slog. I've been tending to take home a briefcase full of work almost every night – like Dad. We could do with a change but this project is beginning to feel like fun already." He and Emily exchanged glances and Sebastian thought he could detect just the slightest blush on her flawless cheeks.

"There is one question I'd like to ask, now we're all sitting down. Just what *is* a 'glebe field'? In all the rush I've been more concerned to look up planning law than I have the definition of what a glebe field is. I 'm sure I should have done that first!"

"Well I didn't do it either, until I found myself on the Planning Committee," said Rose. "Until then we just went there for picnics and walks and it never occurred to question what the name meant. I thought it just meant 'a field belonging to the church'."

"Well isn't it?"

"According to Wikipedia, until 1978 it actually belonged personally to the vicar of the church concerned. After that, the ownership went to the Diocesan Board of Finance to which the parish, or 'benefice', belonged. In some cases that could be even in another county!"

"How confusing!"

"Yes – the position of vicar in most parishes is controlled by a 'patron' who owns the 'gift' of that parish. Goodness knows how it all came about but it's like the rest of our history: a real tangle. I expect a monastery would send a few monks to some heathen area to acquire land and build a new church to 'get things going' – and then keep possession of the building but you'd need to check that out. Lords of the manor on which a church was built, owned the patronage for that church – the right to appoint a vicar – with the agreement of the bishop. Long ago you could buy and sell such a patronage and people did. The parsonage was often somewhere for a wealthy family to place a second or third son ...

... but I don't think patronage is going to affect our battle here. What counts is that the PCC – Parochial Church Council – has persuaded the church hierarchy in Truro that this field needs to be sold off if the church is not to fall down!"

"So did it mean that all vicars were officially 'farmers', before 1978?" Emily asked. "I'm not being facetious: it just seems to be outside their remit."

"It meant that some of them were land-owners," said Rose. "The glebe belonged to the benefice and was originally supposed to provide part of the priest's income. Most of their money came from tithes – a percentage of the produce of all the farms in the parish, which would be stored in the tithe barn and sold off in due course to finance the church's work and maintenance. Glebe land was either granted by the lord of the manor – often for one of his relatives appointed as vicar – or donated by grateful landowners who owed the Almighty for some deliverance or another – or perhaps absolution for the usual human failings."

"Like what?"

"Use your imagination, Emily! Murder, robbery – secret love?"

"So old Miss Weeks pays grazing fees to the Bishop of Truro?"

"I guess so – or to his treasurer; but it's not going to be very much but if the field is sold off it would affect her, for a start. We ought to go and see what we can learn from her. I'll phone and see whether it's OK for us to drop round tomorrow – or the next day, if you can stay that long, Sebastian?"

"I was hoping to stay until the weekend, if you can put up with me."

"That's what I was expecting and it's fine. You won't mind, will you Emily?"

"No Mum." Emily busied herself plumping up a cushion next to her, trying to look nonchalant.

"I'll phone Miss Weeks: see if we can go over in the morning."

"And I'll turn in, if that's OK with you? It's been a long day," said Sebastian.

§

"Do you want to come with us, Emily?" Rose was clearing away breakfast, aided by their guest. "You don't need to do this, Sebastian," she said.

"It's habit: I do it every day at home otherwise it wouldn't get done except Tuesdays and Fridays when our cleaning lady comes in. Dad's not good at domestic chores. He disappears with the Times as soon as he's finished."

"I'll come, yes please. I've got nothing to do here and it will be nice to see Miss Weeks again. It must be a year since we met."

"Good! You can help me show Sebastian the Glebe and the church and then we can drop in to see her. She's invited us to coffee at about eleven."

Visiting The Glebe made Sebastian understand why Rose was so determined to try to defend it's peace and uniqueness. It was like stepping back into history – there was nothing to remind him of the Twenty-first Century, looking across the meadow towards the ancient church. Sebastian took photographs and made notes; then they drove back down the lane to the first cottage with its granite and slate garden wall. Miss Weeks straightened her back from weeding by the path up to the door, the top half of which was hooked open, allowing the visitors a glimpse of polished furniture and plates on the dresser.

"What a delightful house," said Sebastian as Rose stopped the engine. "The kind you might expect to see on a Cornish calendar."

"I think it was, not long ago," said Rose. "Miss Weeks is a super gardener. She wins prizes at local flower shows."

The old lady welcomed them at the gate and they spent some time hearing about the various blossoms and unusual plants in the garden as they moved towards the door. Miss Weeks enjoyed talking about her hobby. Once inside she settled them into the armchairs and sofa before going off to the kitchen. It gave Emily the chance to tell Sebastian more about her: she spoke softly:

"She must be nearly eighty. And goodness knows how old the pony and donkey are. I can remember them in the Glebe as long as I've been coming here!"

"Her family has always lived in Lantrelland and owned the next-door farm until her father died, before the Second World War," added Rose. "The Rouses bought it and have let it run down ever since and I've heard it's now being sold. Eddie is taking 'early retirement', which means he's going to do more of the same, without making a mess over such a large area. I haven't got much time for him."

"Who's that, dear?" Miss Weeks was back, with the coffee.

"The Rouse family: We were telling Sebastian about the farm – having been in your family before the war."

"A sore point, I'm afraid, Rosie. Eddie Rouse *has* let it run down, hasn't he? Let's hope the new owner tidies it up and makes it productive again. My father used to make a good living there and it's wonderful soil, and there's hardly any frost, so near the sea."

"So it *is* being sold?"

"Oh yes, although I'm not sure to whom. It's being done by sealed bid and the auctioneer hasn't been very forthcoming about the result although I'm sure the bidders will know by now."

"It must have been sad for you to leave the farm," said Sebastian, joining the conversation. "I understand your family was there for a long time."

"Hundreds of years! Yes it was a blow but I kept this cottage and managed to get the tenancy of the Glebe so that I could at least have somewhere for my two favourite animals. I feel the Weeks family still has a foothold in Lantrelland." She laughed. "Although now, we're about to lose it!"

"That would be so sad!" said Emily. "Do you remember years ago, Mum, we used to come here often for picnics and then go swimming down in the bay. When I was about twelve. We used to see you in your garden and you always waved."

"I remember," Miss Weeks said. "I thought at first you came from abroad: tourists, perhaps."

"That was partly true. My grandmother is from China, and Mum and I look a lot like her. My grandfather came down from London in the forties, with his parents – the Johnsons. They lived down on the quay in Polperris."

"The artists? Oh yes, I was one of the first to buy one of their pictures. It's in my front parlour. You are an artist too, aren't you Rosie – as well as a councillor?"

"Yes and I'm wondering whether I've taken on too much!"

"I'm sure you'll manage, dear. You've kept things going for all these years! It can't have been easy – what with having your grandparents *and* Emily here to look after too."

"I'm sure I was no trouble," laughed Emily, "but there is one thing I've always wanted to tell you, Miss Weeks; and this Glebe business has brought it back to mind. It's about this ring." She held out her slender right hand to show off the bright gold.

"I found it one day in the Glebe; on one of our picnics and I was allowed to keep it after Mum had reported it and everything."

"I remember that, too," said Miss Weeks. "The local policeman asked me if I'd had anyone enquiring about lost property and it caught my imagination."

"Oh: why was that?"

"I wondered whether it might have had something to do with one of my ancestors – I don't know how many greats – great aunt. It was the younger sister of my umpteen-greats grandmother: a very poignant story – so sad."

"Oh do tell us," said Emily. "We do have time, don't we Mum? I'm sure you won't mind, will you Sebastian."

"Of course not! I'm just as interested as you and I've only a few questions for Miss Weeks. They can wait."

"Well: this however-many greats aunt was only seventeen when she fell madly in love with the oldest son of the lord of the manor at Carnhill on home leave from abroad. In a whirlwind romance he asked her to marry him. Funnily enough she too was called Emily. She was one of the vicar's daughters at Lantrelland and her elder sister, Elspeth, eventually married my ancestor Henry Weeks. Later, in Victorian times, the vicarage burned down and was never re-built because everyone around here was joining with the Methodists and other chapels." Miss Weeks paused as she handed round the coffee.

"Emily's fiancée was called Hugh Olver," she continued. "The oldest son at the manor was always called Hugh and still is today – although they hyphened on the 'Blythe' because they were so pleased when one of the Olvers married the daughter of another rich Cornish family about a hundred years ago. Both families originally made their fortunes from the slave trade and sugar estates in the West Indies."

"I wondered how the Olver-Blythes had become so wealthy," said Rose. "It's not something they talk about in their guided tours around their lovely mansion."

"I suppose it wouldn't be very nice having paintings in the tea-room of slaves being flogged in amongst the sugar-cane," said Sebastian.

"No indeed," said Miss Weeks. "Emily Tregrove – her father was the Rev Paul Tregrove – was due to marry Hugh and go with him back to Jamaica to live with him on one of their estates there. He was back in England to find a wife and according to Emily's diary, which her sister found after Emily's death, they first saw each other at Lantrelland church. He was supposed to be meeting 'suitable' young ladies from around the county and his parents had arranged all kinds of balls and parties for him but the young couple were introduced at Matins one Sunday morning and it was love at first sight. He refused to have anything to do with any of the other girls. In a matter of weeks he had asked her to marry him and she had agreed and was wearing his ring. Everything was wonderful: preparations began for their wedding. The vicar, Emily's father, was delighted at the splendid match that had been made. He was more pleased than the Olver family at first realised, because despite his vocation as priest, he had a skeleton in his cupboard. All the parishioners knew about it – as did the people in Polperris; but since they did not move in the same circles as the Olvers, the family at the manor took some time to find out. I can imagine it was the servants who tipped them off."

"What was the skeleton?" Emily asked.

"Well, the vicar was himself a local man. His father had been Rector of Polperris. He and his brothers were educated locally until they were old enough to go away to boarding school and on to college. When Paul was a theological student he was home for the summer and became involved with one of the Puckey girls. She was well known in the village for being 'rather wild'. The Puckeys were descendents of prisoners taken during the Spanish raid on Cornwall in 1595. They were probably of Moorish descent. When the Rector discovered that the two had been together un-chaperoned for many afternoons, he insisted his son marry the fiery and beautiful young woman. She in turn gave birth to Emily – incidentally more than a year after the marriage – and became a pillar of society, even though villagers always joked about her family and her frivolous youth."

"That's hardly a skeleton, surely?" Said Sebastian.

"It was in those days! At least in 'county' circles. Old Squire Olver was enraged and told the younger Hugh that if he married Emily, he would be disinherited and sent off to Australia or

59

worse! You can imagine the young man's predicament and his instinct for survival quickly overcame his passion for Emily. Emily's sister Elspeth discovered what happened when she found the diary sometime later. The last entry describes how, one terrible autumn evening, in the middle of one of those raging south-west gales, Hugh arrived on his horse at the vicarage and asked to speak with Emily alone. He then told her it was all 'off' and explained why; and without waiting even to comfort her he fled back to the Manor, leaving her in a state of shock and outrage. Emily was distraught; snatched her cloak from the hall and fought her way through the wind and rain into the churchyard. She went to the corner of the graveyard where some yew trees, leaning over from being constantly pressed by the West winds, hid part of the wall from the view of the church and its surroundings. It was where she and Hugh used to meet when he was supposedly 'out riding' and she was 'tending the flowers in the church' during their short and beautiful courtship.

"I'll show you what she wrote the next day. I've got it here."

Miss Weeks went to a bookshelf and carefully took out the remains of a leather-covered diary. She opened it and allowed her visitors to see the faded writing.

"It's very hard to read," said Emily.

"It is indeed," said Miss Weeks, "but years ago I spent ages working out what she had written. Her writing was so shaky and I'm sure those marks must be tears. I'll read it out – it finishes: 'I cannot believe that Hugh, who told me he could not live without me, now denies any future for us together. It is as if he has become someone else, not the Hugh whom I love. He spoke to me like a stranger. I cannot bear it...'. "

"Does it just stop?" Rose asked, with concern.

"Those are the last words in the diary," said Miss Weeks. "It's so sad, isn't it? Family records show that she developed a high fever that same morning, and died of pneumonia two days later, having hardly stopped weeping. Elspeth wrote in her own diary that when Emily had finally come back to the vicarage that awful night, soaked to the skin and icy cold, she was no longer wearing the ring. "

Emily Johnson now looked disconcerted; she began to take the golden ring from her right hand.

"I'm sure this must be the ring," she said. "It's the one I found in the Glebe, down in that corner near those yew trees. You ought to have it, Miss Weeks. It belongs to your family."

"Emily, dear; my sweet child: I don't want it! I want you to keep it! When I heard that a ring had been found by a young girl I thought it was providential and that at last it might bring some happiness once again, as it must have done when Hugh first gave it to the other Emily. Isn't it extraordinary that it's your name too? I purposely didn't mention anything to the policeman because I wanted you to keep it – and I want you to keep it now. It looks beautiful on your lovely slender hand and it gives me pleasure to see it every time we meet."

"So you knew, all the time?"

"Oh yes, dear! And enjoyed knowing! The policeman said it was you and praised you for being so honest."

"That's so kind of you Miss Weeks!" Rose took the old lady's hand. Emily was too overcome to speak and had tears brimming in her eyes; she found a hankie to wipe them away before asking:

"And what happened to that Hugh Olver? I hope he died at sea!"

"No he didn't: much as he might have deserved to," smiled Miss Weeks. "He married a young lady from Saltash two months later and took her off to Jamaica, where they had four children – and became very rich. They returned to Cornwall thirty years later when he had various ailments that made it hard for him to stay in a hot climate. They finished their days at Carnhill and were the ones who added the grand west wing and the extensive outbuildings now used as a museum and tea-room. When they died, the oldest son came back from the West Indies to become squire and one of his brothers stayed on to run the estates, which he did very successfully. When he in turn died, never having taken an 'official wife' but leaving various light-brown offspring, his older brother's family here sold off the Jamaican estates, slaves and all, for a huge sum of money just a year or two before slavery was banned in the eighteen thirties. Once that happened,

61

of course, the profit went out of the sugar so they had got out at the right time."

"So Emily Tregrove's older sister went on to marry the son of Farmer Weeks your ancestor?"

"She did – and I'm the last surviving descendent with that name; and this cottage is the last little bit of Cornwall our family owns, although there are still families of Puckeys living in Polperris – mostly fishermen and builders; very distant cousins, I suppose. The Weeks side of the family died out, except for me: a bit sad – although I enjoy life and my garden and pensioner animals keep me busy and active; and of course visits from people like you are always exciting. It's a pleasure to see you. I've watched you grow up into such a beautiful and sophisticated young lady, Emily! It has been good to know you 'inherited' that ring."

"Well it has certainly not brought *me* bad luck," said Emily. "Touch wood, I've been amazingly lucky ever since I found it: passed all my exams, caught all my flights and arrived safely in all sorts of exciting places when visiting my grandparents and now having a great job and nice flat in London – as well as Mum down here always glad to see me!"

"I'm glad you appreciate me, Emily," said Rose, laughing. "How kind of you, Miss Weeks, to let Emily keep the ring. It was most generous."

"Well I had no means of identifying it and I don't think the police would have been very convinced by a two-hundred-year old diary, do you?"

"You never know! They might have; but the least we can do now is to help make sure that your animals don't lose their grazing; and that you don't find yourself over-run grockles and emmets," said Rose. "Sebastian, do you have any questions for Miss Weeks?"

"Well I do, Miss Weeks, if you have a few more minutes," said Sebastian, taking out his large, lined notebook and pen. "First, of course, is to ask whether you would agree to appear as a witness for the CPRE at any public enquiry we might be able to obtain?"

"Of course I would, Mr Trenleven; but before you all go, I'd like to show you Emily Tregrove's grave – if you haven't seen it before?"

"Oh yes, please; we might have seen it but without knowing its relevance," said Rose. "Meanwhile, I'll eaves-drop on your questions and answers. The more I can learn about The Glebe, the better."

"One more question – what's a grockle?" Asked Sebastian.

"It's what we in Devon and Cornwall call holiday-makers: most disrespectful, considering how important they are to our economy!"

It was nearly lunchtime when the Johnson women and Sebastian Trenleven gave Miss Weeks a lift back to the church and followed her to the east end.

"Her father had her buried as near the altar as he could," said Miss Weeks. "They used to leave spaces in the graveyard for 'special' people – usually incumbents who were particularly beloved by the parishioners and I understand Emily's untimely death was a blow felt not only by her family but by the whole congregation from the surrounding farms. After that, the Olver family more or less stopped attending the church here and built their own chapel."

"With their own ill-gotten gains!" Emily sounded quite angry. "And now they're up to something fishy again. We saw Hugh in the Glebe with Eddie Rouse and Brian Rogersson. I wonder what they are up to now."

"Well Hugh Olver-Blythe is no longer chairman of the Church Council. It was his father who started coming back to the church here. He was quite a nice man and it was the first time for generations that any of them had ventured back: it took so long for the ill-feeling to fade. The present squire is very different from his father and only took on the church responsibility until his father died. I've always found him very cold and calculating, although he's always perfectly charming and polite."

"He's always immaculately dressed, too," said Rose. "He was wearing a very expensive suit when we saw him here yesterday."

"He seems to spend most of his time in London, although I don't think his family here misses him very much!" Miss Weeks gave a wicked smile. "I gather they are never short of guests over at Carnhill – mostly Mrs Olver-Blythes friends from the golf club. Now – here we are. This is Emily Tregrove's grave."

"No epitaph?"

"Only what you can see: simply her name and 'Born 15th May 1802 Died July 29th 1819'."

"Her poor mother," said Rose. "Her poor family."

CHAPTER 6

Breakfast in the dining room at Carnhill House was unusually conversational. The previous day, Hermione Olver-Blythe had met Brian Rogersson at Looe Golf Club and learned of her husband's site visit at Lantrelland.

Hugh rarely told her much about his business and she had to follow up any tip-offs concerning his financial deals or extramarital dalliances that might come her way. She did have one or two particular friends who took malicious pleasure in keeping her informed mainly of the latter. Brian Rogersson had his own motivation with regard to Hermione and she knew how to exploit this.

Some of Hermione's friends also had husbands who spent most weeks 'up in London', supposedly 'making an honest bob'. Occasionally she was able to score off her chums when Hugh self-righteously reported seeing another member of their county set 'playing away'. From Brian Rogersson she had learned about the intended purchase of the Rouse farm and the machinations over the Glebe, although he had taken advantage of her interest by finding a quiet spot in the bar where he might, as he would put it 'chat her up a bit' and perhaps attain knee contact. Hermione was all he had ever dreamed of – titled, great looks, immaculately dressed, beautifully spoken and part of the 'county set'. She was, to him, still in perfect condition, well groomed, elegant and desirable. His hope was that she might appreciate his attention (some might describe it as 'a bit of rough') at some time in the future.

Back at the breakfast table Hermione, by careful questioning and a less chilly approach than Hugh usually expected at that time of morning, had dredged up a little more information about the recent meeting that had accounted for his suit having to be sent to the cleaners for removal of mud and manure. She was pleased about his investment in yet more land but suspicious of his involvement in helping Eddie Rouse to get planning permission for development of The Glebe. Hugh had told her as little as he could about his longer term objectives but she understood that getting planning permission was going to be delicate but important to other, more ambitious plans.

"We were just talking about our options when that wretched Asiatic woman councillor turned up – right there in The Glebe," complained Hugh Olver-Blythe as he looked up from the Financial Times on his Kindle.

"Which Asiatic woman? Another of your fancies?"

"Oh do give it a rest, Hermione. Anyone would think I'm some kind of Lothario, which I'm not. In this case, however, one might be tempted: she *is* rather splendid – well-spoken, smart; and built like a fashion model. I might take up your suggestion!"

"Very droll! Do you think she was there in her official capacity?"

"Probably not: her daughter was with her – a younger version: lovely shape but rather haughty I thought."

"Unless your charm was slipping…. Did you try to sell her your plans for Lantrelland?"

"Absolutely not! You can just imagine what she would do. She's the councillor for Polperris and Lantrelland, freshly elected and new on the planning committee. She will be out to make a name for herself and this is just the kind of project that some of these incomers really hate! I want to get as much of it in place before I go anywhere near the planning office."

"I thought you and that planning man had it all sown up? Wasn't he round here?"

"That was absolutely on a private basis. We didn't even mention business!"

"Of course not, Hugh! Don't worry, I understand."

Hugh considered whether he should broach the subject of his mega-plan for the new 'authentic picturesque Cornish harbour and marina' at Lantrelland. He decided not to: Hermione was sensitive about her social position. She loved being 'lady of the manor', having full use of his credit cards and the prospect of becoming 'the wife of the Lord Lieutenant of Cornwall', which, all things being equal, was a possibility, due to the long history of the Olver-Blythe family. Hugh's father had had that honour, which had led to splendid receptions at Carnhill and even a visit from David, Prince of Wales, before he got mixed up with the American woman.

Hugh doubted whether Hermione would welcome a new and busy road passing within a mile from Carnhill House, bringing weekenders and yachties in their hundreds. A friend of hers from Bridport, two counties to the east, had confided to him one night in bed in his London flat that the picturesque town had lost a lot of its social shine when a television series had been made about West Bay, Bridport's own haven for fishing boats and yachts. She said one couldn't go there any more for fear of being jostled off the quays by myriads of London and Cardiff TV fans eager to 'see the place for real'. Hermione might (correctly) surmise that the masses might tire of Lantrelland and Polperris's attractions and descend on the gentile tranquillity of Carnhill's gardens, lake and superior tea-room. Whereas this might provide Hugh with funds with which to replace Carnhill's leaky gutters, ailing oil-central heating and pay for another much-needed gardener: it would certainly 'lower the tone'. It might even make it worthwhile to set up a souvenir shop, another of Hugh's ambitions, which Hermione could never contemplate. She would feel that the Olver-Blythes were becoming 'shop-keepers'.

Hugh understood Hermione's sensitivity: shop-keepers and theme-park owners were still several notches above 're-cyclers', (better known as rag-and-bone men). Being the daughter of Lord Poynsworth, known in the House of Lords – not to his face during his lifetime – as Dustman Dick, made her very touchy about her lineage. Perhaps her father *had* been rewarded as a hero of the Coalition Government, during the Second World War, for collecting redundant cookware and other recyclable materials for the War Effort but The Honourable Hermione did not like to be reminded of it. It had taken all those years at Benenden School for her to truly *feel* like a lady.

Hugh decided that now was *not* the time to talk about the marina. He would have to ensure that she was away on a cruise –

when the planned launch was to take place in The Square Mile of London.

"So – what *did* you talk about?" Hermione persisted.

"Talk about?" Hugh pretended he had returned to his Kindle.

"With the foreign lady and her daughter?"

"Oh – Councillor Johnson! She's not foreign, my dear: she just looks it. Her father is Charles Johnson, the fellow who works for the United Nations. We met him once at the Royal Cornwall Show. He was giving a talk on natural fibres or something."

"Oh God! I remember – it was your chairman-year at the Country Landowners Association. It was interminable and so *boring*! I've avoided those lunches ever since."

"Well I found his talk most interesting," defended Hugh. "Our members around here – especially up on the Moor need a bit of inspiration and Charles Johnson had been introducing some new breed of sheep to Chilean peasants. They've created a whole new market for coarse wool used in house insulation. You mix it with a little adhesive and boron and it becomes resistant to all kinds of insect and fungal infestation once you've packed it into the walls and roof cavities."

"Riveting! I was bored out of my mind! So where does the Japanese lady come in?"

"She doesn't. Johnson married a *Chinese* expert out in Africa somewhere and Councillor Johnson is their daughter; she runs a gallery in Polperris – took over from Charles' parents."

Hermione was now able to put some of the threads into context. The Johnson Gallery in Polperris was quite an up-market affair and was one of the few local 'attractions' to which she sometimes took her friends from London and Cheltenham. It showed them the quaintness of an East Cornwall fishing village and gave them the chance to buy something tasteful to take back to impress people with their Cornish sojourn. Perhaps a visit to the gallery might prove interesting? She might learn what was prompting the councillor's activity regarding Hugh's schemes; and Hugh's interest in the exotic artist.

"They must be up to something!" Rose Johnson said to Sebastian Trenleven and Emily as they cleared away the table at the studio in Polperris. It was low tide and the gulls were particularly noisy as they squabbled over tasty residues left on the harbour bottom by the retreating sea: stranded fish, discarded sandwich crusts and small crabs pursuing the same mission. Across from the gallery, on the quay opposite, the refrigerated fish lorry was collecting last night's catch. Box after box of pilchard, mackerel, pollock and shellfish landed rhythmically with a muffled bang as it was stacked inside.

"That was an unholy alliance if I've ever seen one," she declared. "Hugh Olver-Blythe, Brian Rogersson and Eddie Rouse? I wouldn't trust any of them."

"It would seem that, from what you say, that they have something in mind," said Sebastian.

"Yes, that's for sure;" said Rose, "big money! They are not small operators – well OB and Rogersson aren't."

"So do we know how they have attempted to do this in the past – individually, I mean?"

"Well," said Rose, "Eddie Rouse usually sells land when he's running short of money; and he owns the land adjoining the church and the Glebe. His farm runs down to the sea on both sides of Lantrelland beach and I can't think why the National Trust hasn't bought it from him. Brian Rogersson is always looking for ways to make a quick buck but I can't believe he would want to set up another of his mega-rubbish stores in an Area of Outstanding Natural Beauty next to an SSSI!"

"But Mummy, he's into all kinds of other schemes, isn't he?" Emily was remembering Rogersson's failed attempt to open of beef burger franchise in Polperris three years earlier. The gaudy shop-front was deemed as completely out of keeping in such a picturesque village and the planners had not given way. Brian had not thought it worth the effort to take the matter to further appeals and began looking at other possibilities. Ideally he wanted something not too far from his 'emporium' near Liskeard because he hated travelling.

"You are right! I wouldn't put it past him wanting to open up a huge caravan park or holiday camp; but why should Hugh Olver-Blythe want to get mixed up with something like that? It's not his style at all."

"What might *he* have that the other two need," asked Sebastian?

"Cash – and stacks of it. I hear he's raked in a fortune in London during the downturn over the past couple of years. He's had cash when everyone needed it, having just sold out of a Brazilian timber company just before it was closed down for illegal logging. There was even a question in the House of Commons about 'British participation in the destruction of the rain forest' but he denied all knowledge and got out just in time. He will be looking for somewhere to invest his ill-gotten gains and I suspect he will want to do it in the UK, where he can keep an eye on things. He very nearly lost the lot, operating in South America where he couldn't understand the language and didn't know the ropes."

"Wherever do you get all your information, Mum?" Emily was surprised at Rosie's knowledge of City scandal.

"Don't forget my water-colour courses! Some of these city types love to come down here and forget their troubles. One of them heard that Hugh OB lived near here and we got talking so I learned a lot, that week!"

"Does he have a reputation then?" asked Sebastian. "It might be relevant if he is behind the application for The Glebe."

"The impression I got was that his record is 'without blemish' but my student touched the side of his nose, knowingly and winked!"

"I see." Sebastian made a coded note.

"What I *can't* see is why Hugh Olver-Blythe should want to back such a tawdry little project such as an ice-cream parlour, car-park and bungalow," said Rose. "He could pay for that and forget it without noticing! He must have something else in mind."

"You did say that this Mr Rouse had sold his farm, didn't you?" Sebastian checked his notes.

"He *wants* to," said Rose. "Don't say it's to Hugh Olver-Blythe? Although, come to think of it OB *has* bought several farms along the coast during the past few years. It hasn't made him very popular with the local people because he screwed the price down so low some of them barely had two pennies to rub together, once their debts had been paid. The chairman of our planning committee, Nancy Libby, told me. She says that Trevor Philp, who's also a councillor on the same committee and churchwarden at Lantrelland Church, is only hanging on to his farm by his finger tips. He can't make enough to live on, keeping a few beef cattle and sheep. Trevor's getting on in years and works all hours. He can't stand Olver-Blythe and says he'd rather drop dead at work than see his farm get swallowed up by Carnhill."

"Why can't he do something different – like some of the other farmers around here," asked Emily. "You know – put up wind turbines or grow willow for fuel?"

"He'd never get planning permission for the turbines and his land is too steep for willow: I asked him. He said he's thought of everything – from milking goats to horses for trekking – but Carnhill's done that already with their stables; and Trevor couldn't afford to buy all the pasteurisation equipment, steel vats and things for the cheese. He said that anyway he was too old to get up and go milking every morning."

"But if he can't get planning permission for wind turbines – how come something like the ice-cream parlour has a chance – especially on an ancient site like The Glebe?" asked Emily. "It's sounds daft!"

"It may sound daft, darling, but Mrs Libby said that several unlikely schemes have got through on appeal; and in the case of Brian Rogersson he just goes ahead and does it – and waits for the authorities to take action against him. He's prepared to spend a fortune on barristers – oh – sorry Sebastian! But you know what I mean." Rose laughed in embarrassment.

"Of course I do Rosie but in this case my father told me I'm 'honorary'! I suspect that he too has ulterior motives. Lady Henrietta Merchant is a most persuasive lady!"

"She's the one who wrote back to me from the CPRE."

"Exactly!" She met Dad at some dinner and I got picked for the job. I believe he's taken her out to the opera a couple of times since then. Perfectly legit – he's a widower – my mother died five years ago. I'm pleased for him really, because he was becoming quite a hermit."

"But Mum, how do these appeals get through. Anyone can see that it's all wrong to spoil that setting at Lantrelland. It would make it like Newquay!"

"They get through because someone is prepared to put a lot of money behind them – and the local councils haven't got enough money to fight back – that's how!"

"Well it's all wrong!"

"Of course it is, Emily," said Sebastian. "Sometimes it's the other way round – when really good things get turned down that would benefit everybody except the multi-nationals, which manage to block them. It makes my blood boil sometimes when I see big business sabotage projects that make perfect sense."

"Like what?" asked Emily.

"Take hydro-power, for example – using the flow of water to produce electricity. For centuries this country's flour mills got their energy from water-wheels. Just about every parish had at least one; or a windmill. Water wheels are only now beginning to make a come-back, even though enthusiasts have been giving us the figures and the logic of it for decades."

"Surely that's a political thing?" said Rose. "Government could have encouraged it – like they have for other kinds of renewable energy?"

"Exactly," said Sebastian. "But they haven't! Why not? Because the electricity companies with their coal-fired power stations and their nuclear plants were afraid of the competition. They put their lobbyists to work in Westminster – and with the civil servants who are often clever but gullible. Nuclear power is subsidised to a huge degree because the cost of decommissioning the plants isn't built into the price they charge for the electricity. It will be our descendents who will have to face getting rid of nuclear waste that will take thousands of years before it's safe. No one pays the proper price for fossil fuels, either: not for all the damage it causes to our atmosphere or our food crops."

"How does it affect crops?" asked Rose.

"It's the ozone, apparently – kills the leaves," said Sebastian.

"But surely you couldn't get enough electricity from water-wheels to make a significant difference, could you?" asked Emily.

"Don't get me going! It's another pet hate of mine – *that* fairy-tale ," said Sebastian. "That's partly why Dad sent me on this job. He says I'm always going on about renewable energy – and what with that and our Cornish name I ought to be able to make a success of an appeal down here!"

"Not much of a vote of confidence!" said Rose.

"Oh, he trusts me all right – and he's made me go through all the boring part of this job but I've never really known where I've wanted to specialise, so he thought putting my Greenpeace inclinations and my legal training together might help me make up my mind about my career."

"In that case we are lucky to have you," said Rose. She noticed that Emily was looking down at her hands. "Aren't we Emily?"

"What? Oh yes!" Emily brushed a dark lock of hair away from her eye and shook her head to make it hang with the rest of the shining cascade, down her back. She and Sebastian caught each other's eye and both smiled, looking a touch sheepish. Sebastian's kiss had been disconcerting. She had put it from her mind, telling herself it was trivial: a one-off moment of lust. Her mother's remark prompted again that same excitement and confusion. She felt *very* lucky.

"Go on, then," said Emily, trying to sound intelligent; "tell us about hydro-power. Is it a good idea?"

"It certainly is," said Sebastian. "Here in the UK it's one of the cheapest ways of producing clean electricity. It's more dependable than solar, wind, or ocean energy and is probably more profitable for those investing in it. Government has put out figures showing that in England and Wales there are still nearly two thousand more suitable sites where you could install hydro-power plants ranging from major ones with dams to small turbos from streams. Hydropower already producers a fifth of the world's electrical energy and ninety per cent of the renewable energy – and gravity is free! That's what drives it."

"So why are they only *now* talking about it? Renewable energy has been all the rage for decades!" said Rose.

"And see how little has happened!" Sebastian is scornful. "It's because the big companies have spent quite a bit on persuading governments to ignore it. If Government had put money in twenty years ago, people would have developed much more efficient ways of producing electricity without destroying the planet. The fossil fuel and nuclear people would be having a much tougher time trying to compete. The boffins say that less than a third of the world's hydropower has so far been developed. It's like so many good ideas – they can be smothered by vested interests."

"And that's democracy?" Emily said.

"That's our version of it!" Sebastian agrees.

"So how can you fight these big conglomerates?" Emily sounded naïve.

"With money!"

"But we don't have any!" said Rose. "All we can do is make a fuss and appeal to the electorate."

"A lot of good that will do", said Emily. "Like banging your head against a fish box, Mum."

"I hope you don't mean that, Emily," said Rose. "I was hoping for your support in this. The Glebe is one of your favourite places."

"I know, Mum but it just makes me feel hopeless. Like taking on something we can never win."

"That's what my father says about my buying lottery tickets," said Sebastian. "But I always tell him, someone has to win every week! I won ten pounds, once!"

"Wow – big deal!"

"Well it's better than nothing and it raised my hopes. I know I'm a very lucky person. There are such people, you know!"

"I've decided I am too," said Emily. "Perhaps I should be buying tickets, too! A friend at college was always on about it. She quoted a Professor Wiseman – I remember his name because it sounded convincing! He was at the University of Hertfordshire and did a study of 'lucky' people and found that it came from their own attitudes and behaviour. You can actually become lucky by thinking positively and being 'open to opportunities'."

"Do you really believe that, darling?" asked Rose.

"I do! The professor reckoned he'd proved it. You can look it up if you don't believe me! I did! He did all kinds of interviews with hundreds of people, asking them about their luck and found that lucky people tended to use various ways of creating situations they might take advantage of. They break out of the ordinary; and learn ways of dealing with bad luck, like imagining how things could have been worse. He gave volunteers a month to carry out exercises and then come back to tell him what had happened. He said the results were dramatic. Eighty percent were happier and more satisfied with their lives and decidedly luckier. Unlucky people had become lucky, and lucky people had become *even* luckier. He quoted the unlucky life of a girl called Patricia. She was one of the first people to take part in his 'Luck School'. After a few weeks of simple exercises, her bad luck went away! She said she felt like a completely different person; she was no longer accident-prone and was much happier. For her, for once, everything was coming right!"

"But how bad was her bad luck, before that?" Rose asked.

"Unbelievable, Mum. I thought I'd told you about it at the time."

"You didn't!"

"Well: this Patricia was an air-hostess; and everyone *knew* she was unlucky. It was always on *her* flights that a drunk passenger made it necessary to turn back. Then it was *her* flight that got struck by lightning. Three weeks later she was on a plane that had to make an emergency landing. Other trolley-dollies didn't want to work with her in case it was infectious! She stopped wishing people good luck before they had an interview in case it worked the other way!"

"Sounds like office chairs making people pregnant, to me," said Rose. "Once you put the thought in peoples' heads they make it come true!"

"Exactly, Mum!"

"I think you are right, Emily," said Sebastian. "The human brain's a very funny thing – you can programme it even when you don't really believe what you are telling it to do! I have to do quite a bit of that in my job! It's part of persuading juries and judges!"

"That's all very philosophical – but we're not getting anywhere, are we?" Said Rose. "We need to find out what they're up to. I shall have to dig around in the planning office and see whether there's anything brewing there. The trouble is I've got to leave someone here to keep the gallery open."

"All right! I can take a hint," said Emily, smiling. "Do you want me to?"

"Oh darling – how kind! Yes please! But what are we going to do with Sebastian? It seems a pity for him to come all this way and then leaving him to his own devices. Do you want to come with me to Liskeard – that's where the council offices are?"

"I think you would probably get on better without me – people might smell a rat if you came in with a stranger, especially if you are trying to pick their brains. If you don't mind, I'd like to hang around here. I must phone the office about various things and if you have any local planning regulations and minutes for me to read, I could keep myself usefully employed until closing time! After that I'd like to go back to Lantrelland – down to the beach this time – to take some photos and fit things in with the map: I've brought the right Ordnance Survey sheet and I think it might be useful to know the place better."

"Well you are most welcome to use the phone and I'm sure Emily can fix some lunch for you – can't you Emily?"

"What? Oh yeah – salad or something? Or we might go out."

"That would be fine," said Sebastian. "And I could bring you some coffee in the studio – I don't want you to feel I need waiting on."

"If you *do* decide to go out, don't be too long," said Rose. "People expect the gallery to be open when it says it will be! Someone may have seen a picture and decided they must have it. I don't want to miss a sale!"

"OK, Mum."

The telephone rang. Rose went into the hall to pick it up. She returned looking less than pleased.

"Damn! That was someone crying off my course next week. They've gone and broken their leg! How inconsiderate! That's most of my profit gone unless I can find someone else at short notice. You don't know anyone, do you, Sebastian? Someone needing a break? New hobby? Rack your brains!"

CHAPTER 7

"You'll never win if you don't buy a ticket!" Sebastian taunted Emily as they stood by the counter in the newspaper shop.

"Well you've only ever won ten pounds – and how long ago was that? You must have spent a fortune to get it."

"But at least I've 'opened an opportunity for myself'. It's a cheap way of being a lucky person if you ask me! From what you say it's that kind of thing that makes someone lucky, isn't it?"

"Yes I suppose," said Emily, "but I don't want to waste a pound!"

"Well in that case, be stingy and stay unlucky! It's all in a good cause – paying for the Olympic stadium and suchlike. I'm not gambling any more than I can afford to lose and for several days each week I've enjoyed thinking about the possibility of becoming rich."

"And probably paying for stuff the Government ought to cover out of taxes!" said Emily.

Sebastian handed over his ticket to the shopkeeper and waited in anticipation.

"Nothing, sorry!" The shopkeeper said. "Do you want the dead ticket?"

"Yes please." Sebastian took it. He always did: just in case the shopkeeper had seen it was a winning ticket and claimed it for himself. It wasn't that he didn't trust people: his father's profession had taught him that precautions against dishonesty were easy to take and sometimes well rewarded. He would leave it in his pocket for a while, then tear up the ticket and dispose of it in a bin of his own choice. "And I'd like two more, please, for next week."

As they walked from the shop Emily was about to make a sarcastic remark about him 'lashing out' by doubling his stake, when he handed her one of the tickets.

"There you are – you *too* could now become a Euro-millionaire! Put it somewhere safe."

"Some hopes! But thank you, that was a kind gesture." Emily tucked it into the pocket of her shoulder-bag.

"Not really: I've been feeling guilty about you."

"What for?" Emily turned to look at him as they went back towards the gallery with the cold meat and yoghurts they'd just bought.

"For….. pouncing on you in the cave the other evening." Sebastian was quite embarrassed about it even now. "My animal side got the better of me! I'm sorry."

"And I was hoping you meant it!"

"Well I did! But that's not the way to behave is it?"

"I didn't stop you, did I? I could've – if I'd wanted. I'm quick on my feet and I've been known to punch someone on the nose."

"Am I forgiven, then?"

"No, because no offence was taken! I quite enjoyed it actually!" She gave a shy smile and walked on more quickly. "Come on, we'll be late re-opening if we don't get a move on."

§

"We can't go on meeting like this," said Sebastian as he dried a plate after lunch.

"Like what?"

"Over the sink!"

"Are you in a pouncing mood then?"

"Well, no more than usual! You know what we males are like!"

Emily emptied the plastic bowl of its soapy water, propped it to drain, dried her hands and as Sebastian turned, after placing the plate on a shelf, walked into his arms, reached up and pulled his head down, raising her lips to his, kissing him firmly.

"I've discovered I'm a primate too," she said as she came up for breath. "I needed that. Now do you want coffee?"

Sebastian's Gallic passion was now alight, his dark eyes sparkling with excitement. Before she could turn away from him he caught her and crushed her in his arms and pressed his cheek against hers before seeking her lips once more. Aggressively but without violence he held and kissed her until he felt her give herself to him, her tongue seeking his.

"Now we're quits," she said, placing her hands on his chest and gently repelling him. "No more apologies! I definitely enjoyed that and I think I should tell you to be on your guard from now on! And before you get any ideas of me being some kind of sex fiend – I'm not and I've never done anything like that ever before! The moment I saw you I knew that something like this was bound to happen – even before you accosted me in the cave! So there! I've had it on my mind since I woke up at three this morning – although I did go to sleep again."

"Your Honour, may I suggest we adjourn for a few minutes for that coffee?"

"A good idea Mr Trenleven. Court adjourned for fifteen minutes. That's all the time we've got anyway before I have to open that door again to the bargain seekers. We can take our coffee and some chocolates back to the gallery if you don't mind sitting in with me for a few minutes?"

"I'd be delighted; as long as you don't mind my coming back in here afterwards to make a few more phone calls," said Sebastian.

They took their coffees to the polished desk in the gallery where Sebastian pulled up a chair into what he learned Rosie and her daughter called the 'cheque-writing position'. He settled comfortably, his long legs reaching under the desk and was thrilled to feel Emily's calf touch his, out of sight of either of them: not moving – just 'being there' and exchanging a little warmth. They looked at each other as they took the first sip of coffee. Something was happening between them that neither could explain.

Sebastian spoke of it first, as he watched Emily's serene face. Her upward slanting eyes were fully open, smiling at him and her neat mouth with its make-up free, Cupid's bow lips expressing contentment. He said:

"It's odd but it was just the same for me, too. When I saw you yesterday, it felt like coming home after a long time away. You were somehow familiar; we'd met before but I wasn't sure where – and it had been very beautiful. Sweet memories were tantalisingly out of reach. It must be what my mother used to call a 'coup de foudre', the 'strike of ze lightning' that hit her when she met my father."

"And were they happy?"

"Blissfully! He's never got over losing her. Even now, after five years he's only just beginning to take the slightest interest in any other woman."

"And you've been struck with me? Are you sure it's not just lust?"

"When you kissed me just now – yes it was, very much so; but now? I feel so content sitting with you like this – being together. I can't say I've experienced anything quite like it before and I'm hoping I won't wake up and feel foolish and ashamed. You have somehow disarmed me."

"Good! I can't stand over-bearing men! I'm relieved you're not put off by my being so un-ladylike. I don't feel threatened by you and I've enjoyed every second of having you around. Don't ask me why but I felt the same as you. It's as if I knew you already and just needed reminding – most odd! It will take time to find out whether it's real. What I *do* know is that I want to know all about you!"

"Oh dear! Not *all* about me? Let's start somewhere uncontroversial." Sebastian put his cup down and sat back, waiting for Emily's first question. Then he thought better of it.

"Why don't you let me start by asking *you* something?" He wondered how she would react – and was acutely aware that if

81

they didn't divert their attention away from their physical attraction, things might get out of hand to the detriment of the gallery's opening hours.

"Go ahead – fire away, said Emily. "You're the expert – but don't forget I'm not under oath!"

"OK! Let's start with my reason for being here – the Glebe Field, and saving it. You seem to feel the same as I do about the air we breath and the world we depend on but what made *you* first get mixed up with movements like Greenpeace?"

"I think it was hearing my grandparents talking about Tanzania and UN work there. It sounded so exciting – they got involved in all kinds of things, farming, music, pagan religion and politics too. My grandmother is an anthropologist and Grandpa is an agric and it's hard to avoid politics in either of those jobs. Then there was 'Blue Peter' on television. It linked up things they talked about with the reality of animals becoming extinct and deserts spreading – and it was never boring."

"But all that must have been when you were a kid. It's more urgent now."

"That's true," said Emily, "I feel I ought to be doing more than 'keeping myself informed'. Sitting here in the gallery is like being back at work except that *you* are here – and that's nicer than I expected – but in London when I'm not writing a press release or sticking envelopes, I spend a lot of time reading. Someone left me a copy of a book by an American, Lester Brown, who calls himself an 'environmental analyst'. He's like an Old Testament prophet and has been around for ages."

"I know who you mean," said Sebastian. "And I can guess the book: was it 'World on the edge'?"

"That's the one! Isn't it amazing? Do you believe it?"

"I wasn't sure when I started reading it. It got more and more depressing and I felt like chucking it away."

"So did I," said Emily. "There seemed to be no hope for the human race. We're so STUPID. We know perfectly well that the way we are living is destroying our support systems: so what do we do? We go on doing it! Did you finish the book?"

82

"Eventually: I was reading it at mealtimes. Dad takes 'The Times' and I've usually got a book on the go. We don't usually say much but Dad got fed up with me exploding about one pending environmental catastrophe after another. In the end he said this Brown fellow was thoroughly irritating and why couldn't he say something useful? Out of curiosity I flicked through the second half of the book and sure enough it's packed with practical solutions."

"I was the same." said Emily. "It was getting me down – all that doom and destruction. I only just made it to where he starts talking about 'Plan B'. There's nothing we don't know already but it needs someone to *do* something before the pooh hits the fan."

"I hadn't realised how much worse things had become – or how quickly. What brought that home was his account of what's happened in Pakistan. No wonder extremist movements spring up there: it must be desperate. When Pakistan was separated from British India in 1947, a third of the country was covered by forests. Now it's only four per cent! Pakistan is only the size of Texas but has more livestock than the whole of the USA! The animals graze the countryside bare and there are no trees to slow the run-off of rainfall, which washes away the soil, destroying the crops and drowning people in so-called 'natural disasters'."

"It is rather warm in here!" said Emily. She got up to push open one of the French doors, letting in not only the fresh air and smells of the harbour but the clamour of the gulls and sounds of the fish market:

"He doesn't hold back either," she said. "Perhaps it's desperation that no one seems to have been listening. He condemns governments for having expanding their army, rather than forestry, farms and family planning. He says that in 1990 the Pakistan military budget was fifteen times bigger than for education; and nearly fifty times bigger than population control. As a result, the place is now a poor, over-populated, environmentally devastated nuclear power where sixty per cent of women can't even read or write!"

"Fantastic book!" said Sebastian. "Is your copy here?"

"No – I'm only down for the week. I keep mine in the loo – it reminds me how important it is!"

"Great minds think alike! So do I – hoping my father will pick it up but he's usually got his mind deep into crime and corruption!"

"Reading that book makes me feel how helpless we all are, in the face of wealth and power." Emily reached for Sebastian's empty coffee cup.

"That's one of the reasons my father won't read it. He says he'd rather be an ostrich and hide his head because there's so little he can do about things; but reading it makes *me* angry and Bolshie. That's why I was glad to take on this brief over the Glebe: it's something useful I can fight for."

"You sound like those surfers who helped clean up Cornish beaches. Remind me to tell you about the SAS sometime," said Emily.

"I thought they were our version of the American SEALS – doing dangerous rescues and fighting terrorists."

"In this case they're not, although 'Surfers Against Sewage' *have* been fighting successful campaigns."

"Oh of course! I've heard about them but not in detail. You'll have to tell me more – but let me take these cups and I'll go and do my phoning. Can we go out somewhere this evening? Your mother won't mind, will she?"

"No, I'm sure she won't. I expect she'll be glad to flop out in front of the telly, after her day's sleuthing."

"See you later, then." Sebastian planted a light kiss on Emily's forehead as he passed. A few moments later, the 'ting' of the studio door heralded the arrival of the afternoon's first visitor.

§

Peter Trenleven is dejected. Outside, the weather was anything but summery. It was one of those wet days that slows London down to an irritable, dripping traffic jam that edges its way from traffic light to roundabout, queuing into the gloom.

84

After weeks of daily battle with the prosecution counsel in front of a testy and hostile judge his client has gone down for ten years.

"I was fairly confident we were going to win," he said to Harry Potter, finalising the accounts. "If only the bloody man hadn't opened his mouth! He just about confessed – it was the first time anyone had mentioned a Swiss bank account."

"I suppose the prosecution waded in?" said Harry.

"And how! They demolished my case and the judge more or less told the jury what they had to decide. I felt such an idiot. The stupid man could have been on the plane to Portugal. Instead of that he'll be sharing a small cell with someone who will probably have him by the throat if he says a word out of place."

"You knew he deserved it?"

"Of course I did – but the prosecution simply didn't have enough to convict: not until he gave it to them."

"Justice was done, then!"

"Harry, don't go all righteous on me!"

"Sorry Mr Trenleven – I was only trying to help!"

"Of course you're right but I was hoping to win that one – right or wrong!"

"Well, you can't win 'em all, sir; as my father used to say but at least you can now take some time off?" The phone rang and Harry picked it up.

"Trenleven Chambers, good afternoon? Where are you? Still in Cornwall? How's it going?"

Peter Trenleven's frown lifted as he watched the expression on Harry Potter's face for any signs of anxiety. He was relieved to see a broadening smile: plainly it was no emergency call.

"He's asking for you, sir!" Harry handed over the telephone.

§

85

"Good afternoon!" A cultured voice brought Emily to her feet. She took a catalogue from her desk and moved towards the expensively-dressed woman who had just come in.

"Oh! I don't think we've met? I usually find Mrs Johnson here."

"She's out this afternoon – I'm her daughter. Would you like a catalogue?"

"Thank you, I would."

"Are you down on holiday?" asked Emily taking her place at the desk again.

"No, I live just up the road – at Carnhill."

"Lovely old house!"

"It is – but a nightmare to look after, we're so near the sea; the wind and rain is always tearing away at the place! But we do our best! And you, do you live in Polperris?"

"Not now. I did as a child but now I'm up in London: just down for a few days."

"You must be the one my husband saw with Councillor Johnson yesterday?"

"At Lantrelland? Then you must be Mrs Olver-Blythe?"

"Yes I am! So it *was* you?"

"My mother had just picked me up from the station and I asked her to take me to the Glebe to blow away the last of the London fumes – we've always gone there for picnics and walks. I love it!"

"Such a delightful place. So's this! I bring friends here to your gallery quite often. I think we've been quite good customers in the past."

"That's good to hear! Can I offer you a coffee? There's still some in the pot," said Emily.

"That's so kind but no thank you. I'll just have a quick look round. I came in on the off-chance of seeing your mother – just for a chat. I have one or two friends who might be interested in exhibiting; but there's no urgency. I'll call again."

"I'll let her know you were here. Perhaps you wouldn't mind signing the visitor's book? And do leave your telephone number."

86

As Hermione Olver-Blythe went over to look at one of Rose's latest paintings of Polperris harbour, Emily could see what an elegant and well-dressed woman she was: not a hair out of place behind the velvet head band; and no attempt made to hide the first streaks of grey in her shoulder-length bob. Hermione looked slim but fit, her loosely fitting linen dress, obviously expensive, hinted at small breasts low on her chest. It revealed the arms and shoulders of a sportswoman, brown and firm. The skirt reached below the knee, above enviably long calves. Her sandals and matching cream handbag had gold buckles. She looked more like the clients Emily expected in Hanover Square.

"Emily! I think I might have got a substitute!" Sebastian's head came around the studio door. "Oh – sorry! Didn't know you had someone in! Do excuse me bursting in." He looked embarrassed and lowered his voice as he quietly came over to the desk.

"I've just been talking to my father and I might have sold him the idea of filling that gap on your mother's course. I'll be back at the office by then and he's just finished a long case and is due for some holiday. I checked up with Harry Potter first – before suggesting it."

Emily laughed. "Now I'm confused! How does *he* come into it?"

"He's our clerk in chambers – in his fifties – not the under-graduate with a wand! He keeps us all in line: salt of the earth!"

"I told Dad how great it was down here and I know he's always had a yen to try painting so it seemed like a good opportunity. There we go again – it might just be his lucky break! A new interest and hobby? At least he'll find out whether he has any talent."

Emily looked across to make sure Hermione wasn't watching them and then gestured to Sebastian to 'watch it'! She scribbled on a piece of paper 'tell you later!' and said:

"That's great. Mum will be pleased. We can send him an introduction pack – with a list of what he needs to bring."

"A mackintosh?"

"Essential! And warm clothes. She likes to get them outdoors as much as possible. None of this copying from photos. She says you need to be sitting there, keeping warm and soaking it all in."

"What, the rain?"

"That too! But no – the 'feel' of a place; and the colours as the light changes. Anyway, it's not always raining here – just look outside now!"

Bright sunshine lit the harbour and the tide was well on its way to reaching the top of the quays. Dinghies and fishing boats alike were bobbing busily after the passage of a boat, loaded with tourists off to 'see the caves and the lighthouse', had churned its way to the narrow harbour opening, the boatman at the tiller, confident in his blue Guernsey and flat cap.

"That's Jack Puckey," said Emily. "He's been doing that for years; charges them seven pounds fifty for a forty minute trip. They go out past the big rock, up as far as our cave – turns round, points at the Eddystone, which you can't always see unless you are on the top of a wave, and brings them back! They love it! He stops at the end of September and goes on The Social until April."

"Sort of hibernation!" Sebastian pictured old Jack by the fire, dreaming of seasons gone by.

"In March he paints the boat and cleans up the engine, ready for the summer."

"Isn't this him, in the picture?" Hermione is plainly enjoying their conversation.

"It is! Mum goes down most years and sketches him doing his spring re-fit. He enjoys it, and chats away to her. She gave him one of her paintings of him and he was thrilled. She said it was only fair he should have a share in his own image!"

"It does make a lovely picture – so full of character," said Hermione. "Too many of the paintings of Polperris don't have any people in them."

"That's just what my mother says. She thinks they're an important part of a harbour scene and she likes drawing them."

"Isn't that you – in that picture over there?" Asked Hermione. It reminded her of the cover of that book she had enjoyed so much, 'The Shell Seekers' except that one of the children looked so much like a younger Emily."

"It is, yes! But that was ages ago: I was about nine. My mother doesn't want to sell that one."

"I'm sure she doesn't," said Hermione; "it's such a good likeness – I recognised you at once – you haven't lost any of your good looks!"

"That's very kind, thank you," said Emily, pleased but blushing. "At that age I was always a bit self-conscious about looking 'foreign' but my mother always used to tell me that she enjoyed painting people of different races and colours and that they were all beautiful."

"I saw a picture of some Maasai warriors, upstairs," said Sebastian. "Is that one of hers?"

"Yes. We used to have a lot of African pictures from when she was going out there to stay with my grandparents. She was born in Tanzania. That's where she got the idea about 'sharing the images' – the Maasai used to insist on being paid if you wanted to take a photo or make a painting. They had seen books and post-cards on sale for high prices with pictures of their friends and relatives and were sure they deserved something for it. She used to pay up – and make a note of their post-box so she could send them a photograph of the finished painting."

"Fascinating," said Hermione. "May I keep this catalogue, to show my friends?"

"Do, yes!" It's got our contact details and I'm sure my mother would be pleased to hear from them."

"Thank you. I'll be on my way. Very good to meet you, Miss Johnson and.....?" She smiled at Sebastian.

"Sebastian Trenleven – just visiting, you know."

"Charming! Enjoy your stay. I'm sure we'll see you again in this part of the world. People usually come back. Such a beautiful place, isn't it? Bye for now."

They waited until the gallery door had closed firmly, giving Hermione plenty of time to be well out of earshot before speaking.

"It *is* a beautiful place at the moment – but it wouldn't be if her husband had his way," said Emily. "Can't she see that?"

"She might not agree with him but she probably likes him being rich," said Sebastian.

"She was determined to find out who *you* were," said Emily.

"It's my irresistible charm!"

"I have to agree with her there! But I don't think that was her motive – you're a bit young for her! She was just snooping and wanted to ask questions, now Mum's on the planning committee; but Mum will be *very* pleased you've persuaded your father to come on the course. Do you think they'll get on?"

"I hadn't thought of that!"

Sebastian walked round behind Emily's chair and put his hands on her shoulders, then slid them under her shining hair, lifting it and letting it fall back. "You have such heavy hair! Gorgeous! It's so good to touch! If my father's genes are the same as mine I suspect he's going to find the Johnson women as exciting as I do! He might even learn to paint!"

CHAPTER 8

"You can't really support Rouse' application to put up a café at Lantrelland, can you?" Brian Rogersson was puzzled.

"Of course not! But if I hadn't said I *would*, he might have sold the farm to the National Trust," said Hugh.

"But the Glebe isn't his anyway, is it?"

"Not yet! But he has told the church parish council he won't buy it unless it's got the planning permission and they're mostly his relatives – and they'd like to 'keep it in the family', so are going along with him."

"So how long will you go on – speaking up for him?"

"My dear Brian, 'for the moment'. There's no particular hurry. Eddie Rouse needs money rather badly at present and the banks aren't mortgaging the way they used to even though land prices have never been higher. They're not even allowing farmers to go on stretching their overdrafts. He needs to sell his farm if he's going to be able to cash in on property prices for his retirement. So I'm being 'very co-operative' on both fronts at present – in buying his farm and in supporting his planning application."

"And when the sale goes through?"

"I think I might be very busy with my own projects," said Hugh, hands clasped under his chin.

"What if he fails to get his permission for the Glebe?"

"I don't think he'll mind! Buying the Glebe is only a diversion to keep the family off his back for selling the last of the Rouse farms. They have visions of him running 'a nice little business', keeping the name alive and bringing some cash into the parish. If *he* loses face, they all lose face: he's always been a bit of an embarrassment but the idea of him 'settling down' is very appealing to such a proud bunch."

"But what if he *does* get his planning permission? Will he go ahead and build his café and bungalow?"

"Knowing him? Probably not! He'll try to sell it off to one of his mates or someone from up-country and they'd most likely do something like you – push all the planning rules over the edge!"

"There's no need to be insulting: you know as well as I do what a bunch of plonkers the planners are around here. They can't recognise a good thing when they see it: something to bring real prosperity into a district. All they want to do is keep it like some picture postcard and hope people will come and look at it. The best they can hope for is a few more folk paying for bed and breakfast – and more celebs buying holiday homes that are shut up for most of the year! It's bad enough already with helicopters coming in like swarms of bees every Friday! It's getting like the old days – taking hours to get in or out of the county: Ferraris blocking up the A30 – even the new bypass over Goss Moor!"

§

"I feel we do have to deal with such applications sympathetically, Councillor Johnson, even if they *are* eventually turned down. Normally our elected representatives are anxious not to appear 'anti-development', especially when they are in rural areas. The farmers are having such a hard time at present. Their costs have rocketed!"

"I'm sure that we appreciate your political diplomacy Mr Ferguson but in this case Lantrelland is protected by national designations. SSSI and AONB are powerful shields, aren't they? With 'Site of Special Scientific Interest' and 'Area of Outstanding Natural Beauty' one would have expected any application to be turned down immediately – so why wasn't it?"

"The coalition government has been trying to relax centralised rules to allow local people take more of their own decisions about their own environment, as you know, Councillor Johnson. Our chief executive's understanding of the guidelines is that if parish and district councillors – the elected representatives – have good reason to waive even the most stringent rules, then they should be allowed to do so. Even 'green belt' protection has begun to be overturned where there are good local arguments agreed by the councils. I think you will find that it has stimulated all kinds of useful development and led to growth that we all need so badly to get us out of the credit crisis." Niall Ferguson's voice had overtones of soothing a troubled child. Rose found it patronising and irritating.

"Are you telling me that traditional planning processes have been completely dropped?" she asked, sharply.

"Oh no! There are still various levels of appeal and review but Central Government has instructed that 'common sense should prevail'," said Mr Ferguson, beginning to sound hurried. "I'm terribly sorry, Councillor Johnson, but would you allow me to go now because I have an appointment the other side of Liskeard – someone wants to extend their bungalow."

"Don't let me detain you," said Rose, "but before you go, I'd like to look at the paperwork that's accumulated so far over the Lantrelland application. Is that possible?"

"I'll certainly ask the chief if that's possible, Mrs Johnson."

"Miss Johnson, actually."

"So sorry, Councillor."

"And as I recollect, as a councillor I can have access to all council files except those relating to personnel matters? I have been reading the guidance notes very carefully."

"Indeed, Miss Johnson, of course you are right. I'll ask the clerk to get the file for you, but will you please excuse me, I have to run now."

"Very well Mr Ferguson. I'll make an appointment when you are less busy. It's something of importance to the people in my ward."

Rose detected a slight wince in the look that Niall Ferguson threw in her direction as he took his leave, picked up his brief case and hurried towards the front of the council offices.

"I had the distinct impression that he was trying to make me feel that I needn't worry my little head about it; everything was in hand and why didn't I run along and play? It gave me the creeps and I didn't take to the man at all," Rosie told Emily and Sebastian, back in Polperris a couple of hours later. "I was sure he didn't want me to see the file on Lantrelland. I smell a rat."

"Mummy, you're such a suspicious person! He's probably had all kinds of ineffectual councillors to deal with in the past and doesn't realise what he's up against. I'm sure everyone at that office will soon get the message that you don't mess about. He won't have noticed the scalps hanging from your belt yet!"

"Well he'd better watch it! That kind of attitude sets all my inquisitive cells in motion and from his performance this afternoon, I don't trust him!"

"Mum, do you want a cup of tea or is it too early for something stronger?"

"I think a sherry might improve things, please, Emily. What about you Sebastian?"

"I've only just finished a fine cup of tea, thanks Rosie. The service here is excellent!"

"Do you mean you didn't have to get it yourself? You *are* honoured! Emily usually waits for me to do it!"

"Mum that's not fair!" Emily went over to her mother and put her arms around her, giving her an unrestrained embrace and kiss. "I wait on you hand and foot because I love you so much!"

"Darling, were it so true! I know you love me but the hand and foot thing is usually restricted to me tripping over your shoes and picking up clothes in your bedroom. On this occasion I'm sure you can impress Sebastian again and bring me that drink – thank you dear. It will help wash planning officers out of my day: such an oily character, that Ferguson. I foresee problems with him. Now darlings, tell me what you've been up to all afternoon. Have you sold any paintings?"

"No, but we've had one of your patrons in looking for you. Mrs Olver-Blythe from Carnhill. She was disappointed to have missed you."

"She's actually quite a good customer," said Rose. "I like her better than her husband! She brings her smart friends in now and again and I've sold them a few paintings in the past. What did she want?"

"Not sure – but she said something about having some friends who might be interested in exhibiting here."

"If I like their work: I hope you told her?"

"No! I thought you would be the one to tell her that. She wasn't sounding too presumptuous – more of a polite enquiry."

"That's all right then. I don't want to sell pretentious rubbish!"

"No Mum! I can see you've had a trying afternoon but now the good news: Sebastian has filled the gap in your next water-colour course."

"Oh I didn't know you wanted to paint? But that's excellent."

"It's not me, Rosie! It's my father! I was talking to him this afternoon and he sounded rather low, having just lost a big case so I thought I'd try to divert him with a tempting week in Polperris. It was a long shot and I didn't expect him to go for it but it caught his imagination. I got Emily to phone him back to tell him more about the course and he's writing to you to confirm things. She told him you would post off his information pack."

"I shall look forward to meeting him," said Rose. "We'll put that in the post in the morning. Well done Sebastian! You're the kind of activist we need around here: you don't hang about."

"It's funny, too, Mum, because we discovered that we've both been enjoying that book by Lester Brown – quoting bits of it to each other. He's always had a thing about the Rainbow Warrior and Greenpeace; and he's even got a Blue Peter badge!"

"So that's why your father picked you for the Glebe job," said Rose. "I suspect he and I will have plenty to talk about when we're out sketching."

"Oh no! Family secrets!" Said Emily. "You'll find out more about us than we know ourselves! Once Mum gets going.... Sebastian, what have you done?"

"I'm sure you've got nothing to hide, Emily; and I've led a blameless life up until now so we need not worry. I was going to ask you, Rosie: would you mind if I asked Emily out this evening?"

"I'd welcome it, Sebastian. Then I can put my feet up, watch telly and be really lazy. Just don't wake me up when you come in! What have you got planned?"

"Nothing much, really. I've looked in the Cornish Times and there's a dinner dance at the Hannafore tonight. I thought we might go there. Emily liked the idea, too."

"Have you brought anything to wear, darling?'"

"No – but I knew you wouldn't mind me rummaging round your wardrobe!"

"I might have guessed! But I thought you were going back to Lantrelland for some photos?"

"I think we've got time for that, too, Rosie," said Sebastian, "if Emily can get ready fast, afterwards. We don't have to be at the Hannafore until eight."

"I can!"

"Thank goodness she doesn't spend hours with make-up," said Rosie.

"So it's just my hair – and I can easily stack that up. I can be showered dressed and coiffured in twenty minutes if it's worth my while! Can we borrow the car, Mum?"

§

The last of the visitors had left Lantrelland beach by the time Sebastian and Emily got there and parked beside the public lavatory – the sole building the council had allowed to be erected near the shore. Even that had taken a while for the various bodies to negotiate. After the National Trust had managed to persuade the Rouse family to allow walkers to use the cliff path through their land 'by kind permission', the Ramblers and the tourist board had both requested that 'toilet facilities' be provided; and the council staff had suggested that Lantrelland would be the best place because it was reasonably accessible for regular cleaning by council staff based in Polperris. A septic tank had been installed to avoid pollution running into the sea – as it had in other bays for generations until Surfers against Sewage had drawn attention to it.

"It's a bit exposed here, isn't it?" Said Sebastian.

"Only when there's a south wind. It normally blows from the west and this bit of sand is quite sheltered by that little headland. It's very safe for bathing though – clean too – and it's the nearest beach that Mum was happy about for me to come to when I was little."

"Oh! What about Polperris? Surely they don't still let sewage go out to sea?"

"No – not now they have the tank – unless there's very heavy rainfall and they have to open the sluices. You hope the bad weather and the tide will wash it all away before anyone goes on the beach by the harbour."

"It doesn't sound very healthy."

"I don't expect it is but the water companies don't talk about it much. Perhaps Mum can find out more, now she's on The Council."

"Shall we have a paddle?"

"The water's jolly cold! You won't like it!"

Sebastian was already taking off his shoes and socks.

"I thought you were going to take photos and make notes?"

"I'm going to take a picture of you – and this lovely bay; to take home with me but I wanted to get you on your own!"

"Am I safe?"

"Fingers crossed, you might be!" Sebastian called over his shoulder as he trotted down to the water's edge. Emily slipped off her sandals and went after him and they stood in the crystal water as the tiny waves flopped on to the grey sand.

"This can't have changed for hundreds of years – sea, sand, waves and cliffs. There's only that loo as evidence of human existence and even that has been nicely designed. It's not obtrusive, is it?"

"Not like some of the old toilets you find – that look like gun emplacements – concrete and iron bars," said Emily. "They all have that characteristic smell of loo and disinfectant. This beach is one of the only privately owned beaches around. It's part of Eddie Rouse' farm, believe it or not. I'm surprised he hasn't started charging people to park near the loo! I wonder what the new owner will do?"

"In theory I imagine he wouldn't be allowed to do much by way of development," said Sebastian. "The coastline is supposed to be well protected."

"I couldn't help feeling that there must be come connection between the planning application for The Glebe and the sale of Rouse' farm when Mum and I saw Eddie with the awful Brian Rogersson and Hugh Olver-Blythe eyeing it all up."

"It's quite possible," said Sebastian. "With the relaxation of planning controls I wouldn't be surprised if people didn't start seeing how far they could push things. You're right, this water's freezing!" He took Emily's hand and led her out of the shallows back on to dry sand. "Sit on that rock and I'll dry your feet – my handkerchief's clean, don't worry!"

"What luxury – Sir Walter! How gallant!" Emily did as she was bid, raising one shining foot. Sebastian knelt and placed her heel on the hankie spread on his knee, mopping her ankle. It gave him the chance of touching her. He even brushed the last traces of sand from between her toes with the corner of the white cloth and reached for the sandal which he returned to her foot, fastening it carefully and setting it back on the ground.

"You've got lovely warm hands," said Emily. "Paddling always makes your feet feel so good when you put your shoes on again, doesn't it?."

"Give me the other one – and while I dry it, tell me about that pretty little ring you wear. I keep noticing it and thinking how nice it looks on your hand."

"Funny you should mention that just now," said Emily. "It's connected with Lantrelland – that's where I found it. Up in the Glebe Field."

"We don't seem to be able to get away from the place, do we? Sit there for a minute. I am listening and I'm going to take a few pictures while you speak." He dried her foot and took his smartphone from his pocket, composing a picture of Emily sitting on the rock, her hands clasped over her knee. In the background he included the east side of the bay.

"Keep it like that – I'm going to do a close-up too, so you can see the colour of the ring. It's so pretty! Tell me about it!"

"So Mr Olver-Blythe's ancestor was already showing a trait towards the necessities of life – like money?" Said Sebastian as he drove back towards Polperris, edging his way round the narrow lanes and blind corners, hoping no long reverses would be necessary if he met anyone.

"Breaking poor Emily's heart, causing her to die! It just shows how much he really cared!"

"Well I suppose life was different in those days – he couldn't have gone for job-seekers allowance if his father had disinherited him. Perhaps the first Emily should have told him earlier on about her mother's dubious parentage?"

"Maybe she wasn't ashamed of it! Who knows, her mother might have had all the nobility of a proud Spanish lady?" Emily's loyalty was to her name-sake. "The Puckeys still in the village are a very fine-looking family, even if they haven't had great opportunities in this life!"

"I suppose the same could be said about a lot of the people of Polperris. Only a hundred years ago many of them were truly on the breadline. Speaking not as 'the barrister fighting change' in this case but as myself I can't help worrying that society should allow mundane developments and new businesses to start up in this area. At least it provides employment and gives people a chance to prosper. Why should East Cornwall be preserved like some kind of private garden for the middle classes and foreign visitors when the 'natives' can't even find a job? If the Puckeys had had the opportunities that you or I had when we were children, they might be living very different lives, might they not?"

"I suppose so," said Emily. "When the Cornish mining boom fizzled out, thousands of skilled people left and went abroad and there were so many of them from the same background with the same accent – and often with the same name – they used to be called the same nickname – 'Cousin Jack'; like Scotsmen being called 'Jock'. For those left behind, with no land, there was only fishing and labouring – and it's not that much different now. Anyone with any ambition has to leave – like I did! I'd love to live and work down here but what would I do? At least in London I've got scope for better jobs."

"Couldn't you start up some on-line business? You can do that from anywhere?" They had reached the main road towards Looe and Sebastian was able to drive a little faster. "It's such a wonderful setting, isn't it? These sudden valleys and then level green fields, neat stone walls topped with turf! I'd love to live here!"

"I suppose we're not the only people in Cornwall needing barristers," said Emily.

"There's one chambers in Truro – I looked them up before I came down. The Godolphin Chambers cover the whole of the south west – so do others like Rougemont Chambers in Exeter. It's not very feasible to just stick up my plates and start from scratch! We're a bit like birds of prey – we need a large catchment area! Some of us specialise and offer our services over very long distances and it looks as though I'm about to become one of those long-distance counsels – if I follow my inclinations."

"Won't you get the reputation of 'resisting change' and find yourself working for NIMBYs all the time? That would be awful!"

"I suppose there would be that danger if I were setting up from scratch. I'd have to take what work I could find. Working from our chambers in London I can afford to be more choosey about which cases I take – or at least, my father can! I don't get much say in the matter. What with him and Harry Potter: and Dad agrees mostly with what Harry suggests."

"Harry sounds great," said Emily. "What's he like? Mum says he sounds like a real Londoner."

"He is! He started decades ago as the tea boy and messenger. He was so bright and willing that everyone asked him to do little jobs for them and after a few years he knew all the ropes and was able to stand in for the clerk. Then the clerk was ill for a while and Harry was able to bring in a few changes, bringing it all up to date. Then the clerk died and Harry was the obvious replacement. He's as sharp as they come, and kind. It makes such a difference when you've got someone like that. He makes us all laugh and helps keep a good atmosphere; in chambers there are often a lot of tired people working too long at their desks under loads of pressure. I don't know what we'd do without him. Now, where's the Hannafore?"

"Turn right just before the bridge and go right out to the point – you'll see the sign," said Emily.

"Do you go there often?" Sebastian had visions of her being a party girl.

"I've only been there once – for a New Year's dinner dance. Mum had a boyfriend who wanted me to go along to partner his ghastly son – a real Hooray Henry who trod on my feet – but the hotel was fine and the food was excellent."

"I'd better be careful about what I tread on, then!"

"You had!"

Emily was right about the food. The fresh air and paddling at Lantrelland had worked up an appetite. Their table was some distance from the band, allowing them to talk without shouting and although the restaurant wasn't full, the dance floor had enough couples on it at any one time to make Sebastian feel inconspicuous as he tried to recall ballroom lessons from long ago. He asked Emily for a waltz after the main course.

"It will make room for pudding," he said, taking off his jacket as most of the other men had done. Emily kept her silk wrap around her shoulders for the moment. She wanted to feel well-covered until the atmosphere in the ballroom warmed up – because the dress she had chosen from her mother's wardrobe was daring. Rose herself had never worn it in public. She had bought it in Paris a few years before in a mad moment, having been taken there by her then beau for a 'cultural weekend'. It had turned out to be the most exciting part of the weekend because the man was really boring and the weather, terrible. The 'little black number' had only been worn in Rosie's bedroom and admired by herself in the mirror. When Rose saw which dress Emily had chosen she sensed that Sebastian must have made a big impression.

Emily followed him into the flow of couples gliding around the dance floor. Sebastian paused, held up his left hand into which she placed her right, stepping towards him until her body touched his, her other hand resting lightly on his right arm. He supported her against him, feeling the firmness of her small waist. They stood, waiting for the music and then he leaned forward, leading with his right foot. It was as though Emily was part of him – no hesitation, no resistance – she simply floated backwards and left it all to him. His legs remembered all the steps he had learned and anyone watching might have thought they were regular dance partners.

"This is lovely," said Emily. "You dance beautifully: I bet you go every weekend!"

"I don't – honestly! But I might say the same about you. I was thinking you must be quite a party girl – it's like dancing with a professional!"

"That's very generous of you. Just wait until I get my feet tangled!"

They laughed and with growing confidence Sebastian tried a reverse turn – a great success; and then a few more steps before another, even quicker spin.

Emily held on to him as centrifugal force pulled them away from each other and as they gracefully slowed they found themselves very close indeed – and very much aware of each other's body and its contact. Emily didn't relax her pressure against him and enjoyed feeling the warmth of his chest against her breasts through his expensive shirt. The music came to an end and Sebastian softly kissed her on the cheek.

"That was marvellous, thank you," he said.

They walked back to their table and found that the empty plates had been removed, the cutlery re-laid ready for the next course. He pulled Emily's chair out for her to sit down, which she did without seeming to notice it but thanking him with a warm smile. Sebastian wondered whether she had always had this natural grace and what she had been like as an art student. She might be a few years younger than him but being with her was so calming. She was such a picture to look at – tonight wearing a headband that kept the long hair directed down her back; her oriental face with a serene half-smile of contentment. When she moved it was un-hurried. Any quickness about her was the way her eyes took in the whole scene and responded to Sebastian, frequently meeting his – expressing amusement, agreement, warmth and sometimes challenge. He could feel himself becoming more and more besotted with this original and enchanting girl.

The waiter was there within seconds, reciting the choices for dessert. Emily chose crème brûlé and Sebastian followed suite, not interested in food but simply basking in her presence. For her part, Emily was enjoying the strong silence of her partner. He wasn't hassling her with bright conversation though she could feel that both of them wanted to spend time – hours, days – always – talking and learning more about each other. On her lap the fingers of her left hand resorted to turning the gold ring on the middle finger of her other hand. It soothed her inward excitement.

"Ready for another dance?" Sebastian asked as they put down the dessert spoons. "It's a slow foxtrot, isn't it?"

"Sound something like that – I can never tell," said Emily. "I just go where I'm led on a dance floor."

"I noticed – it's wonderful: you're a pleasure to dance with."

"Thank you Sebastian: and so are you!" Emily stood up and allowed the cream silk wrap to slide off her shoulders and drape on the chair. As she turned to walk towards the dance floor Sebastian's breath was taken away when he saw why Rose had never dared wear the dress. It was backless and swept down, almost revealing – well – what in a chap would be called a builder's cleavage. It emphasised the superb lines of her body, reminding him of Pippa's shape at William and Kate's wedding a couple of years ago – but with far less fabric.

As they sank into each others arms and started flowing with the music, Sebastian's right hand had nowhere else to rest but on the flexing muscles of Emily's lower back. As she nestled to him, she could feel his response to her choice of gown, through the fine cloth of his trousers.

CHAPTER 9

"I was in Polperris the other day," ventured Hermione Olver-Blythe, as she sat with Hugh on the terrace at Carnhill, watching the August sunset. She had suggested a night-cap of port: the colour of the sky was such a dark red it reminded her of Hugh's collection of vintage ports, of many hues, in the cellar.

"See if you can find one the same," she had said. With reluctance, but wishing to maintain good relations before his departure for London the next morning, he had decanted a suitable bottle and now brought two glasses of ruby liquid on a tray, which he now placed on the cast iron table.

"These new cushions are so comfortable," said Hermione. "I'm glad I got them for these chairs. They're cold, otherwise, don't you think?"

"Yes, my dear." Hugh's thoughts were elsewhere: he was visiting his architect tomorrow. Antique-style lamp-posts would look good along the main breakwater of the new Lantrelland Harbour, which would be perhaps something like The Cobb at Lyme Regis but less stark. It would have friendly handrails and good lighting, yet be solid enough to resist the mighty waves of the Atlantic reaches of the English Channel.

"It's not often warm enough to sit outside like this in the evening, is it?" She asked, wanting to keep his attention.

"Makes you wonder whether they might be right about 'climate change'," said Hugh. "Mostly codswallop, though! This kind of weather happens from time to time. I remember it like this here when I was a kid; my parents sitting on these very chairs. No cushions then! It seemed to rain most of the time so we didn't mind a hard seat if it was nice enough to sit out. "What did you say you were doing in Polperris?"

"I went to look at that gallery up the Warren – you know – the Johnson woman's place. I've got a couple of friends who are thinking of exhibiting there."

"If she'll have them! She seems to have very definite views on things," he said; remembering, too, how good she looked at their unplanned meeting in the Glebe field: single, too.

"I didn't get to speak to her; she was away being a councillor but her daughter was there with a young man who turned out to be some kind of legal eagle, from what I could gather. I overheard him talking about 'chambers'. They said Mrs Johnson was 'up at the council'."

"Don't like the sound of that," said Hugh. "She's one of these greenies and I imagine, a bit of a left winger. She's stirring it on the planning committee, just when we could do with a bit of cooperation from them."

"Well that might make my idea appeal to you, Hugh," said Hermione, homing in on her next move.

"What idea?"

"Well, it occurred to me that we're not getting any younger. I'll soon be forty – not far behind you – and the long room has no paintings of us. I wondered whether we might commission a painting – or a couple of portraits."

"It would cost a packet, wouldn't it?"

"I've no idea – but it never seemed to dissuade your ancestors. Just about every previous generation had itself 'made immortal' by an artist of the time – even if some of the early ones are a bit quaint in style." She didn't say so but the earliest painting – one of Squire Hugh Olver and his inelegant bride in the early eighteen hundreds, painted against a background of palm trees, looked as though it had been done by a rank amateur.

"Were you thinking of getting one of your friends to do it – or Councillor Johnson herself?" Asked Hugh, now more interested.

"Well it did cross my mind that we might discuss it with Mrs Johnson. I like her work."

106

"I think you mean 'Miss' Johnson, or 'Councillor Johnson' as she wishes to be known. She told me off for calling her 'Mrs', the other day."

"Really? Although I did wonder how her daughter came to be called Johnson as well – but of course being illegitimate means nothing these days, does it?" It was one of Hermione's secret worries – that Hugh, in his dallying with other women – might make one of them pregnant – and go off with her.

They had been married for nearly twenty years and she had had two miscarriages but they had not been able, so far, to have any children. She knew how important it was for him to produce an heir; the thought of all his estate and considerable fortune being handed on to a distant cousin bugged him – he had mentioned it once only, early in their marriage, before there was any doubt about her fecundity, or his. Since then it was a subject that neither mentioned and their 'love-making' had become an uninspired, occasional ritual that gave little pleasure or satisfaction to either. Hermione still made the effort to get him to perform at a time of month when she ought to be most fertile. It wasn't difficult to arouse him and he knew what was expected of him when she was still awake by the time he went to bed. Her slightest touch prompted him to waste no time in relieving his lust.

It had crossed *his* mind too that if one of his more respectable girlfriends in London did 'forget the pill' he might consider legalising its birth after the event, especially if it were a boy. Hermione, he sensed, was more interested in her expensive life-style and 'county' status than in him personally and although it would be expensive for him, she would probably agree to split up. The down-side might be that his chances of becoming Lord Lieutenant would be set back by a few years, if not permanently. Being married to the daughter of a member of the House of Lords was a definite plus but propriety was expected before any royal appointments were made. Gone were the days when buccaneers like Walter Raleigh could hold the post.

Being realistic, Hermione suspected that her title would not be enough to earn Hugh's loyalty. She also knew that his reputation in county circles was not what it might be. She had the social skills needed to stay on friendly terms with the women of the set but his aloof coolness and steely ambition had always kept him apart from the more aristocratic old families of the far south-west. For the moment, however, both Hermione and Hugh took care to keep up appearances, living their separate lives but tolerating each other's presence when Hugh was in residence at Carnhill.

"If you think that's a good idea," said Hugh, "I'd certainly consider it. Her grandparents' pictures are fetching good prices at auction, I noticed recently." Hugh could already see two appealing possibilities. It might help in getting Rose Johnson on-side for his big planning application; and secondly there was the intimate contact with her as he and Hermione sat for their painting. The need for separate sittings was already flitting across his mind – Hermione might be busy with a golf tournament at the only time he could manage to be available …….. Rose Johnson was such a desirable woman; he couldn't resist those oriental looks. Her daughter was even more gorgeous but out of reach, like most of the younger generation. For him, only money could procure the attention of young women and there were attendant dangers, as he had discovered in the red light districts of London. Another idea – if he played hard to get over conceding a painting it might give him some leverage over his souvenir shop. He decided to resist the painting proposal and stick out for something in return.

"I like the idea but of course it would cost thousands," he said; "and at a time like this there are probably much better investments."

"Like stocks and shares? Bonds? I think that's dubious," said Hermione. "'My father was saying only recently that one might just as well go back into artworks, or bricks and mortar: interest rates being so low."

§

108

"Emily? Is that you?"

"Sebastian! Where are you?" Emily tucked the phone between her shoulder and ear so she could continue listening while manipulating the frying pan. It was such a relief to hear his voice. She had almost given up hope of seeing him again after returning to London together. He had seemed so quiet and withdrawn on the train back to Paddington she felt his initial interest must have been short-lived and was resolving herself to put it down as a passing, if pleasant interlude. He had been full of chat as they trundled from Looe up to Liskeard on the sprinter train but no sooner had they taken their seats in the The Cornishman, stopping only at Plymouth, Exeter and Reading, than he disappeared into paperwork collected during his stay in Polperris. He had been polite and friendly but it was as though the spell had been broken. This was Sebastian the barrister on a working trip and Emily felt restrained to interrupt as he made notes, hardly aware of her presence except when they stopped at a station. At Exeter he raised his head and gave her a pleasant smile, remarked on the Sunday evening crowd of people returning to 'The Smoke' – before becoming absorbed again in his work.

He had kissed her warmly before they headed for their respective tube stations but that was a week ago. Since then she had waited for him to call. The last thing she wanted was to appear as though she were trying to make the running. Her reasoning was that if he was still interested he would phone. She wanted it desperately: there was so much to say and she wanted to be with him, talk and be held by him; touch him, kiss him – and more. The first few days she made excuses to herself. Each time the phone rang her heart leapt, only to be disappointed.

Sebastian for his part, had come home to a crisis that seemed to fill his life, driving all thoughts of Polperris and The Glebe – but not Emily – out of his mind. He was conscious of a new thrill of love and affection that Emily had brought but it didn't seem to be urgent. It had taken him by storm – without any logic: he couldn't possibly know enough about her to make any sensible decisions but these had already been made. He was going to marry her and they were going to live as one. The constant presence of this knowledge gave him constant joy and he kept meaning to pick up the phone, to hear her voice and share everything with her. Events, however, took over.

At the chambers and at home in the evening he found himself enmeshed, entangled, consumed by what was happening to his father. The fraudster, whose case was lost when Sebastian was in Polperris, was now blaming Peter for 'gross negligence'. The man had been sent down for five years and was in Wandsworth Prison but from there was pursuing vengeance on the legal team that had 'failed to save him'. His solicitor was bombarding the chambers with letters that questioned the advice Peter had given his client. They threatened civil proceedings for incompetence and complaints to the Bar Council.

"That solicitor knows as well as I do that the man blew it when he insisted in going into the dock. I told him silence was his best defence but he's so convinced he's done nothing wrong he completely ignored anything I said. Now he's blaming me and his solicitor is enjoying himself writing snotty letters and sending more bills to the accused."

The fraudster had also activated some of his less savoury friends and the Trenlevens had been receiving abusive and sometimes silent calls on their phone at odd hours of the night. The first of these had occurred the same evening that Sebastian returned from Polperris. He was about to ring Emily when the phone went. He hurried to pick it up, hoping it was her. It would be a relief from his father's problems – but his cheerful 'hello!' was met by a man's voice telling him: 'you're fucking useless! You *and* your old man' and the phone being put down.

That distraction had driven Emily not out of mind but into a cherished background in Sebastian's thoughts. He still felt connected to her – not out of touch – and would phone her as soon as he had a minute: she would understand.

Emily, however, didn't. She hadn't known him long enough to know how steadfast he could be but how was she to know what was happening?

The next morning, after further calls during an interrupted night, Sebastian took on the task of arranging an intercept on their home number so that anyone calling had to talk to an operator long enough for the call to be traced. He also tried to find out how the fraudster and his accomplices had managed to get the Trenleven's home details. It was quite frightening, especially to Sebastian who had never experienced this kind of thing before, although Peter took it less to heart, having dealt with criminals for so long. There was plenty one could do to protect one's privacy and safety but all these things took time and trouble and Sebastian was given the job of undertaking them.

Hence a week raced by before Sebastian realised he still hadn't called Emily. It was a shock: like waking up suddenly after heavy sleep. Whatever would she think of him?

"Emily, I'm at home and I'm feeling awful for not having phoned you before. It's been a horrible week and I completely lost track of time. I'm so, so sorry!"

Emily's relief was so great she burst into tears – a weakness she had inherited from her Chinese grandmother. The tears streamed down her face: she was glad he couldn't see her. It didn't denote any failure on her part but gave release to so much pent-up emotion in a physical and immediate way. Neither did it detract from the steely will she had also inherited. It did mean that she was unable to speak for a few moments, which was punishment enough for Sebastian, whose mind went into overdrive. Was she going to slam the phone down on him?

"Emily? Are you there? Can you hear me? Please say something! Let me explain – things have been really bad here at home. We've had problems!"

He waited, sure she had not put the phone down and hearing the other handset's mouthpiece being covered. The suspension was unbearable, especially since he knew he deserved a good kicking.

"Emily?"

"I'm here: give me a moment – I'm cooking!" She tried to sound casual. Her relief at the sound of his voice had broken her sadness, blowing it away but now she was filling with righteous indignation. Anger took the place of defeat. She left it to him to continue the conversation as she turned off the gas, put down the pan and went over to sit at the table. "And yes, I *can* hear you."

Her fury rose: the bastard! A whole week – leaving her wondering whether it had all been a wishful dream! How dare he? She could kill him! It was enough to provoke another flood of tears. She reached for the hankie tucked into the sleeve of her cardigan and blew her nose. 'Get a grip Emily', she told herself – waiting for Sebastian's next humble approach, which was not long in coming. He related the alarming tale that had been the cause of her distress and anger, using all the skills that he had learned during his training. It wasn't long before she was feeling sorry for him. His summing up ensured her forgiveness: he was acquitted – almost.

"In my head," he said, "I've been phoning you all the time. I've been telling you that I've fallen in love with you. You've been beside me all through this fuss and I've been asking your advice and you've been reassuring me just as though we were together. It's just that … as soon as I've gone to pick up the phone something else has plunged in, forcing me to go off and make statements to the police or check up with Dad about what to do next. It's been truly awful! When I saw what today was and realised I still hadn't been in touch with you – I was almost scared to phone because I knew you'd be upset – or at least I hoped you would be!"

"What do you mean by *that*? Charming!"

"That sounds terrible, doesn't it – but I hoped you cared enough to be worried that I hadn't phoned! Oh God! I'm making it worse, aren't I? I need to be in front of you so I can apologise properly. Can I come round? Can I take you out to supper?"

"I've nearly cooked it here. I could probably expand it a bit if you deigned to come and join me?"

She was relenting: a smile had returned, along with her feelings of excitement and relief. She would soon have him in her arms again.

"I'm almost out of the door already. I'll be there in just a few minutes – and I've not forgotten my mobile, just in case I get stuck anywhere. I promise I'll call you if I'm held up."

He wasn't held up: Emily did not continue her cooking but whizzed round her flat tidying up before attending to her hair and

112

changing into 'something more suitable', a favourite low-cut red top and close-fitting mini-skirt.

§

At about the same time the telephone rang at the gallery on the quay in Polperris. Rose Yi Johnson thought it might be Emily. She had been a little concerned at Emily's subdued voice the night before but had not liked to ask what the matter was. With Emily it was better to wait until she was ready to tell you: any probing would bring the 'I'm fine, Mum, really!' response.

"Rose? It's Barbara Weeks."

"Oh Miss Weeks – how nice! Are you all right?"

"Yes thank you, very well but I hope you don't mind me phoning late like this. I've been wondering whether to or not for the past half-hour!"

"But of course you can – what can I do for you?"

"Well it's about The Glebe. I knew you are doing your bit to defend it and I've found out something you ought to know."

"Oh, do tell me! I've not been getting very far as yet," said Rose. "I'm still gathering information."

"I know it sounds silly but I still don't really trust the telephone – I'd much rather come down to see you, if you had a moment. Not now, of course – but perhaps tomorrow morning? I can't forget the days when the operator used to listen in to one's conversations! Ridiculous, isn't it?"

"Perhaps it's not – bearing in mind what's been happening – all that phone-tapping; although I can't think why anyone would want to hear what we've got to say!"

"Well what I've got to tell you will make your hair stand on end," said Miss Weeks, mysteriously.

"I can't wait to hear. Would you like to come to coffee in the morning. I shall be in the gallery and for most of the time there's no one around. We shall be able to have a good chat."

113

"About ten, then?"

§

"Emily? It's me! Are you all right? I was a bit worried last night – you sounded low."

"Mum! No I'm fine, thanks! Just cooking supper for Sebastian: he's popped round. We're both sipping a sherry – very formal, you know."

"That's all right then. I thought I'd give you a quick call. Miss Weeks just phoned and is coming round tomorrow to tell me 'something important' about The Glebe. It's made me all excited!"

"Promise to phone immediately she's gone!"

"I will, my darling; but for now I'll go away before you burn the omelette."

"How did you know it was an omelette?"

"I didn't – it was a guess! Bye for now! I love you!"

"Me too! Bye!"

"Good news?" Sebastian asked as Emily put the phone down.

"Not yet but it might be," she replied, remembering to switch on the cooker's extractor fan as the pan began to smoke. She moved it aside and turned down the gas. "Sorry – I should have done this sooner. You can open the big window if you like."

It was warm, the sun having come out in the afternoon and London was enjoying a perfect summer evening. Sebastian did as he was asked and then went over to stand near Emily as she prepared the food.

An hour and a half earlier he had offered a bunch of flowers at her front door. She had accepted them and invited him in formally, shutting the door firmly and hitching the safety chain out of habit while he stood awkwardly waiting for a cue. He wanted to hold and kiss her but knew he still had to show he was truly sorry for excluding her. He did not have to wait more than a

114

few seconds. Emily took his hand, pulled him through into the sitting room, put the flowers down and spun round, throwing her arms around his neck.

"You rat-bag! I could murder you! Leaving me like that – all week! You.... you.....". His passionate kiss silenced her tirade and she abandoned herself to his arms as they held each other almost motionless, aware only of each other's scent, the feel of her silky cheek, his prickly chin, their soft lips and tongue tips mingling. This was passion not to be denied a moment longer. Emily broke free and reached to undo his tie.

"I don't know how you can bear to wear this," she said, hanging the tie over the back of a chair; "and give me your jacket!" He obeyed before releasing his cuff-links to roll up his sleeves. She stopped him, unbuttoned his shirt, pulled it open and revelled in hugging herself against his bare chest. They kissed again; more softly and longer this time until Sebastian reached inside her top. She responded by slipping it off, then her bra. He pulled her close again, sensing her firm breasts against him and then releasing her so that he could kiss her shoulder and downwards as she leaned back. His mouth paid homage to her perfect figure and youthful nipples that reminded him of a Greek statue. Emily's hands were in his hair, pulling his head against her. Her heart was beating rapidly and she felt a weakening in her body that called her to lie down.

"Come through here," she said, breathlessly, tugging him through to the bedroom, falling on the wide divan, arms above her head, her dark hair spread over the pillows. Sebastian hesitated a moment, then undid his belt and slipped out of his trousers, shoes and socks, leaving them piled beside the bed before lying next to her, leaning over to continue his appreciation of her body as she stroked his neck. She found herself moving against him uncontrollably. He kissed her on the mouth once more before paying attention to the fastening of her wrap-round skirt that fell open revealing no underwear – simply the rest of her slender and shapely body.

"Don't be shocked – it was warm and I changed in a hurry," laughed Emily. "I usually wear them! Take it as a compliment." She reached over and put her hand over the bulge in his Y-fronts, feeling around. She placed her hand on his stomach, slid it down taking hold of his rigid penis, bringing him almost to instant ejaculation but letting go to push the pants down and away. In turn he put his arm under her back and leaned over to continue his kiss on her mouth – so softly, his lips brushing hers to relish their smooth warmth, the tip of his tongue seeking hers. His left hand stroked her flat belly, working down to her neatly trimmed mound of Venus, pressing and exploring for the parting into the warm, moist interior that welcomed his finger. Emily raised her hips against his hand, encouraging penetration and uttered a sharp intake of breath as her lower body pressed for more. She pulled him over on top of her and turning slightly towards him so he could mount more easily and then guided his penis until she could press its head sensuously up and down over the lips of her dewy vagina. Sebastian couldn't wait: only one thing restrained him: his golden rule of using a condom.

"What about ……. ?"

"I don't care!" She said. "I must have you – now!"

She cupped both hands on his buttocks, pulling him down into her. He had no alternative but to slide deep into the warm tightness. It was only seconds before she was enveloped in wave after wave of ecstasy as her body took over and devoted all its energy to drawing into itself anything and everything he had to offer. He too, now experienced an explosion that took command of his whole self, pumping and pumping with a power he had never experienced before – almost frightening him with its intensity. To both of them it felt as though it would never stop. They were gasping between kisses and then Emily laughed infectiously, sucking in gulps of air, now gripping his muscular flesh with fingers like a vice – before flopping back, spent, happy and replete.

"Don't move"! She commanded.

"But I must be heavy!"

"You are – and I want you to be!" She couldn't get enough of the roundness of his buttocks as her hands ran back and forth over them, giving the occasional press, to refresh the delight that she could feel between her legs. She wrapped her heels around him and drummed them against the back of his knees, wriggling with pleasure.

"That was absolutely – amazing!"

"Me too! Phew! I couldn't hold it any longer! But what have we got ourselves into?" Sebastian sounded concerned.

"Like what?" Emily still didn't care.

"You don't know I'm not HIV positive?"

"You're not are you?"

"I've no reason to be! I haven't had sex with anyone for over a year – except myself," he added, embarrassed.

"Me neither! What about blood transfusions or dirty needles?"

"No! And what if you get pregnant?"

"What a lovely idea! Would you mind?"

"Mind? NO! There's nothing I'd like better – except it might upset the parents! A bit sudden?"

"My mother couldn't say anything – that's how I came to be! It's sudden but so was my finding *you*. It's all – crazy – but I'm sure it's right!" Emily propped herself up on one elbow. "Aren't you?"

"I am - I was from the moment I saw you. I couldn't believe such a thing could ever happen to me!"

"That's just how I felt!"

"Will you marry me, darling Emily?"

"Not unless you promise to phone me every day!"

"I promise!"

"Then yes! I will marry you – right now if you like!."

"But I haven't got a ring!"

"You can borrow this one – you know all about it – I did tell you didn't I?"

"You did! Darling Emily – are you sure?"

"Of course I am. I *never* make rash decisions! Well – this is my first." She sat up, slid the gold band from her right hand and gave it to Sebastian. He put it to his lips and held it there with both hands for a moment, before taking her left hand and easing it on to her ring finger.

"I, Sebastian Trenleven, take thee, Emily Johnson to be my wedded wife, to have and to hold until death do us part."

"And I, Emily Johnson agree to all that, taking you, Sebastian Trenleven as my beloved husband for always! There! We are engaged: married and might even be pregnant all in about five minutes! Do you think that's a record?"

"It certainly is for my family," laughed Sebastian.

"Personally, I don't care," said Emily, "but I enjoyed the ceremony and I'd like some more. Let me nip out and get a towel – I don't want to muck up this bedspread."

By the time she was back, Sebastian was ready for her and this time everything lasted much longer and the omelette supper was eventually very late.

CHAPTER 10

The architect's office in Bayswater was as Hugh remembered it: impressive. Once past the outer Georgian door and tiled hallway, you entered a brightly lit space surrounded by glass and green leaves. How they had managed to get permission to change the elegant Georgian residence and its garden into this equivalent of a forest glade was a mystery but it gave him confidence. The airy space had the appearance of open plan but subtle divisions allowed each of the five casually dressed but trendy-looking architects to have their own privacy: none overlooked the other's paired computer screens. The focus of the whole space was in the centre, like the dance floor in a night club where an octagonal table displayed detailed models of buildings and developments, even down to green lawns and miniature trees.

"Those are our ongoing projects," said his host Clive Goodman, the senior partner. "They give us a reference point when clients are visiting. We shall need to make a lot more room on the table for yours, Mr Olver-Blythe. It's under construction already, if you'd like to see it, in the studio upstairs – or would you prefer to talk first?"

"I think it would be good to get an overall picture, don't you, Clive? By the way, do call me Hugh – it's quicker." He followed Clive to a double glass door leading to stairs that took them to another large working space mostly taken up by half finished models, racks of cardboard sheets, drawing boards and, on one side, the largest card guillotine Hugh had ever seen. On the wall a panel of computer screens displayed moving videos of three-dimensional drawings.

"It's over here." On a wide bench near the window, a model the size of a singe bed was taking shape. Still unpainted, it was in pale cream card, although the shadows cast by its various shapes gave some contrast to the general outline.

"This outer breakwater is the key to the whole project," said Clive Goodman.

"It's going to have to put up with quite a battering, isn't it? We get some frightful gales and storms down in Cornwall," said Hugh.

"We commissioned a team of maritime civil engineers to give us the basic design, using the materials you suggested, Hugh. They liked the idea and thought it would work well."

"It struck me that the granite blocks were not far from Lantrelland; they weren't wanted by the quarry people and had been rejected for one reason or another: just sitting there in an ever growing pile – some of them quite huge! I'd seen other breakwaters based on them and it seemed like a reasonable suggestion," said Hugh, pleased he had been right. "I assume the expensive bit will be moving them and settling them in place."

"The engineers were quite happy about using a barge-mounted crane and there must be plenty of suitable transport for granite available in Cornwall, as long as there's a suitable road down to the bay."

"So far, so good, on that score," said Hugh. "I'm buying the farm that would allow us to construct a better road down from the main highway – as long as I can get the planning."

"That, of course, is the make or break factor, as we both know," said Clive.

"Thanks to your ambitious investment plan we've been able to bring in some planning consultants who have experience of working close to National Parks, Areas of Outstanding Natural Beauty and the like. In my opinion they've come up with some very promising suggestions. They work from the premise that you offer the authorities benefits for the whole area that hadn't even been considered and would be hard to refuse. Of course the other requirement is that whatever you build must merge with the surrounding environment."

"I think I could have worked *that* out for myself," said Hugh, slightly testy that his expensive initial outlay might have been squandered on granny being taught how to suck eggs.

"Yes it seems obvious," said Clive, sensing the irritation, "and perhaps I haven't related this very well – but they've come up with some very original suggestions. For example the design of the 'outer quay' as we're calling it – partly for public relations reasons – other ports in Cornwall use the term 'quay' and it brings traditional structures to mind, doesn't it?" He looked at Hugh who nodded in confirmation.

"The 'outer quay' could be constructed to be twice as wide as might appear necessary. This would give us a lot more flexibility as to its use. They suggest that we could build into it wave-powered air turbines, such as they've got on the Scottish coast. The quay would be built in deep water, anchored at its base with reinforced concrete piles. When finished, most of the quay would be permanently under water and as solid as a natural headland. The design has artificial caves facing out to sea allowing waves to enter them. Each time a wave comes in it compresses the air in the cave forcing it past a turbine. As the water pulls back it sucks the air out again almost as strongly. The turbine is kept rotating by the compressed air – and the power comes from the waves."

"Surely that means the turbine has to stop and reverse each time a wave comes and goes?" Asked Hugh.

"No: they use something called a 'Wells turbine' that keeps spinning in the same direction whichever way the air is travelling. The turbine blades change their angle automatically – very clever!"

"It all sounds terribly expensive", said Hugh. He had visions of vast outlay for the wide quays and generating stations. "Not very sightly, either?"

"The generators can easily be disguised as net or lobster-pot stores, built on the quay. Electric cables can be built in and linked to the national grid at its nearest point. As for the cost," continued Clive, "it's offset partly by Government grants, and partly by a subsidised price for the electricity you produce and sell to the national grid. It will break even in about six to eight years, after which it becomes very profitable. The most important benefit, though, is the weight it gives to the argument for allowing planning permission. It creates construction jobs; and after that at least one professional post, maybe more, for an engineer to supervise and maintain the generators."

"Hardly a full-time post," questioned Hugh.

"Agreed: but as part of the responsibility of the harbour-master's office?"

"Ah – quite a prestigious job – just right for one of the locals?"

"Exactly – someone who's been away and got the qualifications – creating a job that will allow him to come home."

"Good thinking," said Hugh. "Any other bright suggestions?"

"Well, on a broader canvas, the consultants came up with one that sounded very appealing – a marine conservation park. Add to that a row of wind turbines to delineate the limits of the park and we become altogether 'green and desirable' – hard to refuse!"

"If I can find anyone daft enough to invest!" Said Hugh.

"Well, that shouldn't be too difficult as far as the wind turbines are concerned; as you know they are quite a hot topic in The City. The marine park doesn't cost much at all to establish and we've been researching some very compelling arguments for it that will appeal even to the most commercial of the Cornish fisherman."

"By putting some of their favourite fishing grounds out of bounds? That sounds improbable," said Hugh, once more feeling that he was being sold fairy tales.

"Everyone thinks that at first but the consultant showed us a DVD of an American project started in 2001 when a famous scientist, Dr Jane Lubchenko, produced a declaration signed by nearly two hundred marine scientists calling for marine reserves to be set up all around the world. It wasn't one of those 'scare your pants off' announcements but stayed very positive. They said 'it's no longer whether we should set aside fully-protected areas of the sea but where we should do it because it has been proved that marine reserves work and work fast!' They gave examples: off the coast of New England one reserve led to populations of snapper fish rising forty-fold. The fishermen, who had fought hard to prevent the reserve being set up, were soon converted!"

"The fishermen in Polperris are always complaining that the Spanish and other 'foreigners' are mopping up all the fish along the coast," said Hugh. "It might prove popular if they could be convinced it would work: the planners would have to listen!"

"Well Dr Lubchenko and her supporters tell another success story. In the Gulf of Maine, on the American East Coast, the authorities banned all fishing methods that might damage the stock of ground-fish. They created three marine reserves totalling over six thousand square miles of ocean and were amazed by what happened: the results were spectacular! The population of scallops recovered so fast in the undisturbed conditions that numbers increased by fourteen times in five years! People couldn't believe it! That wasn't all. Fish population densities went up by nearly a hundred per cent and average fish size rose by a third, with species diversity up by a fifth. I looked the figures up again just before you arrived because I thought they were so impressive. Look, I've made some notes for you. After what happened to cod stocks off Canada, even the fishermen had to agree that it was worth doing."

"Whether it would impress our planners is another matter," said Hugh. "I've been trying to get one of them over to our way of thinking but he's not the most imaginative of brains."

"Showing the DVD to the fishermen and local councillors on a chilly winter evening, followed by a few drinks and canapés could be a useful bit of public relations – it would begin softening them up. The consultants suggest a lot of activity of that nature as part of a political build-up to promote economic growth in the face of NIMBY opposition. They've had quite a bit of experience!"

"Fight them with their own weapons? Out-green them? Sounds right," said Hugh. "I agree; as well as designing the whole complex and raising capital, our most important task is to build up such a strong case for permission that the local people and politicians will back us up. The trouble is there are people who have come to live in the area who are politically active and becoming influential. We've got one half-Chinese artist-woman who's just been elected to the Council in the local village – and is now on the planning committee. She's already snooping around Lantrelland and I've heard she's been on to that 'stop everything in the countryside' society in London."

"The CPRE?" Clive offered.

"Something like that!" Said Hugh. "My wife's trying to find out a bit more but she got the idea that they've already begun to involve lawyers. It's quite worrying."

"But not unexpected," said Clive, trying to calm his client. "We get it for practically every project of this nature. I don't think one needs to worry too much about it at this stage – except by doing as we *are* doing – coming up with good reasons for the development and spreading the word. In fact, Hugh, I'm so confident that I'd like to come in with you on this one. We've had a couple of winners in the West End recently and I've been looking for somewhere to re-invest our capital."

That evening, as Hugh settled into his First Class seat on the train at Paddington, he opened his evening paper and ordered a large gin and tonic to celebrate the way his grand project was developing. So far, so good!

§

"Sebastian!"

"What?"

"It's nine o'clock!"

"So what? Where am I anyway?"

"You're in my flat – and it's time we got up; otherwise we'll miss all the best bits of the Farmers' Market."

"Do we *have* to go? Sebastian groaned.

"If you want some lunch: come on, lazy-bones!"

Emily, full of life, pulled the single sheet away from under his chin and exposed his long, strong body. He rolled up into a defensive position but she continued her assault with prods and

124

pinches, provoking him to retaliate. Now fully awake and joyously remembering their night of love-making he turned the tables on her and straightening out, pulled her over on top of him, her long hair falling over his face and shoulders. He revelled in it, hugging her to him before rolling over, holding her tightly. She surrendered and threw her arms above her head.

"OK I give in – but we must get up! It's nearly ten o'clock."

"And it's Sunday and we don't have to go to work."

"And there's nothing to eat! We shall starve!"

"You Chinese are always starving!"

"I'm only quarter Chinese and maybe less: and it's all lies about them starving!"

"I'm going to eat *you*! I shan't starve!" Sebastian snarled like a lion and to Emily's shrieks of laughter, pretended to take a mouthful of her shoulder.

"You bully! Get off me," she giggled, struggling feebly to escape.

"Not until you prove you still love me," said Sebastian, taking her hands in his and holding them down against the pillows.

"Let go of my hands and I'll show you," she said.

The next twenty minutes was taken up in passionate release of all their new-found happiness; being able to see, touch and feel each other's body anywhere and everywhere; kissing, stroking, hugging and finally merging themselves together, attaining a rhythm of movement that once more brought them to mutual climax of body and self. They fell apart, replete and at peace.

"What are you smiling about?" Asked Emily.

"Am I?"

"An inane grin!"

"I guess it's because I'm so happy. Did I ever tell you I love you, Emily?"

"I think you did mention it. A good job too, otherwise I'd have sent you packing!"

"I wouldn't have gone – I'd have stalked you!"

"I should hope so too because I love you more than I've ever loved anything or anyone – except Mummy."

"So I'm second best?"

"No – first equal – but different."

"I'll settle for that, as long as you will still marry me?"

"It's a deal – now let's see if we can fit in the shower together; but it will have to be rapid."

§

Rose Yi Johnson woke up at five, that Saturday morning. She had been having a vivid dream: missing the plane from Dubai to Nairobi where she was supposed to change flights for a Fly Tanzania connection to Mwanza – but her luggage had already been loaded. She woke up in a panic, relieved that it was light and that the gulls were calling outside her window. Visitors often couldn't sleep through their racket but she found it comforting and homely. Her childhood fears of flying and long-distance travel to see her parents quickly faded. She was home and safe: Emily was in London, apparently madly in love with a most charming young man (with good prospects) and Honeysuckle Weeks wanted to tell her something. Lost luggage and missed flights gave way to thoughts of breakfast followed by a quick lick and a polish of the gallery before Miss Weeks was due.

In the back of her mind, however, something niggled. For a moment Rosie couldn't think what it was. Something slightly uncomfortable had to be done: now what was it? She reached for her bag and dug out the diary that ensured she attended council meetings, dentists' surgeries and no longer, thank goodness, parents' days at Emily's school. There was only Miss Weeks at eleven today. She turned the page: 'Sunday, 22nd July 2012 – 4.30pm, Tea Carnhill, Mrs H-B. So that was it: not so irksome after all but why had her subconscious given it such a negative slant?

Living alone was all very well but things got out of proportion when there was no one else to take your attention, remind you of things and need your consideration. Why couldn't she meet someone nice, as Emily seemed to have done? Better get up and put the kettle on – drive away all these niggles. It was a lovely day and the scene outside was magical – bright colours, sparkling water, everything moving – the odd cloud, the gulls, the boats rocking and the first holiday-maker jogging out towards the cliff path, the other side of the harbour.

"Activity! That's what you need, my girl," Rosie told herself out loud. She took her own advice and in the next few hours achieved a great deal: taking a bath, doing her hair and dressing; dashing out for a couple of croissants and some cup cakes from the baker's; and opening the gallery promptly at nine. By the time Miss Weeks arrived, Rosie had actually sold two paintings and was feeling more than satisfied. She was about to fill the gaps on the wall with suitable pictures from the large cupboard by the door, when the old lady breezed in.

"Good morning, my dear!" She said, kissing Rosie on the cheek. "How kind of you to let me come and see you!"

"Not at all: I've been looking forward to it," Said Rose. "Come through and we'll bring a tray back in here, if you don't mind, in case I get any customers. I have to make the most of my summer season, as you can imagine."

"Certainly, Rose; let me carry something for you."

"First, could you stand back and tell me whether I've got this picture level?"

"Up a tiny bit on the right! That's it! Perfect! What a lovely picture. It's the view from this window, isn't it?"

"Absolutely! I still love it: and it changes every time you look out. I don't feel my harbour pictures are pot-boilers for tourists because I enjoy painting each one even though I seem to know every slate and chimney pot as well as all the boats. They are never quite the same, though, and the light's always different."

"There are a lot fewer fishing boats than there used to be," said Miss Weeks. "It's sad really. On the way here I met two or three fishermen up who I know are out of work."

"I've heard them complaining it's not worth going out: they can't catch any lobsters and crabs; the mackerel seem to have disappeared and there are already too many boats doing sight-seeing trips."

"I've noticed that the harbour's filling up with these ugly white speedboats, too," said Miss Weeks.

"I know. They roar around at the weekends and the harbour master's always having to remind them about speed restrictions and proper mooring. The owners don't seem to know anything about boats; they're not local. I suppose the only good thing is that they stay bed and breakfast and eat out at the cafes and restaurants. The village needs them really."

"I don't expect they buy pictures, do they?"

"I have to admit, one or two do! Especially if I've included their boat in a painting! I try to leave them out but now and again it does add to the composition to have something white and shiny."

Rose placed the tray of coffee things on the desk and Miss Weeks put the plate of cup cakes beside it as they sat opposite each other.

"Well – now there's no one to over-hear us, let me quickly tell you what I've learned, Rose dear," said Miss Weeks. "After you told me you'd seen Mr Olver-Blythe and the others in The Glebe I thought I'd do some sleuthing – like that lady detective on television – so yesterday I went round to visit Eddie Rouse' wife. I knew he was out because I saw him go down on the tractor with a hay-turner hitched up. It was going to take at least a few hours before he came back.

"Judy Rouse and I are old friends. When she was young she used to come and help us on the farm: she loved animals and I think that's why the Rouses bought our farm eventually, because the family thought she might keep Eddie on the straight and narrow: she's a lovely girl, although not to look at: no beauty I'm afraid and a lot younger than Eddie. She's the salt of the earth but the poor thing couldn't get him to concentrate on farming. He was always trying to find easy ways of making money and at best, has been 'foolish'. She's had a terrible time, one way and another. There was nothing suspicious about me visiting her because we do drop in to see each other from time to time. She usually comes to see me when she's really down and I go over there when I feel I haven't seen her for some time. Anyway, we had a good chat. It turns out that she's relieved that Eddie has finally agreed to sell the farm because it might pay off most of their debts. She doubts whether there would be enough money left over to buy The Glebe *and* build a bungalow and café there; and she can't quite understand what's going on but she knows that Eddie has frequent meetings with Mr Olver-Blythe and has been seeing that Brian Rogersson quite often. Eddie keeps telling her he's got a deal pending that will see them safely retired with a little business at Lantrelland Glebe Field. He's trying to convince her that it won't make it look like another Lands End pleasure park and says Mr Olver-Blythe is helping him. They've got a London architect to come up with tasteful plans that should get permission."

"Personally, I think that would be very difficult," said Rose. "The Glebe and the church haven't changed in hundreds of years and it's such a special place, don't you agree?"

"I do! I just love it as it is. My two animals are happy there and it keeps them all year long if I buy a few bales of hay for January and February time. I know they're on the fat side but I don't have the energy to exercise the pony like I used to: I've got so lazy in my old age! I take a taxi to come down here these days. I haven't been down in the trap for years and the bike is such an effort!"

"So you think Eddie Rouse is serious about his plan to buy The Glebe?"

"I'm not sure," said Miss Weeks. "Judy said she had heard Eddie and Brian talking about 'the marina' and 'waterside flats with their own moorings'. When she asked Eddie about it all he would say was that Mr Olver-Blythe was thinking about 'a bit of a development' for Lantrelland Bay when he'd bought the farm."

"A marina? Can you imagine? It would completely change the whole coastline between here and Fowey!" Rose was quite shocked.

"It would! That's why I phoned you, because now you are on the planning committee I thought you ought to know about it."

"Well thank you very much Miss Weeks for letting me know. I'm surprised we have heard nothing about it. No one at the Council has mentioned it. The trouble is the planning staff don't seem to have much to do with the councillors and we don't know what's going on until a formal proposal comes up in front of the committee. I really must try to get to know some of the planners better; then at least we could get early warning. This way, developers can have complicated proposals all prepared and we on the committee are put under pressure to give permission without understanding the implications."

Rose didn't say it but she had her doubts as to the integrity of at least one of the planning staff. Niall Ferguson's shifty behaviour had set all her suspicions going and she decided that she would keep him under surveillance as discretely as she could. She decided not to mention anything of this to Miss Weeks, who might innocently alert Judy Rouse.

"I'll certainly take this up at The Council although for the moment I think we'll pretend that we don't know anything about these other plans, don't you? Let's try to learn more about what they have in mind before alerting them that we have found out, shall we?"

"How sensible, Rosie! I knew you would put my mind at rest. I've been feeling so helpless about the whole thing. Once these developers get started they are so difficult to stop! See what's happened where Brian Rogersson built that monstrous shopping centre like a cross between a Spanish fortress and a fairy village – absolutely ghastly!"

"I have to be careful what I say about that," said Rose. "Half my constituents seem to have jobs there! They can't find work anywhere else locally and most of them are happy working for Mr Rogersson. Apparently he looks after them well, even though the wages are low. He employs a lot of those who don't have any qualifications."

"That's the thing, isn't it? If you are not farming or in some kind of holiday business there's nothing much else for them to do without trailing up to Plymouth every day."

"If they *did* build a marina it would presumably make jobs for anyone connected with the sea," said Rose.

"Well exactly! They tell me there are several fishermen who have had to give up recently because there's nothing much left to catch in the sea. In any case, I'm glad we have had this little chat. My mind feels easier now I've told someone in a position to do something about it; but I'll do as you say – try to find out what I can and let you know. I must go now, my dear, because I've got stacks to do – all my shopping for the week: a list as long as your arm. Thank you so much for the coffee and for your time."

"It's been a pleasure, Miss Weeks. You should drop in more often. It's lovely to have someone local in the gallery and I always enjoy a chat with you. We've known each other for so long!"

"Oh yes! And I remember your grandparents when they first came down from London – such nice people! They made this into a beautiful little art centre. Before, it was so rough-looking – just sheds and stores, apart from the dwelling house. Goodbye my dear and we'll be in touch!"

CHAPTER 11

"When are you going to tell your mother?"

"What about?" Emily's mind was on her shopping list as they walked down to Islington farmers' market.

"About *us,* darling Emily!"

"Oh that!" She held up her ring finger and kissed it. "I'll phone her as soon as I've got lunch on the go – unless you volunteer to cook, in which case it could be sooner."

"You haven't tasted my cooking!"

"I have every confidence in it. You are in good condition – not too fat; and you are delightfully athletic – especially in bed."

"In that case, how can I refuse? What do you have in mind?"

"Pasta: and salad; followed by the freshest fruit we can find. You can usually get strawberries here; and now Wimbledon's over the price will have gone down."

"Are we allowed cream?"

"We certainly are: they even have Cornish clotted cream here. Someone sends Rodda's best up on the train."

"We ought to go over and tell Dad, too. I haven't seen him for two days."

"He knows where you are, doesn't he?"

"Yes; he pretended to be shocked and didn't believe me when I said I'd sleep on the sofa. We can go after lunch, can't we? But hang on a mo'. I'll check out my lottery ticket in here." They were passing a stationer's.

"I'd forgotten about that. I've got mine in my purse," said Emily. "Do we have to buy something as well? Like when you want change? A box of matches?"

"No – course not! The shopkeeper's getting his cut!"

132

"Sorry mate! Nothing on this one. Do you want another?"

"Might as well – make it a lucky dip, EuroMillions! I'm lashing out again but I enjoy the wishful thinking." Sebastian folded his new ticket and put it in the special place in his wallet, saving the dead ticket to throw away later.

"Now let's have a look at yours, dear!" The shopkeeper took Emily's ticket and held it in front of the bar-code reader. It didn't stop him chatting: he seemed to have pent-up need for conversation. Emily wondered whether every customer gave him the opportunity to become part of his world. Perhaps he was lonely? He sounded like a football commentator during the build-up of a forward attack, speaking fast while enunciating his consonants.

"Oh! Now that's interesting! Hang on a minute! You realise it's a jackpot this week – nearly two hundred million? Frightening isn't it? You know The Lottery's made nearly two thousand five hundred new millionaires in this country since nineteen ninety four? My goodness!"

"Well I doubt very much I'll be one of them!" Said Emily, taking out her purse to find some money for her next ticket. She had enjoyed the faint hope of winning since Sebastian had given her the first opportunity and it was fun, mildly: no big thrill: but it was not as if she was spending beyond her means.

What, though, was holding things up? The man was not offering to return her dead ticket. She felt a sudden apprehension – not unpleasant; not so much nervous but more a frisson of expectation. Perhaps she *had* won something.

"I think you might have been lucky here," he said. "You'll have to ring this number when you get home." He pointed out a telephone number on the ticket as he passed it back to her.

"How much is it?"

"I don't know dear. All I know is that it must be more than five hundred pounds! That's all I can pay out in cash. Above that – up to fifty grand – you have to go to the Post Office.

Congratulations anyway – it's certainly better than a smack round the face with a wet fish! You can pop in and tell me what happens next time you're passing!"

"Fantastic! I might be rich!" Emily took the ticket, handling it with reverence as she tucked it back in her purse. "I feel all jumpy! Come on Sebastian – let's hurry up with the shopping and get home to find out how much it is. It should be yours really – you bought the ticket."

"But I gave it to you."

"Can you prove that?" Emily teased.

"Just wait 'til I get you home!"

Even the weather looked brighter and better as they left the stationers and made their way to Baron Street and the rows of stalls in Chapel Market. The next half hour was sheer pleasure as they exchanged small talk with the farmers at their stalls, picking out the best-looking lettuces, carrots, fresh peas and new potatoes. They found one stall with extra large punnets of strawberries, and discussed whether to buy one, or two. Emily was extra careful about her shoulder bag, keeping it tight under her arm. To have it snatched today would be the ultimate disaster. She might lose thousands!

"Come on, Sebastian. I can't wait any longer. Let's go home and find out the news."

By the time they arrived back at her flat they were decidedly warm, having walked briskly in the hot sun and as Sebastian prepared a cold lemon drink with water from the tap, ice cubs, fresh lemon juice and sugar lumps, Emily phoned the number on the lottery ticket. She had no idea what to expect as she read out her ticket number to the bored-sounding operator at the National Lottery's headquarters. She found out afterwards that the operators are trained to sound casual when speaking with winners so that their secret is kept. Another operator might tip off the press if they overheard over-excited declarations.

"Can you give me your name, please?"

"Emily Johnson."

"Your address and phone number?"

Emily spelled them out.

"Before I tell you how much you have won, will you allow me to give you a little advice?"

"Oh yes, of course," said Emily, the tension rising. Her feelings were verging on panic. How could such a nice thing make her feel so awful? Her heart was beating and she felt short of breath.

"Just give me a moment," she said. "Sebastian! Can you come here, please?" She called through to the kitchen. He was already on his way and appeared in the doorway with the two glasses of lemonade. He had even picked two small mint leaves from the bunch they had bought a few minutes earlier and floated one on each glass.

"Whatever's the matter? You are quite pale! My poor darling, is it bad news?"

"No – I just want you here. You can listen too." As he put the drinks down at a safe distance, she held the phone up and they put their heads together next to the ear piece. "OK, can you go ahead – sorry to keep you waiting," she told the operator.

"Ready for the advice, Miss Johnson? The first thing I'd say is put the ticket in a safe place – right now – and then make a note so that you don't forget where you have put it. Have you got a pen and paper?"

"Yes!" Emily picked up the phone pad.

"You have won two hundred and four million pounds." The calm voice sounded even more bored. Emily's head was reeling but she managed a reply.

"Thank you," was all she could say.

"Now please will you write down this phone number I'm going to give you. Then the place where you are going to put the ticket. When you have finished speaking to me, I suggest that you call the number and speak with one of our counsellors who can tell you what you have to do to collect your winnings. You can phone now, even though it's Sunday – the counsellors work from home and are on twenty-four hour alert, so don't worry. If you would rather wait, that's all right too – but I have to warn you that unless you proceed within one hundred and eighty days, the ticket could become invalid."

"Oh, don't worry about that! I'll phone straight away. Is that all you need to know from me?"

"Yes – that's all; but do you have any further questions?"

"I'm sure I do! But I can't think of anything just now!" Emily was on the point of fainting and at the same time had a strong urge to scream and jump about.

"Shall we end this call then? You won't need to call us again – just that number I've given you. Would you like to double check it?"

"Oh yes of course." Emily read the number back and it was confirmed. She said goodbye and put the phone down before giving Sebastian the shock of his life by throwing her arms in the air and allowing her pent-up emotion to rip, first as a triumphant yell and then by breaking free of his supporting arms and doing a kind of war dance around him. This was a side of her he had not yet experienced and made him realise how little they knew each other, though it didn't seem to matter.

"Did I hear correctly? Two hundred and four million pounds?" Sebastian could hardly believe his ears.

"That's what she said! It's got to be a record! I can't believe it! Me? Well – me and you – because I feel it's yours too. Do you still want to marry me?"

"I can't afford not to! I hardly dare phone my Dad now – I can't tell him all of our news at once; he'll have some kind of seizure!"

"And how shall I tell Mummy? She'll go bananas! It's not that she's hard up. My being engaged will be more of a shock than the money. Shall we do it straight away?"

"Let's eat before we phone anyone. I'm sure we'll calm down a bit with a little food – but we could celebrate with a drink first, couldn't we?"

"I shall need a clear head before I speak to a counsellor but yes, let's have a sherry or something."

"I've done these lemon drinks – won't that do?" Sebastian sounded disappointed after his efforts as barman.

"Perfect!" Said Emily. "How lovely!" She reached for the lemonade.

"This is going to change our lives," she said. "I can't really believe it yet. Two hundred and four million pounds! That's a fortune! It's so much money – whatever shall we do with it?"

§

Carnhill, July 23ʳᵈ 2012

Dear Miss Johnson,

I hope you will forgive this scribbled note – and that I'm not addressing you as 'Councillor Johnson'. Let me explain why. It is because this is simply a private enquiry to you as an artist, regarding a possible commission.

My husband and I are interested in discussing with you the possibility of having a portrait – or possibly two separate portraits – of ourselves, to go with those of his ancestors in the long gallery at Carnhill.

We wondered whether you might be interested in bringing some samples of any paintings you may have done of this nature so my husband could see them? Or we could make an appointment to come down to your studio if you would prefer. I was very impressed with your work on my recent visit.

Neither of us is au fait with the process of portrait painting but I'm sure you will be able to give us all the details. After that we can decide whether we shall be able to go ahead.

I do look forward to hearing from you. Perhaps you would like to call me on my mobile? The number is 07700 900 496.

By the way, I <u>did</u> enjoy my visit to your studio. I'm sorry I missed you but it was a pleasure to meet your charming daughter.

Yours sincerely

Hermione Olver-Blythe

The note was on un-headed paper but Rose noticed the Carnhill crest on the flap of the envelope in which it had arrived the day before and underneath it, in very small italic print *From The Hon. Mrs H. Olver-Blythe.* The lady was not being entirely informal, thought Rose, snobbily: being the daughter of 'Dustman Dick' was showing through Hermione's veneer. It seemed she could not resist reminding the recipient of her title.

Truth to tell, in this case, it was an unfair assumption. Hermione had written the note in a moment of enthusiasm; and thinking it wise to clear the idea with Hugh, had shown it to him before sending it off. She had been surprised at quite how willingly he had agreed and wanted to keep up the momentum. In retrospect she regretted suggesting separate portraits because Hugh had been rather *too* easy to convince and Hermione suspected it might be that her promiscuous husband might have ulterior motives. She was not wrong: his interest in Rose Yi Johnson was prompted by various fantasies. The thought of 'sitting' for hours being able to stare at her and persuade her of his growing affection had definite possibilities and Hugh was all for it; the sooner the better. His reaction to her suggestions confirmed Hermione's suspicions.

"I'm not sure about having one painting of both of us," he said, having read the note. "There aren't any other couples in the gallery."

"All the more reason for us to have one together," said Hermione. "We could include the house in the background and it would make the picture oblong – landscape instead of portrait – and it would go nicely about the fireplace instead of those two little ones, which even you don't like."

It was true. Not all the Olver-Blythes, or the Olvers before them, had had Hugh's good looks. The two paintings she had mentioned were not good. They dated from the late nineteenth century during a period of financial hardship. The artist must have been someone local whom they could afford.

"I must say that's a good idea," said Hugh after a moment's consideration. "We might ask for a really large painting; something impressive: it's a huge fireplace."

It had flashed into his mind that they wouldn't necessarily have to sit at the same time although he wouldn't mention that just now; it would become obvious once the work had started. How could an artist paint two people at once? He might still be able to arrange sittings for himself when Hermione had a golf tournament or committee meeting. He had visions of being in Rose's studio on a hot afternoon; being too hot and having to take off his jacket; showing the physique about which he was so vain: a result of those hours in the gym in London. His daydream was interrupted when, most unusually, Hermione, who had been standing behind him while he read the note, began massaging his shoulders.

"Oh – that's rather good!" He said, moving his head and flexing his muscles.

"I thought you were looking rather tense," said Hermione, moving her hands to his neck, finding those soft parts at the back of his head. He leaned back against her.

"Oh that's lovely – don't stop," he said. "I can feel it relax me straight away. I didn't realise you had such strong hands. You have hidden talents."

"It comes from smiting the golf ball down the drives over at Looe," she laughed. "You have the shoulders of a weight-lifter! I don't know what sport you get up to in London!"

"You know I play squash! And I go to the gym. Ow! That's good – over a bit to the right! That's it!"

"Just a moment," said Hermione. "Slip off your jacket and I'll give it a real go."

Hugh could hardly believe his ears and wasted no time in obeying. Hermione was fully dressed and made-up, ready to go off for the day. Her perfume and closeness were having an effect that normally took her some effort to arouse, late at night.

"Esme's not coming in today, is she?" He asked.

"No – it's not Tuesday or Thursday," said Hermione, pleased with the effect she was having on him.

"Oh good! If I lie down over there on the chaise longue do you think you could go over my back, too?"

"Of course: but I'll have to take off some of my finery," she said.

Hugh went over to the tapestry-covered chaise longue and sat taking off his shoes and loosening his trousers before peeling off his shirt and vest. He looked up just in time to see Hermione advancing on him in her bra, skirt and stockinged feet. She pushed him backwards, leaned over and kissed him aggressively, her hands exploring his chest, stomach and below, focussing on that most important centre of sensitivity. It was too much for Hugh. He pulled her over beside him, then deftly mounted her, returned her kisses as she pushed down his remaining clothing. He took her almost violently and with a passion she had not experienced from him since their honeymoon in Biarritz twelve years earlier. It was the first time for ages that she nearly achieved orgasm with him and it was with mixed feelings that she released him very soon after he had delivered what she had been seeking – his seed – into her body.

Her plan that morning had been twofold – to get his agreement for the painting and to seduce him during the time she was most fertile – as she had been doing for several years. She never mentioned this, for fear of making him feel he was being used simply as a stud – though that was the case. Her ambition was to get pregnant before anyone else with whom he was 'having a relationship'.

"I'll definitely hire you as my physiotherapist," said Hugh, picking up his clothes and making his way back towards his dressing room. "Thank you Hermione. That was a delightful way to finish breakfast: and if it was prompted by the thought of posing for a painting then I suggest we commission one as soon as possible."

"I'll send off this note, then," she called after him. "You could drop it off in the post-box as you go to the station."

She hurriedly grabbed the nearest envelope, inserted the note, addressed it and attached a stamp. She had dressed and put on her shoes in time to meet him by the front door a few minutes later, looking every inch the successful city gentleman, not a crease in his suit or a hair out of place.

He took the letter from her and bestowed on her a smile that was unusually warm before descending the wide front steps to his car. With some satisfaction she went back to her room and sat at her dressing table. She congratulated herself on the success of a tactic that might help conserve her current status and life-style.

§

"So – you are being prodigal today, are you?" Peter Trenleven said as he heard Sebastian open the front door of their Putney home. "I thought you were going to be away for the whole weekend!" He came out of the kitchen.

"Careful what you say, Dad – we have a guest." Sebastian opened the door wider and offered his hand to welcome Emily over the doorstep.

"This is a surprise! You must be Emily: at least – I hope you are! If not I shall be most confused – Sebastian said he was staying with you this weekend."

"It *is* me, Mr Trenleven," laughed Emily. "How do you do?"

"Delighted to see you in person, Miss Johnson: or can I continue to call you Emily? I hope you will call me Peter and make me feel a little less aged."

"Oh come on, Dad, you're only young middle-aged!"

"I'll have you know I'm only four years off my State Pension! Sixty-one is nearly old – and often feels like it."

"Only when you've been doing daft things like running half marathons or winning tennis tournaments." Sebastian was proud

141

of his father's sporting achievements and wanted Emily to know about them.

"Do come in, Emily. This is a surprise. I didn't expect to see even Sebastian until late tonight. I was going to have cocoa ready for him!"

"Ha ha, Dad! But we wouldn't mind some tea if there's some going?"

"There is if you make it. I've just been re-potting the geraniums and I want to clear up but I'd love a cuppa, too. You two carry on and I'll catch up with you when I've finished. It won't take a minute."

Sebastian gave Emily a whistle-stop tour of the ground floor, showing her the dining room, study and drawing room with its leafy conservatory, before taking her through to the spacious kitchen overlooking the garden. She sat on the window seat and watched him. The kitchen, she observed, had a worn appearance. Nothing was sparkling and every surface was cluttered. She itched to put things away. Sebastian's mother, she suspected, would not have wished to see her kitchen like this.

"You must miss your mother," she said.

"I do," Sebastian replied. "We both do. It doesn't do to think about it too much. In many ways I'd like to move away from the sadness here but I haven't the heart. Dad's only just beginning to come to terms with things. It's less acute than it was but last year was awful."

"It must have been." She was going to ask more about his mother when Peter reappeared from the garden.

"Tea ready? Good! Let's have it in the conservatory. It's cooled off in there now. It was boiling earlier."

Sebastian carried a tray through and they sat in the cane armchairs around a low coffee table.

"Well," said Peter. "Have you two had a good weekend?"

"Unbelievable!" Said Sebastian. "Literally! We've got *so* much to tell you.!"

"Oh? Perhaps you had better pour out some tea, Emily? I think I might need it and the boy doesn't sound quite himself.

You are not usually so eloquent, Sebastian; I hope it's not going to shock me!"

His son's face told him it couldn't be bad news. He hadn't seen Sebastian as happy since before they learned of Françoise's fatal diagnosis. What he now heard, though, was indeed a shock. Sebastian's news struck him like bolts of lightening, twice in succession.

"Well, Dad: I know this will come as a surprise but Emily and I are going to be married!"

"But you.... When did you meet? It must be only a couple of weeks? Emily, don't get me wrong but isn't this a bit sudden!"

His hand was shaking so much the cup rattled in the saucer. He put it down on the table and sat forward in his chair, hands tightly together.

"It must sound crazy but we are both sure." Sebastian for his father's approval.

"It happened so fast it took us both by surprise, didn't it Emily? We feel we've known each other for ever. I never believed in love at first sight but it really did happen."

Peter looked across at the beautiful young woman. He could quite understand why Sebastian had been so struck. She was remarkably attractive with her long shining dark hair, Chinese features and fair skin. Her smile had already captivated him and on first meeting it had been like shaking hands with a princess.

"Do you feel the same, Emily? It's a bit drastic, isn't it?"

She blushed and cast her eyes down. She hated herself for being unable not to. She knew exactly how she felt, with a determination as strong as that of any man but on occasions like this, her body took over and made her look shy and retiring. She forced herself to meet Peter's enquiring eyes.

"I do feel the same; don't ask me why; I know it's illogical but it's like meeting someone again with whom I used to live. I feel safe with him; and happy. I just know I can trust him and want to be with him always! I've never been like this before. I've never been engaged, although I've had a few relationships that didn't come to anything. It must be a bit of a shock for you, too, though!"

Having been so brazen in expressing her feelings, Emily once more lost her confidence and looked down at her tightly clasped hands. She missed seeing the twinkle of love showing in Peter's eyes as he took in the news, which was so romantic. It registered his acknowledgement of the impetuousness of the son he loved and this lovely creature who had come into their lives so suddenly.

"You can say that again! *What* a shock! It's hard for me to take it in: it's *so* sudden! All I can do is to wish you both, every happiness. It's amazing and I'm very happy for you. What a lucky man I shall be – to have such a beautiful daughter-in-law! How long do I have to wait? Have you decided on a date yet?"

"Do you know we haven't had time to discuss minor details like that," said Sebastian. "We are a bit overwhelmed by the enormity of the whole thing – but that's only part of what's happened this weekend. You'll NEVER believe the rest of it!"

CHAPTER 12

"But Mum, you met him: you could see what he's like!"

"Yes I did, and I liked him. He's good-looking; he seems to be intelligent and resourceful and he's certainly charming, but my darling – you hardly *know* him. How on earth can you be *engaged*? You've only just met! Don't tell me you've been to bed with him already?" Rose changed the telephone to her other ear so she could reach for the drink she had poured for herself before it rang. "Hello? Are you still there?" she asked but the silence confirmed her suspicions. "Well I hope you took precautions!"

She waited again. "Emily – please say something!"

"Mum, he's lovely!"

"So is Prince Harry but you wouldn't marry him within days of meeting him!"

"I might!" Emily giggled – the way she used to when she was a little girl and Rose remembered the times it had dissolved her annoyance having caught the child in some mischief or another; but this was serious: admission of guilt was one thing but marriage? And the possibility of pregnancy! God! Emily might be turning out like her mother! Like me! That had to be prevented.

"Well for goodness sake go and get the morning-after pill – unless it's already too late."

"Mum please! It's most unlikely that I am and even *if* I am it's what I want! I've told you, I'm quite sure about Sebastian: we are all right together."

"All right? That's not enough."

"Mum – *you* can't say much – if you had taken such advice, I wouldn't even be telling you all this!"

"That's just why I *can* say a lot, Emily. Believe you me, bringing up a child on your own is no joke."

"But I wouldn't be on my own. Sebastian's not going to go away."

"Isn't he? How sure can you be of that? You know what men are like!"

"Not *all* men. Not this one; and I've met his father now, too. He's such a nice man and very well respected. He's given us his blessing."

"Huh! How generous of him! What's he got to lose? I expect he fancies you, too!"

"Mum that's horrible! I'm beginning to wish I hadn't told you."

"I'm sorry, darling, I don't mean to be horrible; it's just that I can see you falling into a foolish mistake that could ruin your life. I ought to know! I'm speaking from experience."

"So having *me* ruined your life? Thanks Mum!"

"No I didn't mean that! Of course it didn't; but it did change my life completely. It meant that I was tied down for nearly two decades, looking after you and keeping house. Any career I might have had was delayed and altered."

"But you were on your own; and I'm not going to be. Sebastian's going to be here; and anyway, neither of us is going to *need* a career now. That's the other bit of news I've got for you."

"Oh my God, whatever next?"

§

As she heard the astounding news about the lottery win it was almost too much for her. The meaning of 'mind-boggling' passed through her consciousness in the next few minutes and she fought to prevent herself being completely distracted by all the possible scenarios flooding into her head. The stars must be in mis-alignment, she thought. This isn't happening – I'll wake up in

146

a minute; but she didn't. Emily had gone quiet again at the other end of the line and the silence was deafening.

"Mum? Are you all right?" Emily's voice was timid.

"Well ..... no ..... of course I'm not. I feel like those signs for a theatre – the smiley face and the worried face both showing at once. I'm finding it hard to believe what's happening."

"That's how I've been feeling too – except that I'm two happy faces. I don't think I've ever been so happy or excited."

"They call that 'being high', my darling; and it's usually followed by a return to reality. You need time to calm down, think – and come to your senses. Can't you come down for a few days and sort your head out? I've got lots to tell you and it might bring you back down to earth. I never expected this kind of thing from you. Which happened first – the Lottery or getting engaged?"

"It was Sebastian and me first. The Lottery thing was next day."

"At least it's not all about money; just the madness!"

"Mum, it's not madness. I can recognise 'the right thing' when I see it – and I've seen it! It's Sebastian and me being married; and we're going ahead with it, whatever happens."

"I'm sorry, Emily, but I cannot let you do this."

Rose's concern was turning to parental authority. It reminded her of having to put her foot down during Emily's first year at secondary school when she wanted to 'stay over' at some particularly dubious boy's house where you could almost smell pot smoke as you passed the front door.

"Mum, I've got to go – but please don't be angry. I couldn't bear it."

"I'm not angry, darling – just worried that you are letting yourself in for a potential disaster that you will regret."

"Mum I can't stop to talk, there's a lady coming from the Lottery to give me advice on what I should be doing with all the money. There's the doorbell – and Sebastian's opening it. I'll have to go."

Rose reluctantly said her goodbyes and both of them put the phone down knowing it was only the beginning.

§

"Miss Johnson? I'm from the National Lottery. You *are* Miss Johnson?"

"Yes, that's me! Very pleased to see you – I've got so many questions – do come in. And this is my fiancé, Sebastian Trenleven – it was he who actually bought the ticket."

"But I gave it to her straight away – there's no doubt as to the ownership," Sebastian said quickly.

"I think it would be sensible to write that down so that – God forbid – if anything goes wrong between you, there's something a judge can use to help him make decisions."

"I should warn you that Sebastian is a barrister!"

"Well I'm sure he won't object to signing such an agreement," said the motherly lady who looked as though she were on her way to the shops for groceries. Emily had been expecting someone dressed rather like herself at work – a sleek businesswoman – but the Lottery representative seemed very ordinary and relaxed.

"My name's Dot Macdonald," she said, shaking hands with both of them.

"I'm one of the freelance advisors who are on call for Lottery winners. They call me a 'winner counsellor'. I only work when I work – if that doesn't sound too daft! I'm on call twenty four hours a day and I'll give you my private phone numbers if you promise to call me whenever you feel you need to. At a time like this, the Lottery organisers realise that things can get too hectic and confusing and people might need help to put things back into perspective."

"You can say that again," said Emily. "We've just been telling our parents and it's left them in a spin too!"

148

"Of course it has. We advise you not to spread it about until you have begun to get used to the idea. I'll explain why. If you make promises to give relatives and friends some of your good fortune, you may be letting them in for big tax bills, so it's better to work out how best to arrange things before even letting them know. People get carried away – first by the news and then by the tax man! I know what it would be like if my kids phoned me up with news like that! I've got a boy and a girl – she's still at college and the boy's doing his 'A' levels. That's what I do with the rest of my time. My husband has a 'steady' job, working in the Post Office so he's the one at home keeping the ship on course, as you might say. I come and go as required. It's very exciting, sometimes!"

"*Too* exciting, perhaps?" Sebastian instinctively liked the lady, whose calm confidence inspired trust.

"At times, yes! I expect it's the same in your job, too, isn't it?"

"Not yet, thank goodness; but my father's a criminal barrister and it does give him some nasty shocks from time to time. Fortunately some pleasant ones, too!"

"I'd like to exchange experiences with him one day! But shall we talk about your winning ticket, Miss Johnson."

"I'm Emily: and this is Sebastian – may we call you Dot?"

"Of course. When you phoned me I was just back from Doncaster – from someone who won nearly a year ago: it was good to learn I don't live too far from you – I can be here quite quickly if you ever need me to be."

"I hope that won't be necessary!" Emily looked puzzled.

"You never know – so make sure you've got my phone numbers on your mobile and perhaps in the back of your diary – if you still use one!"

"It's all so new to us; but come through and I'll make some tea or coffee," said Emily.

"Let me do that," interrupted Sebastian. "It's your win – and you are the one who ought to be first to hear all the good news."

"But I want *you* to hear as well! I'm too excited to remember everything. Hurry up and put the kettle on; and come back to sit with me. I need you!"

"How nice! I feel wanted!" The look that Emily and Sebastian exchanged warmed Dot's heart. Young love: how beautiful. She hoped the money didn't disrupt it and knock if off course. She had had clients whose lives had been shattered by sudden riches and this girl was now *super* super-rich.

"There's one more thing I must ask straight away," said Dot, going through her mental check list. "Does either of you have to take any medication at regular times? Anything like diabetes or blood pressure? We've found that people can forget to take their pills in all the excitement – and some have even finished up in hospital. It's just so I can remind you from time to time, if necessary."

"Neither of us – yet! We're both fine, thanks. Nothing a cuppa won't fix!" Said Emily.

While Sebastian was pottering in the kitchen, making tea, Dot and Emily learned more about each other and it transpired that Dot's secret ambition was to paint landscapes, especially in the West of England. She and her family spent time there every year although some of her holidays had been interrupted by phone-calls forcing her to leave for a day or two; or by hours on the phone soothing a winner faced by a crisis.

"Well, now you are back, Sebastian, perhaps I can ask you both some more of the routine things I ought to know; then I'll try to answer your questions," said Dot. "I assume you have a bank account, Emily?"

"Yes I do; and I've photocopied details for you."

"There's something else I must get out of the way. That's just making sure that you are who you say you are! We do have to be so careful, as I'm sure you understand. Can you show me your passport, for example."

"Of course! Let me dig it out," said Emily, heading for the small escritoire by the window. Dot produced a portable hand scanner, switched it on and passed it over the relevant pages.

150

"When we've had a chat I can email your details through to our office and they can transfer the money immediately – so it should be in place by this time tomorrow. We have a special arrangement with most banks – including yours," said Dot, looking at the paper Emily handed to her.

"The bank will wonder what's hit it!" Sebastian tried to imagine a clerk receiving the information.

"I've no doubt they will be pleased – because it's going to mean a lot of business for them – especially in this case; and that brings me to the next thing. It's something that needs very careful consideration on your part and I'd advise you to take a few days before making up your mind about it. It might seem a simple decision for you personally but some people find it hard to make up their minds. It's about publicity or secrecy."

"I'd wondered about that," said Emily. "My gut feeling is to keep as quiet about it as possible. I've heard that you get pestered terribly by people asking for money and financial people trying to sell you into schemes."

"That is a danger," said Dot, "but some people have always wanted to become 'a celeb' and in your case, having had a record win, it would be easy to get on telly and in the papers. Yours is a much bigger rollover than that Scottish one last year, which was 'only' a hundred and sixty million pounds – a bit more actually. The people allowed their names to be published and take the consequences but were apparently happy to do so."

"Will Emily be under any pressure to go public?" Asked Sebastian. "That would concern me. Do the Lottery people want it?"

"Of course the organisers would prefer the news to be shared because it will increase their sales of tickets but the law makes it water-tight, that if the winner wishes to remain anonymous, it must be so. Even within the company they take every precaution to prevent any leaks. I'm under the strictest possible instructions not to divulge any information about you or your business."

"That's reassuring," said Sebastian. "What do you think Emily? You won't want to be a celeb will you? Or *will* you?" He

151

suddenly realised how little he knew of Emily's ambitions and dreams. Her reply surprised him.

"I'm not sure," said Emily. "It came to me in the night. I've not been sleeping a lot the last night or two."

Sebastian suppressed any reaction. He wanted to take her hand and re-live the memory of their love-making. He wondered when she had had time to get good ideas and was tempted to make a joke about 'lying back, thinking of England and the Lottery' – but did not allow his face to change from that of a serious listener.

"Being such a big win: a European and perhaps even a World record, it puts us in a strong position to get a huge amount of publicity for any cause we'd like to support, wouldn't it? I've been wondering about that," said Emily.

§

Rose Johnson was not at all happy. Normally, the prospect of a new group arriving to start their week's adventure into painting would be stimulating. You never knew what the people would be like. She had celebrated some outstanding weeks when several of the pupils had been especially talented; challenging her ideas and leading her to change even her own techniques and thinking; and she had endured other weeks when students were grumpy, quiet, sarcastic or over-critical of each other, leading to a bad atmosphere in which little progress was made by anyone. As she finished phoning all the bed and breakfast proprietors booked for this week's visitors, passing on times of arrival, she wondered what she was going to say to Sebastian Trenleven's father who, if the young couple persisted with their crazy dream, would soon become 'family'. Would he agree with her that their offspring ought to give each other more time before taking any more momentous decisions?

Peter Trenleven, as he travelled westwards, was having similar thoughts. What would happen if Emily's mother opposed the young couple's marriage after such a short courtship? He was about to spend a week in Sebastian's future mother-in-law's company and it could be very uncomfortable if she disagreed with him about letting them find out the hard way – or with luck, achieve their romantic dream. It might be hard to concentrate on the water-colours, although that could be safer than trying to convince the mother of an only and precious daughter that his son's intentions were honourable.

§

By the time Dot had left, Emily and Sebastian felt quite exhausted. They didn't even have the energy to take the tea tray back to the kitchen but left it on the table and flopped back on the sofa.

"Do you want some more tea?" Asked Emily.

"I'd love some!"

"OK, just give me a minute. First, I need to just lie here." She leaned over towards him, and put his arm around her shoulder, tucking herself close to him. "I'll put the kettle on in a moment." At which she dropped off to sleep. Sebastian didn't like to move but looked down on her serene face. He couldn't get enough of its symmetry; the eyelids that closed without a wrinkle, and their lashes resting on her golden cheeks. Her nose set so perfectly above her Cupid's bow mouth and its full lips. He could not resist kissing her softly on her forehead, savouring her cool skin against his lips; his right hand sought her breast, resting there, feeling its shape and firmness. Thus he sat, fully aware of how happy and content he felt in the midst of this whirl of mental activity. It was not long before he, too, slept.

"I'm so glad you were all able to come," Hugh Olver-Blythe tells the Lantrelland Parochial Church Council, all seated in the drawing room at Carnhill. None of them has been invited here before and each is dressed as though it's an important Sunday. Churchwarden Trevor Philp is sitting next to Hugh.

Mr Philp lives at 'The Barton', the farm to the east of the church and, as in so many parishes in the South West of England, The Barton has always had close connections with the church, the incumbent often being churchwarden. A sensitive and thoughtful man, Trevor Philp is one of the best farmers in the district. His rolling fields are not defaced with patches of weeds; the top of his ripening corn is free from weeds and level as a billiard table; the hedges on The Barton are stockproof, protected by barbed wire and trimmed into an 'A' shape to give maximum protection to birds.

The Philps' farm roads and tracks are passable even in the wettest winter; each tree in the woods that cover the steep sides of the valley through the middle of the farm is given sufficient space in which to collect light and nutrients to grow tall and straight. Trevor and his sons invest time during the winter, thinning out and clearing unwanted undergrowth. This work yields firewood, fencing stakes and kindling for the fire at home. Their children and grand-children will eventually reap the benefits of selling the mature timber.

Other members of the council are retired local people and a few are incomers from up-country, some as far away as Sheffield. Between them they form most of the congregation of Lantrelland Church, where the Eucharist is celebrated once a month, with the vicar, now resident in Polruan, trying to keep up with his Sunday rounds at the end of which he hopes he won't be breathalysed, following so much communion wine.

"It's very good of your chairman to accept my invitation to Carnhill this morning – especially since I have now stood down from your committee. It is as a parishioner that I've asked you to spend a little time considering the situation in which we find our Church at Lantrelland – a mediaeval treasure for which you are responsible to the people of this parish and indeed, Cornwall and the nation." Hugh clears his throat before continuing. He is enjoying the drama.

"As you know, last year's PCC agreed that the church needed essential repairs to its roof. Both the vicar and I spend a great deal of time approaching bodies such as English Heritage and a host of trusts and charities, asking for grants and donations towards the roof; and I have to say we did achieve some success – although nowhere near enough to carry out the complete job. The committee reluctantly decided to sell The Glebe to raise the full amount necessary. It seemed appropriate that a favoured buyer would be a neighbouring farmer who was about to retire – Mr Eddie Rouse, whose land lies next to some of Carnhill Estate's.

"I should confess straight away that I *do* have a personal interest in this whole matter because I would very much like to buy his farm to consolidate my estate. The sale of the Glebe to Mr Rouse would be of great benefit to both himself and me: giving him a home and occupation for his retirement, while at the same time strengthening an estate that I think you will agree is doing its part in bringing at least *some* prosperity to this part of the County. If Mr Rouse can become established at The Glebe it will doubtless provide paid employment for local tradesmen and parishioners who at present have to travel some distance to find work."

Hugh Olver-Blythe had worked out a strategy on his recent visit to his architect (and now business partner) as to how much he should reveal of his ultimate plans. They had decided that, at this juncture, it would be safe to mention the new road.

"As you know, Lantrelland beach belongs to Eddie Rouse – much to the envy of The National Trust, which, along with Prince Charles, our Duke of Cornwall, owns much of the coast in this county. If I am able to buy his farm, with the beach, I hope to put in a road that will allow tourists and holiday-makers easier access to both Carnhill, where, as you know, we have various features to attract business in the summer; and the beach, making this part of the coast more of a draw for this important aspect of our local economy.

"My problem – and this is why I decided to ask you for help – is that if Eddie Rouse cannot get planning permission to make changes to The Glebe, enabling him to enhance his living and give up his farm, then he cannot afford to give up his farm!"

What Hugh *doesn't* say is that Eddie Rouse will have his farm taken from him by the banks if he fails to sell up and pay off some of his debts, although it's likely committee members know this already. He has given Trevor Philp a briefing before the meeting, without divulging his master-plan, and Trevor has confirmed the reasons for Eddie Rouse' urgency in selling up.

"I thought it only proper that I should declare my personal interest in this matter before asking for your assistance because I have no wish to hide things from you. The truth is that it is unlikely that permission can be obtained for development of this particular field, however appropriate, and we are facing tough opposition. A group of district councillors and some of the people of Polperris village have decided they don't want *any* development at all. In my opinion they are ignoring the needs of our local people – for jobs and opportunities that are so limited in this area. They are also depriving all the visitors and tourists on whom – let's face it, so many of us depend for our living – from having new facilities. To me it makes sense to provide these people with everything they need to enjoy their stay, having travelled so far for a holiday in Cornwall."

Some time later Esme appeared at the door of the drawing room with a trolley on which were laid out coffee cups, plates of chocolate biscuits and the silver coffee service that Hugh had inherited from his grandparents.

"Ah, Esme, how timely! Shall we take a short break and enjoy some coffee, ladies and gentlemen? If none of you is in a hurry we might spend a little time seeing more of the house. We have several interesting paintings in the long gallery next to this room. We can resume our discussions after stretching out legs. By the way, the lavatory is just through that door." He pointed.

"The meeting will have to close by midday because I'm greeting a group of New Zealand tourists who are here looking for traces of their Cornish ancestry."

He suspected the PCC would be more likely to give him their backing if their experience were positive, not boring, and decided not dwell too much on the protected status of The Glebe although he did give it a mention. During the coffee break and the following whistle-stop tour of the long gallery Hugh made every effort to be his most charming until members of the committee felt they were truly 'county figures'.

§

"Emily, my darling – I'm going to have to wake you, or it will be bed time again!"

Sebastian gently rocked Emily in his arms until her eyes opened.

"Whatever is the time?" She asked, trying to remember where she was and what was happening. "I feel so muzzy! I must have dropped off."

"So did I – and that was over an hour ago. It's nearly eight o'clock and I'm hungry!"

"I've got an idea," said Emily. "Let's have a shower to wake ourselves up – then we can pour ourselves a drink, get supper and have a good chat about what happens next. What do you think?"

"It sounds perfect – as long as we don't get side-tracked in the shower."

"I shall reject any of your amorous advances, if that's what you mean – at least until ten o'clock!"

"It's a deal." Said Sebastian extricating himself from under her, standing up and offering her a helpful hand to stand up and embrace him. "Let's go!" He led her towards the bathroom.

Considering how little time it took to shower and prepare supper, it was surprising how enticing the dining table looked when they sat down to eat a short time later. Sebastian lit two candles and brought out a bottle of white wine from the fridge. The sparkle of glasses, cutlery, and water jug made the plates of scrambled egg on toast look like the first course of an elaborate meal. Emily had found two linen napkins in the sideboard, giving it the feeling of 'dinner' rather than 'supper'. The plastic pots of yoghurt waiting as pudding might look a little ad hoc but the general atmosphere had become that of an elegant restaurant.

"I still can't believe our luck!" Emily said, enjoying her scrambled egg.

"Two hundred and four million pounds! It's incredible"

"Incredible but true!" said Sebastian. "You are an instant multi-millionaire."

"What a responsibility!"

"What a relief, though. You'll never have to work again! That's an end to your financial worries."

"Or a beginning of them! It's never been a real problem. I've *always* been lucky – Mum's always given me everything and now I'm earning quite good money."

"Are you going to go on at the gallery?"

"I think I should, at least until they can find someone else. It's the busy time and I've already had a week off."

"Have you thought any more about whether to keep it secret – or how you might spend it?"

CHAPTER 13

"How do you go about it?" Asked Hermione. "Do you take photos?"

"I do – but I also need quite a few sittings, if we can agree on dates and times. The photos are useful when I'm working on the painting in my studio but I'd like to get general outlines and pick up the atmosphere from working here with the two of you. Have you any idea of what you would like in the background?"

"Well yes: I was hoping we might be outside, with at least part of the house and some of the landscape."

"That's fine. Perhaps we could begin to look for somewhere suitable for you to pose. Then we can begin thinking about how you might dress. Perhaps Mr Olver-Blythe would be standing, with you seated; or you could both be standing?"

"If we were both standing he would need to be on slightly higher ground. I'm nearly as tall as he is and I don't think he'd like to see that recorded for posterity!" Hermione smiled. "We're a bit like Charles and poor Diana – and I have to wear flat shoes when we're out together. By the way, has my husband discussed fees?"

"Not yet but I'm happy to explain about them. They're based on how much time I expect to take and the cost of materials and expenses like transport, which in this case won't be much because we live so near. I can estimate fairly accurately how many visits I will need for live sittings and then work from there."

"Hugh asked me to suggest to you that you drop us a line with an estimate and a timetable for sittings. If we decide to go ahead, it would be rather good if the painting were ready for next summer season – if you think that might be possible?"

"That sounds like ample time and I can certainly send you an estimate."

"There is one question I'd like to ask," said Hermione. "Will you need both of us every time, for a sitting?"

"Oh no; only for the first once or twice. After that I can make appointments as necessary."

"That's good – because Hugh is quite hard to pin down and I'm often away at the golf club or some committee."

"That's a bit like me. I'm new to the 'meetings thing' and they take more time than I expected."

"I understand congratulations are in order? I saw that you had been elected to our district council? Quite an achievement – well done – although I have to admit I support the other party!"

"Thank you; and I won't hold your party against you! That's the benefit of living in an experienced democracy, isn't it? I have a leaning towards the greens although I'm a LibDem."

"It does seem that politics is going 'three-dimensional', doesn't it: left and right, red and blue, orange and green?"

"I'm very much a beginner and have a lot to learn," said Rose. "My best teachers so far have been people at their front doors. I've been surprised at the kind of things they want to talk about. It's usually concerning their daily lives. I don't think any of them mentioned the state of the world or global warming."

"Do you believe in getting involved in that aspect of politics?" Hermione asked.

"I'd like to. My parents still work for the United Nations; my father's British and my mother is Chinese – so we're that kind of family! I've been brought up to the sound of airports and African drums, not to mention being dragged around conferences and exhibitions in funny places."

"How interesting!" Hermione thought it best to leave it there. She would leave the lobbying to Hugh, who had much stronger feelings about the ambitions of 'greenies' and the way they impeded growth. "Shall we go outside on to the terrace? You might like to have us standing on the steps for the painting. That could give Hugh the height he needs! It's just out through these French windows." She opened the door and they stepped out on to the terrace.

"My goodness, that's an ugly storm building up!" Hermione was looking westwards where dark clouds were piling up, high into the sky, contrasting with the rich blue they were beginning to blot out.

"I used to enjoy seeing a good storm," said Rose, "until those floods at Boscastle did so much damage."

"I seem to recall that it happened in Polperris a generation ago, too. Your grandparents would have remembered that."

"They used to talk about it," said Rose. "It must have been terrifying – our house is so close to the sea and the little river went quite mad, roaring down through the village. They finished up with several cars in the harbour, upside down! I haven't heard the forecast for today, have you?"

"No – but that storm is going to be no fun. I think you should be making your way home. I don't want to sound inhospitable but there's another reason too: you'll have to forgive me because I feel a little queasy."

"Oh dear! It's time I got going anyway. I have a course starting this afternoon – my students will start arriving after lunch. Is there anything I can do for you before I go – is it serious?"

"No, no – I'm sure I'll be fine." Hermione tried to sound convincing but she felt distinctly sick.

§

Peter Trenleven, travelling at speed across Hampshire on his way to Polperris by train, also felt uncomfortable on two counts. Firstly he had just taken a call from Harry Potter saying that his ex-client, now residing in Her Majesty's Prison at Wandsworth had taken on a particularly unpleasant firm of solicitors to sue him for negligence. The man would also be putting in a complaint to The Bar Council; an enquiry from *them* would need careful attention. He much preferred to fight in court rather than defending himself to his own professional body.

161

The other matter that was troubling him was what kind of reception to expect from Emily's mother. Sebastian had warned him that Rose Yi Johnson was not happy about his sudden engagement to her daughter. It wasn't as if Rose hadn't met the boy. They seemed to have got on so well when she was briefing Sebastian on the CPRE case but it had now become too complicated by half. His son was representing a prospective mother-in-law – a politician embarking on legal action over an emotive matter and about to become his father's art teacher. What a situation! A dangerous mix: he was not looking forward to his arrival in Polperris. As the train flew across the Somerset levels seemingly downhill towards Exeter, he too could see the clouds of a gathering storm far to the west. By the time he reached Cornwall it looked as though he would be in for a drenching. The very elements were against him.

§

"Shall we leave the secrecy thing on one side for the moment," said Emily. "I'd like to get some idea of what we *might* do with all this money and then see whether secrecy, or maximum publicity would be the best strategy."

"Go on," said Sebastian, wanting to encourage her to feel creative. "That sounds sensible, although I'm very cagey about being on telly and in the papers!"

"So am I, but it's a resource that we've collected along with the cash!"

"That's true: and it must be worth millions in itself. Just imagine if we wanted to buy that kind of publicity! You could have the media eating out of your hand for the next few weeks – and probably beyond, if you play your cards right."

"I think we need someone like that awful Max Whatnot – who handles public relations for kiss-and-tell celebs. He would know how to extract the last ounce of news out of our win."

"He may seem awful," said Sebastian, "but he's very good at his job. He usually comes out smelling of roses – and his clients often don't smell as bad as they might, once he's given them a makeover."

"We might even consider getting *him* in, then!" Emily was laughing. "I wouldn't rule anything out yet, would you? Dot was saying we ought to mull everything over for a week or so. In the meantime she will make sure it's all secret. I was incredulous when she said she couldn't even tell her husband where she was working. Do you believe her?"

"Well, I hope you'd tell me where you were, Emily! I'd be worried to death if you disappeared for days at a time."

"I suppose they can still talk, using her mobile? She could let him know she was all right."

"Even then – I don't like the idea. I suspect she would tell him *where*. I know I would!"

"Good," said Emily. "I hate to think of you being kidnapped by a bunch of greenies – or worse, Russian oligarchs wanting to build a palace in Hyde Park! I shall keep tabs on you when you are out on dangerous missions! I think Dot's too careful *not* to tell her husband where she's going – even if she won't admit it."

"And I must say that I like her suggestion that we take up their offer of a small advisory committee."

"Best of all, her idea of an immediate holiday – somewhere warm, lying around on a beach, thinking and talking about it – away from anyone with an axe to grind. Do you think we could do that?"

"Not immediately – like tomorrow or the next day – if you *are* going to keep on with your job!"

"That's true! And you can't just drop Mum's case now, can you? It wouldn't make for good relations with your future mother-in-law!"

They both laughed.

"In that case we shall both have to go on working and keep our mouths shut – but the advisory committee does sound like a good idea." Sebastian reached out, taking her in his arms and stroking her long hair. "It's your money, you know – not mine! I shouldn't have any say in the matter: you must do what you think is best."

"Half of it will be yours as soon as we get married! Let's do that first, shall we?"

"Get married? Yes please! I'd like us to be 'legit' – especially if you are carrying our child."

"I don't think I am! But it *is* possible – and I don't want to have to go around making up stories about 'early arrivals'. How quickly could we get married?"

"I think it's two weeks but I'd have to check that with our specialist. Harry will know who to ask."

"Let's do it then!" Emily hugged him hard. "I can't wait!"

"We're not getting far with spending your two hundred million pounds."

"Two hundred and *four* million pounds. I'd have been pleased just to get those last four!"

"It could become a bit of a burden, couldn't it?" Sebastian is now serious.

"And I think we've got to avoid that. Dot's committee does sound right. They must know good people with experience of loads of other winners."

"It's so much money," said Sebastian. "It needs someone working on it full time; we could easily afford it and whatever we do, we can't afford *not* to employ people to manage it. There are so many implications – tax, investment, security and keeping an accurate track of it all. I expect the committee will be able to advise on that, too."

"Where do we want to be? London? Or Polperris? Yet another thing to think about," said Emily.

"That sandy beach and sunshine where we can talk things over properly sounds ever more enticing," said Sebastian, kissing her.

"Well, if we can book up our wedding straight away, the honeymoon might be two weeks from now. That would give me time to find a stand-in at the gallery. Meanwhile, we can practice for the honeymoon!"

164

"I second that! But we promised each other we'd lay off until we'd had a proper talk. We're having that, aren't we? So let's make a few notes." He reached for his briefcase and took out his notebook. "I'll start at the back, so it doesn't get mixed up with the CPRE and Lantrelland. Come on – give us a few preliminary possibilities."

Emily put one finger against her chin and thought for a minute.

"Well, I've been having one or two ideas ever since you gave me that ticket – day-dreaming about a win – but Dot says we should set aside a few thousand *now* for things like the wedding, honeymoon and a few treats for ourselves and our parents."

"That's a great start! That leaves two hundred and three million and umpteen more thousand pounds to spend. What next?"

"I wondered about starting a shipping line!"

"That's original! But why?"

"Ever since I saw 'Windstar', the computer-controlled sailing ship. I've thought how good it would be to have a fleet of sailing ships to carry freight and passengers around the world: save all that carbon dioxide and fumes."

"Where did you see it?"

"My grandparents were working in St Lucia, in the Caribbean, and Mum took me over to spend a holiday with them. It was marvellous – we went in January, when there aren't any hurricanes and it was so warm! You never saw anything more graceful: she had four masts all the same height and her mainsails were all triangular. They all get larger or smaller by winding themselves around the rope that goes from the top of the mast down to the end of the boom – what do they call it?"

"A halyard, I think!"

"That's it! They told me the captain just sets the course and the computer takes over: steers and sets the sails on its own – no one has to haul ropes unless something goes wrong. I watched the four sails grow larger all at the same time when the ship left port. I think they must have an engine for getting them in and out of harbours but can switch them off once they are in the open sea."

"I seem to remember my mother boasting about them. The Wind Star and other Windstar yachts were designed and built in France. There's one that can take more than three hundred passengers and has five masts as well as a large jib. Do you realise you can now afford to go on one of their best cruises? We can find out what's available."

"Maybe we could do that instead of finding a warm beach?" Emily suggested.

"I think that's about all we could do, though. To set up a shipping line would cost more than you've won! That might only buy one ship."

"So how did shipping lines ever get started?"

"I expect someone bought one ship and ran a good business – was lucky, worked hard and built up from there. Perhaps they rented other ships or borrowed to buy more? I really don't know – cargo ships are just so huge, aren't they?"

"And they use enormous amounts of fossil fuel, too!" Said Emily. "That's why I was thinking we need sailing ships to move stuff around the world. It worked very well before steam, didn't it? But I see what you mean – I don't think we could afford to make a global impact with that idea! It would take years."

"Are you sure you want to do something that has 'global impact'?"

"I'm quite sure, yes! Having read that book I really believe the world *is* on the edge of catastrophe and I sometimes lie awake at night worrying about it. Lester Brown confirms so much of what I've heard my mother and grandparents talking about for years. Now I've got the chance to make a difference I don't want to miss it. Only big money can make things happen fast."

"So does a big fright! A catastrophe like that Christmas tsunami in 2004 made governments set up warning systems that people had been wanting for decades!" Sebastian paused, stroking Emily's hand absent-mindedly. "Talking of tidal waves, Dad's on his way to Polperris today, to your Mum's water-colour

166

course – and the weather forecast down West is terrible. Did you hear it?"

"I didn't, no."

"They are talking about storm force winds tonight over Devon and Cornwall."

"I expect they'll lower the baulks to block the harbour entrance. That's what they do in big storms," said Emily.

"What are baulks?"

"Great beams of wood that block the waves from bashing into the harbour. The fishermen lower them down with a crane into grooves in the quays and they stay there until the storm is over."

"What about your house? Might it get flooded?"

"I don't think so – although it did when the river went mad. My great grandparents had quite a bit of damage then. The ground floor isn't very high above sea level. But they've built all kinds of flood protection channels and barriers now, further up the valley, to make sure it doesn't happen again."

"Another example of a 'big fright'? But you can't blame the tsunami on the activities of humans," said Sebastian.

"No but we can blame ourselves for allowing people to build houses close to volcanoes and in flood valleys; or even on the beach. It's usually only the very poor or the very rich who do that. The rich because they want to and the poor because they can't afford to build anywhere else." Emily was beginning to sound strident.

"*Someone* has to get things going if we want change," she continued. "I remember my grandmother telling me about all the frightful disasters in China when the Yellow River used to flood, killing thousands of people. She said that after the revolution millions of people were organised with spades and buckets to move soil and build flood protection measures. They built dams, too and used them to produce electricity."

"A bit like the idea for the New Thames Barrier – the original one's not big enough now to save London if we get the wrong tides and wind. Thousands of houses could be ruined, including our chambers. But let's get back to the subject. Have you got any more ideas about how you want to spend the money?"

"I suppose we ought to set up our office first: then at least we can do something about any decisions we make," said Emily, thoughtfully.

"That's sensible. We can get a recruitment firm to find people – and then take part in the selection. We could get my father on the panel – he's good at sniffing out baddies!"

"Talking of your father, he's about to meet my mother – any minute now! Let's hope it's not the clash of the Titans!" Emily put her hand on Sebastian's shoulder. "Anyway, enough work for the minute – let's have a shower – then we can start our evening activities. You can cook me a candle-lit supper!"

"Yes, Madame – and will there be anything else?"

"There might be, if the supper's good!"

§

The five participants in Rose's water-colour course were meeting for the first time in the gallery. She always began the course on the first evening with a drinks party, followed by supper at one of the local restaurants or pubs.

This week's would-be artists looked as though they would get on well together. There were three men and two women all dressed as though they moved in similar circles. In the past she had once experienced a mixture of stockbrokers and ancient hippies and, as she told Emily by phone after two days, the mixture curdled – they didn't get on well and she had to get strict about some students going out to smoke spliffs on the quay.

So far, Rose had been able to avoid Peter Trenleven except to welcome him as a student. Now, however, with everyone beginning to talk to each other, she saw him approaching, a glass of sherry in his hand.

"Well! Here we are then!" He said, self-consciously. He felt strangely nervous as he walked up to this upright and elegant Oriental woman who was plainly still in her prime. This evening she had piled her hair up and pinned it in a swirl, displaying her long and graceful neck. Her black dress followed the curves of her slender body, reaching down far enough not to be called a mini-dress but still well above the knees. Her shapely legs and small feet looked very long, elevated as they were by high heels. Miss Johnson looked more like a fashion model than an art teacher and painter. Her smile was polite and formal.

"Yes indeed! I hope you will find the course useful. Have you any experience of painting or drawing, Mr Trenleven?"

"Very little, I'm afraid; but I've always wanted to be able to preserve some of my visual experiences on canvas or at least in a sketch book."

"Let's hope you will begin be able to, this week. We always start with a day's drawing and it's something you just have to keep practising, month after month, trying to analyse what you need to do to make a realistic reproduction of what you see."

Peter plucked up courage to broach the matter of his son and her daughter.

"I believe we have family matters to discuss," he suggested.

"I'm hoping we don't!" Rose sounded abrupt and stern.

"Oh?"

"No: Emily is still so young and, I'm afraid, impetuous. I don't know about your son – that's part of the trouble. I'm not a bit happy about them 'getting engaged' after knowing each other for a matter of days. They've been watching too much television."

Peter ventured to put another view.

"I agree it is all been precipitous but during the past few days I've seen them together and they are already behaving like a married couple. I was pleasantly surprised at the way they treat each other. It seems to be a well-balanced relationship with a good deal of give and take on both sides. It's not been a simple time for them, either – what with their windfall!"

"That worries me even more. Large sums of money do strange things to people and I'd hate to see Emily lose all the independence she has built up for herself. She's only recently settled down to a regular job in London; found a nice flat and made some friends."

"From what I gather, neither of them are planning to give up their work, at least for the moment. For example Sebastian is very committed to the cause of preserving the integrity of that ancient meadow. He's been telling me about it; and from what Emily says, she is anxious not to let her employers down, either. They seem to be doing all the right things."

Rose found herself irritated by the calm confidence of this man. How did *he* know what was the right thing for her daughter? He couldn't have any idea! Yet here he was, talking as though he too had known her always. He didn't know how fickle she could be – or how wilful. It took a long time to know Emily. Rose was beginning to get the impression that here was an arrogant man who blindly admired his son.

"I hope you will support me in trying to get them both to see sense. It's really stupid to talk about 'getting married straight away'!" Said Rose vehemently.

"I'm not sure I agree with you," said Peter. "They seem very grown up and are certainly well over the age of consent. There's nothing much either of us can do if they really have made up their minds. It's the stuff of fairy tales! My inclination is to wish them luck and give them as much support as they need."

"I'm sorry you feel like that: it seems to be a mistaken and, if I may say, unwise line to take." Rose flushed with anger and wondered whether she should be speaking so strongly to someone who was also a client; but her beloved daughter's future life was under threat and Mr Trenleven could like it or lump it! "I intend to actively oppose this hasty marriage and I hope you will back me up. They haven't known each other long enough even to need a shotgun wedding."

"Thank goodness such events are in the past for civilised societies," said Peter calmly. "I believe there are many good reasons for having children before one is too old – and it's one of the quandaries facing today's young women. They have to work

170

so hard and for such long hours that before they realise it, their reproductive lives are nearly over. The pursuit of profit and 'growth' has become today's pernicious ailment, don't you think? It ruins lives and causes all kinds of negative side-effects. I feel sure you and I would be in agreement about that, wouldn't we?"

"I was hoping you would support me over this but you will have to excuse me as I must spend some time with the others. No doubt we shall be able to continue this conversation." Rose's mouth was not showing any smile as she excused herself and moved to speak to other people in the room. Peter was left feeling still uneasy.

Outside, the harbour master was directing the work of putting the baulks across the harbour entrance in defence of the impending storm as the sky darkened.

CHAPTER 14

"What are you so cheerful about?" Harry Potter had rarely heard Sebastian whistling as he entered the office.

"Oh, nothing!" Sebastian dumped his briefcase on his desk and smiled over at Harry. "It's a lovely day, though, isn't it?"

"Looks like a scorcher, if you ask me," said Harry. "I prefer it a bit cooler, thanks."

"Well it's going to be later, if that storm comes up this far. Have you heard the news this morning?"

"I watched it on telly before I came out. Your Dad must have copped it soon after he arrived down in Cornwall yesterday. I'm glad I'm not down there."

"Let's hope it doesn't last long or he won't get much landscape sketching."

"But it will do him good to get away. That jail-bird is trying to make his life a misery."

"There's nothing in it, is there?"

"Personally, I don't think so and we've got plenty of evidence to back up our side – but you never know with these things. Appeal judges can be funny sometimes."

"I'm sure they wouldn't like to hear you say that, Harry!"

"I'm sure they wouldn't but I've been in this business a long time and I've seen some strange decisions. But what about you? Are you going to go on with the law, now you're marrying one of the richest women in the land?"

Harry's question was asked kindly; he was very fond of the young man whom he had watched grow up as a close member of his father's family trio. He had seen how devastating the death of Françoise had been to both father and son but the change in Sebastian since he met Emily had lightened his heart. Add to that the fantastic lottery win and Harry was hoping that the Trenlevens' fortunes had changed for the better.

"We're trying not to get swept away by all the excitement, Harry! The lottery people have a policy of keeping us calm until we've got our heads around it all – but Emily and I have the added shock of getting engaged!"

"You could have knocked me down with a feather when your Dad told me! I couldn't believe you were such a fast worker, Seb!"

"It wasn't just me! Emily's the same! We just clicked – like a pair a magnets!"

"The mind boggles!" Harry laughed.

"Well you know what I mean."

"I think I might! But what next?"

"We want to get married and go away on honeymoon in two weeks time – to do a bit of thinking."

"I hadn't heard that's what people did on honeymoon," said Harry. "Not in my day! They used to go away for a bit of fun and be together. I know my missus and I did!"

"That too of course, Harry; but we want to make the most of the opportunity that's landed on our lap – and try to do something about the way the world is going."

"That sounds like famous last words! I don't believe there's much any of us can do; things generally work themselves out, given a bit of time and a few wars."

"I think they have done in the past, Harry; but these days I think it's much more urgent and both of us feel we ought to at least try to make a difference."

"Like rescuing a few more crooks? We're doing our best already and see what happens! They still come back and bite us. And don't think you'll stop rich developers from building on the Green Belt or knocking down ancient monuments. You're right about one thing, though – money talks!"

"Well exactly, Harry; but it depends on what the money says and who's got it – and we've now got a fair chunk and intend to have our say."

"Well you could settle that Cornish business pretty quickly if you paid for repair of the church roof. They wouldn't have to sell the field: if I've read the brief properly."

"Emily has already suggested that and I'm sure we'll do it if it's not too late but we want to try to do something on a larger scale. We're really worried about what happens to our children and grandchildren – and yours!"

"Already? Sebastian: it's a bit early for that isn't it?"

"It might not be!"

"My goodness! I don't know: the younger generation.!"

"Come off it, Harry: I bet you were the same."

"Not like today, Seb! And definitely not like my father's day. They were lucky if they got a kiss goodnight until they'd been engaged a good while. That was just after World War Two; things were looking pretty bad then, you know. There were millions of people displaced and cities around the globe were in ruins – but look around now – the world got over it. We've just had all kinds of global crises – banks going bust and whole countries unable to pay their way but it'll blow over, you'll see!"

"Not this time! That's just it: we don't believe it will, unless something drastic happens," Sebastian found Harry's complacency surprising. "Just take a look at the facts: it's really scary. It's only a year or two since the British Government's top science advisor put it on record that the world was facing 'a perfect storm' of food and water shortages, with energy prices going crazy by 2030. The following week Jonathon Porritt wrote in the paper that he predicted this would happen by 2020 because things were even worse than that. He talked about 'the ultimate recession' from which the world would not be able to recover."

"I can't take what these greenies say without a pinch of salt," said Harry. "Porritt's been rabbiting on about that for years. It sounds as though he's muddling the economy up with global warming and all that twaddle. We've heard it all before and nothing much seems to have changed. And there's that other American chap you've been quoting at us for the past couple of months – he had the same name as that useless prime minister – Brown."

"Lester Brown? I believe him; and he isn't a bit like Gordon Brown – he hasn't changed his warnings for the last twenty years. I've been looking him up on the net. He says the only thing that's changed is that everything is speeding up and it's all going to happen sooner than everyone expected. I've just been reading his latest book and right at the beginning he tells the riddle that teachers in France use to impress the need for urgent action."

"Go on then – tell us!" Harry's scepticism goaded Sebastian.

"It's about conveying the meaning of 'exponential growth'. They ask the children: 'if a lily pond has one leaf on it the first day, two the second day, four the third and the number of leaves continues to double each day until, on the thirtieth day, the pond is completely full with lily leaves: when is it half full?'"

"Is this a trick question?" Asked Harry.

"No – not at all!"

"I give up! Day fifteen?"

"No, Harry – it's half full on the twenty ninth day – the day before it's full. What Lester Brown is saying is that we on earth may have already gone beyond the thirtieth day. He's saying that it might be a single, comparatively small factor that tips us over the edge. Something like a crop failure in one major farming area – caused by a heat wave. What we humans have done is to chip away at the very heart of what keeps us alive as a race."

"Like what, Sebastian? You're sounding like a fanatic now!" Harry was irritated by such vehemence. "I mean – come on – humans have come through all kinds of terrible things: the Black Death, influenza pandemics, tsunamis, earthquakes and two world wars. So what if the climate *is* changing a bit. I go along with the Americans – we'll find technical ways round it. I think a lot of the fuss is being made by scientists who need research money and the easiest way to get that is to frighten the shit out of the public. Then what happens? Politicians put the taxes up and the scientists can go on looking for trouble that's for the most part imaginary."

"I wish that were true, Harry; but I wish you'd read the book. He's not looking for funds – or trying to help others get them! What he's suggesting would more than pay for itself. It's not twaddle, talking about the world economy and the environment – they are tightly linked. We are changing the climate and driving some states into ruin: and other countries will fall with them."

"Now you are sounding like a trailer for some horror film! Give us a break, Seb!"

"That's what I'm trying to do, Harry! If intelligent people like you don't get the message all kinds of things are going to happen that will completely wreck our lives."

"Oh yeah? Like what?"

"Like the heatwave they had a couple of years ago in Russia. In 2010 the temperature in July went fourteen degrees above average. For seven weeks the people in Moscow went through Hell with it going over a hundred degrees Fahrenheit – that's thirty eight Celsius in new money. They had forest fires and farmers went bankrupt – they reckoned that losses totalled about three hundred billion US dollars. Only last year the Russian grain harvest fell by nearly a half and they banned grain exports to try to keep internal prices from going through the roof. It had the effect of raising grain prices across the globe."

"The market will put that right, though, Sebastian. We all know that. The Americans and Europe will plant more and then there will be a glut again – you'll see."

"The trouble is, Harry, it only takes a day for everything to go pear-shaped. Something like a flood, an earthquake or even a new plant disease – happening in important grain-growing regions and you have instant global disaster because no one has sufficient reserves to keep us going for more than a week or two. What you *can't* do is speed up the time it takes to grow another crop. *That* always takes at least four months or more."

"Sebastian, I just don't believe it's like that. They'd have to produce a lot of evidence if a judge was going to convict humanity of such gross negligence!"

"And that's just what Lester Brown has done. You can check out his facts and figures: 2011 was the second warmest on record; all seven of this country's record high temperature have been in the last decade and 2006 was the warmest: you can't deny that."

"It could be simply a quirk of Nature."

"That's true – but added to all the *other* facts it is significant and that's what Lester Brown is saying. His book is not one of those boring scientific papers: he's made it dramatic and backed it up with evidence that would be very hard to discount!"

"Like what, Sebastian?"

"Like newspaper and TV reports of things that have really happened. For example, at the same time as the Russians were in trouble with their heatwave there were cloudbursts of rain in the Himalayas and the mountains north of Pakistan. There was so much rain it just formed a wall of water that flooded down the Indus River, bursting all the defences like soft cheese and went on to cover a fifth of the whole country. Two million homes were destroyed; twenty million people's livelihoods were ruined, with two thousand dying; six million acres of crops were destroyed and a million farm animals, drowned. Rescue services couldn't move around to help – with so many roads and bridges washed away. People had to wait as the huge mass of water made its way down to the sea."

"But Seb, there's nothing new about natural disasters! You've only got to look through history. Go back to Noah if you like!"

"Things like this are not *'natural'*. It's a direct result of what we're doing in our pursuit of profit at the expense of natural resources. Lester Brown presents evidence that would stand up in any court. He alleges that twenty years ago Pakistan made decisions that led directly to disasters. Instead of investing in planting forests, conserving soil, teaching people to read and to use birth control, they spent national resources on building up their army. In 1990 their military budget was fifteen times that of education and forty four times what they spent on family planning and health. As a result Pakistan is now a poor, overpopulated, environmentally devastated nuclear power where more than half the women can't read or write! It's on the brink of becoming a 'failed state' – and failed states are a threat to all of us *now* – let alone future generations. No one seems to know what to do about them. Just look around you, Harry – Afghanistan, Yemen, Somalia and other African countries. People haven't got enough to eat and in the end they have to break out. Mostly they die before they can bother us but when they do get organised into something like Al Qaeda and Boka Haram we most certainly feel the effects. The trouble is we don't recognise these movements as desperate attempts to stay alive. We put them down to religious extremism but I believe that religion is just a vehicle being perverted by promises of instant paradise and everlasting life."

"Sebastian, you sound like one of these extremists yourself and you are beginning to worry me," said Harry. "I don't want to fall out with you but I do think you should be a bit careful about ranting like this – especially in front of clients. They'll think you're going round the twist. As a barrister you are supposed to be able to present the facts in a convincing manner so that 'reasonable people' will believe you. I'm not sure I'd want to hire someone to represent me in court if he started blasting off like that."

"Harry I'm presenting you with evidence that I believe to be true and verifiable and if you are blocking it out because you can't face the truth, then that's your problem!"

"Not if I'm the judge it's not! It's yours!"

§

Far from the refuge that Peter Trenleven had been seeking his visit to Polperris was proving more than a little disturbing. Outside, the weather was raging. The evening drinks party was proving uncomfortable too. He could see Rose was trying to do her best to be civil as she offered the canapés or wine but her Oriental face was anything but inscrutable. Despite her antagonism, however, her beauty attracted him: he felt stirrings that had been suppressed for years. He could not stop watching her as she moved around the room, at ease with her other guest-pupils and exuding a warmth and welcome that he was being denied. The way her slender figure – dressed for the occasion in a richly decorated and vividly patterned cheongsam – moved, (occasionally exposing a perfectly proportioned thigh,) sent tingles down him and aroused what he had to admit was pure lust. Yet he felt excluded and far from home.

The noise of the storm outside was unsettling as it rattled the windows; and he was conscious of some deep, almost inaudible thuds: more feelings than sounds, as though his body was being softly shaken. It was waves slamming against the baulks; and the sound of their power was threatening, making him want to move away from this place.

"Miss Johnson," he said, having deposited his glass and plate on the table provided. "I do hope you will excuse me but it's been a long day and I'd like to turn in and rest, ready for the course tomorrow."

"Oh – leaving already? I had hoped we might have a chat." The frustration showed through her polite tones. "There's so much we need to discuss."

"I'm sure we shall be able to, over the next few days but I'm too tired to think straight at present and I will be better company after an early night."

"Very well – but do take care on your way back to the Claremont, this wind is blowing slates off and I'd hate to lose a student on the first night! Just watch how you go."

"I shall indeed!"

Peter put on his coat and hat and stepped outside on to the narrow street. He was not prepared for what hit him. His hat was ripped from his head and went bouncing and rolling off down The Warren like a mad thing. The wind hit him from behind almost knocking him off balance and he found himself almost running to stay upright, being driven after the hat. The flickering light from the street lamps was reflected in every wet surface around him: the cobbles, the walls and windows. Bed-and-breakfast signs and thrashing electric cables were trying to free themselves from any kind of fixing. The cables sparked as they short-circuited – forced together by the gale – while rain pelted down horizontally. The noise was frightening, with wind howling and shrieking in the roofs and around the chimney pots; leaves, torn from trees flashed past him. There were falling slates and once, the sound of a window smashing as it was shaken open to be driven off its hinges.

Turning the first corner, he nearly tripped over his hat, lying upside down, soaked through. He bent over to pick it up, squeezing out some of the water. He wondered whether it would ever regain its shape. The sound of a sliding slate was followed by a moment's silence and then a smash, as immediately ahead of him, it shattered in pieces on the cobbles. If he hadn't stopped to retrieve his hat it might have caught him on the head. The sooner he was back indoors the safer he would feel. He lengthened his step and walked as fast as he could up the high street and climbed the steps into his hotel.

This was no ordinary storm and once back in his room Peter stripped off his wet clothes and steamed himself in a hot bath before putting on dry clothes and going to the dining room. He wished he was at home in London, lonely as it might be, with Sebastian spending so much of his time at his new love's flat; and notwithstanding the underlying niggle about what a vengeful convict might be planning for him.

Polperris, its weather and the formidable – if desirable – Rose Yi Johnson seemed less than inviting.

§

"I hope your Dad's OK," said Emily, as she and Sebastian sat watching the BBC news, late in the evening. "They're talking about hurricane-force winds in Cornwall and I know what that's like. The whole village shakes and rattles. It's scary."

"He'll be all right. He went through the blitz in London and that must have been a lot worse. Anyway, he's old enough to look after himself and he's got your Mum to keep an eye on him."

"I'm not sure what will be worse for him – the storm or Mum. She's hardly speaking to me. She started by warning me not to 'be rash' and got increasingly angry until she rang off. It's going

180

to take her a while to get used to the idea that we're getting married so soon."

"I do hope she'll come to the wedding?"

"I'm sure she will – even if it's to try to stop it going ahead. She won't want to miss anything and we did plan it so she *could* come, between painting groups. Has your Dad phoned?"

"Not since he got to the hotel but he was due to go for drinks and meet his fellow pupils, wasn't he?" Sebastian was absent-mindedly twiddling a lock of Emily's thick hair between his fingers; her hand was resting on his knee.

"That's partly what's worrying me. Mum might be having a go at him – trying to get him on side."

"But he's OK about it: given us his blessing. I think he envies me – you are so gorgeous!"

"I've had enough of this gloomy news," Emily picked up the remote and switched off the television. "But not enough of this," and she slid her hand up his thigh and began to undo his belt, pausing to lightly press and prod what she might find when she released the trousers that were growing increasingly tight. That didn't take long; nor did it take more than a few seconds for him to follow suit, loosening her jeans and kneeling on the floor in front of her as she lay back on the sofa.

He deftly removed her jeans before revelling in the pale and silky softness of her inner thighs, kissing and nuzzling upwards towards her pale green pants. She raised her knees so he could pull the pants off and away; then rested her hands lightly on his head, running her long fingers through his hair as he explored her with his mouth. He found what he was seeking and circled it very softly with the sensitive tip of his tongue. She could not stop herself from lifting her hips to meet him. It was too much for him and he rose up, invading her, covering her body with his and kissed her passionately on the mouth. She reached down and took his erection in her hand, guiding him first to brush her eager opening and then raising her body again to impale herself on him. He pressed down, entering her slowly, as far as he could until their bodies were tightly together. He could feel the waves of pressure coming from her vagina as it tightened around him,

181

warm and provoking; he pulled back very slightly before pressing down once more to reach yet deeper into her body; then again and again, faster and faster until she gasped and caught her breath, half laughing half crying as she lost control, writhing and shaking while hugging him powerfully and falling away but coming back for more and more. He was unable to hold back any longer and felt himself ejaculate into her with unstoppable power as his whole being was driven into her, not once but again and again, ever more strongly until he was drained, satiated, released by being entirely at one with her – body, heart, everything – all of him joined and mingled irrevocably as part of Emily Johnson. They were one; and inside Emily, two of his sperm were well on their way to finding the egg that was waiting for them in her womb.

Emily ran her fingers over his back as he lay exhausted on top of her. She revelled in feeling the weight of him, pinning her to the sofa; the pressure of his pelvis on hers; the retreat of his diminishing member moving by tiny degrees inside her as it shrunk back, leaving her body glowing and comforted; celebrating the radiant experience of perfect intercourse. She knew at this moment that if ever she were to conceive it must be now. It felt so right, so natural and good. They dozed off in each others' arms, still joined at the hip.

Outside the wind had got up and it was beginning to rain. After an hour the fall in temperature woke them and they made their way through to bed, entwining their bodies to get warm again before sinking into deep, contented sleep.

§

"What about it then? Are we going to be celebs? Or are you going to be 'the anonymous winner of the biggest ever EuroMillions prize?" Sebastian had fetched two mugs of tea and they were sitting up in bed. It was already light and the storm had passed with the night, leaving London fresh and clean after a brief but heavy downpour.

"I never wake up this early! Do you realise we went to sleep at half past nine last night? I don't have to leap out of bed and dash for the underground for another whole hour. Let's talk about things?"

"That's just what I was saying," said Sebastian. "We've got to work out roughly what we want to do so we can decide on whether it should be kept quiet or whether we make a big splash? Are you sure you want to become a target for all the paparazzi?"

CHAPTER 15

Towards the end of the course, Rose was going to have to try a different approach to Peter Trenleven. Whenever she had tried to raise the subject of their children's engagement he became a different person: still polite and charming but unapproachable in any but a superficial way, answering her with 'I'm afraid there's little we can do – young people today have such a will of their own, don't they?' and 'My late wife and I were equally foolish: I'm in no position to criticise Sebastian in his choice of life partner: mine turned out to be so happy'.

The wretched man made her feel guilty about judging the wisdom of the young couple in rushing into marriage and even having a baby when they barely knew each other. Peter's apparent naivety, based on his own beautiful but tragic experience, made her appear orthodox and heartless. Whether she liked it or not, she had to get closer to this man if she were to influence his attitude. She felt so inadequate before such a confident and accomplished gentleman about whose reputation she had read so often in the newspapers. She needed to impress him so he would take her seriously.

Apart from the art itself, Miss Weeks' revelation about the clandestine plan to construct a new harbour and marina at Lantrelland was the only subject she had to gain his full attention. Out sketching on the last afternoon, her pupils dotted around the village, she made her rounds, visiting each one in turn, offering advice and encouragement. On this occasion she spent little time with most of them, saving her energies for her next foray with Peter, about whom she discovered she had mixed feelings.

Whether she liked him or not, her body responded to his presence on every occasion. He made her blush as soon as he looked at her with those soft and friendly eyes that seemed to tell her so much yet so little. They seemed to say he knew she wanted to come into his life; that he was admiring both her looks and her abilities; he understood her anxiety though it was unnecessary; and that she would get used to being an 'in-law' to him and the son in whom he had every confidence. Damn it! He was treating her as though she were some kind of eager teenage fan!

To be honest that's what she felt like. Today she had taken extra trouble to appear her best; with a broad-brimmed straw hat, sleeveless blouse – nonchalantly fastened low as if by accident; and jeans that fitted like a glove, showing off her shapely behind. Her sandals were not the easiest to walk in but raised her heels sufficiently to give her the extra inch in height she felt she needed before assailing this castle of a man.

"Peter, I know it's not really your concern but Sebastian's," she began, having exchanged a few remarks about the rough drawing he was making of the Victorian chapel in the high street, "but I thought you would be interested to hear a bit of news I picked up from a dear old lady who lives next to The Glebe at Lantrelland. Her family used to own the farm next to the church and she's always lived there and knows everyone."

"I would indeed be interested, Rose," he said. They had begun to use first names after the first three days of the course; Rosie had felt this was a minor gain on her part although everyone else used Christian names from the first evening so it was no great achievement. "If you remember, I heard about this business even before he did from Lady Merchant and I've been taking an interest ever since. Quite a relief after the kind of work I usually do."

His enthusiasm encouraged Rose; she now had his attention – a foothold on his ramparts.

"There's nothing official yet but apparently this planning application for The Glebe is only a front for a much bigger enterprise that is likely to hit all the national newspapers, once it gets known. A local businessman – incidentally the biggest local landowner from a very old family and part of the county set in Cornwall– is hoping to construct a completely new village, with harbour *and* marina in Lantrelland Bay next to the Church. Can you imagine?"

"He must be thinking terms of millions of pounds and several years of public enquiries and appeals," said Peter.

"Millions, yes – but probably not years before he gets his own way," said Rose. "The present government has been blunting the teeth of planning laws and guidance ever since it came to power. The Tories have always had to listen to the big building companies and developers and the recession has given them a strong argument to 'allow growth' with minimum intervention from central government."

"That's true even where we live in Putney," said Peter. "Jobs and investment are getting priority and I can quite see they are needed but I suspect we shall come to regret some of the new developments, in retrospect."

"Like Plymouth," said Rose. "After the blitz in World War Two they allowed a complete re-design of the city centre, based around the private car. Broad boulevards and high-rise buildings – open spaces and fountains. You should give it a try! One has to walk miles to reach the next shop – usually in a howling gale and rain while the traffic roars past. The concrete is cracking and steel windows are rusting and older people are wishing they still had the original city with its narrow streets and varied buildings instead of these vast boxes and flyovers."

"I must admit it did look a bit bleak when I changed trains there," said Peter sympathetically as he sketched in the shadow cast by the high roof of the chapel on the yard and houses to the east of it.

"Don't forget under the porch as well," pointed out Rose, "although I'm sure you wouldn't! I hardly need to mention such a detail to my star pupil."

It was an effort for her to say this, although it was true – he *was* the star pupil not only for this week but for the whole season thus far. It was only fair to tell him so, even though she felt she was saying it through gritted teeth. 'Oh well', she thought; 'in for a penny, in for a pound'; a bit more praise might let her gain ground on other fronts. Until this moment, her reserve towards

186

Peter Trenleven had not changed. It was not without cost to her; not allowing herself to express all her fears for Emily; neither had Peter given her the opportunity to do so. Every time she broached it he changed the subject.

It wasn't that she didn't *like* Sebastian. When he had stayed with her and Emily at the studio she had grown to like and trust him but not sufficiently to agree that her beloved daughter could commit herself so irrevocably so soon. Marriage? After just a couple of weeks? It was ridiculous – potentially tragic. Yet Peter, so confident and unyielding, refused to join her in intervening to prevent such foolishness.

Standing next to him, looking at his sketchbook and forcing herself to be professional, she had no option but to praise his achievement with the charcoal stick.

"You definitely have talent and I think you should go on with it, if you enjoy painting."

He was a natural and she could hardly believe he hadn't already attended art school. In his water-colours he seemed to know just how much paint to include in his initial wash of the thick paper to depict the Cornish dawn or distant hills. His skill in drawing had led her to enquire where he learned it.

"Oh I've always doodled," he'd replied. "You know – long court cases and people sitting still long enough for me to take my time. My notebook's full of criminal faces and somnolent judges. That's what prompted Sebastian to suggest I came on this course. He has often told me I ought to have a go at painting."

Rose was itching to say more about his son's intrusion into her daughter's life – just when the girl was finding her feet in London. Once more she restrained herself. Whichever way things went she needed to be on reasonable terms with Peter Trenleven; be it to pick up the pieces after a short but passionate affair between their offspring, or as an in-law. She had managed to corner him during previous sketching trips and raised the matter of the engagement but he had immediately clammed up, avoiding any responsibility (in her opinion). On one occasion she had said:

"And what if there's a pregnancy? If they have got engaged in such a hurry they might fall out equally as quickly – then what?"

Peter's was tempted to retort: 'well you ought to know!' He did not, hoping to avoid open warfare but found himself saying:

"They are both old enough, surely, to know better? It's quite a while since Sebastian has had a girlfriend but I think he knows all about the birds and the bees. We tried to make sure he did as soon as he began showing an interest. My wife was French, you know, and they seem to be able to discuss such things with their children without too much embarrassment – Françoise could, anyway."

"And I made sure Emily knew the facts of life as soon as she started enquiring about them but these two seem to have become quite irrational about each other, don't you think? I mean – they've hardly met more than a few times."

"Don't forget they both work in London. I've hardly seen Sebastian since he came back from his few days here. He seems to have spent most of his time with Emily, although he has not been neglecting his work on The Glebe Field. I believe she has been helping him with that, too. They have so much in common and both of them are very intense about 'saving the planet'. This extraordinary win on the lottery has made the everything surreal but I have every confidence that Sebastian can keep his balance. He's very stable."

"I'm sure he is; and Emily is generally very sensible but on this occasion I feel it's all much too hasty." Rose felt frustrated and angry that this self-contained and rather smug man could not see the possible hazards. He was so impregnable: charming and polite but perfectly defended and unyielding to reason. What annoyed her even more was the softness of his smile, expressing warm tolerance of her anxiety as if to say 'never mind, you'll come round to the idea'.

When she had opened the door to him on the first day of the course, and before she knew exactly who he was, her immediate reaction was: 'oh what a dishy man!' The attraction was mutual and she was aware of how he watched her, as if sketching her in his mind. More annoying still, she enjoyed his surveillance; finding herself moving carefully and standing attractively;

making sure he could see what she was wearing; and choosing clothes each morning that made the most of her figure.

Rosie resented his implacable resistance to even attempting to dampen his son's ardour, while she herself was unable to control her own response to the sight, sound and behaviour of this poised and elegant man whom she could but admire. Normally she could win over any man who fancied her and although it was a year or two since she had even considered a long term relationship she discovered that her natural longings for a mate were by no means extinct. Peter Trenleven, however, was hard to shift. His paintings had been by far the best and everyone was full of praise for them. Now he was about to leave but she would have preferred to keep him around – have it out with him; provoke a good row and make him see sense. Instead, here she was coolly telling him 'well done' and 'do come again'.

"I'm sure it will be worthwhile, your painting is most promising," she said, pretending to herself he was just another pupil and guest.

"And if I may say so, you have a real aptitude as an investigator and politician! I can see that Sebastian will be getting plenty more useful information from you concerning this planning application. He will be grateful and I will pass on what you have told me. He will get back to you as soon as he can: the plot thickens!"

'Yes,' thought Rosie, 'my political and conservationist plot, but not what's really important – Emily's future.' It would be foolish to raise the subject again, having finally gained a little of his attention. Now was the time to cultivate his confidence, not to antagonise and nag him. People talked about inscrutable Chinese: *he* was the inscrutable one! He seemed to be able to read her like a book while remaining completely private and confidential. Shifting his opinion or getting him to change his attitude was still way out of her reach – or so she thought.

Peter's years of experience dealing with persuasive people who were trying to get him to believe and trust them had taught him the value of inscrutability. He had learned never to reveal his thinking or judgement unless he was ready to do so. On this particular occasion, however, he was glad his true feelings did

189

not show because Rosie Johnson might be shocked. He understood her qualms about Sebastian and Emily and their headlong dash into marriage but he knew Sebastian very well indeed. The boy had never behaved this way before and until now, once his mind was made up – that was it. He was steadfast and single-minded. There was nothing Peter could do to change the boy's determination to make Emily his wife.

Far more urgent, at this instant, was the effect that Rose's delicious cleavage was having on Peter himself. He was finding it very difficult to concentrate on the shadows around the chapel; his eyes kept returning to the pearly skin at the top of those magnificent, neat breasts – or the little he could see of them. However often he surreptitiously snatched glances his sight couldn't glimpse the nipple that he knew must be there and his body demanded to know what colour it was – rose pink, rich brown – even black? A lacy edge to her bra kept his eyes at bay but the curves and texture of her skin were playing havoc with him. This woman was so desirable in every way. Like her daughter, she looked predominantly like an aristocratic Chinese. He could imagine her as an empress. It was depressing that he could never aspire to capturing her. She was much too young for him; at least twenty years younger. Wrenching his eyes away yet again he told himself not to degenerate into being a stupid old fool. 'There's no fool like an old fool,' he muttered. Things had become so complicated. He could not possibly make advances to this woman – his teacher, a sort-of client and future in-law. What was his testosterone getting him into?

Rose, on the other hand, having planned this assault, was observing his efforts not to be caught peeking down her front. She was comforted that he was at least subject to the laws of nature and gratified that her tactic was working. She made it worth his while by changing position as if by chance, so that his frequent looks could get a different perspective of her curves. What did *not* please her was her own physical response to his attention. She suddenly felt a need to sit down and was glad of a low wall right behind her. She propped her bottom on it and leaned forward ostensibly to take another look at the sketch on Peter's knee. It was not incidental that this allowed his eyes even better access to her bosom. Taking the weight off her failing legs was a relief. Time to retreat, though, before things got out of her control. With a final compliment about the perspective he had so successfully captured of the chapel's lean-to kitchen, she put her hand on his shoulder while saying "see you tea – at about half past four."

This was bold of her: the first physical contact apart from shaking hands on the first day of the course. The effect on her hand was electric. She felt the warmth of his body through the cotton shirt and though it was so brief, she could also feel the muscle there: no bony shoulder, this.

Peter too, reacted – though he endeavoured not to show it. This was a contradiction to the coolness and aloof manner that she had so far shown him. His heart picked up speed as he felt her light touch. She might take him to be 'the opposing side' but her body seemed to be calling for an alliance. Peter took heart that his son's future mother-in-law might some day become a much closer acquaintance.

§

As soon as the last student had set off for home, Rose telephoned the Olver-Blythes to make an appointment for her first sitting. It was to be the largest oil painting that she had so far attempted and the canvas was primed and ready for her first charcoal outlines. She would, however, wait until the summer courses were over before setting it up in the studio. Until then, she would draw a series of sketches; first of the layout and design and then make studies of the faces and their characteristics, deciding posing positions for the two subjects. She spoke with Hermione, enquiring at the same time if the storm had caused any damage at Carnhill.

"I think it was just a few trees down," said Hermione, "and we lost some slates off the roof – but I hear we're not alone in that."

They then took out their diaries to make arrangements for the portrait to begin.

§

"It all depends on what we decide to do with the money," said Emily.

"What does?" Asked Sebastian.

"Whether we remain anonymous or become celebs. I must say the temptation is to become famous. I've always dreamed of doing something like becoming a prima ballerina; or to get a leading role in a soap. Even when I was quite small I used to dress up and pretend I was going to a film premiere. I used to borrow Mum's feather scarf and high heeled shoes and walk up the passage towards the mirror at the end, smiling at the photographers and other stars."

"I have to admit I wanted to become an Olympic hero but could never make up my mind which sport to choose. I did go mad about ice-skating for a while but that was mostly because a girl I fancied was always down at the rink. But I did want to become famous – don't we all, at some time? The trouble is, now that it's easily within our reach, I can see the *disadvantages*. One's life becomes public property if you are not careful. You can't be seen going out with anyone without provoking some kind of comment and everyone wants an exclusive interview. You can be misrepresented because of some silly remark or by being seen with the wrong person. It's no fun and I'm not sure I'm very keen!"

"That's why I say it all depends on what we decide to do," Emily repeated. "We could invest the lot in the safest bonds and things, and then spend the interest; we could invest in our own enterprises and make things to sell; we could endow some society or institution so they could appoint some particular expert or research fellow –or we could decide to set up some kind of foundation."

"Or we could go for a grand slam – do something spectacular and exploit the news element of the record winnings; in which case we need to get on with it otherwise it will become old hat," said Sebastian. "We'd become celebs but for a purpose – for part of our cause, whatever it was. Then, with a bit of luck we could maintain the celeb status and keep promoting our cause into the future – making a difference."

"Any ideas?" Emily looked at him for inspiration.

"Well, I did have a thought," said Sebastian, putting an arm around her shoulders and moving her closer towards him, kissing her neck.

"You've always got *that* thought; and I'm glad you have; but tell me there's something else too!"

"Well – the second half of Lester Brown's book is all about Plan B and that has a really appealing ring about it. How about us starting a foundation called 'Plan B' that actually *does things*? There are loads of good ideas around but so few of them get started because no one's prepared to put money behind them. We could work out how much we need to invest to ensure a steady income for ourselves and running the office – and how much we could risk on projects."

"I can't remember all the things he was suggesting, can you?"

"No but we can make ourselves a list. It's a pity my fleet of freight sailing ships is too expensive."

"I can't help thinking that Dot Macdonald's advice on having a committee to advise us is a good one. That would give us brainpower to cope with day to day matters *and* time to think – do some research," said Emily.

"I agree. We can tell her that straight away. The other thing I'd like to get settled is our wedding! Wouldn't you?"

"Yes! Very much yes! I can't wait – and we still haven't invited everyone, have we? I'm so relieved Mum says she'll come. I was afraid she wouldn't!"

"I think she and Dad have had a council of war and decided that it's no good opposing the idea and 'if you can't lick 'em, join 'em' so they can pick up the pieces afterwards when we break up and divorce."

"I would be surprised if they had," said Emily. "I don't think Mum took to your Dad very well during the course even though he was her star pupil. She said things like 'I couldn't get him to understand my point of view' and 'he was very reserved'. It sounded to me as though he was refusing to come round to her way of thinking. My period's late, by the way!"

"Really? Very late? Is it significant?"

"Just look in my diary! I always put a cross in it on the day it starts and until now you could almost do it in advance. I never vary at all – but I'm four days late."

"A good job we're getting married on Saturday then, isn't it?" Sebastian swept her off her feet and twirled her around as she held on tightly, laughing with delight.

§

For the next meeting with Dot Macdonald the engaged couple went to Emily's bank. Dot thought it wise for her bank manager be on the finance committee, fully involved in over-seeing the proper management of such large sums. She had also arranged for Emily and Sebastian to meet other specialists from a leading firm of accountants. These included a tax expert, a fund manager, and an investment analyst

"It's great to be given VIP treatment by the bank, isn't it?" Said Sebastian as they waited in reception. The manager himself had been alerted and was 'on his way'.

"It is for me," said Emily; "usually I'm lucky if he has time to see me! Not long ago he gave me a talking-to about my overdraft."

"I hadn't thought of you as a spendthrift," said Sebastian. "What had you been up to?"

"It was a mix-up," she replied. "I thought I had plenty in my account, having saved up for a car, so I wrote a cheque, which resulted in a phone call asking me to come in at once. They kept me waiting for nearly half an hour; then finished up by apologising for not having transferred funds out of my savings into my current account when I'd asked."

CHAPTER 16

"It doesn't have to be an accurate depiction of the background," said Rose. "If you want the house *and* the sea I can easily include them both. From here it's only visible in the distance and I can fit it into the composition with no difficulty."

"Won't people criticise?" Asked Hugh Olver-Blythe. He sounded concerned.

"I don't think so. Anyway – let them! What we are trying to do is to convey the feel of Carnhill and its present owners – a grand mansion near the sea, set amongst the green hills of Cornwall. I can show you many examples where different scenes and views have been included. It's quite a tradition."

"Like including a favourite horse or couple of hounds," said Hermione.

They were sitting in the sun on the terrace and Rose had brought a large drawing book on which she was making outlines – of the house; of the small beech grove in the surrounding parkland; the hills, the valley leading down to the sea; and the geometric line drawn by the horizon between the hills, dividing the sky from the English Channel. In the foreground she now sketched tentative outlines of two figures –Hugh, standing, dressed in a jacket and plus-fours and Hermione sitting on one of the cast iron chairs.

"Can we have a set of golf clubs on the ground beside me," Hermione asked. "I want to look as though I *do* something, rather than just being decorative. "Hugh looks as though he's just going rabbiting."

"That's easy! Here's a golf bag – let's have a couple of clubs sticking out, like this….." Rose made a few strokes with the charcoal and magically, there it was in the foreground.

"I must say I like the general composition of the painting. It will scale up well, won't it? We need a large canvas to fill that space above the fireplace," said Hugh.

"We've measured it all up, darling," said Hermione, "and Rose has prepared an enormous canvas. She's been waiting for her course to finish before coming up to see what we want to include."

"At least I'll have made a start," said Rose. "There's only one more course planned but before that, I'm going up to London for my daughter's wedding."

"Really? Who's the lucky man! She's so beautiful: remember we met when I came down to see you about the portrait? Is it anyone we might have met?"

Rose was on the point of saying how much she was against the wedding but stopped herself. She needed to retain a certain distance from these people. Her very reason for accepting their commission was to gather information from them, not the other way round. She wanted to get to the core of Hugh's plans for Lantrelland. Hermione may not know any more than she did at this stage and Rose needed to tread carefully.

"It's a young man in London."

"Not that charming boy I met when I popped into the gallery, was it?" Hermione asked.

"Yes, I'd forgotten – of course it was," said Rose. "You did meet him."

"I got the impression he was some kind of lawyer: is that right?"

"Yes he's a barrister."

"I thought so. Did they meet through some court case?"

"Darling, you are getting very personal now," interrupted Hugh. "The poor lady doesn't want to tell you all her family history. We're here to discuss portraits: let's stick to the subject."

"You are right, Hugh. I'm being a real inquisitor. Please forgive me Miss Johnson – it's just that it's so romantic! Such a good-looking couple."

Rose smiled with relief. She certainly did not want to explain why Sebastian had been there. She decided to change the subject and take more control over the conversation.

"Now, I think I should take a few close-up photos of your faces, if you don't mind. They will be helpful as a reference when I'm back in my studio. I don't want you to pose but I'll take some snaps as we talk, if you don't mind, so I have a range of expressions – an all-round record of how you both look from various angles."

"I'll try not to look grumpy," chuckled Hugh. He found that Rose's oriental looks pleased him a great deal and was conscious that his face seemed to be fixed in his most charming smile. He wanted to catch her eye all the time and when the slight breeze ruffled his hair he carefully patted it back into position, wanting to look his best.

To Rose, through the eye of the camera, Hugh's smile was lascivious, even predatory and she felt a shiver of revulsion. She took two quick pictures and lowered her camera. She needed to get them talking so that they would forget what she was doing.

"Do you think we are coming out of the recession at last, Mr Olver-Blythe?"

"I certainly hope so! It's been dragging on since 2008 although personally I've been very fortunate – otherwise we wouldn't have been considering this portrait. I do feel that Cornwall has been dragging its heels. We haven't kept up with the rest of the UK or indeed of the wretched EU, although I must curb my tongue about that – what with you being a LibDem and all that!" He laughed rather loudly.

In retrospect it wasn't the time or place to express his right wing views to someone about to record his visage for an admiring posterity; he was wishing he had been less forthright.

"You can attack the EU: I can take it," said Rose, joking. "I'm not going to start political arguments when I've got a paint-brush in my hand – it might get messy! Or even a camera – I don't want you to look cross!" She raised the camera and caught him looking a little more relaxed with a benign smile.

Rose turned the camera towards Hermione, who was plainly not following the banter. She was looking into space, an expression of calm satisfaction that made her look somehow noble, thought Rose as she clicked the button. Hermione's chin had been slightly raised and the picture was not quite side-view so she had captured her pale blue eyes open wide, collecting any vision or movement in the sky or landscape. It was a most striking pose – if you could describe it as a pose: a private moment, happy but short-lived. The tranquil look changed and her face tightened. Rose clicked again, recording this difference and wondering what had caused it.

"I'm afraid you'll have to excuse me," said Hermione. "I feel slightly odd. I'm sure it's nothing; give me a minute or two and I'll join you again." She stood up and hurried indoors.

"I'm sorry your wife's not feeling too well; perhaps I'd better leave?"

"Don't worry, Miss Johnson. She's been like it for a few days: nothing to worry about; just slightly bilious." He sat in Hermione's chair.

Rose managed to take another couple of photos of Hugh playing down the situation. She noted that his air of supreme control had left him; he was now showing slight annoyance as though Hermione was letting the side down. His mood passed as he took advantage of being alone with Rosie. He turned on the charm, leaning towards her.

"Now *do* please tell me more about yourself, Miss Johnson," he crooned. "It seems so strange that you have been living in Polperris for so long and we've never met before."

'Here we go,' thought Rose. She was wondering when he would start chatting her up. She had heard tales of his exploits with good-looking women and took it as a compliment that she was being targeted.

"For future sittings, where would you rather we met?" He asked. "Here? Or down at your studio?"

§

"I hope you don't mind my asking you to come so early before our scheduled meeting," Dot said to Sebastian and Emily as they sat in the waiting room at the bank, "but I wanted to catch up with you both before we go in front of all these experts. From my point of view the most urgent thing is whether we can treat this as a momentous piece of publicity – it being a record win – or whether we have to keep it secret. If you are going to allow us to go public, you'll have to decide soon, otherwise we'll have lost the impact. At the moment we are making a lot of noise about 'the biggest win, ever' – and how the winners have not yet made up their minds about allowing their names to be revealed. It gives us a kind of tension to keep people's attention; but it won't hold for much longer."

"It's such a life-changing decision," said Emily. "We don't want to be hasty."

"I understand you are getting married next weekend?" Dot enquired. "Have you been engaged long?"

"Hardly! We only met a couple of weeks ago!" Emily laughed out loud. "You can't complain about us being slow over *that* decision. It shocked our families but it was far easier than making up our minds about facing all those flashing cameras."

Sebastian intervened: "I think if we can wait until we come back from our honeymoon – couldn't you swing that? It will give us more time to decide?"

"I think I could persuade our publicity people. It's a story in itself: 'lovers' dilemma! Winners' whirlwind romance'; you could spin it out without giving any names away. I might be able to persuade them – if you can hint that it might be to their advantage. It would build the whole thing up. Even if you decide against it, they could make a story about 'lovers decide to stay silent'. It could be good for our reputation for privacy."

"My present feeling is that we are definitely leaning towards making a big splash so we can make an impact for the causes we're thinking of," said Emily. "We're almost sure we want to start a movement – a non-profit organisation to promote ecological and social awareness. Both of us are very concerned that we are heading towards catastrophe with the environment. *Someone* has to do *something* otherwise we're all in real danger of all going down the pan – much sooner than anyone expects. This win seems such a fantastic chance to make at least *one* more effort to help change our ways."

Dot had not expected such vehemence from so young a woman. It wasn't something she'd come across with her other new millionaires. The couple seemed to have been *waiting* for something like this to happen.

"My goodness:" Dot said, "you *do* seem ready for action. I hadn't realised what we've let loose! I'm not decrying what you have to say – I must agree with your aims although I've never felt that anything that I personally could do would make much difference."

"That's just it!" Said Sebastian. "Most of us know perfectly well what's going wrong and what needs doing but none of us have the confidence to get stuck in to make changes. Neither of us has ever been really hard up and all this money is amazing and wonderful but having money is not *that* important to either of us. I know, to some people, it's the ultimate success but I'd like to think that in spending most of it we might make a difference." He stopped abruptly. "Oh dear! That must sound so idealistic but it's truly what we feel."

"Not at all – I'm getting used to the idea," laughed Dot. "You are different but I shall enjoy working with you! The last couple of days have already been refreshing: I can't wait to find out what happens next. Do you have some rough ideas of what you want?"

"We do, yes," said Emily. "We're thinking of setting up an organisation called 'Plan B for action'. Having done a few calculations on the back of an envelope we've worked out that two hundred and four million pounds isn't nearly as much as we thought when it comes to making major changes around the world. Big companies can spend that much on a campaign for a bar of soap! I wanted to launch a fleet of sailing ships to carry freight but it would only buy about one and a half ships! People would hardly notice! We want to make the biggest possible impact with whatever we do, so good ideas will get picked up and taken forward. The question is how!"

"Quite so," said Dot, sympathetically; "but it sounds exciting and very laudable. Maybe I should prompt our publicity people to be ready for some real news?"

"Probably," said Sebastian, "but we'd like to hang back just for a couple more weeks."

"I hope I can rein them that long," said Dot. "Let's see what the meeting brings. We've put together quite a team for you. They'll be able to fill in quite a lot of detail straight away – like how to set up a non-profit organisation and how it might affect tax liability; also how to register a charity, if that's what you want it to be."

"I've already asked a few colleagues about that," said Sebastian. "Being a charity does impose quite a few limitations. We feel that much of what we need to do is political – rather like Greenpeace – and they've never been able to become 'a charity' in some countries. We'll need to look into that."

"We wondered whether it might be better to give the whole lot to Greenpeace and have done with it," said Emily, "but we believe we might have something different to offer. We've always looked on Greenpeace as activists trying to turn companies and even nations away from destructive activities and towards positive and sustainable ones. They so often have to confront authority by putting themselves in real danger and carrying out stunts. They produce the 'push', if you like, and we believe there's room for an organisation to provide more 'pull' – motivating the wider public to join in."

"I have to admit I've always been a bit suspicious of Greenpeace," said Dot. "There have always been hints and rumours that they are subversive. People have suggested that they get donations from sinister sources."

"My mother used to get furious about that," said Sebastian. "She was convinced those rumours were put about by the American and British secret service, prompted by the big companies who were finding Greenpeace difficult. She said the Canadians were especially to blame. When Greenpeace and other conservationists were drawing the world's attention to the clubbing to death of thousands of seal pups on the ice-flows off Newfoundland, Ottawa did everything they could to play it down. We believe that 'the silent majority', whose contributions keep Greenpeace going, – and whose next major strength is their vote – need help in making up their minds about campaigns and movements."

"Like 'NICE' – the National Institute for Health and Clinical Excellence – does for doctors," added Emily.

"Oh yes," said Dot. "Not always popular! They do their best for the most patients and get slammed by the drug companies."

"Unlike the politicians, the people at NICE don't have to worry about being re-elected – although they probably have to defend their backs – but as long as they can back up their decisions with good arguments, the public will support them. The politicians, on the other hand, tend to respond to the lobbyists, paid by drug companies. We have the advantage that with *our* bank account we can resist the lobbyists; make our own assessments and endorse what we like. We'd be helping people make up their own minds – about things like conservation, clean air and climate change. We're looking for cross-party politics to save the human race."

"But aren't people going to ask 'who do you think you are, deciding what's right?" Asked Dot.

"Of course they are," said Sebastian. "We shall have to invite a group of fair-minded experts to endorse causes that we want to support and offer guidance; respected people like the judge Sir William Macpherson, who produced that report on the murder of Stephen Lawrence. What he had to say about the Metropolitan Police was not kind but needed saying. In the end they had to accept it and make changes. The public is quite able to make up its mind if the facts are fairly presented – just as they can come to the wrong conclusions when so much spin is put on by greedy commerce or power-mongers."

"And religious fanatics!" Said Emily.

"Now you're getting on to dangerous ground," said Dot. "I wouldn't want to mess with them! People who are prepared to blow themselves to pieces aren't likely to welcome being opposed by logic and reason; you might have to spend a lot on protecting yourselves. I remember my parents telling me how Russian and other revolutionaries at the beginning of the last century used to attack those who tried to be reasonable – because they were the ones who helped preserve the status quo – persuading the masses not to rock the boat."

"If we allowed ourselves to be put off by things like that we'd soon talk ourselves out of doing anything and just go along like another pair of lemmings, towards the brink," said Sebastian. "The trouble is that 'reasonable people' don't usually have the funds to pay for good marketing of their message. We've had the luck to win a huge sum of money that should allow us to promote Plan B projects; and ideals put forward by people like Lester Brown and other modern-day prophets. We are incredibly lucky people and I think we have to be prepared to take risks!"

"I have to admit I'm lucky, too," laughed Dot. "My whole life is spent helping lucky people like you cope with gi-normous strokes of luck. I must say, though, that you aren't just unusual in the size of your winnings: you are a first to want to spend their money this way! It's refreshing! A change from new houses, cars and cruises!"

§

"Mum, I'm *so* pleased you've come!" Emily embraced Rose with such a hug that Rose was left breathless.

"Well don't hug me to death as soon as I arrive, darling! You knew I'd come in the end, didn't you?" Rose freed herself and picked up her overnight bag, carrying it through into the sitting room at Emily's flat. She halted to look around:

"I might have guessed it! Chaos! Do you want me to start clearing up?"

There were clothes everywhere; shoes, underwear, dresses, and other essentials such as hair dryer, make up, hand-bags and hats.

"You could help me make up my mind about what to wear. I thought I knew but now I'm not so sure," said Emily.

"What's that lovely new dress there? I haven't seen that before."

"It's what I bought yesterday. It cost a fortune but now I think it makes me look fat."

"Darling you are never going to look *fat*. You are willowy and always have been. Put it on and let's look."

"But you haven't arrived properly yet! How was your journey? Shall I put the kettle on?"

"My journey was fine. I slept most of the way. The last painting course was really hard work; then I had to make a start on that big commission for the Olver-Blythes *and* make arrangements to keep the gallery open this weekend – but now I'm here!"

"I'm sorry I've given you such a shock, Mum. Really I am: but I'm still sure it's the right thing – me marrying Sebastian. He's lovely, you know!"

"I hope he's not *too* lovely and not just a pushover. You know what you are like – always wanting your own way!"

"I know I do – and usually get it – but we've already had our first squabble and I had to give in. He was right, really, and put his foot down. I made a terrible fuss but he didn't budge. Afterwards I had to admit I was wrong."

"Whatever was it about?"

"Several things, actually; the most difficult one was agreeing for both of us to have an HIV and other blood tests. He said it was only fair to both of us before we began a life together. As far as he knew there was nothing wrong with him but he dreaded the thought that he might give me something he hadn't known about – or that might affect our baby."

"What do you mean *'our baby'*?"

"Mum – I've missed my period – and you know I never do. I think I'm pregnant."

Rose stared blankly at Emily; it was as she had feared but still shocking. Part of her wanted to hit Emily; part of her was thrilled at the thought of a new life – an extension of her own; while part of her wanted to weep at the loss of Emily's childhood – soon, irrevocable.

"Mum? Say something! You're making me feel awful!"

Rose still couldn't speak but stopped even trying. She swept her daughter into her arms and returned the welcoming hug even more strongly. Emily knew instantly she could stop worrying: her mother was going to back her up. Rose, in turn, felt the girl's tension leaving her as she snuggled against her. Both of them found themselves crying with relief.

"You wretched girl! You worry me to death! You are so stupid and so stubborn! But I love you so much!"

"And I love you too, Mum – you are so important to me and I know I've been driving you crazy – but I inherited a lot of it from you and you turned out OK, didn't you?"

"Well at least *you're* getting married! It's more than I've ever managed. I'm just an old biddy now – truly on the shelf. But at least I'm going to be a granny – so I ought to be grateful; and I agree with Sebastian: it's only sensible to make sure you are both in good order before you sign the dotted line. Neither of you have led pure unblemished lives and you never know what you might have picked up."

"I know you are both right, really. I was afraid something might turn up to keep us apart."

"The results were OK, weren't they?"

"Yes – and I'm waiting until after we're married before I do a pregnancy test! I think I am but I want to keep the records straight so that my daughter won't be able to quibble about being legitimate."

"Don't *you* feel legitimate?" Rose was smiling as she wiped away her tears – and Emily's.

"I do *now* – but there were times at school when other girls were having a go at me at having no father that I felt resentful."

"I remember that! You came home and gave me a hard time too. There's one thing: I can't say you can't *afford* to have babies yet!" By now they were in good spirits.

"Mum – help sort me out! Look at this muddle!"

"Let's tidy up a bit – have a bite to eat – and then we must get you dressed. You can't march in to the Registry Office late or you'll miss your slot – we must get a move on."

§

Only one thing was worrying Hugh Olver-Blythe about what Hermione had just told him. He couldn't think how to tackle the uncertainty that refused to leave his mind. After all these years, how had Hermione become pregnant? Was he the father? How come she had suddenly conceived? Was it possible that she, like him, had been 'playing away'? She must know that he had not been faithful and he assumed she didn't mind – as long as she maintained her status and bank balance.

It had never been a love match between them: he had married a titled, educated lady and she had found herself a rich, handsome man from an eminent family. They had lived their separate lives, dutifully attempting to produce an heir but silently blaming each other for infertility. Suddenly she was expecting a child at nearly forty. What had been going on?

Hugh couldn't bear the thought that she had been sleeping with another man – or indeed 'other men'. Ladies didn't do that! But how could he be sure? Somehow he had to ask her but she might raise the matter of his infidelities. He realised how little he knew her and how little, until now, he had even tried.

It was the portrait that had begun to bring a change: thinking about how they wanted to be perceived by the world. It was hard to hide behind a façade of marital bliss during the sittings with Rose Y Johnson. Part of her depiction of the lord and lady of the manor involved observing their feelings for each other. Rose's very presence seemed to have acted like a catalyst to Hugh himself and to Hermione. It had certainly raised their libido that first day when they coupled with such passion as soon as she had left. Perhaps that was when it happened? He must try to work out the dates – at least that might remove some of his doubts: unless she had gone to her lover – if she had one – the same day. Damn!

CHAPTER 17

"Is it far to the Registry Office?" asked Rose as they settle into their taxi.

"Not very, and we should have got plenty of time," said Emily, looking like something from Tatler. Rose had added the finishing touches: choosing the right necklace and hurrying out to buy some flowers for a posy. She had also taken a strand of hair from each of Emily's temples holding them together at the back with a plain gold clip. It kept the cascade of dark hair away from her face, showing off her perfect complexion and slanting, pencil-line eyes. She couldn't hide behind her hair now; and had no need to keep pushing it back during a conversation, which she normally did – much to the distraction of any man talking with her – with a graceful upward sweep of her fingers. She could now hold her bridegroom's hand and still have one free, facing the registrar and witnesses. From behind, the gold clip gave a spot of colour to the stream of shining hair that covered her back, down to the waist.

"I remember what I was going to ask you," Emily said mischievously. "How did you get on with Sebastian's Dad? He came back full of it! His sketches and paintings are great, aren't they? We were most impressed."

"Oh – all right," said Rose. "I don't think we had a lot in common but yes, he seems nice enough. Certainly he has talent and should go on with his art. If he continues making progress I'd consider hanging some of his paintings in the gallery."

"As good as that?" Emily was surprised. "He's terribly good-looking, isn't he?"

"I suppose he is, for his age."

"You don't sound very enthusiastic!" Emily was disappointed.

"Don't I darling? Never mind that for now – have we got everything?"

"Sebastian told me just to bring myself and not forget my ring," said Emily. "He will see to the paperwork; but Mum, are you sure you don't like Peter? He's been so nice to me. I was hoping you might hit it off with him."

"Emily – I wanted to hit him! I found him absolutely immovable about some things and he just refused to see my point of view. I got so angry and it was very difficult because I couldn't show it, with him being a paying guest. I just had to bite my tongue."

"What were you falling out about?"

"I'm not sure I ought to tell you – on your way to getting married."

"Oh go on, Mum – it'll come out in the end – I know you!"

"Well if you must know, I wanted him to take my side in dissuading you two from marrying in such a rush."

"I knew you would try! And he wouldn't have any of it?"

"No! He kept saying it wasn't our problem but yours and Sebastian's and he had complete trust in Sebastian's judgement and he too had fallen for you and was delighted you were going to be his daughter-in-law. There – now I've told you!"

"I told you he was lovely!"

"He was infuriating! So I've had to shut up and accept something I still think is hasty: although I do trust you, *really* – and I love Sebastian – or the little I know of him. You look so right together I've begun to feel it might not be so daft after all! It's not as though he's marrying you for your money! He did ask you before you won all those millions, didn't he?"

"Yes he did, Mum – and I said yes. It was on our first weekend together in London: it was bliss! But I'm so glad you are happier about it now. Perhaps you'll begin to take to Peter after all this?"

"I don't think I will. He's much too old for me anyway."

"Mum he's only eighteen years older than you – and you know you've always got on better with older men. He's just your type except that you wouldn't get your own way with him all the time."

"Huh! Let's not talk about it! Here we are, anyway. Be careful as you get out."

Emily's efforts at playing Cupid were not over. Rose was mildly surprised to find that not only was Peter the groom's father but was standing with his son as best man and first witness. After the simple ceremony, lined up outside the Registry Office, the bride and groom, the best man and bridesmaid, and the parents of the bride and groom still added up to only four people. Emily's boss, who had come along to take photographs, remarked that they made a very handsome group: "almost like two sets of twins – one pair slightly worn". Emily made him promise not to repeat that to her mother.

§

"So sorry," said Harry Potter, "but Sebastian's away on his honeymoon; could anyone else help, Lady Merchant? I'll see if his father's available."

Peter Trenleven's ears pricked up.

"I'll speak to her, if she wants," he said, across the room. Henrietta Merchant sounded pleased to speak with the senior Trenleven so Harry transferred the call.

"Henrietta: good to hear you! Are you well?"

"I am, Peter – although very annoyed! You remember the planning application for The Glebe Field at Lantrelland? Well – they've *got* it! Isn't that unbelievable?"

"Well on the face of it, yes it is! Are you absolutely sure? Sebastian hasn't been called to appear at any appeal yet."

"Apparently there isn't going to be one! We're appalled! We intend to make a great fuss about it. The Glebe is supposed to be protected by all kinds of laws and they're walking all over them.

There must have been some dirty work at the crossroads! It means it will all go ahead. It's such a shame."

"I agree with you!"

"We must do *something* to stop it," said Lady Merchant. "Do you think you could get in touch with your son? I know it's not fair on him but the situation really is desperate."

"Can you leave it with me for an hour or two, Henrietta? I'll phone you back when I've had a little time to see what we might do."

"Very well – and I'm so sorry to bring such disturbing news."

"We're used to that, in this office," said Peter. "Yours isn't the worst we've had today: that's the trouble with representing the 'less conventional members' of our society."

"Of course – I remember now – your work with villains! You must be ready for just about anything!"

"Quite so: perhaps we should have lunch soon and share our woes? Meanwhile, let me see what I can do about The Glebe."

§

Emily was rubbing suntan oil into Sebastian's broad shoulders, which had browned even just after a day at the island's remote beach lodge. Her strong hands were enjoying the feel of his skin and the depth of his muscles.

"For goodness sake relax, Sebastian! Don't you ever stop worrying?"

"Of course I do! I'm not *worrying* now – just 'saying'."

"Well it's not what I want to think about on my honeymoon! Let's change the subject."

"OK but it's true what I said and if you see the sea pulling back too far before the next wave – go like Hell for higher ground because there's a tsunami coming."

Sebastian raised his head from the beach towel and glanced at the sea, checking it was not behaving strangely. It wasn't – the

212

clear water hardly had the movement to make more than the tiniest wavelets that flopped on the sand then drew back – just a few feet.

"I suppose you checked there was higher ground by the beach before you booked up to come here?"

"I did, actually, Emily. I didn't want to lose you so soon after we were married."

"You mean you actually asked?"

"Of course! I Google-Earthed it. This is the one island in this group that's got a decent hill on it! The others may be more luxurious but they're far too flat to be safe."

"Next you'll tell me there's a risk that the hill here is a volcano!"

"It's not! I checked!"

"You are *so* funny!" She laughed. "It's like having my own security firm!"

"Well having you is like guarding the Crown Jewels except more difficult because I can't lock you up in The Tower! You are my precious treasure!"

Emily stopped laughing and moved against him until it was impossible to get any closer. A tear trickled down her cheek. She put her arm over to slide her fingers through his hair.

"That's so lovely," she said. "No one's ever said anything so beautiful to me!"

"You *are* a softy," murmured Sebastian, collecting the tear on the tip of his tongue. You cry at the slightest thing – but I love it – and I love you, so, so much."

Emily sniffed and rubbed her nose with the back of her hand.

"Here," said Sebastian, "take my hankie." He reached over to take it from the pocket of his beach robe. "Hang on – I'd just like to adjust your bikini." He looked both ways: there was no one else on the tiny beach or on the winding path up the cliff.

"Seb – not here!" Emily protested as he undid her bikini top, revealing her firm breasts and neat dark nipples. She didn't try to stop him, however and raised her arms above her head, allowing him to kiss her shoulder and neck; and then brush his lips ever closer to the nearest nipple. She felt a tingling all over and raised one knee, turning her body to meet him.

"And there's something else I discovered," said Sebastian, raising his head to kiss her on the cheek. "Mm – this suncream tastes nice."

"Is that what you discovered?"

"No – what I *was* going to say, before you interrupted, was that the other islands over there," he pointed with his chin, not taking his hand from where it had moved, stroking the front of her bikini bottom, "may well disappear within the next five years – under the sea – tsunami or no tsunami!"

"Sebastian! You are *the limit*! I was just beginning to feel really randy and you start going on about *that*! For goodness sake!"

"But it's true, my treasure! Global warming is leading to sea levels rising. Partly because when you warm it, water gets bigger – and partly because the ice-caps are melting much faster than people expected. They now think the sea could rise by a whole metre during our lifetime! Already, more than six hundred million people live no higher than about ten metres above sea level. That includes two thirds of all the world's major cities. People like to live near the sea – so much trade depends on ships – and we like eating fish!"

"Sebastian you are putting me off!"

"My darling – just listen to me a moment! You call me a worry-pot but you wouldn't stand in front of a high-speed train – not unless you wanted to wipe yourself out, would you? But that's what we're doing! I know we're on our honeymoon but I can't drag my mind away from the reality – especially when we're lying so close to the water on such a perfect beach. Just let me tell you one more thing and I'll change the subject."

"You had better!" Emily sat up, pushed him back onto his half of the beach towel and straddled him. She brushed the last traces of sand from her breasts, sensuously stroking herself to distract his attention. A long lock of hair slipped forward over her shoulder, hiding one breast. She lifted the hair back, tucking the last strands behind her ear. She then lowered her eyes to his swimming trunks and began feeling their contents through the cloth – very softly.

"That's nice," complained Sebastian. "It's also provocative! You don't need to stop but I'm still going to finish what I was saying. Mmm that's lovely – whatever's happening?"

"I've seen it happen before and I usually enjoy the results," smiled Emily, exploring him a little more firmly.

"Well, as I was saying..... But what was I saying? Oh yes, I remember. It's not just the rise in sea levels but the increase in stormy weather. If you get a typhoon it can drive the sea in front of it, making the level rise by the height of a bungalow. If that happened in the Bay of Bengal it would force ten million people to move or drown. It's very frightening!"

"Sebastian – I'm putting a ban on that kind of talk for at least twenty minutes or until someone appears on the top of those steps, because I want you inside me and I don't want to hear any more until we have enjoyed each other as long as we can hold out. We're on a honeymoon, remember?" She leaned over and put one hand over his mouth, while the other pulled down the top of his trunks, releasing his erection that, once liberated, sprang up.

"I'm going to study this for a moment," she said, moving off to kneel beside him. She shook her hair forward and held her head over him so that her hair covered him, hiding his lower body. Lowering her head she sought the soft top of his member with her lips and moistened it with her tongue, taking him into her mouth, tasting the salt of the Indian Ocean. She pressed with her tongue and moved her head slightly up and down as he raised his hips, finding it hard to maintain self control.

Emily interrupted things before he came to a climax. She leaned past him to pick up her silk beach robe, put it on and removed the remaining half of her bikini before resuming her riding position, kneeling. She pulled the robe around her so that, to any onlooker, she was simply sitting across her lover, protecting both of them from the sun with her robe. What no-one could see was Emily's hand resting on her own soft bush, collecting the dew-drops of passion that wetted her fingers. She caressed his penis down to the hilt so that it was all lubricated

215

with her juices before raising herself and with her hand, guided the dark head to enter her vagina. She was so aroused that it was a tight fit and she had to press down with her body to force complete penetration.

For Sebastian it was mind-blowing. He stretched up to touch and fondle her breasts, taking their points between his thumbs and fingers, gently pinching and teasing. It was impossible for any more of him to enter her. Their groins were pressed tightly and Emily felt herself gripping him in waves of pleasure. She raised herself, feeling him inside, sliding against her. She raised herself a little more, and put a hand down to touch that part of him that had emerged, feeling its hardness and girth, like a strong bone protruding from her own body. She pressed down again, forcing it back into her and, for a moment, enjoyed its sheer presence before rhythmically rising and lowering herself as if trotting a horse in slow motion.

"Ride a cock horse to Banbury cross," she crooned, smiling broadly. "I *am* enjoying this! Be ready! I'm coming up to a jump!" She increased the pace and almost immediately they both experienced heart-stopping orgasm and ejaculation. When their bodies had stopped pulsing and pumping Emily flopped forward onto his chest, straightening her legs to continue gripping him inside her. They lay exhausted and still, wet with sweat and emissions; hardly breathing: at total peace in loving union. Only the sound of the wavelets on the sand linked them to where they were lying, back on Earth.

"If that's being married," said Sebastian, nibbling Emily's ear. "I like it! Don't you?"

"I do – and I'm glad I said yes!"

In the distance the sound of a gong broke the spell.

"Lunch! That's what we need! Let's have a quick dip and then go up?"

"I'm not sure I have the energy," said Emily. "You've drained me right out!"

"I think you could say the same for me. There's nothing left – and my thing's disappeared!" They both laughed but began getting back into their swimming kit for a cleansing plunge into the warm ocean.

§

"Is that Miss Johnson? It's Peter Trenleven here, Rosie. Lady Merchant has just told me the news."

"Peter! Thanks for calling. I've been wondering what to do because I didn't have the heart to interrupt the honeymoon. Isn't it preposterous? I find it hard to contain my anger. I'm absolutely furious! How *could* they grant permission like that? There were only two of us who voted against but we were completely ignored!"

"Did you protest?"

"Of course I did – and after the meeting I went on local radio and slammed the District Council. I've been interviewed about seven times this afternoon and I'm due to take several more phone calls tonight. I'm trying to make this a national issue. It's a disgrace!"

"On what grounds did they grant permission? It seems such a hasty decision! I thought I'd gather as much information about this as I could so that Sebastian can update himself quickly when he gets back next week. It's new ground to me but from what I gather, it smacks of the kind of work I usually do. Have you any evidence of anything illegal going on?"

"Peter, if I had, I would have already phoned you – but it seems that the whole thing was a *fait accomplit* fixed beforehand. I protested at the meeting that I had not been properly informed but they called in a clerk to show me that the appropriate notices *were* despatched to me by post at least a week ago. I never saw those notices and goodness knows what happened to them. I can't believe the postman would have been in on this, although I'm beginning to wonder. The Parochial Church Council met and endorsed the planning application 'wholeheartedly', adding that they applauded 'this initiative by a member of one of the oldest

217

local families, who was bringing not only employment but other desirable economic activity to the parish that would revitalise local businesses'. They were fulsome in their praise for Eddie Rouse' plans too, and that was read out in full at the meeting. I spoke as forcefully as I could, reminding the committee of the legal protection The Glebe was supposed to have but I was on my own. Two of the people who would normally have supported me at the meeting were absent – whether by chance or not, I don't know – but they weren't there and the committee spent hardly any time on it! They said that the latest advice from Government was that economic benefit was now the major criterion because the nation faced such a financial crisis: they simply passed it. I protested but they said these were exceptional circumstances and they were 'following the new guidelines'."

"It *can't* be legal. This isn't my area of expertise but I can't believe they can get away with it," said Peter, as soon as he had finished making more notes. "I smell a rat – no – more like two rats! If I come down on the train tomorrow, will you have time to help me collect some more facts? Sebastian will have to take this whole thing much further."

"I've been counting on the CPRE to back me up over this – but as I said: I couldn't bring myself to phone him, even though I've got an emergency number for them. They are so far away, though!"

"I expect you've had a text, though, haven't you: to say they'd arrived safely? I had one two days ago and it just said 'bliss! Much love, S and E'."

"Emily sent me very much the same. I was so pleased, although I'm still holding my breath that things won't go wrong. It was such a frightful rush."

"Rosie, I really think we should bury the hatchet over that while we hold the fort until they get back, don't you? They are now married and it's up to us to support them. I'm very sorry you have not found me co-operative but I have every confidence in these two young people."

"I wish I did! Your talking of hatchets and forts makes me feel I'm under siege – like some anxious settler waiting for the cavalry to arrive! I dote on Emily and I can't bear the thought of

218

her getting into a hasty marriage and then living to regret it. I expect you know she has a child on the way? We're due to be grandparents in about nine months time."

"I do, Rosie: it was a bit of a shock to me, too. I was going to discuss it with you when the time seemed right but they are grown-ups – both of them – and I feel we must have faith in their judgement. You and I will have to agree to differ. I suspect we shall be seeing more of each other if we want to spend time with our grandchild."

"Well it's too late to do anything, now," said Rose, exasperated. "It should be all right for the first few years. It's later I worry about, when they've got to know each other."

"They might find that it's even better than they had hoped!" Peter's tone was light-hearted and Rose found it, as usual, irritating. This man was so bloody smug! She felt a surge of anger that he might have encouraged his son and Emily, the only person who truly mattered to her, to embark on a lifelong commitment, instead of joining her in advocating prudence. She curbed her tongue but her silence spoke for her.

"Rosie? Are you still there? Do you think it might be helpful if I came down? I could collect more facts; between us we could make quite a fuss with the press and media – at least try to get them on side. What do you think?" He waited anxiously, hoping they hadn't been cut off but could hear movement at the other end of the line.

"Rosie? Are you all right?"

"Of course I'm all right!" She sounded petulant. She *felt* petulant. She was torn between attacking him and accepting his help in confronting what seemed to be a plain case of collusion between councillors, civil servants and others.

In a way, having him come down instead of Sebastian could be an advantage because he was such a well-known figure. Several high-profile cases had put his face on front pages of the tabloids and appear on TV. His very presence would ensure plenty of media attention. She controlled her annoyance. He was always so damned confident! Infuriating! It made her feel like some helpless female waiting to be rescued. She decided to blame her mood on the council.

"I'm just so outraged at what's happened about The Glebe – you'll have to excuse me." She forced herself to speak more calmly. "I think it *would* be helpful if you came down; although I've no idea whether the CPRE can afford to pay your expenses."

"My dear Rosie, I wouldn't dream of charging for this. I feel it's such a personal thing now. We are, after all, 'family' – aren't we?"

There was another pause while Rose fought her annoyance. She knew it would be stupid to reject his offer. It felt as though the whole world was conspiring against her. What else could she do but wait for him to arrive and then work to dig out the truth?

"I would certainly be grateful," she said, between clenched teeth. "If you let me know what time you arrive I can come and meet you at Liskeard or Looe; and you can stay at the studio – there's no course on at the moment."

"In that case I look forward to seeing you tomorrow. It will be such a pleasure to see you again so soon, Rosie; and I do hope we shall find ourselves more 'on the same side' than during my last visit. I feel I have a lot of ground to make up."

Bloody man! He certainly did! Rose's unspoken curses bode for an uncomfortable visit: oh well: "I'm sure we shall be able to work together," she said. "I am determined to save The Glebe from these greedy people despoiling such a national asset."

Peter said his goodbyes and turned his attention to making arrangements for the next day. Harry Potter agreed to get the tickets and suggested Peter take himself off home to pack, having dug out Sebastian's papers on the case.

"You can read these on the way down," he said, cheerily. He was pleased Peter was going to be away for a few more days. He had been avoiding showing him the latest vitriolic threats that had arrived by post that morning from Maidstone Prison. It wasn't as though Peter needed to do much about it, although he could apply to the High Court for an injunction to silence the ranting criminal. Harry thought it better to let his boss have a few more days concentrating on something less personal. On second thoughts, if Rose Johnson was anything like as good-looking as her daughter, Peter had every reason to go back to Cornwall.

CHAPTER 18

"BBC, BBC: you are listening to News Hour on BBC World Service, this is Julian Marshall."

" That's good! Clear as a bell," said Sebastian. " I wasn't expecting that."

"I was," said Emily. "It's in the brochure. It says 'satellite TV in every room'. Let's listen."

"The United Nations Food and Agriculture Organisation in Rome has just released figures for last year's global grain harvest. Here is our Rome correspondent David Willey with more:

"The FAO says that during 2011 the world's farmers produced more maize, wheat and rice than ever before. The total was over a quarter of a billion tonnes – fifty-three million tonnes more than the previous record of 2009.

"Today's report points out, however, that this does not make us any better off in terms of grain reserves because world consumption rose by nearly a hundred million tonnes. This follows the pattern of seven out of the past twelve years. World stocks have now been reduced from sufficient to feed us for one hundred days to only seventy-five days.

*"Every year, the 'carry-over' stocks – the grain that's left in store as we wait for the next harvest – have been less than **that** and in 2006 it was only enough for 62 days. The consequence of this was a sharp rise in grain prices in 2007 when they doubled and tripled for a short time. Commenting on the situation, Dr Lester Brown of the Washington-based 'Earth Policy Institute', warned that this had driven some forty-four million **more** people into extreme poverty and hunger. He said that protests had erupted in thirty-five countries, as the number of hungry people climbed above a billion.*

"The year before last – in 2010 – global grain stocks were pushed down again by drought, wildfires and a scorching heat wave, which decimated Russia's wheat crops. Russia banned grain exports and prices again began to rise, prompting warnings of a second food price crisis within three years. Dr Brown says that prospects for the world's poorest people remain grim because even last year's record production has failed to outpace consumption. It's not enough to rebuild stocks."

"We can't get away from Lester Brown! Perhaps the media are beginning to listen to him; but it's very worrying, isn't it?" Said Emily. "Those poor people can't just wait around while their children starve: no wonder there are riots! It looks as though things are getting worse – what with global warming and climate change."

"Everyone *says* that – but just before the wedding I was listening to the radio and they were saying that last year, average global temperatures were unchanged from the previous five years!"

"I thought everyone agreed it *was* changing?" Emily was puzzled.

"They do – except for a few. They believe we're just seeing natural fluctuation and that records haven't been kept long enough to make proper comparisons. But whether it's changing or not, we humans are still in trouble because we're running out of land to grow our food!"

"Is that really true, though?" Asked Emily.

"It depends who you believe," said Sebastian, "but many governments plainly do, if you watch what they're doing – banning food exports or trying to control grain markets. Lester Brown has been warning for years that if more than one of the world's four major grain producing areas have a bad year, it can tip the whole world into crisis."

"I thought we were producing more and more every year? Those figures they quoted just now said that, didn't they?"

"Yes but we're using more, as people get more prosperous. They want more meat; and that needs more grain. Then the world's population is still rising – more mouths to feed, every year – and we come back to land shortage. Lester Brown says that although in the past thirty years there have been fantastic increases in grain yield – and production has risen by fifty percent – these increases are beginning to level off or even shrink. They went up until about 1990 but since then, increases have dropped off."

"But what about these four major areas? Where are they?"

Sebastian went over to the desk and collected a piece of the hotel's headed paper and a pencil.

"Let's sit outside;" he said, "this air conditioning's making me feel quite chilly."

They slid open the glass door and went out to the balcony, overlooking the sea. Coconut trees hardly moved in the breeze. Sebastian pulled up a chair for Emily and began to sketch a world map.

"The four areas would probably surprise most people," he said. "The world's biggest grain producer is..... can you guess?"

"America? But I suppose that's a catch question?"

"No catch! Where's the biggest population?"

"China? Or is it India? I heard theirs is growing fast."

"It's China!" He drew a circle around the rough outline of the sub-continent on his map. "They're the world's biggest producer – they have to be: to feed everyone. I remember their production because it's four-five-six – four hundred and fifty million tonnes every year. America produces about sixty million tonnes *less* than that but is the world's biggest *exporter*; India's harvest is only half what China produces – but about the same as the total harvest in all the EU. It's staggering!" He finished his four circles with a flourish. He continued:

"If I remember right, three countries produced nearly half of the world's grain last year: China, the USA and India. After that, the whole of the EU actually harvested a bit more than India. The trouble is, more and more countries have to import grain to meet their needs."

"But the Americans export the most – you said."

224

"They do. It's about a quarter of the global grain trade – but the worry for those depending on the Americans for food is that nearly half the US grain crop is now going into ethanol for motor fuel."

"So we come back to energy!"

"All the time! Japan's the world's biggest grain *importer*: they don't have enough land to grow it; and needed to buy twenty five million tonnes last year; but they've got real energy problems too because their nuclear plants are all having to be overhauled, after the tsunami disaster. The whole world's got energy problems but using *food* to make energy won't be able to continue!"

"Grain for ethanol is surely renewable and sustainable – capturing the sun's energy?"

"Not if you need to *eat* the grain: you have to find other energy."

"Back to nuclear?"

"Not if we want to avoid piles of radio-active waste that take thousands of years to get rid of! But that's where Plan B comes in again – there's plenty the world can do if only the politicians, bankers, and engineers can be persuaded to listen."

"That's one of the things Mum has found so frustrating," said Emily. "She's convinced that the nuclear and oil people have purposely sabotaged efforts to develop renewables. My grandparents are always full of stories from other countries – especially China – where they're making great strides with hydro-power, wind and solar energy; Granny says our climate in UK is ideal for growing biomass for energy – trees and fibre crops – but nuclear and fossil fuel companies have always managed to block things."

"To be fair, the USA has been one of the leaders with renewables and energy saving but they just don't seem able to talk about it! George Bush used to grin away about 'technical solutions' to global warning but it would have been much more convincing if he'd talked about the actual improvements they've been making – like fridges being twice as efficient and buildings that produce a lot of their own energy as well as costing much less to run."

"If people knew about things like that they could pick up the new ideas and we'd all benefit," added Emily. "I think we are right with our Plan B for Action – it's the best we can do with the money we've got. I thought we must be the richest people in the world until I started looking up the figures! I was staggered at how much Bill and Melinda Gates are giving away but they have that huge company with all its brains. We're starting almost from scratch!"

"Come on Emily! We're not doing badly. Your UN connections are worth a lot; and we've got all sorts of bright people in our Chambers – people like Harry Potter, for one!"

"And he's a magician! I bet they haven't got one!" Emily had always loved the other Harry Potter and still hadn't got over meeting a real one.

"He is a magician in his own way: he comes up with all kinds of brilliant solutions. He overhears a lot and drops in some suggestion that solves everything! On top of that *we've* got the Blessed Dot! She's marvellous: and our committee is great. Those people are as enthusiastic as we are about Plan B – or at least in outline," said Sebastian. "It's just that the Gates Foundation can throw so much money at things. In 2010 they said they'd be donating ten billion dollars for vaccines for the poor. We can't compete with that!"

Emily took the pencil and drew a large star on Seb's map over what might be California. She drew rays out across the Southern Hemisphere. "But with our mere two hundred and four million pounds we can spread the word, if nothing else! And we can add a positive spin to stories like that."

"We don't have to spend *all* of it on that, though," said Emily; "I still feel strongly we ought to pay for that new church roof at Lantrelland – to save the Glebe Field. Don't you – husband? It's your money too, now!"

"Of course I do, darling wife of mine; and that's just the way we should be thinking – globally, while acting locally. Now let's go for a swim."

226

"And I'll keep an eye out for any tsunami: that's a 'natural disaster' – not man-made. We can't complain about this weather, though: it's just perfect."

§

The weather in Bayswater was very different from the honeymoon island in the Indian Ocean. Hugh Olver-Blythe and Clive Goodman were talking about the latest developments in their East Cornwall project.

"So Eddie Rouse got his go-ahead for the Glebe! Now it's got planning permission he'll sell us the farm."

"It all seems a bit hazardous, though. I mean – those CPRE people aren't going to take this lying down, are they? Permission went through very fast – without the usual appeals and enquiries. How on earth was that done – or shouldn't I ask?"

"Nothing illegal, as far as I know. I had a word with a few people here in London and in Cornwall and they all agreed that economic development must have priority, even if it means giving up a little picture-postcard scenery. I've got one or two friends in the Department for Communities and Local Government and they've assured me the Coalition is serious about loosening controls to get things moving. I think we've persuaded the local authorities to go along with it."

"I've been doing my bit, too," said Clive Goodman. "You know I was suggesting we should sweeten the application with additional proposals? Well, Whitehall certainly like the idea of a marine conservation project *and* the wind and wave-power plans, too. I think we'll get their backing if we play our cards right. We shall have to get those proposals out before we start talking about this lot." He gestured towards the model of Lantrelland Village and Marina on which progress had plainly been made.

"It looks so much better now you've added some colour," said Hugh.

"We can film it close up and it will give a good impression of the finished job. I'm trying to avoid it looking like the usual marina, with straight lines of yachts and launches, by incorporating several small harbours within the main sheltered area. Then I can put 'ye olde worlde' town houses on each quay, rather than modern town-houses in blocks around the edge. It will be a sort of 'Cornish Venice' with not too much white fibreglass showing. We'll use traditional materials – slates coming from local quarries, rather than China: that sort of thing."

"That's expensive!"

"Yes but it's about creating jobs locally!"

"See what you mean!"

"We can even grout some of the slate roofs with cement, the way they've always done to stop them being blown off in a gale. It breaks up the colour monotony, too. Look, we've done some in the model." He pointed.

"Can you include the wonky house designs – make it look more original." Hugh was smiling.

"I think that might be going a bit far. I suspect some of the local builders still haven't mastered the art of the right-angle – so they'll probably do it for us, free."

Both men laughed: in little danger of causing offence, so far from Cornwall.

"We shall have to go public soon because it's bound to come out before long – now that you've been asking for quotes. That granite quarry owner, for example; I bet he was surprised when you asked about his 'offcuts'," said Clive.

"Not particularly – although he picked it up that I might be building a road or some kind of marine defences; but you are right, he might well be chatting with some of his mates – especially if we start asking about Cornish slate as well."

"How about striking while the iron's hot, then? Put in for permission for the whole shooting match?" He offered Hugh a chair and took a seat himself, facing the miniature village of their dreams.

"I'll have a word with my backers – see if it's auspicious to launch the new company on the money market. We're going to have to find a *lot* of investment to keep the English Channel out!"

"I'm only too aware of that," said Clive. "I've been studying as many local sea defences as I can find, especially in the West Country."

"You've been down, then? You should have given me a call: come to stay."

"I didn't like to: some of the local architects know me – we meet at the RIBA from time to time and I didn't want to have to answer questions about what you might have in mind."

"Good thinking. Well, next time, once things begin to move, you can book yourself in with us. It will save on my costs, too! Can't afford all these hotel bills!"

"You're so generous!" Clive's sarcasm was risky: one didn't push Hugh's sense of humour too far. He changed the subject. "I think perhaps we should go first for permission to 'widen the road' down to Lantrelland beach, don't you?"

"I like the description – it shouldn't draw too much attention. It's a job we can get done by local firms – help keep up support for our application."

"Local farmers and tourist people will like it, too. Holiday-makers find it hard to reverse back to passing places in these narrow lanes. A lot of them can't drive backwards. It will certainly boost visitor numbers to Carnhill – and goodness knows we need them."

"The downturn affecting your margins?"

"I should say so. I was fifteen per cent down last year and it's not looking much better so far this year. I'm pinning my hopes on the September and October 'granny breaks'. They love their cream teas and a trundle round the gardens and they're increasingly important to local farmers, staying bed and breakfast when the families are back at school. A new road will let me get coaches through, too. I can easily widen the car park. I suppose that will need planning, too?"

"It will – but that seems to be the right approach," said Clive. "Getting the backing of the local people for development. The politicians are much more likely to come along."

"Except the greenies! We've got real problems with one councillor. She's half foreign anyway and she's stirring up quite a fuss, backed by the CPRE. Somehow or another they've picked up a London barrister to take on their case. I'm waiting for storms from that quarter. They're not going to take The Glebe's instant permission lying down. However – I'm working on the councillor: we might get her on side yet!" Hugh straightened his tie and patted his hair.

§

Peter Trenleven felt distinctly uneasy as he approached the door to The Studio. His relationship with his son's mother-in-law had been 'delicate' during the week during which his natural gift for drawing and painting had become evident. Rosie had been forced to be nice to him because he was a client; and because of his obvious talent, recognised early-on by his fellow students. He knew she found his faith in Sebastian exasperating. One couldn't tell what was going to happen to the fairy-tale relationship that had smitten the young couple. It could go either way but if ever a marriage could jell it was this one – if Emily was the person Sebastian judged her to be.

It was Rose's apparent uncertainty over her child's commitment that was Peter's only concern – the usual ones, about how they would make a living and where they would want to live were not now an issue.

Today he was going to be the only guest at the studio – as far as he knew – and Rose no longer had to consider 'the group'. Would her true feelings emerge and give him a hard time? He hoped not: after all, he was here on mission on her behalf, with the blessing of the CPRE and its supporter, Lady Merchant. He pressed the doorbell.

When Rose heard it, she too felt an adrenalin rush. It must be him: and she would have to be civil despite his adverse manly characteristics. She had decided *that* was what made him so

230

infuriating: he was so *male*: assuming he was right all the time! He didn't seem to have a clue about women – especially young ones. If only he knew how Emily had behaved during her teenage years he wouldn't have been so smug about his precious son's choice of bride. Not that she would hear a word against her daughter. She did seem to have grown up lately: growing into her new image of authoritative businesswoman and art specialist. Rose remembered too, that Emily had achieved first class honours with her degree in fine art: more than she herself had managed. Add to that Emily's success in securing a husband to go with a pregnancy. Perhaps she wasn't such a bad bet after all – despite being nearly perfect.

Rose was no longer 'my art teacher'; she was 'Councillor Johnson', briefing a lawyer about what was rapidly turning into a scandal involving local government, potentially corrupt dealings and almost certain infringement of the law. This was a completely new relationship. As she approached her side of the door, having spent some while on her appearance, to make herself less like an artist and more like an elected representative of the people, she was able to walk tall and with dignity. It had been worth the extra few minutes, pinning her hair up, giving herself extra height and making her 'more significant'.

"Peter, how good to see you!" Rose stood back and opened the door wide to allow him in. They exchanged polite pecks on the cheek, during which each noted the pleasing scent of the other. Rose liked the fading traces of after-shave and that aroma of travel one picked up on a journey. Peter remembered Rose's perfume: he must ask her what it was: it seemed to carry echoes of happier times.

Over tea, Rose related the rebuttals she had met at the planning meeting and since.

"I was ignored, despite bringing the chairman's attention to the formal complaints we had received. Someone had been marshalling a lot of support for that application and even the interviewer on Radio Cornwall seemed hostile. She wanted to know why I was opposing a project that could provide employment to at least a few more people in the district. It made me look like a NIMBY!"

"Have you had time to go through the guidelines they are supposed to follow?" Asked Peter. "I'm afraid I'm not au fait with this side of the law and was hoping you might be. I need a good briefing before I can speak up for you."

"I've done my best and they have definitely ignored quite a few basic rules. I can point them out to you; but the general mood was gung-ho and the reports in the papers afterwards seemed to welcome the council's decision. We're going to have an up-hill fight if we want to reverse it. At this stage, I think the best I can do is to find a holding position until Sebastian and Emily come back. They might be able to apply some of their new-found riches to remove the *need* for such planning permission."

"I'm not quite with you?" Rose wanted more explanation.

"They might, for example, offer a better price for buying The Glebe! Or make a direct donation to repair the church roof. Meanwhile, perhaps you can take me through these guidelines to see whether there's anything we might do immediately to slow down the developers."

"I've picked out some clauses that I thought you might like to pursue," said Rose. "I'll get them." She stood up and moved towards the door into the rest of the house. Seeing her slim body and graceful motion reminded Peter of an idea he'd had on the train.

"Before you go;" he said, "I was wondering whether I might take you out to dinner this evening?"

"Well I've prepared something for supper – but your invitation sounds very pleasant, thank you: my arrangements will keep. You might get them for lunch instead!"

She could feel part of herself remonstrating. 'What are you doing? Caving in to the first bit of charm – accepting an invitation that could easily undermine the reservation you were so determined to show this man. Too late now – you've agreed. Anyway it doesn't mean anything: he's old. Better to keep a more formal relationship, at least until Emily's marriage looks more secure.'

"Sebastian told me The Hannafore was rather good; would you like to go there?"

"Yes I'm sure that would be very pleasant – thank you," she replied, repressing her doubts.

§

"If I *am* pregnant, do you think we should stick to having only one?" Emily stirred on the firm bed, allowing one hand to run lightly over Sebastian's buttock as she lay on her back contemplating the stars through the open window.

"Well certainly one at a time!" He turned his head but remained lying on his front.

"If the world population goes on growing at the present rate we'll soon reach ten billion."

"How many are we at the moment?"

"It was supposed to reach seven billion last October," Emily reminded him.

"They made quite a hoo-hah about it in the media and various babies were declared to be the seven billionth! Daft really – although it did help get the message across. I remember them saying that back in 1810 there were about one billion people on Earth; and it took more than a hundred years to reach two billion. After 1920 it leapt up. The third billion only took thirty years; and the fourth, only fourteen years. Since then it's been twelve or thirteen years for each of the following increases of a billion."

"So we ought only to have one child? Is that what you're saying?" Sebastian couldn't resist Emily's caresses and moved to embrace her.

"You're all sweaty," she said; "but I don't mind: it makes you nice and slippy: as long as you're clean! I'm not *saying*; I'm only wondering. What do you think?"

"I suppose that if *everyone* agreed not to have more than one child, the world population would fall, or at least stop rising. The danger is that the people who are better educated and more able to help preserve humanity would become an even smaller minority. The poor would keep breeding, to have at least *someone* to look after them in their old age."

"The Chinese are successful in slowing down *their* population growth, aren't they?"

"I suppose they have been," said Seb, "although they allow loads of exceptions – minority groups and excuses for the elite. I know one way of getting permission to have more than one was to claim the first was unlikely to survive – especially if it was a girl."

"It was *me* who told you that!" Emily gave him a push. "And it was Granny who told me. I was doing a project for school when they were home on leave."

"Before we came away," said Sebastian, "I read that a lot depends on fertility levels. Overall it's been dropping. In the nineteen fifties it was about five births per woman and today it's only half that! Many countries don't have enough babies to replace the people who die!"

"So population is falling?" Emily sounded doubtful.

"Statistics show that they are but not everywhere. In Japan, for example, they only have an average of less than one and half children per family. On the other hand in Niger, in Africa, where they people have little money, they have an average of seven children per family. In the USA it's nearly two – but they also get lots of people wanting to come and live there from poorer countries."

"I wonder if those women in Niger actually *want* so many children?" Said Emily.

"The article I read said that there's evidence that they *would* restrict the number of babies if they knew how and could afford to," said Sebastian. "That's especially when they've begun to get a little more prosperous. They would like to be able to educate all their children, which costs money. Also, when family income picks up, fewer children die."

"So poverty is as big a threat as food shortage and air pollution?"

"According to some people it's what needs the most urgent attention of *all*; because once people are liberated from it they can start making the changes we've all got to make if we are going to survive."

"So if *we* have two – or even three children; and bring them up properly – they could carry on what we're trying to start!"

"We could hope so! We're lucky! We've got the money," said Sebastian.

"If we use it right! But goodness knows how our children will turn out." Emily sat up. "My mother worries about me! She keeps saying: 'I never brought you up to be like that!' I tell her it's in my genes! I got them from her – and my father but who knows what he's like? Now hold me tight and let's make sure I *am* pregnant. We are on our honeymoon after all: not in some UN Security Council meeting."

CHAPTER 19

"How long have we been here?" A nut-brown Emily adjusts the top of her bikini, showing a pale division between covered and uncovered breast. She pushes down the other side to allow the sun access both sides: just low enough to keep Sebastian's favourite details hidden. Hotel staff were around with clean towels, and fresh fruit.

"Two weeks today: two days left but I'm not a bit bored, are you? By the way – you'll have to be careful about what you wear when we get home – no plunging necklines or people will think you are a panda!"

"That's why I'm trying to even it up!" Emily gave him a push as he lay on his recliner on the terrace of their grass-roofed chalet. "This is bliss!"

"Mmm, it is; but we're going to have to face the future now. Are we agreed: we go public as soon as we get back?"

"Yes: we can make a real splash. Dot would appreciate an email, wouldn't she?"

"That's what she asked for if we came to a firm decision," said Sebastian; "then we can get a welcome at the airport. It's ideal there – with studios and everything. We haven't got much detail on Plan B yet, though."

"We know the general outline and as long as we don't commit ourselves to specifics until we've had time to think about it, we should be OK. You could email the bare bones over to Dot and I'm sure she will get their PR people to make something of it. The story might bring some good contacts out of the woodwork. We can say we'll call a press conference just before the launch, can't we?"

"I hope we're not going to regret this!" Said Emily.

"What? Getting married?" Sebastian was teasing.

"Stupid! You *know* what I mean: getting involved in 'trying to save the world'."

"You make it sound so desperate!"

"Well isn't it?" Emily sounded earnest.

"I suppose it is – although I keep having my doubts. Looking out across the sea like this – you would never guess that anything has changed or is changing."

"Unless you were a fisherman; or someone who counted whales and dolphins. We've killed off whole populations of fish and sea animals over the past fifty years or so. Four out of every five fishing grounds are being pushed to the limit or are about to collapse."

"I wonder if that's true around here – we're hundreds of miles from anywhere!"

"Let's ask someone. We see fishermen in their canoes often enough."

"I think they come around here in the hopes of seeing you with nothing on!"

"Oh shut up Sebastian! More like they want to catch you taking advantage of me – a poor refugee!"

"They must wonder why you aren't calling out for help!"

"They know I'm terrified – you would beat me up."

"Well from now on I'll wait until it's dark!"

"Don't be a spoil sport!"

"You ought to put some sun cream on there." Sebastian stretched across to place a finger on newly revealed pale skin.

"It's not dark now and you're not going to have your way with me in broad daylight again. We're going to walk along the beach until we come to a fisherman – they can't be that far off: this is a small island."

Emily went into action mode, folding up her towel and putting on her beach robe. They set out along the white beach, past the point that gave their little bay so much privacy and strolled past the first palm-thatched houses towards a line of battered-looking boats with long, rising prows."

"You wouldn't get many of *them* into the harbour at home," said Emily. "Those out-riggers make them so wide!"

"And the sails look huge for the size of the boats," added Sebastian.

"They look a bit shabby up here on the beach but once on the water they don't half shift! Let's talk to someone."

They approached the first boat where two or three men were baiting a long line of hooks. After some smiles and nods one of them asked:

"English? American?"

"English," replied Emily and Sebastian with one voice. The men wanted to know where they were staying and all nodded and agreed it was an excellent hotel. One had a brother who worked there. The man who spoke English said he helped out at the bar during the height of the season.

It didn't take long for Emily to ask more about their daily work. They had finished for today but had been out since before dawn and travelled for many hours before setting their long-line.

"That's a long way out to sea." Suggested Sebastian.

"Every year it's further," said the fisherman. He told his companions what he was saying to the English people. They all agreed with him and one made a gesture indicating a long way beyond the horizon. "All the fish near the coast have gone. The big boats have taken them in their nets. Two boats – one each end – they pull it along and catch everything – nothing left."

The honeymooners learned that this group were seriously considering giving up fishing except for a hobby. They said it was hardly worthwhile – they couldn't compete with the industrial fishing by 'the foreigners'. They pointed out to sea at two large motor trawlers, almost out of sight. Sebastian wanted to know if it had always been like this.

"No – when we were boys we could fish almost from the beach here. Plenty fish; around the coral. Now coral gone too."

"I bet some of the fish lands up at Billingsgate," said Emily.

"And in our favourite restaurants," said Sebastian. After more exchange of information and pleasantries the men suggested the young couple might like a photo of themselves by the boats.

238

"We will do it for you. After, you take our photo: you can send to my brother?" "That's great," said Emily, first posing with Sebastian and then standing with their new friends.

"We'll print some out," said Sebastian, "and post them on. What's your brother's name? I'll write it down. A pity we did not meet you before – we could have gone fishing with you. We are leaving soon."

"Next time, then," said the fisherman. "If we still have the boat."

§

It was one of those wet, grey days as Sebastian and Emily arrived at London Airport. They eventually passed immigration control – when, as usual, Emily had to answer very specific questions as to where she lived, while her passport was subjected to extra scrutiny: much to Sebastian's indignation – but he managed to say nothing until the ordeal was over. Having collected their luggage, he was about to express his feelings when a uniformed stewardess approached them carrying a plaque seeking 'Mr and Mrs Trenleven'.

"Excuse me – is this you?" She asked with a welcoming smile.

"Yes," said Emily.

"Can you come with me, please? They're all waiting for you in the VIP lounge."

They were led to a small room where Dot was waiting. She kissed them both in greeting.

"I expect you would like to wash and brush up before facing the cameras, wouldn't you? We've got some make-up and a hair stylist but people are expecting to see a couple dressed for their honeymoon – nothing fancy!"

Looking much fresher than a few minutes earlier they were then ushered into the VIP press hall and sat behind their name

239

cards at a table at the front. Someone from the lottery introduced a senior director who gave some facts and figures about their record win and then said the company had been happy to hold back on news about records being broken until after the honeymoon. There was warm applause even from usually cynical journalists and photographers when he said:

"And I'm sure we all wish them the very best for their married life! What a way to start – winning The Lottery!"

After this, the event became more relaxed. The lottery executive asked who would speak first, Sebastian insisted it was Emily.

"She's the lucky one," he said, "not me! My luck is that I married her!"

Emily addressed the now silent room.

"It's me who's the *lucky* one," she said. "Sebastian bought the ticket for me and I accepted it to humour him. Then see what happened! And before you ask, yes he *had* already asked me to marry him and I had agreed."

There were several questions about how long the couple had been going out together. The whirlwind romance was plainly going to be a strong element of the newspaper story. The PR man guided questioning through the personal details, including Emily's background, mentioning her grandparents, who were 'working abroad for world development'. Then someone asked: 'how are you going to spend it?'

Emily left it to Sebastian to read from the notes they'd made during the flight home.

"Well – all the usual things. You know: a house, a car and a pension. We've had the holiday! It was fabulous and I've finally persuaded my wife that she's a lucky person. I bought her the lottery ticket to help prove that luck comes from taking opportunities as much as anything else – and this time I was proved right!"

There were a few more questions about luck, as individual journalists followed up lines for their stories. Then Sebastian went on to reveal their major plan.

"They say money talks," he said; "and we want to prove it's true. We are setting up an organisation called 'Plan B' – and we might add a couple more words like 'for action' once we've discussed it with everyone. You realise this is all so sudden and so exciting that we've had very little time to think about it."

"And I refused to let him talk about *that* all the time! We were supposed to be on honeymoon – not at the office!" Emily's intervention created peals of laughter and applause.

"I was going to say – before being reminded of my marital duties – that part of the reason for our meeting in the first place – last month, as you have heard, was our mutual interest in conservation issues. We were both brought up on Blue Peter and 'Planet Earth' has become very important to both of us. What worries us is that big business and governments won't listen to the warnings of scientists, geographers and strategists, which say: 'We can't keep on like this, destroying the planet on which we depend.' If it's true that money talks – we'll see how loud we can make two hundred million pounds!"

He went on to describe how, with the help of the lottery people, they were setting up an advisory group. Next they were going to create a foundation with a governing board and professional staff. The hope was to establish something that could go on beyond the present generation.

"We want to do something practical, like Maude Heath, the Wiltshire lady who died in 1473, said Emily. "She's always been an inspiration since I first heard about her. She was a childless widow who lived several miles away from Chippenham where she sold eggs every week on market day; carrying her basket she would walk along muddy paths and wade through streams to get there. After many years she found it more and more tedious but she had became comparatively rich through her poultry business and before she died, set up a charity 'with land and houses' to create an all-season footpath, even including a long river foot-bridge, 'for the good of travellers'. Today it's still all passable on foot and there are still funds to keep it maintained. That's five hundred years of public service: marvellous! If we can come even *near* that, we shall have done our bit for 'saving planet Earth'.

This statement brought a host of questions – were they going to set up a charity? Neither of them were sure yet; they needed to find out whether it might stop them from taking political action.

"Are you going to support any political party?" Asked an ITV reporter.

"No particular one – not permanently anyway," said Sebastian. "If Labour comes up with a good idea – or even the Tories – we might support it; but I think your question gives me the opportunity to explain how Emily and I met."

He gave them a potted version of how he had been sent to Cornwall for the CPRE when Emily's mother, newly elected to local politics, had taken up the battle to prevent The Glebe being lost as a nature reserve and part of the living history in such a special part of England.

"This may not sound like hot news to you but I've been horrified to learn, since we landed, that the local council has given planning permission for this national treasure to be turned into a car-park with ice-cream kiosk and bungalow. This happened without my ever being able to bring a strong case for refusal, to court. It makes me ask 'what are things coming to?'"

In answer to further animated questioning, Sebastian explained that this was not Plan B's first project but continuation of his professional work.

"I feel so strongly about this that I couldn't miss an opportunity like this to bring the matter to your attention. I mean – one must take opportunities! Otherwise we wouldn't be here now, would we?"

This brought further warm response from a by now, enthusiastic press corps.

"It's not just any old field. It's The Lantrelland Glebe Field – supposedly protected by two of the strongest pillars of planning: the SSSI and the AONB – yet these have been completely ignored."

There were more questions about what the initials stood for and Sebastian was able to explain. The PR man then intervened. He wanted the lottery story to hit the front pages and not get lost in scandal. He called for final questions and photos after which the young couple had to submit to several gruelling but good-natured TV interviews; some conducted by 'celeb' presenters and others with Emily and Sebastian peering into camera as they spoke to studios in Plymouth and Exeter.

It was during one of the interviews that someone noticed the unusual gold ring Emily was wearing. She related how, as a child, she had found it in the Glebe – and how it had become her engagement ring. It strengthened her personal connection with the meadow – and it might have belonged to another Emily, long ago. After the interview she was asked to take the ring off and hold it close to the camera so they could get some close-ups, getting Sebastian to slip it back on to her wedding finger.

"Lovely!" said the interviewer. "That will cheer people up!"

§

In Polperris, later that evening, Peter Trenleven and Rose Yi Johnson watched the TV news with pride. Rose's rather formal and stiff attitude to Peter relaxed a little, helped by the champagne Peter had managed to find in the supermarket. Parental pride and sentiment won the day as the two exchanged reminiscences of their offspring's' former achievements.

The same TV bulletin appeared in an open prison in Suffolk, where an angry fraudster pricked up his ears as he heard the name 'Trenleven'. So *that* cocky little bugger was a barrister too, was he? The bastard Peter Trenleven had to be related and the prisoner was by no means finished with *him*.

Emily and Sebastian, by now exhausted and hungry, submitted to Dot's invitation to 'a small supper' at the Savoy in The Strand, hosted by the lottery executive, who turned out to be very good company. The four of them parted at about eleven after the honeymooners had accepted the last surprise of the day – a luxurious double room in the same hotel for the night, three floors above the restaurant.

"Bliss!" Said Emily as she collapsed on the bed.

"Mm!" Was all that Sebastian could manage as he lay next to her and they both went to sleep – not even waking to undress until just before breakfast, when they once more endorsed their love with slow and sensitive physical union.

It was nearly mid-morning before they thought about going back to Emily's flat. They had decided to live there until they had time to move into 'something more suitable'. Emily was packing her case and Sebastian was still shaving when the phone rang. Emily picked it up: it was Dot.

"One thing I should have mentioned last night," she said. "I hope you don't mind but we decided to take on a security firm to keep an eye on you until you have made your own arrangements. It's just that you are so high profile at the moment – and will be for a while – that you might be sitting ducks for kidnap or attack by some nutcase and we don't want to take any risks while we still feel we have some responsibility for you."

"That's fine by me," said Emily. "Do we have to do anything?"

"No – except meet them down in reception when you are leaving. They've got identity cards." She named a company that Emily recognised. "They'll take you home and 'be around' full-time for a few weeks, if it's OK with you?"

"I'm sure it is," said Emily. "I'll tell Sebastian. See you later."

§

Whether it was because Sebastian was tired – exhausted by the travelling, the press conference, interviews and nights of love-making – or whether something had disagreed with his liver; Emily couldn't work out – but for some reason Sebastian took it the wrong way.

"What?" He sounded truly annoyed. "Who asked them to do that? Security men? Bodyguards? How ridiculous!. *They* can go home for a start!"

Emily was taken aback. She hadn't seen him like this before.

"It seems only sensible to me," she said.

"I never heard such crap," said Sebastian, with venom. "Anyone would think we were the Beckhams."

"This week – in the media, we shall probably get more publicity than they do, or even William and Kate," said Emily, trying not go get annoyed with his irrational attitude.

"Well I'm sending them away," said Sebastian. "We've had brushes with the media – and the underworld – ever since I was a kid and we've just learned to live with it. They're never going to bother us."

"But it's not just you, Sebastian – *I'm* part of the Trenleven empire now – or hadn't you noticed?" The atmosphere in the lush hotel room had changed from that of marital bliss to icy antagonism. They continued their preparations in silence until it was time to take the lift down to reception. The two heavies – although well-dressed and very respectable – were easy to spot and before Emily could intervene, Sebastian had politely asked them to return to their base. He told them he had not commissioned them and would not be requiring their surveillance. He would be taking a taxi home.

By the time they were sitting in a taxi edging their way through the dense traffic, Emily was nearly in tears with frustration.

"Sebastian: Dot has loads of experience of this kind of thing and she wouldn't have laid on security unless the lottery people thought it was necessary. There are so many unpleasant people around: you ought to know!"

Sebastian wouldn't even reply. He appeared not to have heard her but stared out of the window. That did it. Emily was so angry she tapped on the driver's window and asked him to stop. She then took her handbag and got out of the cab leaving her suitcase and slamming the door.

"What shall I do, sir?" Said the cab driver.

"Just keep going," said Sebastian. "She'll come round."

He was trying to sound nonchalant but his guts were in knots and he wondered whether he'd make it to the loo in time. For the first time in an otherwise blissful month, his world had gone spinning out of control. Desperately, he wondered what to do: where would Emily go? They both had keys to the flat so she might go there: otherwise he had no idea. He thought it unlikely she would land on any of her friends for fear of them finding out that the marriage was already rocky. He told himself to 'act natural' and though feeling awful, forced himself to settle back in the cab to complete the short journey. On arrival he carried the two suitcases up to Emily's flat. Though he'd been living there it felt like breaking and entering as he let himself in. He could not remember feeling worse since his mother had died: a black void blocking out all the sweet memories of the past two weeks; and all over such an insignificant disagreement. Why couldn't she see how ridiculous it was to hire bodyguards? Really!

He closed the door behind him, making sure that the catch was not on: Emily must find she could unlock it when she turned up.

§

That evening, Rose was tidying the studio when there was a tapping at the front door. Who on earth could it be at that time of night? It made her quite nervous; until she remembered that Peter Trenleven was upstairs: she wasn't alone in the house. She took off her apron and went to the door, making sure the restraining chain was in place before she opened it a few inches.

"Mum – it's me," said a tearful voice. Rose quickly released the chain and within a second had taken the weeping girl into her arms.

"There there, my darling: whatever's happened?"

"I've left him! You were right – I've been so stupid – unbelievably, unutterably completely fucking stupid!"

246

Emily never swore in front of her mother: not since Rose had washed out her errant daughter's mouth with soap so things must be serious: Rose said nothing but bundled Emily into the kitchen and sat her down while she took two glasses and poured a small brandy each.

"Here, come on, take a sip and tell me what's the matter," she said, putting a comforting arm around the girl's shoulder.

"I can't drink – I'm pregnant," said Emily.

"This is only a tiny bit and it won't hurt either of you," said Rose, feeling increasingly awful as she saw the exhaustion in Emily's face and her drooping shoulders. Emily took a sip: swallowed, coughed and then burst into floods of tears, stuttering out what had happened and trying to answer Rose's anxious questions.

"So where is he now?" She asked.

"I don't know," sobbed Emily.

"Would he have gone to your flat?"

"I don't know and I don't want to know. I didn't realise he could be so horrible – acting like some kind of dictator. I can't live with him and I wish I'd never met him."

"Look – we can talk about all that in the morning. I'm going to make you some hot milk and digestive biscuits while you have a shower and get into bed. Have you got a case with you?"

"No – I left it with him in the cab."

"Well it's a good job you've got plenty of clothes here. Just a minute and I'll give you a hot water-bottle. I'll come up in a few minutes."

Once Rose was sure she could hear the shower running, she quickly phoned Emily's flat in London. It was answered in a flash.

"Hello: Emily?"

"No, Sebastian: it's Rose. I thought I'd better tell you that Emily's here and she's quite safe but very upset. I just hope that this is not going to cause her to lose the baby."

Rose was livid on behalf of her daughter and the potential peril to her grandchild. Having talked herself round to being

247

pleased about Emily being married and pregnant it was like going back to the beginning of the whole wretched business.

"Thank God for that!" Sebastian's relief gave Rose some hope that not all was lost and brought some common sense to bear. Of course they couldn't split up after only two weeks. Emily was probably tired and hormonal; they'd both got off the plane straight into what must have been a gruelling press conference. Having heard Emily's side of the fuss, Rose had found it hard to believe that Sebastian could be so intransigent and foolish. This was reflected in the tone of her voice.

"I'm not going to discuss anything with you now, Sebastian. That's up to you and Emily but I thought you ought to know that she's all right. Now I'm going to take her up something to eat and drink so I'll wish you goodnight." She put the phone down without giving him the time to express his thanks for the call. She wanted to show him just how she felt!

CHAPTER 20

Rose had laid breakfast for three when Peter Trenleven appeared, dapper and ready for the day's rearguard action against the dubious granting of planning permission for The Glebe. He was thinking in terms of an injunction to prevent any rapid action that might damage the delicate flora and fauna of the ancient meadow.

He detected a return to a cooler atmosphere than had prevailed the previous evening. He soon understood why as Rose put him in the picture: it was like the beginning of the painting course – a prickly environment.

"Peter, is Sebastian often like this?"

"No; I would say it was most unlike him. He's normally very calm and logical: I can't think why he should object to having extra security while they are so much in the media focus. They're going to have to be very discreet if it's not to get into the papers."

"Just the kind of thing the tabloids would love – I dread to think of the headlines," said Rose.

"At least she has come home to you and not gone off somewhere," said Peter, "but is she all right?"

"It depends what you mean by all right. Last night she was in great distress and it was better not to talk about it then. She needed sleep but I expect I'll hear the whole story today, in her own time. I'm so angry, though, I'd like to strangle that son of yours."

"I see," said Peter, with a chill in his voice. He couldn't believe it was entirely Sebastian's fault. "I'll phone him."

"You can go into the gallery – we don't open for another forty minutes," said Rose. She ate very little of her toast and noted that neither had he: she was longing to say: 'I told you so', but didn't.

§

"Hello, Seb? It's Dad. Where are you?"

"I'm at Emily's flat – that's where we're staying. Do you want to call me on the fixed line?"

"No – I'll stay on the mobile – I haven't got much to say but I wanted to hear what happened with you two yesterday. Poor Emily arrived here late last night, very distressed and tired. I've been hearing about it from her mother and I can't believe you would have behaved in such a way. What on earth was going on?"

"OK – we were both pretty tired, I admit; and were about to leave the Savoy when Emily said the lottery had phoned to tell us to expect our *bodyguards* in the hotel lobby. I had visions of being escorted out of the place by a couple of heavies – as if we'd been arrested or were some kind of underworld bosses. What made me angry was not being consulted. They seem to think they *own* us, now we've 'gone public'. I said they'd have to call off their Big Brother squad because we didn't need it or want it. That made Emily flip and she said I was stupid because it was a sensible precaution. She refused to phone Dot back. Anyway, I told these two men – who actually looked like plain-clothed policemen – to go back where they came from and we piled into a cab with Emily not speaking to me. After a while Emily made the driver stop, got out and walked off.

"Weren't you worried about her?"

"Of course I was, Dad – but I didn't know what to do and decided to wait for her to come back – you know – begin as you wish to go on: I wasn't going to be dominated by my wife. It was perfectly reasonable that these people shouldn't have carte blanche to take over our lives and she had to see that. I didn't want to finish up like some sort of puppet – either theirs or hers!"

"So you still think you acted rationally and sensibly? Come on Sebastian!" Peter purposely kept his voice persuasive. There was a silence before his son replied.

"I suppose in retrospect I was a bit hasty. We'd had a hell of a day *and* a late night. It caught me off balance and perhaps I did over-react."

"You don't really mean all that crap about 'starting as you wish to go on', do you? That's what some of your 'yah' school mates might have said but I never thought I'd hear it from *you*. Your mother and I didn't have that kind of relationship as well you know. What ever were you thinking about? Have you been watching too many old films?"

More silence, so Peter continued:

"Seb – I've got to go now. As you can imagine things are pretty tense here and I'm trying to fill in for you on the Glebe Field business. Rose and I have agreed to keep out of your domestics but as far as I'm concerned, if the Lottery people have organised protection for you I'm glad. You might like to know I'm still receiving little reminders that our friend in prison has not yet finished with us. Before I left yesterday, an obscene card was dropped through our letterbox at home and I had to alert the police again. I've been quite concerned about your safety too, because it won't have gone un-noticed that you and Emily have become celebs and ours is not a common name. It will have been like a red rag to a bull to our friend in prison. I suggest you get back to the lady at the lottery who's been so helpful – apologise – get the security restored, if they've actually called them off – and then try to put things right with Emily. My impression is that you might have blown it – and if you're not careful it will be all over the papers within a couple of days unless you are pretty sharp! You have a lot to lose."

Still no reply; but Peter's experience of Sebastian since childhood indicated that the boy was coming off it and admitting to being wrong. He waited a few seconds and a more humble Sebastian said:

"Dad, I don't know what to say to Emily. I've been so bloody stupid!"

"Well that's your problem, son; but try to stay in one piece, for all our sakes – and whatever you do, keep in close touch. There's nothing worse than not knowing what's happening to someone you love."

251

"Tell me about it, Dad – and I'm sorry – to be giving you all this hassle."

"Well don't hang around feeling sorry for yourself or me – just get moving: which is what I'm going to do, right this minute. Bye Sebastian." At which he put the phone down. Seconds afterwards, Rose came through into the gallery.

"I see you've finished," she said, coldly. She knew he had: she had been listening outside the door.

"Yes – and I hope I've managed to make him see a bit of sense," said Peter, pushing his hand through his hair, feeling tired. Rose quite relished the sight of such a proud figure looking so worried. Perhaps he was human after all. Despite her earlier feelings of frustration at his arrogant confidence she still felt herself drawn to him. He was beginning to come down to her size now that things weren't going right for him or his son. It must be horrible, having crooks out to get you; and worse, when your son, who a couple of days ago was euphoric about love and marriage, was now alone, distressed and upset. She began to feel sorry for them – until she remembered Emily upstairs asleep: her darling child whose life had been turned upside down by that smart-arsed young barrister. It served them both right! Bloody men! Which reminded her too, that she had been out-manoeuvred by Mr Hugh Bloody Olver-Blythe. Despite having put herself in the dubious position of working on a commission for him (in the hope of finding out what he was up to), Hugh was getting away with his ruthless quest for profit.

Anger hardened her resolve. The Glebe would be despoiled only over her dead body! Now, though, was the time for diplomacy: she didn't want to lose the advantage of a having famous lawyer on her side. Those bastards must not get away with it! She controlled her fury .

"I think we shall have to let Sebastian to mend his own fences," she said. "Of course they never knew each other well enough to rush off and get married like that but we'll see, won't we? Now: I suggest that I get on the phone to try to find out exactly how they managed to pass that planning application for The Glebe without my objections apparently being heard – and in contravention of the law. If I get the cordless phone from the kitchen, you can listen in. If any customers come I'll take the call through into the other room, if you wouldn't mind dealing with enquiries. I'll just creep up to make sure Emily's OK. I'm hoping it won't have affected her pregnancy."

"Quite so," said Peter, looking worried. "I'll unlock the outside door, shall I?" As a former student he knew his way around and could at least be of some use. He smiled hopefully at her.

"I don't think it's worth opening this morning – there don't seem to be many people in the village at the moment," she said returning his smile. "I usually play it by ear at this time of year and if anyone's really determined they'll ring the bell. I was going to leave a note in the window saying 'open after lunch'."

He looked so worried Rose wanted to hug him: tell him not to worry because her Emily was much tougher than she looked. Men caved in so easily and now she had seen the great Peter Trenleven QC toppled from his pedestal she wanted to look after him: pick up the pieces. With a kindly look she left to get the cordless phone.

Rose's conciliatory smile gave Peter the kind of thrill he hadn't experienced for decades. Never mind all the fuss and fury: here was such a lovely creature – still in her prime, full of drive and energy – sending him a message that said: 'I'm here! Come and get me!' It set all his neglected emotional and physical systems stirring. He sat up and checked his tie, then shirt-cuffs. Perhaps he wasn't *so* much too old to win such a beautiful creature's affection – especially one with the heart of a tigress.

§

"Dot? It's Sebastian Trenleven."

"Oh – good: I was hoping you would call. I wasn't sure where you were."

"I'm at Emily's flat."

"How is she?"

"She's fine, thanks." Sebastian tried to keep his voice 'normal'. "I've rung up to apologise about yesterday."

"Oh?" Dot could play at that game too.

"Yes: I expect you've heard that I sent the security men away?"

"I did, yes. I think perhaps we had better get together to talk about it, don't you? I'm not too sure about talking on the phone these days: you never know, do you? Shall I come round?"

"That's very kind, Dot: and I'm sorry to have caused such a hassle – I wasn't thinking clearly."

"Oh, don't worry! It's not the first time this kind of thing has happened – I expect you were tired. The press conference went well, though, didn't it?"

Sebastian hadn't given their great ideas a thought since he woke up that morning – alone in Emily's bed and Dot's reassuring voice made him feel a little better.

§

"Peter, I've got an appointment this morning with Hermione Olver-Blythe. She's sitting for a portrait. I shall be out for a couple of hours but I've left all the paperwork on the desk. Perhaps you can go through it and make any phone-calls you need. Will that be OK? I'm glad you are here – someone around when Emily emerges; keep an ear open for her – just in case." Rose breezed out, paint box and sketchbook in her bag.

§

"How many sittings is this? I can't remember – is it three or four?" Hermione was embarrassed to have forgotten. Something had taken the edge off life and she felt 'mellow': that was the word. Apart from being sick in the morning – although now infrequently – she had never felt better.

"This is the fourth, Hermione," said Rose, kindly. "My goodness you are getting forgetful! To tell the truth you are less intimidating than I originally thought! I'm sure that will come through in the portrait. You're less haughty than I feared!"

"I'm not stuck up, really," laughed Hermione. She was surprised at how close she had become to Rosie Johnson. "And you are not nearly as inscrutable as I expected. I know what to look out for these days!" They both chuckled as Rose looked up, paint brush poised, to check on just how Hermione's eyebrow tilted and for how far it extended. She wondered whether that was the natural shape or whether it was a result of plucking. In years to come, fashions would change and she didn't want today's look to date the painting. The more naturally she could portray this fine-looking woman, the more lasting the portrait's impact. Looking around the long room at Carnhill Rose had sensed the atmosphere in which the paintings had been made – soaked up by perceptive artists. Some of them would have been flattering to the sitter, though in this case no flattery was needed. Hermione's bone structure was that of a classic English beauty. What noble blood might be represented in her? Hermione's father was from humble background – but quite possibly related to one of the great families in the English Midlands; from some secret dalliance between 'his lordship' and one of the domestic servants perhaps?

"And what are you thinking about?" Asked Hermione.

"Oh nothing!"

"Yes you are! Don't forget I'm studying you, too!"

Over the past few weeks they had learned a lot about each other and were less afraid of airing their thoughts. The first sitting without Hugh being present had been quite formal but by the end of it the two women had begun to exchange quite personal information: Rose expressing her concern about Emily's sudden marriage; and Hermione hinting that she didn't really trust Hugh. She quite surprised herself that she was allowing someone else to see her intimate concerns but somehow she felt safe with Rose's air of discretion.

By the third sitting Hermione had found herself looking forward to the time she would spend, entirely focussed on Rose, who gently probed with questions, finding out as much as she could about her subject's life and upbringing. Rose knew that to encourage a sitter to confide she had to be frank about herself too, making it an exchange rather than an inquisition. With Hermione, she felt oddly as though they were on the same side: here was another woman who had had to fight her own battles and maintain her position within the community. She owned up:

"I was just wondering where you got your lovely face," said Rose.

"What do you mean?" Hermione was grateful for such a compliment but curious as to its motivation.

"Well – after you told me of your father's origins – I hardly dare say this because it might sound insulting – you are surprisingly noble to look at – and beautiful too! I wasn't going to mention it but you did ask me! I wouldn't be surprised if you didn't have royal blood somewhere in there! You never know what the aristocracy got up to in their chilly castles, do you?"

Hermione could no longer keep still. She gave way to uncontrolled laughter and both of them took a minute's break as they shared the outrageous moment.

"I think I'd better *not* ask you what you are thinking next time," said Hermione, "you might tell me!" More laughter.

"I'm going to shock you, now," said Hermione, suddenly serious. "You may have been wondering about my ancestry and the aristocracy having their way with some poor housemaid – but let me tell you they haven't changed! These Olvers and Blythes are a bunch of lechers! Going back through the records you can find all kind of evidence that payments are being made to support illegitimate children. I'm quite sure that Hugh is unfaithful to me and has been ever since we met. He has that cockiness that makes him sure that he's entitled to help himself to any woman

256

he fancies. I expect he's already made advances to you, hasn't he?"

"Not that I've noticed," laughed Rose. "I've been more concerned about whether to include a wrinkle on his ear lobe than detect lechery in his gaze! No – so far he's been the perfect gentleman but we don't chat like you and I do. He keeps himself very private."

"That's because he's scared of you," said Hermione. "You are a red hot Communist as far as he's concerned. He's only going through all this portrait business to try to keep you on side – you realise that, don't you?"

"I guessed as much but it doesn't worry me. It can work both ways, can't it? I'm a great believer in the benefits of spying and intelligence – as long as it doesn't play dirty. Conflict can often be avoided if one knows what the other side is truly thinking."

"A woman after my own heart," said Hermione. "I know you'll keep this to yourself – or I hope you will. I have a fear that Hugh will dump me if I don't produce him an heir before long: especially if he makes one of his London totties pregnant. I'm already passing my sell-by date and we never discuss it but his heart is more like a cash-register than a centre of affection and passion." She paused.

"There: now I've said it! I've never told anyone else, Rosie – and it's such a relief."

Hermione's laughter had left her face and she now hid behind her hands, and broke down in tears.

"My dear Hermione!" Rose put down her palette and went over to put her arms around the distressed soul, so much in need of comfort. "It must be horrible for you: but you *are* pregnant, aren't you?"

Hermione stopped crying and pulled away.

"How did you know?" She sounded indignant. "Who told you?"

"No one has said a word," replied Rose; "but I'm not blind! It's what I do – observe people. I can see your face has filled out – so has your bust: you've gone up two cup sizes! Did you think no one would notice?" She laughed again and the tension between them passed. Hermione retrieved a hanky and dabbed her eyes.

"I suppose I did," she giggled. "I'm sure Hugh wouldn't have noticed if I hadn't told him!"

"And did you really think I couldn't add two and two together – with you having to nip off to be sick. You haven't complained every time of 'having eating something'. What was I supposed think?"

"I thought you would be too polite to ask!" They both enjoyed another good laugh. "But it's odd, isn't it – we're both sort of 'double agents'."

"You *have* told him? About the baby?"

"Only recently: I wanted to be sure I wasn't going to lose this one. I lost the first two, ten years ago."

"That must have been dreadful: but you've seen the doctor?"

"Of course! All's well so far; and he's not predicting any trouble. I've been for a couple of scans."

"Is it a boy?"

"They're not sure but they think so. That's top secret. I don't want Hugh to know. Apart from the doctor you are the only person who does know."

"I bet the local people know you are expecting," said Rosie. "Someone will have picked up the signs – the same as I did – and you don't expect them not to discuss it, do you?"

"I expect they will be wondering who the father is, after all this time! So will Hugh! He will assume I've been behaving like him! What a laugh – but I haven't – ever! He'll find some excuse or another to get a DNA test done – I can just imagine it – something like: 'to make sure there are no hereditary conditions'."

"We'll never get a portrait at this rate – there's so much to talk about."

"I think you're right. Let's get on with the painting! But I do feel better now. Are my eyes all puffy?"

"A bit, yes, but we can leave them until next time. Turn you head just a fraction to the right." The sitting continued in silence for several minutes. Rose broke the silence.

"It's been a bit of a shock, the PCC getting permission to change the Glebe Field. You realise I can't take that sitting down. I will have to take it to court?"

"Now who's being a double agent?" Said Hermione.

"I am – and I'm not being very subtle, am I? As you can guess I'm pretty fed up about the whole thing and I know your husband's been helping Eddie Rouse put his case together. How ever did they do it?"

"My dear, I honestly don't know! He doesn't tell me anything. I learn more about what he gets up to from Esme – our lady what does – when she comes on a Tuesday. All I do know is that Hugh's been spending a lot of time on the phone to his friends up at Westminster."

She was careful not to say anything about his frequent visits to Liskeard during the past few weeks, although she suspected it had been to meet people from the council. She didn't want to be disloyal.

"What I can't understand is why your people are getting so worked up about The Glebe Field. It's only one more little meadow. OK it's pretty but surely it's not much different from all the other fields? What Rouse wants to do could be done very discreetly and designed to fit in with the landscape, couldn't it? We need the jobs down here and things are pretty desperate. Surely someone can plant all those herby weeds and things in another meadow?"

"That's not the point," said Rose, trying to be patient. "That meadow is supposed to be protected by two of the strongest planning laws we've got – but these have been ignored! It's a real example of what's going to bring our own downfall – the end of the world as we know it!"

"Rosie, how can you be so dramatic?" Hermione was incredulous.

"It's true! When you've got your baby you'll begin to think more about the future. What kind of life will he lead? We face real threats of invasion by populations who can no longer survive on their own land – because it's been destroyed by droughts, floods and pollution. People will only tolerate hardship and death of their children for so long before they rise up."

"I suppose that's true enough – when you think of recent revolutions."

"And there's always something new when it comes to war. My grandparents have always said that. It went from horses to tanks – and now to drones and computers. Remember how Al Qaeda used passenger planes as missiles. The under-dog always has to find new tactics: Grandpa Charles says it was foreign fishermen who were responsible for the Somalis becoming pirates. Koreans, Spanish and other Europeans were plundering the fish in Somali waters illegally. Finally the Somali fishermen had to take unilateral action – no one else was helping them uphold the law and they had no navy – so they went on the attack with fast ribs driven by outboards. It proved so successful they went on to start taking hostages and demanding ransoms. Anyone sailing within a thousand miles of Somali without protection is mad! I expect someone will begin piracy in the air, next. It would only take a couple of jet fighters to force down a few airliners."

"I wouldn't put it past them," said Hermione, trying to hold her head in the agreed position.

"It was injustice that's triggered it! People with sufficient education to know that they are being unfairly exploited are no longer prepared to accept it. Look at the Arab Spring! It's by no means over – Gaddafi may have gone but there are still others trying to keep the lid on things. Not just in the Middle East, either: the poor in India and America will get the message too."

"What about China? They must have got millions of poor peasants."

"That's true but for the past fifteen years they have been trying to do something about it. They've created millions of jobs out of nothing. Go to Beijing or Shanghai and count the number of street sweepers – a leaf only has to fall and someone pounces on it! It's not necessary – except that it keeps another family fed and children educated. Meanwhile they're putting on courses in computing and literacy, training people to do other things other than dirt farming. They want to move at least a quarter of the rural population to work in cities, using their brains instead of their brawn. It's a massive undertaking!"

"Aren't you biased, though? What with your family connections?"

"Course I am!" Rose laughed. "But I know where I'd rather be poor! Look what happened to those poor people in New Orleans when the sea defences broke down! Many still haven't been able to go home. We don't know how lucky we are, living in Europe!"

"So why get worked up about just one little meadow? It's not as though Eddie Rouse is going to rise up and smite us!"

"Because we're ignoring the rest of the inhabitants of the planet – the animals, plants, insects – every other living creature. I can't believe how stupid we are. You hear of governments issuing licences for more and more drilling for oil in national parks and protected areas. Then they're talking about 'fracking' and 'the new era of shale gas' and how important it's going to keep us supplied with fossil fuel for another century; and all this time climatologists telling us that we are making the Earth unfit to live on; and that we're spoiling the very resources that keep us alive! It's crazy!"

"It makes you wonder whether Mother Nature will revolt and take matters into her own hands!"

"She's already giving us a few warnings! Not all the disasters you hear about are 'natural' – they are the consequence of our 'planet abuse'. Anyway, it's time for me to clean my brushes – I must get back. Emily has come home for a day or two and I've got another house guest. They'll be wondering where I am."

CHAPTER 21

Emily woke up with a start. Something was badly wrong but she couldn't recall what it was. Her bedside clock said one o'clock. It certainly wasn't night-time, though the sky was overcast and she could hear rain and wind outside as well as the incessant seabirds. Then it all began to come back. She had walked out on Sebastian. She had come home in rage and devastation. The blackness of her feelings overwhelmed her and she felt her abdomen tightening up and an urgent need for the loo. Intolerable Panic was gripping her. She fought to get a grip as she stepped into her slippers and grabbed a dressing gown before hurrying to the bathroom.

Sitting on the lavatory, waiting for her gut to stop griping, she recalled the details of last night; her sudden arrival here; the relief of being comforted by her mother. It was now past midday and she knew her mother would be out – up at Carnhill, painting. Rose had explained she couldn't afford to miss any opportunity of a portrait sitting. Peter was here, too. He was the *last* person Emily wanted to encounter: he was so nice and she felt awful about leaving Sebastian. She couldn't bear to think about it at present but she knew she couldn't spend her life with someone who rejected good advice, over-ruled her decisions without consultation and then took actions that affected both of them *and* their embryo baby. She clasped her hands on her stomach, fearful that the pains were nothing to do with the precious child she was carrying.

She couldn't face Peter Trenleven and she didn't want to have to talk with her mother about the consequences of breaking from Sebastian. Then there was all that money she had won – needing to be sorted out. She must think: she had to get out of this house without Peter seeing her and before her mother came back. As soon as her gut settled a little, she dressed, rummaging her wardrobe for the biggest sweater and old duffle coat. Using her mobile she called for a taxi to meet her by the fish market.

§

Peter was quite startled when Emily appeared, dressed for bad weather.

"Just dashing out for a bit," she said, not stopping to explain or even greet him properly. Peter barely had time to get to his feet by the time she had left and as he returned to the planning documents a feeling of disquiet came over him. He had hoped she might wake up calmer after a night's rest but her hasty retreat and anxious look were very disturbing. He wished Rose would return. Perhaps mother and daughter would meet, along the Warren?

They didn't; though Rose, travelling back from Carnhill, did wonder who it was in the taxi she passed coming the other way, as it turned off towards Lantrelland.

§

"I think we've got to strike while the iron is hot," said Hugh Olver-Blythe. He and Clive Goodman were standing by the finished scale model of Lantrelland Harbour and Marina. "We've got to get more backers so that when we come to present our application we can say the finance is all in place and we can go into action in a matter of weeks, rather than months. This month's unemployment figures have put a lot of pressure on government and we can offer work for at least twenty people straight away and hundreds within a couple of months – builders, electricians, plumbers, the lot; and of course all kinds of work for fishermen and transport workers. We'll have to emphasise that."

"And of course all the goodies we've got worked out to go with the project," said Clive. "We'll out-green the greenies!".

"Are you working on the planning people?" Hugh enquired.

"We've taken on that PR group from Plymouth and they've been building up some good relations with most of the councillors concerned, especially the chairman of the planning committee, Mrs Libby. I believe she's related to some of the local farmers around Lantrelland and, once we've gone public, they will find they own several lucrative building sites. When the core of the new village is established people are going to want to set up other businesses to service them and will have to find sites on the mainland next to Lantrelland. Of course most of that land will belong to you but your neighbours inland will still have some good opportunities. I can think of winter boat storage as an example – small caravan sites, too: there are all kinds of things we could talk about."

"What about Councillor Johnson? She's quite a Rottweiler on that committee and she's hand in hand with the CPRE."

"The less said about her and *that* lobby, the better. If papers have been lost in the post that's not our concern, is it?"

"Quite so, quite so. I shall not concern myself with her affairs – except in an artistic sense?" Hugh smiled at the prospect of a sitting in a few days time when Hermione would be away for an ante-natal clinic. "Perhaps I should concentrate on the local party members?"

"That proved successful over The Glebe application. Your local treasurer seems to have good connections in Westminster – and we're going to need them when it comes to fighting the appeal, which is bound to come. They've smacked on an injunction blocking any ground work until it's settled. You knew that, didn't you?" Clive need not have worried:

"I'm well aware of what's been going on and I'm beavering away trying to bring influential local folk to our way of thinking. I think we'll be all right, in the current climate. The Government's really rattled about the recession."

"It was quite a coup – getting that initial permission," said Clive. "Do you think we can hang on to it?"

"Certainly as long as we need to. I'm happy to let it blow up into a really big row while the other application is being slipped through. We'll have to make sure we emphasise all the peripheral benefits and play down all that 'outstanding natural beauty' nonsense. For goodness sake don't tell me about anything I mustn't know! I don't want to finish up being grilled like a Murdoch in front of a Parliamentary committee."

"I'm sure I don't know what you're talking about!" Clive's expression was that of a schoolboy accomplice. Changing the subject he drew Hugh's attention to the heavy rain splattering against the windows. "This weather's pretty foul, isn't it, for the time of year?"

"Yes," said Hugh. "It's not good for my garden tours, although it does drive people into the tearoom earlier; and makes a good argument for opening a souvenir shop – if I can get it past Hermione! I've got my own planning restrictions at home, you know!"

"If my eyes didn't deceive me, on my last visit, haven't you got a family event to celebrate before long: which might entail some 'building alterations' at home?" Clive was stepping very gingerly – Hugh had not mentioned anything to him as yet.

"You mean getting a nursery ready? You noticed, did you? We haven't talked about it much and I'd be grateful if you kept it to yourself for the moment – just until we're sure everything's OK."

"Of course, of course, old man!" Clive knew when to back off. Hugh was uneasy about the exchange. He hadn't thought Hermione's condition was so obvious and if Clive had noticed it, so would many of the local people and they, like him, would be wondering who the father was. If only he could be confident: he couldn't blame Hermione for having an affair – perhaps in desperation to provide an heir for him – but he preferred to think of her as still being 'a lady' in the traditional sense: someone who understood the needs of her menfolk while remaining chaste. For a heart-stopping moment he wondered whether Clive might be involved. He had, after all, visited Carnhill when he himself was away. He dismissed such a suspicion.

"Yes quite so – er – foul weather isn't it? The disadvantage of these glass walls makes you want to reach for a raincoat even though you're warm and dry, doesn't it?"

"Yes it does, rather," said Clive. "That's why we've included these extra lights." He walked to the doorway and flicked a couple of switches. The spacious area that a moment ago had looked gloomy and wet now lit up as though a beam of sunshine was penetrating the clouds. "Raises the spirits, doesn't it?"

"I can even feel the heat," exclaimed Hugh, unbelieving. "That must be a pretty powerful light source? And very greedy on energy?"

"It isn't actually!" Said Clive. "It's all done by mirrors," he laughed. The lights themselves are LEDs and we've added a tint of yellow filtering. The heat you can feel is radiated out from those black pads you can see. It only comes on for a few minutes – until the room temperature rises to where it was before the weather deteriorated; then it goes off again. You'd be surprised – people don't notice it going off but it makes them feel good when you switch it on. It's all in the mind!"

"It sounds very much like town and country planning!"

"Quite so!" Clive was pleased with the impression created.

"By the way, Clive, I wonder whether you would like to join me and a few friends at the House of Lords tomorrow evening? A couple of chaps I was at school with rather liked our idea and suggested putting a dinner party together. I know it's short notice but wondered whether you could bring a few enlarged pictures of this model with you – and perhaps say a few words? There will be some very useful potential investors coming; as well as a few people from the Government side."

§

"Can you drop me off here," said Emily. She had hardly said a word to the taxi driver. She was afraid of bursting into tears and losing her dignity. The driver didn't mind; he was new to the

266

area and as far as he was concerned she was just another fare –
probably some tourist from abroad; she looked foreign. The car
pulled up in the parking area by the lychgate at Lantrelland
Church. It was pouring with rain but Emily ignored it once she
had paid. She opened the door and stepped out into the wind and
wet, making her way to the limited shelter of the gate.

As the car drove away she huddled against the side post of
the gate, hiding as best she could from the buffeting gusts that hit
against the ancient construction with such force it scared her. She
now gave way to the grief, shame and anger that filled her. She
could not forgive Sebastian. She hated him and never wanted to
see him again. She didn't need him, though she was carrying the
child he had fathered. Her wrath surged up and she screamed at
the wind: no one could possibly hear her.

"You bastard! You are NOT going to govern my life!"

That felt good but the force of the storm rammed it back at
her. The wind enraged her more: again she yelled at the top of
her voice:

"And *you* can sod off – too!"

She visualised Sebastian's supercilious look as he had told
the security men 'they would no longer be needed'. She cursed
the anonymous God of The Wind, allying himself to Sebastian,
trying to knock her down and dominate her. She was *damned* if
they were going to win and stepped out into the full blast of the
howling assault and, bending over nearly double, forced her way
to the leaning yew trees at the bottom of the graveyard. She
stood, looking across The Glebe, recalling the story of the other
Emily, all those years ago – who must have felt much the same –
desolate and so alone. She reached towards the rings on her left
hand – feeling the golden scrolls and oak leaves on the ring that
had become her engagement ring and began to ease it from her
finger. The rain was soaking through her duffle coat and its icy
touch reached her shoulder and back.

She paused to pull the hood up, too late to protect her hair,
which was already dripping as it trailed away in front of her,
whipped by the wind; then resumed removing the ring, which
was a tight fit. She had a strong urge to tear it off and throw it as

far as she could into the field. It was nearly free when she heard a woman's voice.

"Emily! Emily! My dear!"

Was it her imagination? The voice was fragmented in the wind. She couldn't tell from which direction it was coming. Such was her state of mind she thought it might be the spirit of Emily Tregrove, come back to comfort her. She left the ring in place and yielded again to the sobbing that overcame her.

A moment later she felt an arm around her shoulder.

"Here she is! Thank God!"

Emily recognised the voice of Barbara Weeks and sank to her knees in a state of collapse.

"Come along my dear – come with me. We must get you out of these wet clothes at once," said Miss Weeks, helping her up and leading her towards the lychgate.

"We'll take her to my cottage: I've got a fire lit and I'll run a nice hot bath for her," she said, addressing two athletic-looking men in long raincoats, standing beside her, looking embarrassed.

That was the last thing that Emily remembered. Something gave way and she blacked out, falling into Miss Weeks' arms, unconscious. Miss Weeks couldn't hold her but before Emily slipped to the ground the two men had caught her – reacting so fast that it took the old lady by surprise.

"Don't worry love," they said to her. "We've got her!" One of them picked Emily up in his arms while the other took Miss Weeks into his care, putting his arm around her and supporting her back to their large black car outside the lychgate. They put their charges gently into the back and the car turned round, making its way back to the cottage down the lane.

Miss Weeks sent them into the kitchen to get the kettle on, giving them instructions not to come out until she called them. In front of the fire she gave Emily the smallest sip of brandy and reassured her that all was well.

"There, my dear: you're quite safe and we'll soon get you dry and warm."

"Miss Weeks? I'm sorry – I must have fainted. I didn't see you?" Emily was so confused and had begun shaking as she regained her senses. The warmth of the fire and Barbara Weeks' ministrations, made Emily feel better; as did the dressing gown and blanket in which Miss Weeks enveloped her, sitting her snugly next to the fire.

"You stay there for a bit and I'm sure you'll be fine," she said. "I'll bring you some tea – would you like that?"

"Yes please," said Emily. "I'm so sorry to have given you so much trouble."

"You will never be any trouble to me, Emily. I feel you are part of my family and you know how fond I am of you. I'm just so grateful these two gentlemen came along when they did. I was wondering what to do when they came to the door. They explained who they were and showed me their identity badges. Earlier, I'd seen the taxi bring someone past, as if they were going to the church – and then it went back empty and I know the church is locked so I was really worried someone might be exposed to this awful weather. When these men knocked and asked if I'd seen a young lady – and described her – I knew immediately it must be you and I guessed where you would be."

"I'd better try to explain…., " began Emily.

"Not now, my dear! You must just rest and get warm. I'll let those gentlemen out of the kitchen now."

As Miss Weeks bustled away, Emily felt the tension leaving her. She remembered what had happened and how she had felt. She checked her left hand to make sure both rings were still in place. Thank goodness she hadn't succeeded in carrying out her protest; and thank goodness the gripes in her stomach had stopped. Perhaps she hadn't endangered her baby. Perhaps all was *not* over with Sebastian? Angry or not, she was still part of him and he was part of her. Perhaps his behaviour had been a one-off? Maybe her hormones *had* made her over-emotional? There was still so much thinking to be done. She drifted off to sleep."

§

"Dot, I feel awful! I'm afraid I've blown it with Emily. She's gone back to her mother's. Do you think you can get in touch with her there? I'll give you the number."

"I'm so sorry to hear things are like this," said Dot. She had come straight over when he phoned on the Monday morning. "It's this weather! I can't remember it being so awful. I've even spoiled my new umbrella: it went inside out and I finished up jamming it into a litter bin. It was a liability."

"Let me take your coat," said Sebastian. "Thank you for coming so promptly: I'm not sure what to do; or even if I can ask you for help anymore – I'm not the prize-winner – Emily is."

"As far as we're concerned you are part of the package," said Dot, taking his hand. "You are husband and wife; and up until whatever happened, which I presume was only yesterday, you seemed to be coming to grips with it all very well. Let me tell you straight away that this often happens and you mustn't let it get out of proportion. In many cases it accompanies a very nasty hangover. You don't seem to have got that! Knowing Emily, I doubt whether she would have been hitting the bottle either."

"I'm sure she wasn't," said Sebastian. "Especially now – she's pregnant. She's booked in again to see the doctor – although I shall have to phone the surgery to cancel. I have to say: it was my fault entirely. I can't imagine why I was so stupid."

"You mean – cancelling the security men?" Asked Dot.

"You know about it?"

"They contacted me straight away – without stopping their surveillance. We knew where you both were and have done all along. Our concern was your safety and that goes beyond some domestic tiff! We assume you'll get over it but meanwhile you still need someone to keep an eye on your safety. Your father's office got on to us, too."

"What about?"

"Apparently your father has been receiving threats?"

"Yes he has – a client in prison."

"Your Mr Potter was worried that your name being in all the papers might give whoever it was some new ideas and so we doubled up your protection. You realise it's only until you take

270

control of the arrangements for yourselves. We're spending *our* money, not yours at this stage. We can't afford to lose winners!"

"You're making me feel worse," said Sebastian. "Heaping coals on my head. How can I have been so short-sighted? What a bloody fool! I'm so sorry!"

"It's not me you should be talking to but Emily, isn't it?" Dot still sounded sympathetic rather than accusing. She smiled warmly.

"You're right – but I'm not sure she'll even speak to me and I don't blame her."

"My suggestion is that you follow her down to Cornwall and try to make it up. Give her a surprise." Dot thought twice before passing on her next piece of information but decided to, anyway. The boy needed to know what his silly behaviour had triggered.

"I must warn you, Emily too has been taking a few risks herself but I'll let *her* tell you what happened to her last night during the storm. All I will say is that it's a good job our security people didn't listen to you."

"Oh God! What happened, Dot?"

"I really feel it would be better for Emily to tell you herself. Enough to say that she's all right."

§

"Has Emily appeared yet? Have you both had some lunch? I'm sorry to be so late but Hermione Olver-Blythe needed me around for longer than usual." Rose bustled into the gallery. "I would have been earlier but I stopped off at the supermarket to pick up a few things for supper. Where's Emily?" She then saw the look on Peter's face.

"Oh God – what's the matter? Peter – tell me at once, please."

"Emily's all right, Rose; she will be home just a bit later – she's at Miss Weeks' cottage at Lantrelland."

"At Lantrelland? Whatever for? Why on earth …..?"

"Rose – we don't know why. You will have to ask her when she gets back. Miss Weeks found her in a distressed state, in the graveyard – soaking wet, about an hour or so ago. She just phoned to say the girl is sleeping by the fire getting over her ordeal and all's well."

It was all too much for Rose. She needed to know exactly what had happened and she took command, getting Peter to close the gallery; the weather was so awful no one was likely to come anyway.

"We'll leave the light on so people can see someone's around. Now let's go through to the kitchen and you can tell me just what's been going on. I'm so worried about Emily – you're sure she's all right?"

Peter did as he was bid and followed Rose after she had deposited her sketch book and paints. He carried her supermarket bag through and over a mug of tea, told her all he knew.

"I didn't *do* anything when she went out because I assumed she wouldn't be more than a few minutes – she gave that impression – and I didn't want to close the gallery until you came back. I was expecting you a bit earlier."

Rose assured him that he had done the right thing and questioned him closely about what Miss Weeks had said.

"So the security men will bring her home when she wakes up?"

"That's what she said," concluded Peter.

"What a good job they were there!"

"It was indeed! Those Lottery people seem to be well organised; but winning so much money *is* very disrupting, isn't it? They must have picked up a lot of experience about how it affects people."

Rose was tempted to say something about the added complications of Emily having been rushed into marriage with a family under threat from the criminal fraternity and now being pregnant but decided not to.

§

It was late evening before Emily was escorted back to her mother's house on the quay. After a tearful reunion, Rose made Emily agree to see the doctor the next day. In the gallery, the two security men began their shifts of keeping watch. One of them went to book in at the Claremont saying that one room would do – because one of them would be on duty all the time. They reported back to their headquarters and to their clients at The Lottery: all was well.

§

Later that night, the security man on duty was surprised to hear a knock on the door at the gallery. He quickly put on his jacket and prepared himself for action, pressing his pager button summoning assistance from his colleague – just in case. The colleague had barely checked in before he was sprinting back towards the gallery.

"Oh – hello! I've come to see Miss Johnson."

"Oh it's you, Mr Trenleven. Remember we met at the Savoy? Do come in. My colleague will be here in a minute but I'll tell Miss Johnson you are here."

"It's all right, I know my way round," said Sebastian, weary from his hasty travel from London to Polperris.

"I think it might be wise if I came with you," said the security man, tactfully. He wasn't sure what kind of reception Sebastian might get from Rose and it was his job to protect his client in all circumstances.

Rose was preparing a hot water bottle for herself, having tucked Emily safely up in bed; and swore under her breath when a soft knock on the dividing door once more delayed things. The sight of Sebastian, looking like death – so apprehensive and scared; with the security man hovering in the background looking uncomfortable – softened her irritation. She had half suspected that Sebastian would arrive sooner or later: indeed if he hadn't she would have written him off as a bad job. She didn't

273

give him a chance to explain or apologise – what everyone needed now was rest.

"Sebastian! You'd better come in. Emily's asleep; better if we leave her alone until morning. You can put up in the attic bedroom, can't you?"

The security man made himself scarce and got ready to explain why he had pressed his 'help' button. A good job he and his colleague understood each other and the exigencies of the service.

§

Emily's appointment to see the doctor was not until after lunch so Sebastian had the whole morning in which to try to put things right between himself and his bride.

CHAPTER 22

It was tense in the kitchen this morning. Rose, first to appear, made sure the security man had a cup of tea. He thanked her and said his companion would be there shortly for the next shift. The gallery smelled musty with a taint of unwashed man and she tactfully offered 'some nice fresh air' and opened the French windows on to the gleaming harbour and village, none the worse for last night's storm. The sun was bright and the gulls gave no sign that anything untoward had taken place. A closer look at the streets found broken slates and glass, dustbin lids and bins separated from each other, sometimes by hundreds of yards; otherwise the village was intact, the stream coming into the harbour not its usual clear self but flowing angrily, muddying the blue-green seawater of the harbour.

Taking a deep breath as she took in the scene, Rose's feeling was that of relief. Emily was safe: Sebastian seeking forgiveness – or so she hoped – and all of them under the protection of professionals. Perhaps life wasn't so bad after all. She made her way back to the kitchen and shut the door behind her. The reconciliation was something she wanted to keep 'in the family'. She found Peter had laid places for four: plates, bowls, mugs, butter and marmalade at the ready.

"I took the liberty….." he began.

"Oh don't worry – your domesticity is very welcome because I'm on edge about what happens next; aren't you?"

"I must confess I am – but in the circumstances I think the less we show it, the better – don't you?"

Rose *had* been thinking that she might offer Sebastian some wise words about how to treat a woman, hinting that Emily was not the kind of person who took kindly to being pushed around or ignored. Now here was the senior Trenleven, whom she had never liked very much, coming in, taking over her kitchen and starting to dictate how she should behave towards her own daughter. She said nothing but felt her indignation rise. Then the toaster popped up, making her jump.

Luckily for Peter it diverted her for a few seconds in which she could reflect. Emily was a big girl now and married – like it or not! Peter was right – the young couple would have to work things out for themselves 'for better or for worse'. Rose and Peter must stand on the touchline and not even shout. Without thinking she took hold of the hot toast and passed it to Peter.

"Excuse fingers," she said. She would have liked to knock some sense into these infuriating men but didn't have time to assemble anything constructive before Sebastian entered, looking ill with fatigue; he was hesitant and apprehensive. His father's heart went out to the boy.

Rose, too, was moved by the pathetic condition of her new son-in-law. He looked so pitiful: no longer the cocky young barrister but a dejected newly-wed.

"Oh – I was wondering whether Emily had come down yet," he said, on the point of retreating upstairs again.

"Come in and have some breakfast," said Rose quickly. "You look as though you haven't slept!"

"I'm afraid I didn't. I was just dropping off after the storm when the gulls started – and I had a lot on my mind. I'm sure you understand."

"I do, don't worry," said Rose, kindly. "Sit down here and eat something – I'll make a little tray for you to take up to Emily later. I gave her strict instructions not to get up until I'd brought it but it's something you could do."

"That's so kind. I've been wondering how to approach her," confessed Sebastian. "I feel terrible. Do you think I'll be forgiven?"

"You'll have to see, won't you?"

"You're going to have to eat humble pie," said Peter. "If it's any comfort, I upset your mother with something I said when we were on our honeymoon and she wouldn't speak to me for a whole day. I thought the end of the world had come but learned the lesson that Françoise was usually right."

"Harry made me feel worse yesterday when he told me about you receiving more threats. He said they must have twigged that we're related – from the papers. How could I have been so short-sighted? Such an idiot!"

Rose had been busy during this exchange and the toaster popped up again.

"Here – eat this and you'll think more clearly," she said.

Revived a little later, Sebastian took the tray, which Rose had made look so tempting – even to a posy of sea thrift as decoration – and climbed the two floors to Emily's room. He knocked gingerly at the door: no reply; so he went in softly and was rewarded by finding Emily asleep, looking beautiful, one arm resting behind her head and her dark shining hair spread over the pillow. He stood holding the tray, loving what he saw and committing the image to his memory. Her face was relaxed, with the slightest of smiles; he watched as her chest rose and fell almost imperceptibly. Quietly placing the tray on the dressing table he went and knelt by the bed. He wanted so much to kiss her perfect face. In the morning light it had the texture of porcelain – not a wrinkle or blemish. She stirred and opened her eyes.

"Oh it's *you*!" She asked. "What's the time?"

"Nearly nine."

"And you're *here*!"

"Yes I got here last night." He took her hand. "Emily – can you ever forgive me? I'm *so* sorry!"

"What for? Oh!" The memory of the nightmare of their parting came back; her flight to Paddington and the hollow pain that only eased in her mother's embrace. Then the ordeal of the graveyard: but now, Sebastian was here! His eyes were anxious and he was haggard: no longer the imperious maker of decisions; not the short-sighted prat but a worried lover asking for another chance.

"I was so bloody stupid, Emily. I don't know what I was thinking about."

"I don't care – now you're here: that's what's important. Come!" She threw her arms open. "I want to hold you so tight you'll never forget!"

"But your breakfast will get cold!"

"Let it! Just take off those clothes and get in!" She moved to make room and lifted the sheet invitingly. Sebastian did as he was bid and in seconds was enveloped in her embrace. For a while their reunion was passionate, joyous, and very vigorous; afterwards, gulls or not, they slept – exhausted, peace restored.

On waking, Emily sent Sebastian down for fresh tea. It was so good to be together again – heightened by having survived the upsetting crisis.

"Come back quick," she said. "We need to talk about how I'm going to convince my mother I haven't married Napoleon; and that its not all over."

"Believe me," he said, "I'll be back as soon as I can – I don't want to be cross examined by those two!" He dressed, and made his way downstairs.

He found Rose and Peter deep in conversation, the kitchen table covered in papers and reports from the district council.

"You took your time," said Peter.

"We got talking – and just dropped off to sleep," said Sebastian, unconvincingly.

Rose silently congratulated Emily as Sebastian fled with two mugs of tea.

§

The younger couple were in for yet another life-changing shock. Rose had lent them her car after the local doctor thought it wise to have an ultrasound scan. He wanted to make sure all was well with the pregnancy 'just to be on the safe side'. He had listened to Emily's womb and was not entirely happy about what he heard although there was no point in adding to their troubles by saying anything. They had explained that Emily had been 'caught out in the storm last night' and had fainted after the ordeal. In general, however, the doctor assured them that Emily and her embryo seemed to be fine so they were light-hearted as they drove to the clinic.

"I can see why your doctor recommended the scan," said the midwife, as Emily lay, holding Sebastian's hand, while the slippery sensor was moved around over her lower abdomen. "I think you might have twins! Look!" She turned the screen so that they could both see; and turned up the volume of the sound. The muddled bleeps from two tiny hearts must have been what made the doctor wonder what was going on.

"It's too early to be sure," said the midwife. "You'll have to come back in a few weeks' time so we can make sure – but I think you should be getting yourselves ready for *two* babies. Otherwise, everything seems to be all right."

Driving home after hearing this momentous news, Emily remembered she was supposed to be back at work the following day. Sebastian persuaded her to ask for a couple more days 'to get over jet lag' and the news they had just received; so she called her boss on her mobile.

"No problem!" She told Sebastian. "He sounded as pleased as we are! The girl he's got to stand in for me wanted to stay on for another week and he'll give me unpaid leave – he said he thought I could probably afford it!"

"That's good," said Sebastian. "If you're feeling OK we could pop in to thank Miss Weeks for rescuing you? It's a good job she did! I'm still feeling awful about the way I treated you, driving you to such risks. Darling, I'm so sorry."

"Yes, let's go and see her; but there's no point in you going on beating yourself up. We were both out of our heads and it's been a lesson, hasn't it?"

"It certainly has! Do you still love me?"

"More than ever! I've learned you can be a complete shit – but that I don't have to put up with it! Honour has been satisfied and I feel I can cope with you even when you are raving bonkers."

279

"But you had a narrow escape: *anything* might have happened!"

"I didn't realise it at the time – I was just so angry!"

"We were *both* very lucky! So were our twins!"

"Oh my God yes! I'd nearly forgotten about *them*: what a lovely surprise!" Emily put her hands on her tummy.

"You won't be so glad when you're the size of a house," said Sebastian, carefully taking a corner. "Where do I turn off for Lantrelland?"

They caught up with Miss Weeks in The Glebe, making sure her beloved animals had come through the storm without ill effects. The faithful animals were, as usual, standing by, in the hope of a sugar lump or extra strong mint from her grubby raincoat pocket – she always put this coat on to go 'out around and see the things'.

Sebastian and Emily, hand in hand came through the kissing gate – taking a quick kiss – Emily said it was a pity to miss such a chance. It would be extra lucky, now they were friends (and lovers) again. They had tried the cottage and, receiving no reply, went on to The Glebe to see that no JCB diggers were ripping up the turf or digging foundations. They spotted the little group by the water trough and strode, light-of-foot across the meadow as the old lady picked out the twigs and leaves blown in by the gale.

"My dears, how lovely!" She said. "You must excuse me – my awful old coat. You've really caught me on the hop; but I'm so pleased to see you're all right, Emily: and that *you*'re here so soon." She gave Sebastian a beaming smile. "I've just finished so you can walk me home."

"We'd love to," said Emily. She took Miss Weeks' arm and Sebastian followed the two friends back to her cottage. He couldn't hear what they were saying but was easy about Emily updating her rescuer – even if it might put him in a poor light. He deserved it and Miss Weeks had long earned Emily's affection and confidence. He felt included in their love and it was good, seeing the two women chat as they stepped round the occasional anthill back towards the gate.

"So what do you think?" Emily asked Miss Weeks later, as they sat out on the lawn at the lee side of her cottage. The sun was so warm they were enjoying a glass of home-made lemonade in the shade. The discussion was about saving The Glebe, now that Eddie Rouse' planning permission had come through. Between them they came up with several alternative strategies and by the time Emily and Sebastian went back to Polperris their tactics, too, had been agreed.

§

During the following month Miss Weeks spread the word among members of the Parochial Church Council, friends and relatives, speaking as a local resident. Sebastian put proposals to the Lantrelland PCC, in writing from London, copying the correspondence to Rose and to Nancy Libby of the planning committee. Rose followed this up with phone-calls to church members, canvassing support for accepting a large donation, which could cover not only repairs to St Gluvias Church's roof at Lantrelland but restoration of the whole site – the church interior, boundary walls and gates – and best of all, the purchase of The Glebe Field for the National Trust. She was able to say that the Trust would take it on if the Church authorities gave their blessing. She went personally to visit Trevor Philp, the churchwarden so she could spell out the proposals clearly and attractively. Mr Philp found this very welcome because the church roof was just one more worry when he was fighting to save his farm. Beef and sheep were not profitable enough to keep him out of the red on the limited scale that his small acreage allowed. He was glad to make it up with Rose, who had told him what she thought of his voting in favour of Eddie Rouse' application. He had only voted for it because there might be some spin-off to benefit his dwindling income – perhaps a few more bed and breakfast visitors during the summer.

At the same time, Sebastian was assembling relevant legal arguments for the planning permission to be challenged in the courts. Aided by the solicitor at CPRE he was able to give Rose near certainty of victory. Rose made sure that the Council and the Chief Executive were made aware of this and would face eventual defeat with damaging repercussions in the full glare of media publicity. The costs of any court case, if they lost, would have to be carried by the rate-payer: not popular with voters.

Rose talked of headlines such as 'Lottery-winners roast Council in bid to save national treasure'. Thus there was plenty of stick to accompany the carrot of Emily and Sebastian's offer that most bishops and district council chairmen could only dream of.

To the young Trenlevens, spending a million pounds, or even more if necessary, would achieve all kinds of benefits. By the time Sebastian was invited to address the Parochial Church Council he was able to present them with a compelling case. If they proceeded with the sale to Eddie Rouse, consequent development would be thwarted in court; but by accepting the endowment fund offered by his wife and himself the PCC could avoid court action and all future worries about church repair. The council applauded loud and long when Sebastian sat down and voted in favour of accepting the generous donation.

Everyone regretted Eddie Rouse's disappointment but were sure he would understand it was an offer they could not refuse. They agreed Trevor Philip should make a personal visit to explain things. It was also decided to play down the lottery aspect because many local people didn't even approve of gambling – even a fund-raising raffle, which some chapel-folk believed sinful.

"I think we'll say 'from a local benefactor'," said Mr Philp.

"Even better," said Sebastian, "Emily and I would be happy to remain anonymous."

§

The diversion created in the media by 'the rescue of the Glebe Field' was playing directly into the hands of Hugh and his financial backers whom he had been wining and dining in The City. His public relations people were able to put around stories about NIMBYs blocking economic development at a time of national crisis'. They found plenty of retired celebs who welcomed a few more minutes of limelight, posing for cameras in their cliff-side gardens to offer their support. Public opinion polls, with carefully crafted questions, demonstrated how people in East Cornwall resented 'beard and sandal interference' blocking their chances of making a living and getting 'off the social'.

In The City, promoting such an attractive investment for serious money gave Hugh and his cronies many openings for other exciting activities 'after work', when they could tell their wives that 'it would be too late after the meeting to get back' so they would be 'staying the night in town'. It also served to keep Hugh out of the Hermione's way, with her moody behaviour during the pregnancy. He did, however, make sure he was home for Rose and her portrait sittings. During these brief visits Hermione found him more malleable regarding the costs of preparing a nursery for the baby; as well as other changes of décor she had long been plotting. The bags under Hugh's eyes also warned her that he was indeed 'very busy' in London. She took her revenge by avoiding his indirect questions as to the parenthood of the child she was heralding as his heir. Let him wonder! It might concentrate action in his head, rather than his usual zone of self-indulgence.

§

Nancy Libby, always diplomatic, was concerned that Judy Rouse might suffer from the consequences of Eddie's frustration once Trevor Philp had delivered his bad news. She was so worried she decided to attempt to defuse the shock by warning Eddie of Trevor's impending visit.

Until Nancy's intervention Eddie was in high spirits, such as he had not enjoyed for a long time. Winning the planning permission had given his dream of a bungalow and little business a great leap forward. He could picture himself in a year's time, opening the field gate to let the public in, paying for his delicious ice-cream (and parking their cars) while they wandered down to Lantrelland Beach. Later he might consider applying for planning to put in another little shop selling beach toys. Mr Olver-Blythe had dropped by to pat him on the back and wish him well with his plans but sympathising over the injunction that was blocking progress. He said he would help by chivvying up the church authorities in Truro to accept Eddie's offer on The Glebe. Afterwards Eddie felt things were definitely looking up: at least until Nancy called.

"Hullo? Morning Nancy! How are you?" He put his hand over the mouthpiece and whispered to Judy: "It's Mrs Libby."

"Oh I'm fine, thank you. Yes, 'twas a terrible storm! I thought we were going to lose our roof! How did you-party get on?"

The conversation continued at a trivial level, as custom dictated, for a couple of minutes before Nancy got down to business. Judy watched her husband's expression change as he listened. She couldn't make out what was being said although she suspected that it was a tale of fallen trees and loose slates – perhaps a damaged cattle shed. Whatever the news was it must be bad. Eddie didn't say much except 'yes', 'no' and 'I see', sounding more and more gloomy. After several minutes he said his goodbyes and put the phone down.

"Well I'll be beggared!" This was strong language for Eddie, who despite all his underhand business techniques and greed, always maintained the demeanour of his chapel background, even though he now attended Lantrelland Church where the services were few and far between, which suited him well.

"Whatever is it, Eddie? Are they all right? Is Mrs Libby hurt or something?"

"Not so hurt as I am," said Eddie. "Would you believe? She's heard the Church people are pulling out over The Glebe. They've had an offer several times what they'd agreed to sell it to me for and I bet I know where that's from! That blimming Johnson woman, down Polperris: her daughter won all that money. Doesn't it make you sick? You can't trust anyone these days, can you? There's no honour in business any more. Even the church council has its price. I say that's corruption! I'll take 'em to court!"

"'Tis shocking," sympathised Judy. She knew it would be pointless to say anything else. "'Tis all money, money, money: I feel really bad about it after all your hard work and plans. We'll have to think of something else for our retirement. Don't worry, Eddie: I'm sure you'll come up with something – you always do!"

It was her one hope – that he still had the capacity to bounce back after a calamity. In the past, such events were usually due to his own ineptitude or lack of attention to the job in hand – forgetting to shut a gate, neglecting to mend a fence, or pay a fine in time. His technique was then to rush about apologising and make excuses, trying to avoid damages or summonses. People generally let him off, grateful to see him finally fulfil his side of the deal or pay his dues. Now, for a change, it wasn't his 'fault'. Self-righteous indignation was not something he'd enjoyed for a long time and he intended to make the most of it. Judy predicted his thinking.

"I think you could 'go public' with this," she hinted. "They've really let you down, haven't they?" At least that would give him something to keep him occupied and raise his spirits. To have right on his side was a chance to gain a bit of respect. It began to inspire him.

"I'm going to get on to the local radio people and the papers," he stormed. "I'll tell them how 'Christian' these people are – breaking their word and forgetting working people: darned if I'm not!"

Judy Rouse was relieved he had taken it this way – with a little help from herself.

When Hugh Olver-Blythe read about it in his *Cornish Times* the following week, he put the paper down to rub his hands. This

285

was just the kind of smoke-screen he needed. He phoned Eddie Rouse to offer condolences and encouragement.

"Pretty shabby, that," he said, "backing out on a deal. I'd have hoped for better from church people, wouldn't you?"

That gave Eddie the chance to vent his feelings once more. Hugh suggested he might like to be interviewed and photographed by his publicity people from Plymouth.

"I blooming well would!" Declared Eddie.

CHAPTER 23

Hermione and Rose had enjoyed a good laugh at Hugh's expense, during a recent sitting when the two women once again spoke with disarming frankness about their most intimate concerns and pleasures. Rose confided that Emily had brought Sebastian into line very firmly at his first signs of imperious behaviour. Hermione approved of this especially when she heard what the row had been about.

"Security is always something that worries me – especially when I'm all on my own here. Hugh's up in London so often. He comes back looking shattered and I suspect he's up to no good even though he swears it's because he's busy on some new scheme or other. He says he has to do a lot of entertaining – new investors – but he can't tell me about it yet: quite infuriating! I can just imagine what's going on. They'll have their meeting over lunch – finish at five, then go out on the town. No wonder he looks tired! You can almost hear them phoning their wives with excuses why they can't get back that evening."

"You're going to have to look less fierce for a few minutes if you don't want your portrait to reflect your present mood," said Rose. "Let's think about something else! At the risk of making you more cross – you must know how pleased I am about Eddie Rouse not getting The Glebe anymore?"

"I thought of you as soon as I heard about it," said Hermione. "Eddie must be livid! I suppose it was your Emily who bought off the parish council?"

"I'm sure I couldn't say," lied Rose, tongue in cheek. "It was an anonymous donation, according to the papers – and even if I did know I couldn't possibly confirm or deny any such rumours." They both laughed. "But yes, I'm delighted!"

"I wonder what Eddie will do next," said Hermione.

287

"He seems set on bringing the Church of England into disrepute: complaining it can no longer be trusted. If he goes on much longer he'll lose any credibility he might have gained by being so heinously wronged!"

"I can't help thinking it's a pity he's lost this chance to start a business," said Hermione. "I would have thought you would have approved of that? We really do need the jobs. Things are so tough for farmers round here."

"Not all of them, I would suggest," replied Rose. "Others have got out while the going was good – and that's freed up land for people like your husband to make a decent return. Hugh has diversified, too, which others *could* have done. Your tea shop and gardens must be quite a draw in summer."

"I must admit they have," said Hermione. "Hugh wants to expand and put up a gift shop. I think that would lower the tone though, don't you?"

"I can't say I do. It all depends what you sell: if it's inflatable whales and beach balls it would be as bad as Eddie's original plans but I think tasteful gifts and things – like in National Trust shops, make a day out at a stately home, more enjoyable. "

Hermione sat quietly while Rose painted.

"Eddie will still have to sell up, from what I hear," said Hermione. "He's heavily in debt. You know he was trying to threaten Hugh by saying that if he didn't get planning permission for The Glebe he wouldn't sell Hugh the farm but would offer it to the National Trust. Hugh humoured him and agreed to go along with 'full support for his application' so I expect Hugh will have to pay more for the farm, if the National Trust really *is* interested but it will be worth it to see Eddie get his come-uppance: I can't stand the man! Mind you, I can't see why Hugh's so keen to get the farm. It's pretty run down." She moved a little to be more comfortable before continuing.

"I think Hugh wants to keep the National Trust at arm's length – and put in a better road down to the bay."

"I wonder *why* one really needs a new road," said Rose. "They always generate more traffic."

"I suppose you *could* say that; but being able to reach the sea more easily from here also makes our attractions more accessible, doesn't it? It would boost our income."

"If your first priority is profit, then yes, a new road will help; but you've got a baby on the way and my daughter's carrying my first grandchild, too. Do we really want them to have to wear gas-masks and carry guns for self protection as part of their daily life? That's the result of unrestrained pursuit of profit. That's what will happen if we go on like this."

"You don't really believe all that, do you, Rose? Surely that's just scare-mongering?"

"I used to think it was; but listening to my parents when they are home on leave; and having had Emily – and now Sebastian, preaching about the dangers ahead I can't help but conclude that if I *do* have doubts, I must take measures to avoid them – in case the prophets of doom are right! It's not as if we greenies are advocating slavery or religious fanaticism – we want to see universal prosperity, rather than the 'super-rich and miserably-poor'; we to be able to breathe clean air and drink pure water – to see wildlife in all its diversity; and our children and grand-children to live in peace."

"Well so do I! Do you think I don't? Or that Hugh doesn't? We're not daft!"

"Of course – but with a straight line objective of 'profit', you simply can't have peace. Profit is not bothered by events such as Bhopal. It's not afraid of war because of all the arms production that war needs. Every shell and bomb that's hurled at the enemy is putting a few more bob in someone's pocket."

"Oh dear, Rose – now you are beginning to scare me! You sound like some rabid lefty." The conversation had gone beyond banter. Rose noted a tightening of Hermione's upper lip. This was how the aristocratic lady had looked during the first sitting – implacable, behind a well-defended reserve. Rose's response was to stop talking and pay more attention to committing this image on to paper.

She had experienced the warmer side of Hermione but now the true face of Lord Poynsworth's daughter resumed its proud expression, chin slightly raised and gaze just over Rose's head. A pity, thought Rose, because over the next few weeks, this is what would appear on the canvass. Fundamentally, Hermione was not going to change.

"Frankly, dear," said Hermione, "I shall do whatever I can to ensure the safety and good fortune of my child – sending him or her to the very best school and university; making sure that he obeys the law and understands that life is about maintaining one's position despite all the competition. No one *else* is going to ensure a bright future for my child. To give him – or her – the best opportunities I need money: that's why profit is so important. I'm sure Hugh agrees. When you look at how the poor live you can understand why they are poor. One can't help feeling they get very much what they deserve."

Rose could feel herself withdrawing. She had needed to get close to Hermione, despite her prejudice. This past few minutes had sealed the way Hermione would look in the new painting. It would be Rose's honest assessment of this fashionable and brittle character, living in an atmosphere that, to Rose, seemed full of suspicion, insincerity, fear of failure and wholly dependent on cash. So be it! The Olver-Blythes were the customers and wanted a depiction of themselves and their property that fulfilled their own self-image. They would get it! The closeness that had developed between the two women was now over. Rose avoided any controversial remarks or comments as she completed the session and took her leave.

Driving back to Polperris she felt sad, though she couldn't suppress an underlying excitement despite the rift with Hermione. It took her time to analyse why. It was about something else altogether although part of her was denying it.

'Peter Trenleven's going to be there when I get home!' Said Care-Free Rosie.

'So what? He's just another example of people at the top. I'm not impressed,' replied Councillor Johnson, responsible world citizen and environmental campaigner.

The two argued all the way through the lanes and even along the last couple of hundred yards along The Warren as Rose carried her bag back towards her family, home and business.

The gallery was open when she arrived and she was greeted by a most charming smile from the elegant gentleman who stood up as soon as she entered. Rose's heart let the side down for Councillor Johnson by missing a beat and Care-Free Rosie took control. The smile she gave Peter went over to him like a ray of sunshine. He had been apprehensive about her return but now he was disarmed.

"Where are the children?" She asked, pleasantly.

"They've gone shopping," said Peter, "and talking about a walk to see the rollers breaking against the rocks. Emily was saying they can be impressive after a storm."

"It sounds as though they've made it up. I'm relieved." The incident between their two offspring had been unpleasantly serious. Rose couldn't bear Emily being so unhappy.

Peter sat down and put his hands behind his head, leaning backwards, his long legs stretched under the desk. Rose could see him unwinding.

"Me too," he said with a broad smile. "I feel like today's weather; calm after the storm. You've no idea how much better I feel!"

"Believe me, I have!" Said Rose, putting her bag down. She felt her shoulders descend by a good inch as the tension left them. It was so good to see this man coming down from his aloof persona. The affection and sparkle in his eyes undermined any remaining resentment she had for him.

He might be quite a bit older but he was still very attractive. She put up a hand to brush her long hair back from her face, returning the smile without reserve.

"They are bound to have some clashes and I hope they've both learned from this one," she said. "With a bit of luck they'll be like the rest of the village – picking up the broken slates and making repairs!"

"I'm hoping I don't feel so responsible next time they suffer from a cold front or gale warnings," said Peter. "It's very wearing, isn't it? I think we all ought to celebrate, don't you?"

"What a good idea;" said Rose, "what shall we do? We can talk about that in a minute but first I must tell you: I've had a

291

most interesting sitting with Hermione Olver-Blythe. It's the last one of her by herself and I have decided how I'm going portray her. Also I think I've learned a bit more about what they're intending to do down at Lantrelland."

"I'd better take some notes," said Peter. "And perhaps you should get busy on that canvass," he suggested.

"You are right – but I have to get it all set up first. That's going to take a while. I still have to do various bits of carpentry to get it in the right light; and I'll need some kind of little platform to stand on."

"Would you like me to help? I'm not bad with a hammer and nails. I've even been known to use a saw! Maybe you'll put me up for a few more days?"

"Peter that's kind. Are you sure you can spare the time?"

"I'll give Harry a call to make sure he's not expecting me. Sebastian's got a lot more to find out before he goes back and Emily says she has the rest of the week to herself – so it looks promising!"

§

"That *was* a bright idea of yours," said Emily as she and Sebastian held each other close, smooching around the dance floor at The Hannafore between courses at dinner, later that evening. "Look at your Dad with Rosie! They haven't stopped nattering since we came out."

"It wasn't my idea: it was their own. They seem to be getting on better and it was Dad who wanted some kind of celebration. I had a twinge of worry when I suggested coming here tonight," said Sebastian; "especially when I said 'on us'. I hoped you'd agree, because we hadn't discussed it and it was going to cost quite a lot: all rather on the spur of the moment."

"I was pleased you *did* invite them; it's the first time I've seen them looking friendly towards each other," said Emily. "They seem to have accepted us as a couple now – and you *are* funny: worrying about spending a hundred pounds or so! It's not as though we're penniless!"

"I still haven't come to terms with all that. It's such a huge change and I was anxious not to be making too many unilateral decisions – upsetting you."

"Oh Sebastian!" Emily threw her arms round his neck and kissed him fiercely. "You *are* a darling!" He looked embarrassed.

"Well it's *your* money!"

"No – it's *ours*. We've agreed we'll have a joint account so let's stick to it. Anyway - we're going to be good for the local economy if we go on at this rate," she laughed. "That champagne we had before we came out was the second bottle we've had in two days!"

"And you only had a sip. I'm so thankful you are all right – and that *we're* together again. It was so awful – that row – and it was all my fault."

Emily didn't comment, she simply moved her right hand further up his back and drew herself even closer as they made a gentle turn in time to the music. Resting her head against his chest she began singing along with the band. Sebastian joined in and they celebrated their return to marital bliss. Emily broke the spell.

"Look at them now!" She giggled. Rose and Peter were dancing together as closely as they themselves had been. "How lovely! Do you ….?"

"Don't even think about it," said Sebastian. "It would be too good to be true."

"OK I won't – but I've always wanted Mum to find someone nice. They look right together don't they?"

"Especially in this light! You can't see Dad's wrinkles;" laughed Sebastian.

"Don't drink any more this evening. I don't mind driving and being on the wagon for the babies but I want you in good order for later," said Emily, pressing her hip against his groin as they did another slow turn.

The atmosphere of celebration continued. Everything seemed to be progressing. After the newly-weds had returned to London, Peter stayed long enough to see the outlines of Rose's major painting take shape on the large canvass. He made sure it wasn't going to move, creating a firm frame to support it. The 'podium' as they both called it, even had a hand rail against which she could lean. It had pads of old carpet under its four corners so she could pull it around over the studio floor without scratching.

Each time she stepped up on to it, long after Peter had gone home, she remembered with pleasure their days spent together as the summer made way for autumn. When she painted the top of the painting, keeping her balance by pressing her hip against the hand rail it was as though Peter was there, supporting her. She would look forward to the phone ringing late in the evening after the day's work, when they had both fed themselves and cleared up. It was surprising how much they had to talk about: chatting and exchanging experiences of the day. Peter followed the progress of the painting without actually seeing it – despite Rose's attempts on Skype with the webcam. They gave that up after a couple of tries and she simply described what she had been doing.

§

Sebastian and Lady Merchant held a council of war at the CPRE and, having consulted Rose by phone, decided to drop any action over what was the plainly 'fishy business' of planning permission being granted to development of The Glebe.

"I think it would be far more positive to show our gratitude to the anonymous donor who has bought the Glebe for the National Trust," Lady Merchant told Sebastian. "I'd be very happy to come and attend an official acceptance ceremony if the Trust were to hold one. I think that the action we all took *did* have an affect and some politicians and even civil servants will be glad the development didn't go through. They must have stuck their necks out rather dangerously."

"You're right," said Sebastian. "I don't think it would have taken too much investigation to have brought out some very dubious practices! We hear, though, that much larger schemes are being cooked up, although nothing precise yet. It seems Mr Olver-Blythe is pulling investors together to build a new harbour, village and marina at Lantrelland Bay."

"Goodness, how appalling! I must get my scouts alerted. The word is bound to get out around the City if that's where he's been looking."

"My father's been in Cornwall and confirmed that something's going on but it's all being kept very quiet. What he did learn was that they are preparing very carefully, selling their ideas to influential people and politicians. Olver-Blythe's been spending a lot of time going up and down to London, too. Even my mother-in-law, the artist Rose Johnson, can't find out much and she's doing a portrait of him and his wife. She did hear that Hugh's been wining and dining various government ministers and senior advisors. I'm afraid we're going to have to wait until the planning applications begin to come in. Rosie is keeping a close eye on that side of things, after the last debacle."

"That was a shock, wasn't it? What made it worse was that it added to such inappropriate permissions being given. The word must have got round. We've got cases all round the country. Some landowners, having bought land speculatively, are now coming back with development plans, having seen that Government policy is being 're-interpreted'. I wouldn't be surprised if they didn't want to start prospecting for oil in Windsor Great Park!"

"What a thought," said Sebastian. "Meanwhile all we can do is to be vigilant."

"Quite so – and we must stay in close touch, Sebastian – if you are still prepared to represent us. I understand you may leave this kind of work now you've had that amazing lottery win. You two have become household names!"

Sebastian said that he would be glad to continue with his Lantrelland brief at least until things were settled.

"Although actually, I think my father may take it over! He seems to be spending a lot of time in Polperris and has been working closely with Rose Johnson."

"I feel quite jealous!" Said Lady Merchant. "He's such a nice man!"

"Well if he does take on the brief, you will be seeing more of him!" laughed Sebastian. "I suspect I'll be spending most of my time on the new foundation we are launching soon. I hope you will be able to come."

"I'll certainly try! Now I really must go."

"Me too but it's been good to meet with you again, Lady Merchant. My father sends his regards – and if you will excuse me, later today we have a workshop with the advisory committee of our new foundation – all very exciting."

"You'll have to tell me all about it when we next meet, Sebastian."

§

It had taken several weeks of intensive research and interviewing for Emily and Sebastian to assemble the two teams that would help them spend some of the capital and as much of the interest as they could from their record lottery payout. For the moment they rented a small block of offices in Liskeard, near the station and were commuting from Rose's house in Polperris. They were surprised at how many of the people to whom they offered contracts, wanted to live in the South West. For example the accountant, recruited from one of London's largest charities, with his book-keeper wife, said that they had been longing to move away from the city and be nearer the sea.

The hardest post to fill had been that of chief executive officer. They had no intention of taking on a large staff but needed someone who knew how to manage large budgets. After advertising in the Financial Times they received an application from someone working at the Eden Project, only a few miles down the road near St Austell.

"Look at this one, Emily!" Said Sebastian. "She's been working for Tim Smit for a long time, on the admin side. She was at the Lost Gardens of Heligan first and then at Eden. I bet she knows all the development ropes."

At interview, it emerged that not only did Hilary Snow know all the ropes but all the people at the end of each rope and many more beside.

"But why do you want to leave such a fantastic enterprise?" Asked Emily when Mrs Snow faced the selection panel.

"Our two children have just flown the nest," she told them, "and it's a chance to begin a new phase of our lives. I am very happy at the Eden Project, which is going from strength to strength but it seems like a good opportunity to take on more responsibility, help build something new and exciting but with parallel aims and objectives. I've discussed it with Tim and he agrees – although he says he'll be reluctant to see me leave. It will give him the chance to promote someone else; he says it will be good for me to be stretched a bit. Don't worry, he's not saying I'm coasting but I see what he means: I need more of a challenge, now there's less to think about at home."

It transpired that she was the money-earner in their household. Her husband, a poet and part-time English teacher, enjoyed the role of house-husband and gardener. Their ambition had long been to sell their house in St Austell and move to a smallholding on Bodmin Moor.

"That will be tough, won't it?" Asked Sebastian.

"Not for me, once the house has been done up," said Hilary. "My husband will concentrate on that – if I get this post. Later we can introduce a few livestock. A modern version of 'the good life', we hope."

The panel, too, liked Hilary Snow, who came highly recommended, and after a second interview, followed by lunch with herself and her husband, was duly appointed. The Eden

Project allowed her time off, during her period of notice, to join the selection process at Plan B so that she too, could participate in choosing the rest of the permanent staff.

By the spring of 2013, Plan B for Action was installed in its offices on the edge of Liskeard and Hilary had taken most of the day to day management off the shoulders of Sebastian and Emily. She was proving to be an able replacement for Dot Macdonald, who had recently told the young couple that she felt they were now nicely launched into their new life as 'rich' and although she would be there if they wanted her, she could now make herself available to The Lottery to take on a new winner.

Hilary's appointment was a pleasant surprise for Rose Yi Johnson, too. Rose knew Hilary from when she had been asked to paint some pictures of the huge transparent domes at Eden. The original request was prompted by Rose's enthusiasm for the aims of the project – of raising public awareness of the value of bio-diversity, in the various climates around the world. Everyone liked the paintings she produced and the project displayed prints of them for sale in their souvenir shop. They were snapped up by visitors. Rose became a regular visitor to St Austell, to sketch new views of the project and later, to bring her classes. Her students always enjoyed moving between the steamy tropical heat of one dome to the dry desert of the next – drawing all kinds of exotic plants and finishing up with a meal in the restaurant. It added up to a memorable day-trip.

Sebastian found that within a few weeks, Plan B for Action took up an increasing amount of his time. He and Emily had also been busy finding and then moving into a barn conversion just outside Pelynt, a few miles inland from Polperris.

"It's pronounced 'Plint'," he told his father, describing the new purchase. "We're only just outside the village and there's a field to go with it so we can 'do things' later if we want to: perhaps keep a pony or something."

They spoke regularly, now that Peter had indeed taken on the CPRE's interest in Lantrelland. Plan B had offered to pay for the presentation ceremony when the Church handed the Glebe Field over to the National Trust. It fitted well with the objectives of the new organisation, whose launch was planned for later the same day.

CHAPTER 24

"When it comes to it, Mr Speaker, the Prime Minister is, as usual, all talk and no action," thundered the Leader of the Opposition, the day before the National Trust acceptance of The Glebe Field, the launch of Plan B for Action and an important meeting of the district council at Liskeard. During Question Time, the Prime Minister was being grilled about planning and local government, a sensitive matter being described as a 'bottleneck constricting national recovery'. Professional lobbyists in the pay of Hugh Olver-Blythe and his city backers had been feeding Opposition members plenty of examples of project failures due to planning delays and dithering.

Pointing an accusing finger at the Coalition front bench and waiting for cheers from behind him to subside, the Right Honourable Member bristled with indignation.

"The Government is *not* interested in reducing the horrendous unemployment figures that are giving so many of our young people the wrong start in life! Where there is doubt – they choose the bureaucratic solution and take so long about making decisions on planning that they miss the moment! Yes, Mr Speaker: the time for investment and action passes! They are refusing to give new businesses the opportunities they deserve and the Prime Minister just loves hiding behind out-dated town and country planning laws. Doesn't he realise there's a world financial crisis? Hasn't anyone told him?"

Packed Government benches drowned his next remarks with a storm of protest. Many members took to their feet, hoping to be called to speak but Mr Speaker was in no mood to consider anything except quiet.

"Order, order! The Leader of the Opposition *must* be heard," he shouted, standing to his full five foot six, as both sides roared their defiance. Members sat down, rebuked for the moment but with the Opposition smelling blood. The Honourable Member continued his tirade:

"There are record numbers of people out of work and many companies are facing ruin, yet, time and time again, we see this government turning down appeals for modest and tasteful developments. Businesses can't expand; jobs cannot be created unless development land is freed from petty restrictions. I have examples of projects for renewable energy, tourism and even National Parks that are blocked by bureaucratic rule-books. Honourable Members can doubtless give us many more examples. How shall we ever get Britain back to work? I ask you, Mr Speaker!"

He threw himself back into his seat with gestures of exasperation.

The Prime Minister tried not to look uncomfortable as he rose to the Despatch Box attempting to defend perfectly reasonable laws that had been passed under many previous governments to protect the integrity and heritage value of British countryside. He was, though, on a loser: the media had been baying for faster return to prosperity and bewailing 'austerity Britain'. Now was the time to 'raise the red tape while calling *ready, steady: go!*' That very morning, perhaps not by coincidence, broadsheets had carried editorials demanding Government to be more flexible in its interpretation of the laws that admittedly were so appropriate during periods of economic growth but which were currently impeding Britain's efforts to pull itself up by its bootstraps.

'Let's get ourselves out of the mire – then worry about the niceties of Outstanding Natural Beauty,' said one paper. 'This is a time of national emergency,' thundered another. 'When we're back in the black we can review the rules.'

§

"Perfect timing!"

Hugh Olver-Blythe and his friends were watching Parliament live at their club. "He's got to back off now! Poor David – he'll have to deliver a few punches below the belt and change the subject – listen: here he goes!"

"Mr Speaker, at least our coalition government is showing leadership and we are not advocating lawlessness of any kind. What does the Right Honourable Gentleman want? Is he calling for motorways to be bulldozed through stately homes and beauty spots? What kind of leadership is that? This is typical of what we have all come to expect from the so-called Leader of the so-called Opposition!"

Hugh and his immaculately dressed companions enjoyed a few more minutes of the Prime Minister attacking the Leader of the Opposition's ineptitude and unpopularity, effectively diverting the assault. By that time, however, correspondents had decided on their stories and were hurrying out to file copy and organise interviews. The calls for 'freedom to work' and 'cut all the crap' would reverberate around the media between now and tomorrow.

"Is everything ready for tonight?" Hugh asked Clive.

"Very nearly. I've got the model set up; nearly everyone we invited has agreed to come along and we gave the press their packs over lunch after some great presentations at The Dorchester. Their editors will get it from all directions this evening – business, parliamentary and countryside reporters."

"It's all a bit hairy isn't it?" One of the richer investors was not quite at ease. He had never been very keen on cozying up to The Opposition even if it was temporary. "Everything's happening at once; our launch tonight, the council meeting in Cornwall tomorrow – and the National Trust having a splash too. It could all go pear-shaped!"

"That's not all," said another. "Those do-gooding lottery winners – you know the ones, the wife's foreign – have got some launch down there as well. My spies tell me they've chartered a hospitality carriage on a train to take the press from Paddington. I think they've even rented the Eden Project for the day."

"So much the better," soothed Hugh. "We've got the business press and a few more fund managers coming to our affair. Don't worry, we've put in a lot of ground work with those councillors. A good majority have pledged us their vote: we're offering so much to their constituents but not too much detail: just a general picture. By the time we've finished all the construction they'll love it! Tomorrow with a bit of luck most of the media will go to Cornwall while the Financial Times and the few business correspondents we really want will be with us in Park Lane. We'll give them the full works so everyone will want a bit of equity. Everything's ready to roll. Once we get that permission we can start at once – the floating crane is sitting in Plymouth, the transporters are lined up to carry the granite to Polruan and I'm chartering two coasters to take them round to Lantrelland. Our new headland – as well as the foundations for its built-in tidal power station will be 'above the water' by October. The rest of it will click into place once all the money's signed up. We're offering a hundred jobs straight away with all kinds of economic spin-off. I'm advertising in the local paper this week for people to work on our new road. That all went through with no problem last month after loads of complaints from tourists not being able to get through to the coast path and Lantrelland Bay. Now, gentlemen, I think we can take ourselves off to catch up with our phone-calls. I think it's going to be a busy evening!" He knew what *he* had in mind but it certainly had little to do with phone-calls. His mobile would be switched off before he set out for a certain house of pleasure in Clapham. What a pity the battery had gone flat. He could disappear until the morning.

§

At Polperris the sea was calm as a millpond; the boats in the harbour seemed to be fixed, motionless; their reflections making perfect inverted images. Rose and Peter were sitting on the quay, well wrapped up against the chilly afternoon, recording the scene in their sketch books. Neither was saying much; they had spent the first part of the afternoon preparing Rose's speech for the council meeting next day; until Peter had looked out of the window and seen how everything had stopped moving. It was too good to miss.

"I don't give us much chance of defeating this one, do you?" Rose said. "The other side are making us look like real reactionaries, fighting progress. It's all so unfair!"

"The trouble is they've wrapped it up in a package full of goodies – wind and tidal power, the marine reserve and all that: and they'll go on about all the business possibilities it could bring. I've almost become convinced myself," Peter replied.

"I hope you haven't," retorted Rose. "It's sheer vandalism! That bit of coastline is a real natural gem, unspoiled for centuries."

"But Olver-Blythe has already made a start on the new road they hustled through a couple of months ago. He's got the bit between his teeth and they've been wining and dining the councillors. Their brochures are excellent – from the pictures you might think Lantrelland Harbour and Marina had been there since the Cornish marched off to England to rescue Trelawney in 1688!"

"You know more Cornish history than I do!" Rose was impressed.

Peter happened to look up at the same moment and caught her admiring glance. A buzz of excitement lifted his attention from his drawing and he smiled warmly at her.

"It's only recent, I assure you," he said. "I've been borrowing books off your shelves and learning all kinds of things."

They were trying to make the most of the light before it faded. Peter sketched the outlines of his picture, shading in some of the deepening shadows. He added written notes about the colours, with reminders to help him relive the atmosphere of the scene when he came to reproduce it in the studio.

In recent days during breaks from Rose's council work he had taken every opportunity to get back to his new-found passion. The moment he picked up a pencil or paint brush and began a composition he became immersed in a suspended state of active tranquillity. It wasn't idle or somnolent and never failed to give him drive and impatience, mixed with lust for colour, shape and mood as the picture in his mind began to take place on the white paper or canvas. Once started it was hard to stop, referring back to his sketchbook, transferring its images and reminders of the scene he was recreating. He kept meaning to stop but couldn't resist the outline of just one more boat; a few more ripples; or lightening that green to push those trees back from the foreground. Hours would flick by. He didn't resent Rose offering advice on the shape of a boat's hull – so difficult to get right – or asking him a question as she worked away on her papers. It just brought him back to the present for a few moments before returning to his contented focus on the picture into which he was downloading his emotions. This afternoon he had only a few minutes in which to capture those mirror images. In a few weeks the sketch would bring it all back to him as he started a painting back in Putney.

"I wish I'd known how satisfying this was," he said, "despite the cold feet."

"You wouldn't have been so rich and famous if you had," quipped Rose without taking her eye off her sketchbook.

"I might have! Who knows?"

"Actually, you might," admitted Rose. "If you had discovered your talent early enough; but I don't think you have a big enough ego to have become a really famous artist. One needs to be absolutely convinced of one's own greatness before becoming truly great – like Picasso or Salvador Dali."

"My wife used to say I *was*, sometimes – *completely* convinced!" Peter smiled to himself as he remembered spats with Françoise, which usually ended up with laughter and, until her illness, embraces and kisses.

"I can see what she meant," said Rose. "The first time we met I thought you considered yourself God's right-hand man. I'd only met Sebastian and expected you to be as obliging as he was – but my first impression was that you weren't – at all!"

"You had 'gone off' *both* of us by the time we met," countered Peter.

305

"And with good reason: *he* had kidnapped my lovely daughter! And *you* had supported him! If you hadn't then turned out to be such a good student, I would have expelled you within a day or two!"

"I hope you don't feel like that now," Peter said, smiling. "We've made it up, haven't we?"

"Only after I saw both of you eating humble pie during the storm back in the summer. That was when I realised you were only human. Since then you have proved to be most useful!" She gave him a cheeky look and saw him chuckle.

"So I might have been reprieved;" he chuckled. "Shall we leave this now and go for a walk? These garden chairs are hard and I can hardly see what I'm supposed to be drawing. We might take some exercise and be fresher for tomorrow? I'm beginning to freeze."

§

It was one of those sunsets that was almost impossible to paint. As they strode along the cliff path towards Lantrelland, the western sky was brilliantly red; the sea mirroring each cloud. The sun, almost touching the horizon, created a shining path across the sea as far as the rocks below them. It was a path of diamonds.

"We'd better not go too far – unless you've got a torch," said Rose.

"I have, actually," said Peter. "One of those little LED key-rings. It's marvellous. We've got about half an hour before it's dark, anyway – let's go quick and look at Lantrelland across the bay – before it disappears under concrete and plastic boats."

"It had better not! I can't believe the Council will let that happen. It's going to be tough but we've got a good case and I've got my best cloche hat ready for tomorrow's presentation: I'm determined to wear it! Let's hope I can impress them; and that the meeting doesn't go on too long. The arrangements are all a bit tight for time. First the planning; then National Trust and The Glebe; finally Plan B."

"When are all the media arriving?" Asked Peter.

"I thought you told me half past two," said Rose, laughing. "Between us we ought to know! Let's hope the train isn't late and the coach people remember to pick them up. I'm going to the station so I can ride back with Emily: we always enjoy a good chat between there and home; and Sebastian's going to make sure the coach goes to the right place. It wouldn't do to lose all those journalists. Then after the Glebe we can all go by coach to the Eden reception and our launch."

"I wonder whether Hugh Olver-Blythe will be coming to any of it," said Peter. "They must have invited him – local dignitary and all that."

"I don't think he is. Hermione told me she will be representing him. He's got some function up in London which he can't miss. Actually, she doesn't believe it and thinks he's having an affair. We're not inviting her to Plan B, though. Not quite her 'thing'."

"I thought you said she was pregnant. You all seemed quite well disposed towards one another, last I heard. Has she been confiding in you again?"

"Yes she has but I suspect that's all over now. We're back to being more formal again."

"What happened?" Peter puffed a little as they climbed the last hill before Lantrelland Bay came in sight.

"We got quite close for a while and exchanged a few confidences but when it came to politics she didn't like my ideas at all. She called me a rabid lefty! The atmosphere has been a bit chilly since but we're still civil, though I'll be glad when I've finished and can collect the cheque. Let's sit on that bench up there and watch the sun. Isn't it glorious?"

The sun was indeed blood red, disappearing fast. As they climbed up to the bench, a couple of steps above the path, Rose turned to look and missed her footing. She flung out her arms and toppled backwards, finding herself caught unceremoniously by Peter who had been standing close behind her admiring her figure.

"Are you all right?" Peter asked, anxiously. "Have you hurt your ankle?"

It took Rose a few seconds to get over losing her balance and finishing up in such a strong embrace. She tried to gather her wits: falling over was something she never did and it had given her quite a fright. Her legs seem to have lost all their strength and she wasn't sure whether it was because of a sprain, or finding herself pressed against such a solid chest, his strong hands perilously close to her breasts. He was carrying her with ease. She found her voice.

"I think I'm OK, thanks. But I feel so stupid! I should have looked where I was treading."

Peter, his face still touching her hair, made no effort to release her, waiting for her to take command of her legs, which she did, planting them safely back on the path. She nearly slipped again and Peter's reflex to save her finished up as an embrace.

Peter breathed in deeply, his face still near hers. Close up she looked even younger. Her complexion was without blemish. When surprised, she looked even more lovely.

Rose was confused. Who was this man? No longer the formal, proud and courtly gentleman – untouchable celebrity lawyer and official advisor to the CPRE – but a sure-footed athlete holding her in his arms as though she was a feather.

She had become more aware of his good looks and the twinkle in his eye over recent visits and was finding him far less irritating than before. Neither was he any longer the crestfallen father of her son-in-law. This new man reacted fast and was strong. His touch was electrifying: it sent tingles to her hair roots. How long was it since she had had feelings like this? It was as though Spring had suddenly taken over her body – out of season.

It dawned all of a sudden: she really fancied this man! She disentangled herself and mounted the last two steps up to the bench, pretending nothing had happened.

In retrospect they remembered it as the moment their relationship changed. During the past few months he had become increasingly attracted to Rose. He had photographed her from several angles on the pretext of 'practising for a portrait'. He was thus able to look frequently at her image, which he did surreptitiously on the train or alone in his room. He was fascinated by those Oriental eyes, sensuous mouth, peachy skin and tranquil expression.

They had danced together at the Hannafore, quite close – but lightly. That was when he picked up the floral scent of her discreet perfume. He recognised it again now. On that occasion they had been shy though the first signs of physical response had begun to stir. Neither had felt it appropriate to take the relationship further, mostly because of Rose's prickly resentment of any dominant male but also because of Peter's memories of Françoise. Such feelings were disloyal even though she herself had said she wanted him to find someone else when she was gone.

This evening it was all suddenly different. Adrenalin flashed through their veins as Rose's stumble flipped them into emergency mode. Their strong, supple bodies reacted fast and effortlessly with Peter becoming sure-footed as a wrestler and Rose, lithe and agile. Landing in his safe embrace she felt the power in his body. In her reflex to save herself she grabbed his upper arms, which were warm and firm as steel.

She hadn't felt like this about him before. He was handsome and dignified, yes; but not someone she would wish to ravish. The dance at the Hannafore had been fun but apart from the occasional pressure of her breasts against his chest, she had not felt any particular excitement. She now had a strong urge to kiss him. He too longed to lean over and feel her perfect mouth on his but felt it might be taking unfair advantage. She had backed away, letting go of his arms, though her hands still wanted to hold them. She had resisted the urge to press herself against him despite the thrills coursing through her body.

As they sat on the bench, shading their eyes from the setting sun, there was suddenly an awkward silence. Peter took the next initiative.

309

"It's a breathtaking sight, isn't it?" He felt bold enough to take her hand – hoping it wouldn't be withdrawn. It wasn't.

Before, Rose would have been outraged at this invasion of her body but her hand seemed to have a mind of its own as it softly entwined fingers with his. She felt herself melting into a state of irresponsible lust.

"Mm, fantastic!" She was fighting to keep her breath steady and willing her heart to slow down. The dry warmth of his hand, which was now responding to the movement of her fingers, undermined her willpower and she was unable to add any further comment on the scene.

Her quietness and his delight at being able to hold her unresisting hand fed Peter's aggressive need to take her once more in his arms and crush her to him. He still resisted and forced himself to become more rational. Without taking his eyes off the last of the sun as it sank below the horizon he asked:

"How can such an adorable woman as you have remained single for so long?"

"Oh I don't know," she said. "I've always been too busy looking after Emily – and making a living – but I've had my moments!" She laughed.

"Well plainly: you had Emily – and what a lovely girl she is! Dare I ask what happened to her father?"

"I have no idea! We were yachts passing in the night – delightful though it was: at a party. I didn't think to ask for his address – I guess we were both slightly high at the time. I knew he was respectable; he was cultured and considerate too. We both let down our guards. I hadn't been expecting to sleep with anyone; neither of us were carrying any other form of protection; there was no worry about AIDS in those days – and apart from a slight headache next morning, that was all I remembered until a couple of months later."

"But.... Emily's been off your hands for quite some time now, hasn't she?"

"Well I suppose she has, although we're great friends and talk a lot. That's why I was so shattered when she suddenly told me she was getting married *and* was pregnant too! I could see her making all the mistakes that I made, only worse!"

"Do you still feel like that?"

Rose's hand began its movement in his again. It snuggled into his broad palm as she sifted her thoughts.

"Not now actually; not since they had their bust-up. It seemed to show that they could survive some of the ups and downs of a long-term relationship. They've both grown up a lot in the last few months and I must say it's a pleasure to see them together. They enjoy each other's company so much; and share ideals and ambitions. I just hope that parenthood won't spoil things for them before they've had time to get know each other properly."

"But what about *you*, Rosie? Are you missing your best friend?"

"Actually I'm not! I don't feel I've lost her and although I've never thought of it in these terms I seem to have picked up two more good friends – despite my initial resentment! But what about you? Sebastian and you had grown very close after losing Françoise. Now he's moved out, you must be feeling deserted."

"Well to be honest, I don't either. I seem to have met up with two gorgeous women, one who has enchanted and captured my son; and another who has almost ended my career as a criminal barrister by diverting my attention in two ways."

"Oh?"

"Well: by introducing me to a wonderful adventure into colour and shape; and by propelling me into to full-time study of a very beautiful, talented and fiery woman – of Oriental and European descent – you might know her!"

"We ought to start back, before it's so dark we *both* start falling over, don't you?" Said Rose, breathless and now in a hurry.

"You're right! Let's go!"

CHAPTER 25

"Firstly, I'd like to welcome Sarah Harrington and all of you to our first 'marketing checkout'," said Sebastian. "It's hard to believe that Plan B has been up and running for only a month but time flies and we've gone with it for a flying start. Hilary, Emily and I have left the arrangements for today to Sarah as our Head of Marketing and, once I've shut up, she'll take the chair for this morning's brief get-together.

"This exercise is to scan ideas and plans before they leave 'the shop'," he continued. "Plan B is selling ideas to the world and we want to be sure they're as good as they can be – fresh and carrying the right message. Are they wholesome and securely packed? Will they be able to sustain knocks and clumsy handling after they've left the store? Will consumers, whether they are academics, investors, governments, the United Nations, or landless peasants understand and go along with our concepts before applying them in the field? That's what we're here to check: so, Sarah: introduce us to our first 'shopping experience' then later we'll face the sliding doors into the harsh world of public scrutiny. You are in the chair!"

The Trenleven's had been lucky to recruit Sarah from the American software company in which she had prospered and progressed so fast. She was taking quite a cut in salary to join Plan B – a result of her own personal career reassessment. At thirty eight years old she had recently met a man to whom she had been strongly attracted. He too, had been smitten: but not for long. He complained she was not prepared to allocate him any time from her mad round of meetings, flights and incessant phone calls and had soon bowed out of her life into the waiting arms of a younger, less successful woman. It had been a blow to her pride as well as her heart and she was now facing the lonely prospect of future promotion and eventual transfer to the USA headquarters – without a life partner.

She had amassed a healthy bank balance, been everywhere, met all kinds of exciting people and spent many evenings with friends, going out for drinks or a run; but still finding no one permanent with whom to share emotions, spend leisure time or physical union.

Plan B had been the beneficiary of a 'review' that Sarah had given herself to plan the next five years. One Saturday morning, she decided that her current life balance was crazy – all work and no play. She decided she was indeed becoming dull. The discovery of a grey hair had finally precipitated her resignation from the multi-national money-making machine. Her new ambitions included buying a house in Cornwall, where she had spent many happy holidays as a child; getting a job that was not all about cash and 'growth' but which contributed to the well-being of humanity. Most of all, she wanted to be part of a community where she met people 'outside work' and could build lasting relationships.

She saw Plan B's advertisement online and sent off an enquiring mail, with a summary of her CV. Hilary Snow snapped it up and showed Emily and Sebastian. From early in the ensuing interview all three could see that Sarah was exactly what Plan B needed. As well as fast intelligence she was elegantly turned out; at ease with senior businessmen and women; and had an impressive track record. Her conclusions about the state of the world were the same as theirs and she understood the ethos of Plan B instantly. Best of all was her creativity. Since joining, she had already come up with some sparkling ideas to get the messages of progressive development across to the world. Her voice and demeanour was full of confidence:

"Thanks Sebastian. Before we go on, could you just turn him round a little, Hilary, so we can all see him? "Sarah pointed to the monitor marked 'London'." Can you see *us*, Seb?

"I can, thanks, and the sound's good. I like the suit, Hilary – you look formidable!"

"I'm not sure how to take that! I'm still caring and gentle but woe betide any journalist who starts getting uppity at our launch, now I'm in my uniform." Hilary said as she went round the table to adjust the monitor. "Is that better everyone?"

"It's a bit of a squeeze but we're all here, so let's make a start," said Sarah, with authority. "Sebastian, I know you have to leave shortly – would you like to begin?"

Plan B's staff were all present; booked for the next hour into the cyber-studio, which also served as the boardroom. The building was a converted chapel with car-parking for only two vehicles, reserved for visitors – who until now had been mostly electronic engineers making everything work. Staff-members who did not arrive by electric bike or scooter, either walked to the office when they needed to be there, or, like Hilary, were dropped off by spouse or partner.

The chapel had everything they needed: a reception area with computer access points and phones for use by visitors. It had a coffee machine, an adjoining lavatory; and even a quiet room with comfortable recliner to allow the travel-weary to indulge in a power-nap. The rest of the bottom floor had more offices while the former vestry made an ample store-room. Stairs led to the mezzanine floor with workstations for those who needed to be 'in the office'. On the top floor, open for the full length of the chapel, a glass-partitioned office at one end had desks for Hilary, Emily, Sebastian; and one for Sarah. The rest of the space, under the high, varnished wooden roof, now with added Velux sky-lights, formed the boardroom-studio where they were all sitting around the long table with cameras, lights and microphones all switched on. Of the bank of four monitors, only one was active and Sebastian could be seen facing his laptop in Emily's flat, which they had decided to keep as a London base.

Most days, it was Hilary who arrived first as her partner included her in his regular rounds. He was well organised – some days delivering produce, others shopping or stocking up at the farm co-operative or builder's merchant. He made sure Hilary was at her desk by eight-thirty, which suited her, being an early-bird; and was prompt to collect her there at six, if she had not phoned to tell him to find her at the hair-dresser or supermarket.

314

Other members of staff had previously worked in Plymouth or Truro and were enjoying a new lifestyle without commuting. Plan B's team was high-powered and ready to engage.

§

"I'd just like to run through today's arrangements before I go off to Paddington to welcome the media," said Sebastian.

"We'll be there with the coach to meet you all at Liskeard," said Sarah. "Your father and Rose will be there too. The Council meeting should be over by then. We'll leave someone here to answer the phones."

"I spoke with Emily a minute ago," said Sebastian. "She's down at Lantrelland. The marquee in The Glebe is looking good and the caterers are setting up for drinks and buffet lunch. She's going to meet the National Trust People and keep them amused until we all arrive. Can you try her on Skype? You've got a spare monitor, haven't you?"

"We have," said Hilary, "and she's expecting us, so hang on a moment."

"OK – but while you're doing that, has everyone seen the news and papers? Apart from a favourable weather forecast, the developers have been pulling out all the stops. There's one headline saying 'Green millionaires try to block new jobs'. They're labelling us as NIMBYs and we're going to have to fight for our credibility. The Opposition is hammering Government for not allowing new business and not keeping their promises about reducing red tape: usual stuff!"

"I heard all that, Seb – hello everyone!" Emily's face had appeared on the second monitor."

"Hello – and go ahead, Emily," said Sarah.

"Well I don't think there's any point in trying to start a slanging match with them, trying to answer every accusation. I feel we must avoid appearing negative but emphasise that we have something better to offer," said Emily; "*without* sacrificing historic scenery and buildings. We're *not* just knocking commercial progress. We're welcoming some of the proposals being put forward – like the marine park and some of the renewable energy projects but I believe the public is fed up with the machinations of big business. I think we can offer editors something more inspiring for their readers. We've got some superb stories for them: the Glebe being saved; the launch of Plan B, which is going to bring exciting job opportunities in Cornwall and around the world; and then the projects themselves. So we've already got loads to show people, haven't we?"

"We have," said Sarah. "For a start the work on Lantrelland Church roof has begun. We've got cameras set up with feeds for TV crews and that can go out live or be filmed. We've cordoned off part of The Glebe so they can get close-ups of the rare plants and all the beautiful flowers that are just coming out; and Miss Weeks is lined up for interviews about the history of the church and its surroundings. She looks great with her pony and her donkey standing each side – they won't budge from her. Lady Merchant and some officials from the CPRE are there – they'll be good for some comment. Then when it comes to Plan B, we've prepared plenty of press packs and video clips for them to include in news bulletins or current affairs programmes."

"Could you just give us a run-through of what the press can expect? Then I can prime a few people on the train," said Sebastian.

"The theme for today is to establish Plan B as an organisation that promotes positive action. Each of our short features begins with *solutions* rather than problems and we've commissioned teams to go out and film them. Several are ready for showing. That in itself has already created work for local professionals – camera crews, photographers, film editors, writers and directors who have been going around the world bringing back reports on people and projects that are contributing to ecological stability. For example, the backing we're giving to promote 'Ahipa' in Africa."

"Are you sure that's the right way round for our presentation?" Emily asked. I thought we were going to first paint a picture of *why* these projects are so urgent?"

"Yes indeed," said Hilary. "I was taking that as read but we're keeping it short: people are fed up with gruesome warnings. We're starting with a realistic reminder of what climate change means to the people who are actually losing the land they stand on. The clip we've got of Kiribass disappearing below the waves of the Pacific is pretty dramatic."

"Do people know such a country really exists?"

"I think that will add to the impact – hardly anyone's heard of it. A group of Pacific atolls with a name that's written as Kiribati and pronounced Kiribass – where the population is trying to work out what to do as the waters rise. None of their islands is more than a few feet above sea level. President Anote Tong is talking about 'migration with dignity' and he's negotiating to buy large areas of land on Vanua Levu Island – part of Fiji's territory – a thousand miles from Kiribass."

"What are they going to do? Move there?"

"That's one option – at least for some of the population. Another might be to take earth and rock from there to raise the level of sea defences; and another might be to use the land on which to grow food for the people on what's left of their home islands. It's a terrifying prospect."

"And we're going to show clips about that at the launch?"

"Yes – the Penzance crew we commissioned finished editing them yesterday. They've only been back from the Pacific ten days and will be there in person to answer questions."

"So it's all going to be very newsworthy;" said Hilary.

"Very! Sebastian's presentation starts with that story, plus a load of shocking statistics about the urgency of what we're trying to achieve. Then we move on to Ahipa."

"What's that again?" Asked Hilary.

"A great new food crop – well, new to most of us," said Sarah. "Emily read about it in *Appropriate Technology*. It's a root crop from South America and was important even before the Inca civilisation. Scientists at 'CIP', The Potato Research Centre in Peru, are breeding from the three main types to produce a high quality food for African conditions. Farmers in Asia and the Pacific have been growing it for centuries but it could be what they need in drought-stricken sub-Saharan countries. It's a legume – which helps produce its own fertiliser in the soil, and has long vines like beans or sweet potatoes. You can grow it up poles or as a mat over the ground, smothering out weeds. We're going to be following how CIP sets up research projects around Africa. After that, if it all works out, we will prepare news features in several languages for TV and radio stations across Africa, the Middle East and India."

"And CIP knows about all this?"

"Yes – we're in touch with a Dr Gruneberg, a plant breeder there, who's been enthusiastic about Ahipa since he first heard of it in 1988. He says the roots are delicious eaten raw but they can be cooked and processed – using all kinds of recipes. They contain lots of energy, like potato, but they're a good source of minerals and vitamins too. When raw they are crunchy – a bit like apple; and go well in salads – or when cooked, they soften, like cassava or sweet potato. When it goes to seed, the seeds can be used as a natural insecticide too. It's an amazing crop!"

"That's a positive story!" Hilary is impressed.

"Yes and we've got photos to hand out with background material," said Emily. "I'm hoping that the Eden Project will even have some Ahipa plants to show everyone, when we go on there this evening. They said they would try."

"I'm afraid I'm going to have to leave in five minutes," said Sebastian. "I don't want to be late."

"Are you on your bike?"

"I shall be in a minute. I'm sure you can run through the rest of the presentation without me – but I'll see you later!"

§

"Welcome to the Eden Project!" Sebastian hailed the assembled media and guests, standing amongst olive trees, palms and a clump of evergreen citrus. What a long day it's been so far! I hope you are not tired out, assailed by so much news and propaganda – because I think you will agree we've kept the best until last. Are you finding the climate in this the Mediterranean Biome to your liking? You will be able to visit the rainforest – where it's much warmer and rather sticky – or the project's other giant climate bubbles, after supper, which follows this short presentation. Then finally we will take you back to Plymouth and you can doze on the train back to London. Follow us now, please, up to the restaurant where you can enjoy a drink; and we'll tell you what Plan B is all about."

Emily and he had wanted the visitors to experience the inside of one of the great domed conservatories before it got too dark so that they could realise the huge scale of the construction. Pictures might make Tim Smit's Eden look like a bunch of bubbles in a quarry but when you were there it put things into perspective, transporting one to other continents. They now led the way out of the biome and across a covered quadrangle to the dining area with lavishly set tables, each place labelled. Sarah had organised it so that, as she put it, 'the hacks won't all get together and gossip'. She had split them up, mixing them with independent film directors, National Trust guests and local dignitaries. Peter Trenleven, Rose Johnson, Dot Macdonald and Miss Weeks were carefully placed next to selected journalists; the harbour master from Polperris had been invited, along with leading fishermen and pleasure-boat owners.

The launch was costing a packet but it was part of Plan B's strategy of 'making it memorable while the iron's hot'.

It had been agreed that Sebastian was the best public speaker and once everyone was comfortably seated, he stood to make his address. Behind him, a screen unrolled from the ceiling; lights dipped and a spotlight focussed attention on him.

"Ladies and gentlemen, friends and in-laws," he began, allowing a few moments for a murmur of amusement at his formality and hint of fun.

"Just imagine what it was like for us to casually drop by a newsagent's shop in Islington to 'buy our next lottery ticket', more or less knowing that at best we might have won a tenner: and then what actually happened. For the next few days life was mad! We had hit a record jackpot – two hundred and four million pounds: unbelievable! What do you *do* when something like that happens? We had to find out! Thank goodness we had Dot Macdonald from the Lottery to guide us. Dot please wave! We owe so much to you – helping us keep our feet on the ground. I don't know who you are mentoring at the moment but whoever it is – they are in good hands – thank you so much, Dot." He paused and led warm applause.

"One thing we did not want was to burden our children – who we don't have yet – with all that money; having seen what happens to trustafarians in other families – not needing to work but not knowing what to do with their lives. At the time we thought we might be expecting a baby – although now we know there are *two* on the way and I won't ask Emily to stand up, disturbing the family."

He had Emily's permission to say this and she waved cheerily as he turned and bowed to her.

"Both of us have long been concerned about the way the world is going and we are now witnessing the predictions of many scientists and observers beginning to come true. The human race is on the edge of catastrophe and yet many companies, governments and individuals still continue to pursue profit, riches and power relentlessly, blind to the consequences for our planet. That's Plan A, in which we destroy the eco-system on which we *all* depend – the intricate collage of air, water, soil and other life forms. It simply cannot continue – except at the cost of millions of lives and untold hardship to all of us.

"We've always been told that 'money talks' and we wanted to say our piece – but when it came to it, the money we had won was only peanuts! Real money – such as amassed by people like Bill Gates and Warren Buffet – cannot be won in a lottery, so we had to scale down our ideas and, with help from family and colleagues, our 'Plan B for Action' evolved. It's small; it's based in East Cornwall; it gives us a job and, we hope, a bit more say in what happens to the world of our children and grandchildren.

"The basis for Plan B is 'think global and act local'. We can't change the world but we can contribute to positive change here in Cornwall while working for the spread of useful and practical knowledge more widely. We are about to enjoy a lavish supper but we acknowledge that millions of people won't eat at all tonight. We here are all very lucky but Emily and I have had the most *amazing* stroke of luck and we want to influence the fortunes of at least some of those who have *not* yet been so lucky. As we see it, 'good luck' needs a little help."

After Sebastian's up-beat opening, he now surprised everyone by a complete change of tone.

"I would like to have begun this evening's proceedings with a taste of victory – but it is not to be. I have to report a defeat! What a way to start: and it's not even our first. Today saw the second of our two failures to conserve the Cornish environment. The first was when an ancient meadow, The Glebe Field at Lantrelland – supposedly protected by law – was about to be sacrificed for 'development'. Inexplicably, the planning committee at the council *gave* the permission. Luckily that battle has now been avoided, as you heard this afternoon, with the Parish of Lantrelland bequeathing the land to the National Trust, whose representatives are with us this evening – and I'm sure they are as happy as we are about this bit of luck! Where are you?"

From around the restaurant various hands waved and there was applause at the mention of the short ceremony everyone had witnessed at the meadow earlier.

"The second defeat was this very morning and I have to say – devastating. You know about it and I need not go into detail but I could hardly believe my ears when Councillor Johnson phoned to say permission had been given for a new village and marina to be built at Lantrelland Bay – completely transforming it into a commercial zone, with a man-made headland, mock traditional cottages and quays. Instead of heritage coastline these wild and untamed cliffs and beach are now to become like Paignton or

Weymouth." Sebastian paused: when he continued it was with anger:

"We have been *stunned* by this decision. Not least by its apparent finality. The developers seem to have obtained the backing of government departments, the press and financiers from the City of London. The current climate of European recession has enabled certain people to manipulate the system and push through something that makes Prince Charles' ten 'carbuncles of awful planning and design' look like pimples!

"The planning committee has allowed classifications, such as Site of Special Scientific Interest and Area of Outstanding Natural Beauty – which should have made the area safe from development – to be brushed aside like trivia. How can this have happened? Whether we like it or not, this has dumped a cause into our lap that we cannot ignore if we are going to 'act locally and think globally'. We *have* to fight this decision – although it's going to be a rearguard action, now it has gained so much impetus. We have been working closely with the Campaign to Protect Rural England – first over the Glebe and lately, over the threat of this new development: and we have failed. I repeat: what a way to start!"

There was an embarrassed silence. Sebastian looked dejected and even Emily was concerned that he may not be able to continue. She took his hand and looked up to him anxiously. The moment was captured by a photographer crouching by one of the nearest tables. It would feature in some of the papers next day with the headline 'Disappointed Lottery Winners'.

Gloom pervaded the room and people wondered what was going to happen next. Was he really saying that Plan B was a non-starter? It was so uncomfortable that some people considered slipping out to find a bar and distance themselves from the depressing mood – until Sebastian shocked everyone by banging the table angrily and declared:

"But it is *not* defeat! This failure is going to harden up everything at Plan B: like tempering steel. It's what we needed to make us realise we are going to have to be tough enough to take a few knocks. We are *not* going to let this incongruous and illegal decision go through. We are going to back the conservationists and those members of the local planning committee who opposed it and we are going to pursue this matter until it is over-turned.

"I know we shall be branded as 'against progress' and that are preventing honest folk getting work but what has happened is helping to define what Plan B is all about. We shall prove that we do *not* oppose 'development' *per se* but we do oppose 'inappropriate development'. Even in the scheme that has been pushed through today there are some aspects that we would support – and if we win the appeal we shall certainly help those to be fulfilled – such as the marine-life reserve and the wave energy ideas."

Sebastian was working his audience as though he were defending an innocent client, with commanding style and convincing argument. It was now time to lift the spirits and put some pace back into proceedings.

"More important than opposition to bad projects is what Plan B can do for fresh and positive thinking. My colleague Sarah Harrington will now show you some short film clips and commentaries on some truly inspiring projects in different parts of the world. You will see that they all connect with us here in Cornwall. For example, new food crops, which you can learn about here at the Eden Project; film and reports made by crews from Penzance and Newquay; and educational resources in many languages, designed and illustrated here locally. We agree that 'every picture tells a thousand words' and much of our work is going to be on television, film and computer screens.

"Finally, ladies and gentlemen, and before I hand over to Sarah – and don't worry, she's promised to keep you no longer than a few minutes – I will answer that question that you must have been asking yourselves. Has today's defeat knocked Plan B off course? Has even bigger money over-ruled fantastic luck and positive resolve? No it hasn't! It's what we needed to show us what we are up against!"

Loud applause prompted a host of restaurant staff to descend with champagne and soft drinks.

CHAPTER 26

"I don't feel like working on this portrait – even though it is my biggest and most lucrative ever," said Rose. "I'm so fed up! I've a good mind to throw it in the harbour. I can't stand that man; and I've gone off his wife!"

She and Peter, both glass in hand, were standing in front of the painting, after midnight, exhilarated by the day's mad dashes from station to Glebe Field, the Eden Project and finally back to Polperris, having dropped Emily and Sebastian off in Pelynt.

"To have Hugh Olver-Blythe sneering down at me *in my own house* is almost too much to bear!" Rose pulled a long nose and stuck out her tongue at the haughty face on the portrait.

"Well you have two alternatives," laughed Peter. "You can change his expression and make him look shifty; or you could take a bit of paper and sticky tape and cover his face until you deliver the painting. Even better, you could paint the price you are being paid on the paper, first!"

"My sympathies lie entirely with Hermione despite her being another right-wing psychopath! She has to put up with him in the flesh. When I think what he and his cronies must have been up to, to get blank-sheet planning permission it makes my blood boil!"

"We're not going to let him get away with it, are we, Rosie?"

"How can we stop him? They even had a message of endorsement from a minister of state as though they were doing the whole nation a favour."

"Whatever the political pressures are, the law is still there and unless Parliament changes it – or unless Brussels legislation, which Britain must have agreed to, over-rules it – that law has to be respected and it's up to us to make sure it is. I'm sure the CPRE will want to take up cudgels over this one and I'd be happy to represent them. I can afford it now: my pension's begun to come in and we're taking on more young blood at the chambers. I'm in an ideal position – having Harry Potter and all of them to do the work while I play Sir Galahad; and since all the family seems to be moving down here I'll be looking for a house too. I might even be able to do some baby sitting!"

"Emily's going to need some of that, I suspect," said Rose. "She and Sebastian are so wrapped up in Plan B I worry that the twins will be neglected."

"That's a bit harsh isn't it? The poor children haven't been born yet and the parents haven't had chance to prove themselves. I'm sure Emily will make a great mother – especially if she's anything like you." He made the last remark with sincerity while taking her hand.

Rose felt herself blushing. Any closeness that had begun to develop between the two of them had been, so far, unspoken. Since dancing together, when their physical contact had revived feelings that had been ignored and suppressed for so long, they were less wary of each other; more relaxed and not averse to exchanging a polite kiss on arrival and departure. Rose now met him off the train at Liskeard rather than wait impatiently at home. Her excuse was that it gave them the chance to catch up on business but the truth was that she couldn't wait to see him.

"You've done a splendid job, bringing up Emily: she's a delightful girl and I'm so happy she and Sebastian are married."

"It was all too quick for me and I'm still half-holding my breath that they won't suddenly realise it was all a big mistake," said Rose. "When the babies are born it's going to be a testing time for their relationship. Sebastian can't expect the attention he gets from Emily now: she's going to be busy with the twins."

On an impulse Peter put down his drink on the work surface between the tubes of paint and swept her into his arms. He held her close, and stroked her long hair.

"We've got to let them go, Rosie," he said softly. "They're grown ups and we can trust them. I promise you that Sebastian is not just some kind of travelling stud who's going to leave Emily while he goes off to find some other young girl to impregnate! He loves babies! He's always been a real softy for them. It's just that you have always had to take so much responsibility. You've got to get used to having freedom to do what *you* want, without having to guard Emily all the time. You're not 'a single mother' any longer: you are simply 'single', starting a new life – and I want to be part of it, if you will allow me even if I *am* being a cradle snatcher!"

That last remark broke any tension that Rose may have felt at being seized in these strong arms. She laughed, relaxing against the broad chest and putting her arms around him, shamelessly pressing herself against him.

"Anyone would think I was some teenager! I don't feel any younger than you and I'm excited there are going to be babies around – and that they'll be as much yours as mine."

She reached up, standing on tiptoes to kiss him passionately on the mouth. He lifted her off her feet as the kissing went on. They needed to be closer and even closer; taking in each other's scent, tasting each other, face against face, hands touching and stroking, caressing and fondling. It was Rose who broke away and, taking Peter's hand, pulled him towards the door and upstairs.

Moonlight gave enough light for them to see each other hastily taking off most of their clothes. Rose pulled back the duvet and nimbly got underneath it. Peter followed, taking her once more into his arms. There was no stopping either of them now; their desire for each other was enflamed by the sensation of their near-naked bodies touching as they revelled in the sensations of heat, impatience and sheer lust. Shedding their last symbols of modesty, pushing discarded underwear down the bed, each felt the years drop away as they came together. Rose was aware of the strong shoulders and tight bottom that she was scanning with her hands and Peter, pinning her to the bed, kissing her breasts, was young again, aroused by their firmness and pertness; thrilled and provoked as she raised herself, hungry for him to become part of her, to fill her and give her his all. She reached down and took hold of his erection, guiding him towards her melting vulva, moistening him against herself.

Peter could hold back no longer, he pressed down, feeling himself slip inside her. He resisted the urge to thrust hard and

326

fast, waiting until he felt her relax, allowing him to move deeper and deeper until she closed tight around him, taking short breaths and murmuring his name. For a few moments they lay motionless until Rose's body began to pulse and he responded with the tiniest movements – up and down. Neither of them could suppress their cries of relief as they both came to orgasm with such power and persistence that, hearing each others cries and gasps, they both had to laugh with amusement and joy.

"Wonderful!" Gasped Peter. "Rosie – you are just wonderful! I'd never dreamed….."

"Now you come to mention it, neither had I!" Rose planted just one more kiss on the face touching hers.

"I have to tell you one thing," Peter was serious again.

"Oh no! Nothing bad, I hope?"

"Well, two things, actually."

"Go on."

"The first is that I love you; and have done ever since you opened the door to me here the first time."

"I approve of that; and you have finally convinced me that I love you too," she said. "It took some time before I realised you weren't some great pontiff from the Eternal City but now I just want to consume you and keep you all to myself! And for your information you feel like a twenty year-old in my arms: your performance is just what a girl wants! What's the other thing?"

"I've never had the snip: no vasectomy. As far as I know, I'm still fertile and do not fire blanks."

Rose put her hands on his shoulders and pushed him up, looking stern.

"And you didn't tell me beforehand! You cad!"

"You didn't ask! And you didn't tell me whether you are still in working order, either. Are you?"

"I don't see why not: I'm regular as clockwork. I'm only forty three - nearly"

"So what have we done?" Peter rolled off her but kept her close. He touched the end of her neat nose affectionately with his forefinger.

"Certainly not set an example to either of our offspring: as if they needed it!"

"I just love your face," said Peter, resting on his elbow so he could look down on her in the moonlight streaming through the window.

"Even though I'm half foreign?"

"What's foreign? One in four people in the whole world looks more like you than me: and I think you and Emily are two of the most beautiful of all those. If we have just made a baby, I hope she's a girl and looks like you!"

"Do you *want* a baby? Because if not, I can take the morning-after pill."

"I'd *love* a baby – as long as I get you too; and as long as you can face all that it entails." Peter leaned over to switch on the bedside lamp.

"Ow! What did you do that for?" Rose covered her face.

"Because I want to see your answer as well as hear it," replied Peter.

"You'll see my wrinkles – and anyway, don't you know I'm inscrutable?"

"That's what *you* think but I have a lot of experience of these matters."

"Well, your worship; as far as I'm concerned not only do I want our baby but I'm prepared to prove it by repeating the act we just tried: it was really rather nice. Now put out that light."

"I'm not sure I can manage it."

"Leave it to me! And tomorrow morning, remind me to tell you something else I've just decided. Now lie back."

§

At Carnhill, the last light went out at almost the same time. Hugh had not been able to enjoy the same kind of triumphant union experienced in the house on the quay in Polperris. He didn't fancy even trying, now that Hermione was so distended and irritable with constant heartburn and tiredness. Feeling benevolent, however, after the triumphs of the day, he took her a nightcap of Bournvita, her favourite, before retiring to the bed in his dressing room to enjoy a last nip of whisky and water before turning in.

Getting the phone-call with news of a full go-ahead for Lantrelland, had brought his meeting of investors and bankers to its climax just before lunch; pledges of financial support quickly followed. With a Jeroboam of champagne they had toasted the colourful model unveiled to them earlier. Clive and Hugh approached a selected few of the most dependable and richest people to invite them join the board of their fledgling company. The responses had been positive and each shook hands on an outline deal.

Clive and Hugh's lawyers had prepared the necessary documentation and Hugh was confident for Clive to see everything signed, while he himself caught the next train for Cornwall. He wanted to be there the following day to cement the political and popular support that had helped to push the applications through. There were 'private chats' to be had with key figures; and promises of contracts to progress so that people felt confident enough to resist the backlash that Hugh was sure would come from interfering people like Councillor Rose Y Johnson and her high-flying barristers who seemed to have begun nesting with the gulls in Polperris. They would be pulling strings to overturn the decisions made at the Council meeting and the Tory hold on East Cornwall, only recently gained, was tenuous. It had only been achieved by the lassitude of LibDem voters whose leadership would not miss this chance to rekindle local support for a cause such as 'saving our heritage'.

As he turned out the light, Hugh remembered with pleasure the soft and pliant body of the young prostitute with whom he had spent the previous night, sharpening up his mind for today's ordeals – most satisfying – while at home, an heir was on the way.

§

"But Peter, they just can't do it!" Lady Merchant was livid. It had taken the senior Trenleven a few moments to answer his mobile phone, tucked as it still was in the back pocket of the trousers discarded the previous night. "It's blatantly breaking all kinds of laws, isn't it?"

"Henrietta of course you are right but I've no doubt there's some clause in the various Acts of Parliament that allows a Prime Minister to waive the rules when he thinks fit."

"Surely not!"

Peter sat on the edge of the bed, glad that Henrietta couldn't see him as he pulled the sheet to cover himself while pushing his hair back from his eyes.

"I'd have to go into it very carefully but when they released some more of Margaret Thatcher's personal papers not long ago, it emerged that in the early eighties when Rupert Murdoch was trying to buy The Times, she had a secret meeting with him. One of the obstacles to his purchase was the law making it compulsory for the matter to be put to the Monopolies and Mergers Commission. Her government was so worried that the Times would go bust and disappear, she simply waived the rules and allowed News International to take it over. It didn't go to the Commission."

"Preposterous! And see what resulted: I suspect we still haven't seen the end of the repercussions. I hope you won't be defending any of them in court!"

"I certainly won't, Henrietta; but you're right – there's a lot more to come out, that's for sure."

"So what are our chances of getting the planning permission revoked?"

"Without some more research I can't give you a dependable answer but my instinct is that it will be very difficult indeed. There's such a head of steam built up to create jobs and business – and the added attractions they've attached so cleverly to the whole project, I can't see public opinion backing us very far."

"When can we have a meeting at CPRE? Where are you? I'm going back to London today – I've stayed the night with friends in Tavistock."

"I'm still in Polperris. I'll be staying down here for a few days but I can make a start. I will get some help from my Chambers but I can fight it just as well from this end. I might pick up some more details."

"Well, do let me know if there's anything I can do, Peter. I was hoping to have a word with you last night but you were so tied up! I thought the Plan B idea was excellent. What a splendid way to spend a lottery win! I'm so impressed with your son and his young wife – she was jolly brave, enduring that long day in her condition. Anyway, I'll be writing to them to thank them for inviting me to the dinner; and I'll be offering to be a volunteer for odd jobs that they may need doing in London. It will be a chance for me to get more involved on the international side."

§

"I couldn't hear everything she said," commented Rosie, relaxing on the other side of the bed, "but she sounded very cross!"

"She is! And I'm going to have to be tactful about the way I work with her. I have the feeling she might have designs on me!"

"She'd better not! She'll have me to contend with!"

"Do you mean that, Rosie? Have you really got plans for me? I must say I was hoping so. By the way, you haven't told me the other big decision you were talking about last night, before we went to sleep."

"Take those glasses off and come back here – then I'll tell you," said Rose. Peter did as he was bid and there was a longish pause as they once more embraced and indulged in each other's presence and touch.

"Well come on then! Stop all this and tell me!"

"I've decided to resign from the district council."

"Whatever for? You've hardly been on it and you've made such an impression. I'm sure you will get elected again. People have been admiring the way you have stood up against big money!"

"There are plenty of other people from around here who could do all that; and I want to devote myself to my new family and my painting. I went into politics because I was getting bored and needed something to break the routine. Things have changed now – I've got grandchildren arriving; a daughter and son-in-law living just up the road; and I *hope* I've got you. I'm not sure if I dare tell you what I would *like* to happen – you might run a mile!"

"Rosie – despite having been on the receiving end of your wrath, I'm still not afraid of you; and any plans you might have for me are sure to be for my own good." He kissed her on the neck.

"Well …. How about moving in with me here? You can have one of the bedrooms as a study – we can install more electric sockets and broadband connections; you could have another room as a den, if you wanted it. I hope you'd sleep with me in here – and I'm even prepared to change the décor to make it less 'pink'."

"Would I have to retire?"

"Certainly not! That never occurred to me: I was hoping you might go on with CPRE – when you weren't out sketching or helping run our summer courses. How does that strike you? I know I'm being daring but you are too good to miss and it's really time I settled down! There – how's that for selfish? Fingers crossed you would like the same!"

"I'd need time to think about such big changes," said Peter solemnly. "Would I be allowed to keep my London flat? If I changed the bedroom to accommodate some of your stuff? I might even get a mirror!"

"I'd thought of that too," giggled Rose. "I didn't like to overwhelm you with it all at once."

"How long do I have – to make up my mind?"

"As long as you like!"

§

Hugh was determined not to panic. He had been dreaming of a member of the Royal Family cutting a tape to declare Lantrelland Marina 'truly part of the Cornish Heritage' when he was aware of someone shaking his shoulder.

"Wake up, wake up, Hugh, I need your help!"

It was Hermione, her face distorted with fear and pain.

"The baby's started to come," she said, sitting on the side of his bed, clasping her abdomen and trying to breathe deeply as another spasm seized her.

"Oh my God! What should I do?" Hugh was fully awake and sweating with shock. He quickly got out of bed and began dressing. "Is there anything I can get you?"

"Just call an ambulance; the number's on the pad by the phone. I'll go back to my room and pick up my things – once this pain stops – oh!" She forced herself to pant.

When the ambulance arrived, dawn was breaking. Hugh followed the flashing blue light back to the hospital in his own car. He had no intention of staying there all day, once the baby had arrived. It was inconvenient enough as it was. He tried to re-organise his plans as he drove. On the one hand, the arrival of a son the day after a triumphant victory was auspicious. No one could blame him for not spending *part* of today with mother and child. He could celebrate with his backers later despite a niggling concern that refused to leave him. Was he the baby's father? If he wasn't, who was? In a frightening moment it even crossed his mind that Hermione may have consorted with someone whose genetic makeup would make it quite plain that Hugh was not the father. Just imagine if she produced a black baby – or a brown one! He dismissed this as 'an intrusive thought' and castigated himself for having so little faith in the wife who, to be fair, did a splendid job at Carnhill as lady of the manor and gracious hostess to the county.

"She's a lady – thank goodness!" He said to himself, keeping the ambulance at a safe distance but not letting it out of sight. He regularly enjoyed the company of girls from different continents and often wondered whether he already had a child of mixed race somewhere. "I'm sure it's my son," he reassured himself. His hope was that she wouldn't spend all day in protracted labour, leaving him in some waiting room. He had his mobile and could cancel most of his appointments: he wouldn't be completely out of circulation.

§

"I've decided!" Peter hadn't moved an inch from Rosie's warm body.

"You can't have thought about it properly; you'll change your mind and regret it. Please give it proper consideration," said Rose. "I'm serious: it's not something I've ever said to anyone else!" She turned her back on him and pulled the duvet close around her.

"Rosie dear, before you get on your councillor's white horse, allow me to put my case. I would like your full attention please – because if you are curled up like that, away from me, I feel excluded and may not say things the way I'd planned."

"What do you mean, planned? You didn't know I was going to say that. I'm feeling very vulnerable, having been so blatant. If you haven't given it proper thought I shall feel awful!"

"For goodness sake hush, woman, and listen!" He pursued her under the duvet and pressed himself against her back, putting his left hand over her mouth. She struggled for a moment, and then gave way, unresisting in his arms.

"Shall I begin?"

Rose nodded and he transferred the hand from her mouth to her breast.

"What a lovely figure you have," he said, "but let me concentrate. What you just proposed was almost word for word what I have been preparing for the past week. I was trying to pick the right moment to put the same questions but what with all the excitement – I suppose it might have been later on today – you got there first. Before you say any more the answer is 'absolutely yes' to all your proposals. I can't think of anything I'd rather do. I realised quite some time ago how much I love you, and …....."

"Do you?" Rose interrupted.

"Yes – I love you very much – is that plain enough? Are you going to let me finish?"

"Well good – because I love you dreadfully and I want to eat you all up and be part of you for the rest of my life! I can't believe my luck at meeting you – it's makes up for all the disappointments I've had in my political career; except that getting elected brought *you* out of the woodwork!"

"Well – there's a complimentary description. What am I? A death-watch beetle or a woodlouse? Not a rat, I hope!"

"You're none of those things – you are just what I've been looking for all my life – even if you are getting on a bit!" Rose laughed.

"That does it! You'll have to be gagged again!" Peter covered her mouth again and held her tight. "I *shall* finish, even if it's not in the most conventional way. I'm not going down on one knee because you might start insulting me again and this mattress is not conducive to kneeling. I want you to marry me: I love you and I want to be your husband so we can be together; make love; fight and bicker; enjoy laughs; look after each other; paint wonderful pictures; treasure our grandchildren and support our son and daughter. I want to do your odd jobs, get your shopping, admire your beauty, laugh at your jokes and hear your gossip. My big worry *was* whether you might turn me down. Rosie, will you marry me?" He took his hand away.

"Well, if you put it like that – yes – I suppose I'll have to!" She said, turning towards him and losing herself once more in his embrace.

CHAPTER 27

"It's a big healthy baby boy! Congratulations Mr Olver-Blythe."

Hugh was instantly alert. Before the senior midwife startled him out of his reverie he had been thinking how useful it was to sit like this. For the first time in weeks he was able to allow his mind to ramble amongst the issues that needed solution in this, the biggest project of his life so far. His vision of Lantrelland Traditional Cornish Village, and its marina was slowly becoming transformed from scale model to the real thing, built of local stone, invading the sea, soon to be teeming with people, boats, boutiques, restaurants and delightful homes – a jewel in Cornwall's tourism crown.

"A boy, you say? Is he all right? Are they *both* all right?"

"They are both fine, Mr Olver-Blythe, and your wife is asking for you."

Hugh found himself shaking: having been shocked back into the present he was once more aware of the odour of disinfectant; the muggy warmth of airless corridors and shining floors. He followed the midwife, hearing the rustle of her starched uniform as she opened doors for him.

"Here we are. I'll leave you together but I suggest you stay no longer than quarter of an hour. Mrs Olver-Blythe needs rest."

Hugh was surprised to find that Hermione and the baby were in a private room. Somehow he had expected a ward with several mothers and babies.

"Oh – you are on your own: that's good!" He felt self-conscious with Hermione sitting up holding the baby. It was her expression that was different. She looked so well: radiant. The guarded but polite face that usually greeted him had softened and her smile was unrestrained, welcoming and relaxed.

"Of course I am, darling," she said, as though she really *was* pleased to see him. "It's what I arranged – we've 'gone private' and you're paying for all this! I hope you don't mind but our son's worth it, isn't he?"

"Absolutely! But you're making me feel so guilty – I did nothing about these arrangements: just left it all to you. Paying up is the least I can do! And thank goodness you are all right. Was it awful – the birth?"

"Well – yes – it was; the pain was like nothing I've ever experienced before but I've been training for it and the midwife was wonderful – she stayed with me for what seemed like ages. She gave me some gas in time to stop me making a real fool of myself – but when the baby arrived it all stopped and I feel completely different! Isn't he gorgeous? Have you thought what we should call him?"

"Well no, not yet. The past few months has gone past so quickly and I have to admit I've been so pre-occupied, names are not something I've thought about. Have you?"

"I have, actually. How do you feel about 'Richard Hugh Olver-Blythe'? He's my father's first grandson and it would make him so happy – and I do like 'Richard', don't you? And we can *call* him Hugh, after you and all the other Hughs – but I'd like him to be called 'Hughie' at least while he's small. It will save any confusion."

"My goodness – you *have* been planning!" Hugh had avoided discussing the pregnancy except in the broadest outline because of the doubts that had made the whole thing so worrying. Could this child really be his – after so many years of Hermione not conceiving: except for that once, which had turned out so sadly.

"That's good thinking: Richard Hugh – or Hughie for short," he nodded. "Yes I like it; I like it very much – and darling Hermione, I'm so proud of you!"

"Doesn't he look like you, too?" Hermione offered the little bundle to Hugh, who forced himself to take it from her. Holding babies was not something to which he was accustomed. He looked down on the wrinkled red face and for the life of him, couldn't see any resemblance to anyone. There was a knock on the door and a motherly woman in a white coat came in with a tray of tea and soft drinks.

"Here we are," she said, placing the tray on the bedside table, wheeling it nearer Hermione on the side opposite the baby's crib. "All part of the service! May I have a peep?" She had a strong Cornish accent.

"Oh what a dear little soul! He's a boy, isn't he? And *doesn't* he look like his Daddy? Oh my! 'Tis the spitting image! Dear of'em! Is he your first?"

"Yes, he is," said Hugh, feeling suddenly parental. If this woman could see a likeness – she ought to know, with her experience of babies. This un-prompted remark undermined his doubts as to Hermione's fidelity.

Hermione was pleased to see the pride in Hugh's face as he studied his son. He no longer looked as though he were holding something that might explode; and after gazing at the child for some while, he gently returned him to her arms.

"He's already been feeding," she said. "He was keen straight away. Look, he's waking up – I expect he'll want some more."

Hugh watched, mesmerised, as Hermione pulled one side of her night-dress open, revealing a full white breast, its faint blue veins and pink nipple stirring him instantly. It reminded him of when they first got married: she had been so young and nubile. She held the baby so that his lips touched the nipple. Baby Hughie took it in his tiny mouth and began sucking lustily.

"My goodness, what an appetite," said Hugh, sitting himself in the chair. "Shall I pour some tea for you?"

"No thanks, but I'll have that glass of orange juice, please. I don't want to drink anything hot when I'm holding the baby – I couldn't bear the thought of spilling it on him! It seems sensible don't you think? I can have a cup of tea when he's safely back in his crib."

"You sound like a professional," said Hugh.

"I've been reading up on it," she laughed. "You should see my Kindle! It's full of baby talk! But how about you? I'm sorry to have woken you up at such an ungodly hour – and then sitting in that waiting room all this time. It seems like yesterday!"

"Well I must admit it was hard, not knowing what was happening but after about an hour I began to settle down and sort out all yesterday's excitement, still milling about in my head. I've made a load of notes of things that need doing, now we've got the go-ahead."

"There's one thought I had between labour pains," said Hermione. "It's about Eddie Rouse. I don't know why he should come to mind but I suppose it was because yesterday Esme and I were talking about his wife Judy. She had been looking forward to having what she called a 'nice new bungalow' on The Glebe Field, if you bought their farm but now that has fallen through, they're in a difficult spot. Will they have to leave the farmhouse? Are you going to let it out?"

"That's what we usually do when we buy a farm," said Hugh. "Our farmhouse holiday lets have been very successful. It's been profitable and we control what goes on: better than selling them off – you never know who's going to come and live there!"

"Have you thought what might happen to Eddie and Judy Rouse, then?"

"Frankly, no! He's never been one of my favourite people and he's never really come up to expectations – he's all talk!"

"Well that's what I thought: he really is a good talker and I've been thinking: we shall need someone else to help guide people around the house and gardens, especially if your development brings a lot more visitors. I was wondering whether you could offer both him and Judy jobs at Carnhill. He would make a very good guide, once you trained him; and Judy could be our housekeeper. I like her and she's had to work wonders to keep them afloat on that farm for so long – she knows how to run a home and I've seen hers – it's clean as a pin and still nice, despite having nothing spent on it. We could offer them the house in part-payment of salary."

"They can't be that far off retirement, though," said Hugh. "Then what?"

"I'd thought of that, too. Some of those buildings on their farm would make ideal retirement homes. We could convert them and rent them out – but made sure they got one, when the time came."

"Hermione, I think I've been under-estimating your management skills for too long!"

"I think you have!"

"Are you going to let Hughie taste the other one now?"

"Now who's becoming a nanny?"

§

"Hello? Mr Trenleven, please."

"It's me, Harry! How are you?"

"I didn't recognise your voice. I'm very well, thank you!"

"That's good: not more disturbing news, I hope?" Peter was experiencing a sinking feeling because Harry didn't usually ring except when things needed attention. At this moment the thought of work, or more threats from ex-clients, were not welcome. Until the phone rang he had been blissfully happy: the first time in years. He and Rosie were sitting out in the September sun, soaking up the tranquillity of Polperris Harbour discussing whether they would have a church or civil wedding and where they might go for their honeymoon.

"Anything but, sir! I thought you'd be glad to hear that the friend who's been trying to stir it for you has suffered a setback and won't be bothering us again. One of his fellow inmates grassed on him with the names of everyone in his network. They've all been mopped up and are inside, awaiting trial for a whole load of offences. We'll be defending some of them; but the word is that he's so angry at being shopped he's forgotten all about you. He must have known it was fictitious anyway!"

"It was entirely his own fault: if he hadn't insisted on spilling the beans in court he might still be a free man! He's still got quite a stretch, hasn't he?"

"It's going to be longer, now – the Crown Prosecution Service is bringing charges of threatening behaviour. They've got loads of evidence and no judge is going to look favourably at a convict trying to take it out on a defence barrister, is he?"

"I must say that's a relief," said Peter. "Although I'd nearly forgotten about it, Harry! My mind's been full of planning law and politics – well – until yesterday."

"What happened yesterday?"

Peter put his hand over the phone's mouthpiece and spoke to Rose. "May I tell Harry about *us*?" He asked in a low voice.

"What a good idea! He's such a nice man! I'm sure he'll be pleased."

"Harry – Rose Johnson and I have decided to get married. You are the very first to know. How about that?"

There was a moment's silence as Harry took in the news. When he spoke it was with genuine delight.

"That's fantastic, Peter! I'm so pleased for you both! I couldn't have asked for better news – so now it's good news in all directions. Things are looking up. Just one more question: when are you coming back to work? It's not that we can't manage but there are a few briefs beginning to pile up that could do with some decisions."

"I was thinking I ought to come up on Monday for a day or two – have a

sort-out with you in the office and do some shopping with Rosie. I'm sure we can delegate things to the new people, can't we? Are they doing well?"

"They've settled in quickly and are getting on fine with the rest of us. There's a good atmosphere."

"Better since I've left?" Peter laughed.

"Not at all! Perhaps more light-hearted – except when necessary."

"I hope I wasn't becoming a drag?"

"You weren't – but you'd been going through a rough time. Things are now certainly looking up!"

"Clive: it's a boy! Richard Hugh Olver-Blythe – born at some ungodly hour this morning. I'm propping my eyes open with matchsticks – up half the night and all the excitement of yesterday. How about you?"

"I'm fine – slightly hung-over. Many congratulations! A son and heir. That's fantastic: you must be so pleased!"

"I am – we both are. Hermione's going to stay in maternity for another day or two and I'm dashing backwards and forwards to see her and the baby. He's quite a little toughie – grips my finger already in his tiny fist."

"That's great! He'll be keeping you busy – but you'll be lucky if you get much sleep for a while."

"I'm making the most of my last undisturbed nights!"

Clive thought it best not to mention, even in fun, what he suspected Hugh had been up to in London a few nights previously.

"Very sensible! I should be with you in about two hours; there's a lot to discuss."

"There is indeed! I'll come and pick you up – what time do you get in?"

The train was on time and Hugh was there to meet it, having first called in to see Hermione and the baby. The two men were relaxed as they headed towards Carnhill.

"Hermione's taking quite an interest in our project, I'm glad to say. I wasn't sure how she would take it. She's sitting there coming up with some rather good ideas." Hugh sounded pleased. "One thing that she's suggested is that we should act quickly to get some job adverts into the local papers so people can see we mean business – and we'll be able to get editorial to go with the ads. She wants to hire a nanny and work with us setting up the project office; you know she's very capable. She'll make a great office manager. I've agreed she can start as soon as the baby can be left. We shall need a housekeeper and she's found someone already – Eddie Rouse' wife: and she reckons Eddie could be trained up as a guide for the main house and gardens."

"What good thinking! Extraordinary: I'd heard that new mothers tended to be completely focussed on the baby," said Clive.

"So did I! But this one seems to have lost interest in golf and shopping and wants to be involved in Lantrelland. It'll save us a lot of money – the cost of a nanny and housekeeper don't compare to hiring a top class office manager!"

"You are right! I've got to make some management changes too, now all this is getting into gear. It was something I wanted to discuss: I don't want to move down here, but you'll have all kinds of queries as we go along. I was wondering about setting up a semi-permanent closed circuit TV link. What do you think? I'm happy to come down every week for a day or two but we could do a lot of the work online."

"Excellent suggestion," said Hugh. "You'll be able to keep in touch with our backers in the City. It's important they stay up to date."

"Of course getting that new headland in place is the first priority, isn't it?"

"Yes indeed – and this afternoon we can give the transport people a call to get them started, taking the granite down to Polruan. The vessels are lying idle and their owners will be very glad to get some work. We can order the floating crane for next week. What about you Clive, have you got any other priorities?"

"We ought to get on with the marine wildlife reserve at the same time. It will help fight off all the flack that's bound to come. The CPRE's been briefing the press about what they're going to do and, I must say, it's quite worrying. If we get things rolling immediately it will be less easy for them to get decisions reversed. I've talked to some of our investors and they're all for it."

"There's not much to do, regarding the reserve, is there? Only defining the outside limits. I'm ignorant about these things – will it mean a ban on angling from the rocks?" Asked Hugh.

"I don't know – I shouldn't think so – it would upset the public; but I can see them wanting to stop under-water harpooning, lobster pots and that kind of thing. We can ask our marine biologist; he's a member of 'Marinet' the Friends of the Earth group; they'll know."

"I'm glad you've been following that up," said Hugh. "I wonder whether they know he's linked with us. It might not make him very popular!"

"They were bound to find out, so I told him to 'own up' and declare his interest early on – then they would know how to treat him. It's not an easy relationship but they're keen to get more reserves up and running and we're paying for this one. They can hardly turn it down."

"How did they like our idea for wind turbines to mark the boundaries?"

"They opposed it at first, saying that submerging the supply cables in the seabed would destroy too much wildlife but apparently there are other ways of connecting up to the grid ashore that don't disturb things on the sea bed. No dredging or fishing will be allowed in the reserve, so the cables will be safe even without being buried."

"Except from the elements," said Hugh, "and the lobsters!" He laughed.

"Well that's true – but there's no telling what the elements are going to throw at you! It's part of the risk: remember – only last year they had a tsunami in Cornwall?"

"Don't even remind me! We could do without anything like that!"

Clive recollected it had been in June; probably caused by an underwater landslide two hundred miles out to sea. The water had suddenly pulled back a long way before surging back as a wave a metre high, scaring people on the beaches. One man, digging for bait at Marazion, across from St Michael's Mount, reported it had been flat calm and one moment he was at the water's edge; but after sorting another forkful of sand he looked round to find the sea had retreated about seventy metres.

"He'd heard what happens before a tsunami – with the sea pulling back first – and rushed off the beach, jumped in the car, heading for higher ground. Very sensible, if you ask me! A load of tourists got wet. They were walking back across the causeway from St Michael's Mount – nice and dry – and suddenly they found themselves knee deep in water. They made it back to land OK, though."

"I remember the time when Boscastle nearly got washed away, too," said Hugh. "But that was the rain! Terrifying! We'd better stop talking like this – people might want to pull out. I just hope these climate change people are wrong! Think positive, Clive!"

"Getting back to those wind turbines; they're trying to work out which is the best bet – to build them like the Eddystone Lighthouse, firmly fixed to the sea bottom; or whether to have them floating, with strong anchors."

"Is there any argument?"

"Not so much argument as 'discussion'. The greenies are wondering whether the vibrations from a *fixed* wind turbine might upset the larger sea life like basking sharks, dolphins or whales – no one knows really and they're calling for research!"

"Preserve us! It will take for ever to get started. We want action!"

"That's just what the other side are saying! Thank goodness we've got the funds lined up to get things moving!"

"The trouble is – so have they! Shedloads of it – from the Lottery!"

§

At Plan B a similar discussion was taking place.

"We've got to move forward on both fronts: fighting bad development and spreading the word about projects to help keep civilisation afloat for a few more generations," said Emily, doodling on her notepad.

She, Sebastian and their colleagues were sitting in their 'quiet space' behind the glass wall of the chapel's top floor.

"I like your idea of having a film crew based here for a few months," said Sarah Harrington. "We can record everything that's going on – even if we eventually lose, and make a documentary about it. No one can deny it's very interesting stuff: visual too: moving all those huge blocks huge blocks of granite from Bodmin Moor to Polruan and then by ship to Lantrelland. Shots of them hitting the water to build up a new headland will be quite something. We could even get under-water clips. I bet it will make a hell of a mess of the sea bottom – not exactly what you want for the marine reserve they keep trumpeting about."

"I don't want to be disparaging about the reserve," said Sebastian. "It's something we might have done ourselves; and it will give us credibility if we don't oppose something simply because 'it's being done by a group we're opposing.' We ought to be doing interviews with proponents from both sides; for the archive – so that anyone making a documentary can have material to draw on when they're putting the whole thing together. For example we could get Friends of the Earth to say their piece – they've got a special group pressing for marine reserves."

"I've heard that Olver-Blythe and his cronies have already got at them," said Sarah. "Our interviewer could ask some awkward questions."

"I suspect they wouldn't find it difficult to answer – so often developments *do* have provisos attached to them. Like 'you can build a housing estate if you pay for fish steps on an adjoining river – helping salmon reach spawning grounds upstream. Most councils make developers put in road improvements as part of getting planning permission – it keeps both sides happy."

"Ouch!" Emily jerked up, surprising the other two. "That was hard!"

"What's going on?" Sebastian was alarmed.

"I think the twins are fighting," said Emily, looking less surprised, now she had thought about it. "One of them must have been delivering a hefty kick. I think it missed – it caught me instead."

"Are you all right?"

"Oh yes, fine, thanks – but I must go to the loo again. That's about the eighth time this morning!" Emily left the room, leaning first on the back of Hilary's chair as she passed.

"Poor Emily! She must be very uncomfortable," said Hilary.

"She's not sleeping well, either – it's a heck of a load she's carrying; and it's not as though they keep still. I dread to think what they'll be like when they get loose in the world!" Sebastian looked tired, too, with dark rings under his eyes. "I keep having to run errands in the night, like getting another glass of water for yet more indigestion tablets. She's been having a lot of heart burn."

"It's no joke, having twins – especially as a first pregnancy," said Hilary. "Not that I've ever experienced it. One at a time was plenty for me to cope with – and thank goodness that was a long time ago. It's not something I'd like to repeat! It's soon, isn't it?"

"Any day now," said Sebastian. We're trying not to go too far from the maternity hospital – a bit like playing music chairs – keeping the empty chair within easy reach."

"Hermione Olver-Blythe has just taken her new baby home, I hear," said Hilary.

§

"My parents are coming on leave at the end of September," Rose was telling Peter, over lunch. She had received a letter with exotic stamps that morning.

"What's more, they say they want to retire here! Would you believe it? I thought they would want somewhere much warmer.

348

They're asking me to look out for a house or cottage they could rent for a few months while they gave it a try. Dad says he wants to get away from malaria and other nasties and Mum says she wants to see snow again but not in Northern China because she was so unhappy there as a child."

"She still goes there, doesn't she?"

"Mum does, most years – but Dad prefers to come here fishing. He says he cramps her style by wanting everything translated and she gets very impatient with him. You know what they're like!"

"You forget I've never met them! I'm a bit nervous about meeting your father for the first time – he's not much older than me, is he?"

"Oh don't go on about that again! You're much younger than Dad – if not in years, in your thinking and behaviour. He used to think of himself as progressive and trendy but now he complains that 'things have gone too far' and hankers for the old days. You might be good for him! Get him to accept the modern world."

"Thank you, Rosie, my love! I'll leave that to you. I can't wait to meet your mother, though, if she's like you!"

"I shall be very jealous so be careful. She's still very attractive but in general, she doesn't like English men – only Dad – and he says it took a lot of convincing before she'd even speak to him!"

"Didn't he rescue her from a hippo or something – on Lake Victoria?"

"That's what finally did the trick, yes. You must get her to tell you about it. It will be good practice for her English if she's going to live here."

"Can't she speak it then?"

"Not very well. She refused to learn for a long time, as a matter of principle. It was 'the language of American imperialism' and all that kind of thing. I taught her most of her English when I was little, coming back from playschool out in Tanzania."

"But you used to speak all sorts of languages, didn't you?"

"I suppose I did – Mandarin, English, Swahili and a bit of Sukuma. People used to laugh when I got them mixed up. When I came back to school here the teachers said I was all behind but I soon caught up."

"Well now you're my own special Cornish oriental flower – and I'm so lucky to have you on my side!"

"Thank you, Peter! I agree – you are very lucky! I'm even giving up a promising political career to devote myself to keeping you happy."

"I rather like the sound of that! Come here!"

CHAPTER 28

"What an exciting idea, Sebastian!" Miss Weeks climbs the stairs towards the mezzanine in Plan B's chapel office. "Let's sit down a moment and you can tell me more about it." She heads for the nearest workstation chair and takes a series of hasty breaths. "That's better! An electric car for Cornwall, you say? Propelled by the wind? Goodness gracious – whatever next? Perhaps my little pony will be able to retire at last."

It was Emily's swollen ankles and doctor's instructions to keep her feet up that meant she was not able to fulfil her longstanding promise to escort Miss Weeks round the new headquarters in Liskeard. She would enjoy the old lady's reactions *after* the visit, over tea at home in Pelynt. Sebastian had taken the afternoon off to collect Miss Weeks despite the frantic pace of everything at Plan B – liasing with his father and the CPRE over Lantrelland; and dealing with a torrent of requests for backing of eco-friendly projects in Cornwall and globally.

"Can I get you a coffee?" Sebastian was concerned he was submitting Miss Weeks to too much pressure.

"That would be lovely, dear. Then I can gather my wits." She relaxed as he went off to fulfil her wish and looked around at the mixture of Twenty-First Century furnishing set into the varnished Victorian woodwork of the chapel windows and scrolled roof supports, which disappeared into the newly-constructed top floor. She wondered how the spirits of the builders and congregation who had celebrated the completion of the building a hundred and fifty years before would be reacting to all this change. At that time, the scourge of alcoholism and its threats to humanity was uppermost in the minds of many of them. Today, equally devoted souls were using the same building to alert the public to even more grave dangers: not only to the morals of society but to death by drowning; wars of migration; foul air and starvation.

"I think they would approve," she confided to Sebastian when he returned.

"Who?" Sebastian asked.

"The people who built this chapel," she said, "would approve of what you are doing here, even though it's not quite what they had in mind."

"That's what we feel," said Sebastian. "Hilary says she gets 'good vibes' when she unlocks in the morning. She puts it down to approval from the spirits of people on the plaques and memorials around the place. You'll notice we've left them, or moved them so they can still be seen?"

"Now you come to mention it, I can see," said Miss Weeks. "What a nice idea! Keeping the spirit of the building alive. I wonder whether it will still be here in another hundred years."

"With a bit of luck our twins will be around to find out! They don't know what awaits them out here in the world, do they?"

"The way Emily has kept working so late in her pregnancy, I suspect they will be amongst the best-informed twins on the planet," chuckled Miss Weeks. "They must have heard her holding forth to you all, both here *and* at home! And they will know a lot of music – she always has something playing."

"She says she wants them to have the continuity of good harmony both inside and beyond the womb! Rhythm too!" Sebastian laughed. "It's a great notion!"

"Now what was this about a car?" Miss Weeks was interested.

"Oh yes! It's a proposal that came to light just the other day. We decided we ought to be using an electric car – if we could get one – for local runs, so I Googled it, looking around Cornwall. I found that the County Council has already begun using battery-driven saloon cars, but I also discovered someone in Redruth with ideas for building much cheaper ones here in the county. I went over to see what he was doing and it turned out he had been trained as a boat-builder, making fibre-glass hulls and fittings. When made redundant he asked his father for a corner of the family service station in which he could develop light-weight electric buggies and cars. He has already built several prototypes – a sand-buggy ideal for ferrying elderly people up and down to the beach or along the prom; a shopper-car for the busy house-wife or husband; and a larger model that might be just what we need."

"But how could they be driven by *wind*?"

"That's just us playing about with marketing ideas. An increasing amount of the county's electricity comes from wind turbines and the cars will get their batteries charged by plugging in, overnight."

"I see: nothing mysterious but appealing just the same."

"The key is to find good batteries, and that's one way in which Plan B is helping. We've taken shares in the business, to give him capital; and we're contacting battery manufacturers around the globe, especially China, to find the most suitable units for his cars. Emily and I will be guinea-pigs with our transport, giving prototypes a good hard trial as family runabouts. We shall be able to put up videos on You Tube as part of our marketing; we might even appear in TV commercials!"

"How strange! Going back to batteries. They were called 'accumulators' in my young days. I remember when we had to take one down to the garage regularly to get it re-charged. They were nearly as large as today's car batteries – but made of glass, with a terminal on the top at each end. You had to be very careful because they were full of acid. It used to run our wireless set, before we had electricity. We kept a spare one so that we didn't miss the BBC broadcasts! It was one of my mother's jobs to take it over to Hambly's Garage in Pelynt in the pony and trap. They had a room full of accumulators, all labelled - with wires going everywhere! That was before we had our own generator – which used to start itself when we switched on a light. It ran on petrol but wind is such a good idea, it doesn't cost anything here – except for repairs after one of our gales! But surely, the problem is when it stops blowing?"

"That's why good batteries are so necessary – and a back-up supply of renewable energy – like the heat from deep below the ground; and from gravity – using the power of the sea's tides."

"But people object to windmills: they say they are ugly and noisy."

"Not when it means there's money going into their bank account!"

"Will it really catch on, Sebastian: I mean, across the world – not just here?"

"We've got figures from the Earth Policy Institute in America that in 2011 there were a record number of wind generator projects in more than eighty countries and there's now enough wind power being harnessed for nearly four hundred million people. That's forty thousand megawatts – and China is leading the way with nearly half of that: it doubled its wind generation every year from 2005 to 2009 and overtook the United States in 2010 – it's now way out in front!"

"Extraordinary! So you feel that your Plan B will be doing it's bit towards helping Cornwall catch up with China! I wonder whether your mother-in-law had anything to do with that?" Miss Weeks gave Sebastian a mischievous smile.

"I suspect we do have a bias in that direction. The women in the Johnson family all have very strong genes – not just for their good looks! You know that Emily's grandmother's hoping to come and live around here?"

"Emily did mention it. I'm so pleased: I used to meet her, years ago when she could hardly speak a word of English. She always seemed rather stern but we became good friends and we've managed to meet when she was on leave. She used to ask me what Emily's grandfather was like when he was young – I knew him when we were teenagers, going to Young Farmers Club – such a handsome boy! But I must stop reminiscing – I know you are busy and this has to be a whistle-stop tour. I've got my breath back – let's start again." She stood up and took Sebastian's arm. "Which way?"

"Up these stairs – we'll go slowly!" He let her take her time but she was enjoying having someone to interrogate and didn't stop.

"I can see that you have found a really stimulating and satisfying way of life. Are you enjoying it more than fighting cases in court?"

"I'm not completely divorced from that. I'm still working with colleagues at our chambers in London; and with Lady Merchant – you've met her of course. We want to see if we can get that marina permission rescinded. It's the other part of Plan B's activity – to oppose unsustainable development."

"That was something I remember Henrietta saying; she came to stay with me, you know, a few weeks ago. She had fallen in love with Lantrelland and the Glebe Field and was very keen to get to know the area better so I invited her down for a weekend. We get on well! I enjoy having someone to listen to my pet complaints. When she was here I told her why I wanted to ban mechanised hedge cutters! I won't bore you with that now. Anyway, she was telling me that Government has been boasting about the removal of nine hundred pages from planning regulations advice, to make it easier for developers to make more money. We both agreed it's that kind of decision that allows people like Hugh Olver-Blythe to turn our wonderful coastline into something like Blackpool – which is fine, where it is – but *we* feel the nation needs to conserve its diversity of habitat not only for wildlife but for us humans too! We don't all want roller-coasters, clock-golf or yacht marinas. Some of us want tranquillity and timeless scenery."

"Quite so," agreed Sebastian; "and what we're trying to do is to divert some of that same enterprise and ingenuity towards projects that might give us *all* the chance to hand on to our children a planet that still works. Now, if you're ready, there's one more floor – the most interesting really – all cameras and lights and things – a little haven of peace for those of us who spend most of our time here. Shall we go up? Then we can go home to see how Emily is faring. She said she was going to bake a saffron cake especially in your honour."

§

"Hermione! What a surprise! Come in quickly, out of the cold – and this must be Hughie!" Rose opened the studio door wide for the pram to come through. She forced it shut against the stiff autumn wind.

"Your cheek is freezing!" Rose rubbed her own after the two had exchanged perfunctory kisses. "Come through and warm up. Is he asleep? He'll be all right if you want to leave him in the pram here – I'll lock the outside door."

"He's due for a feed so I'll take him out and bring him too, if that's all right. I hope you don't mind my dropping in like this but I was down in the village and couldn't resist the urge to come to see how you are getting on with the painting. I would have phoned but you know how it is!"

"I do indeed! And you are very welcome and I'm nearly there. That's one of the problems with painting, knowing when to stop! There's always something you'd like to change – even ages afterwards. I think it ought to be in a contract – being able to come and tweak things for at least ten years after delivery! Anyway – you can take a good look and force my hand if you like. Make the decision for me!"

"I would never dare! But I'd love to see it." From where they were standing only the back of the frame supporting the long painting was visible and the two walked round to the front."

"My dear it's MARVELLOUS!" Hermione was thrilled at the panoramic view of Carnhill, Lantrelland and Cornish scenery, all in rich greens and greys, with the sea in the distance, light blue against rolling white thunder clouds soaring up into the pale sky. In the foreground, a dignified Hermione, seated on a cast-iron chair, her back straight, her chin high; and behind her, standing tall, Hugh, proud and confident: not a hair out of place, his tweed jacket giving him a breadth of shoulders she might have wished he really had. His right hand supported the barrel of a twelve-bore, the butt of which rested on the grass beside him. Both of them were looking out of the picture into the distance, every detail of their proud expression depicted with fine brushwork – an almost photographic likeness; Hermione with the faintest smile, as though remembering a recent triumph; and Hugh, master of all he surveyed.

Rose admitted to herself that, in the end, she had painted a portrait in which the clients could see themselves as they would like to be seen, rather than how she, the artist saw them. The faces and postures had changed somewhat, during the past few weeks. Rose hadn't been with the Olver-Blythes for nearly two months, during which a lot had taken place in her life – finding the love of her lifetime and preparing to become a grandmother being the most seismic aspects. Her anger – at Hugh and Hermione's pursuit of wealth and power, regardless of the consequences; their determination to maintain their 'upper class' separateness, their airs and graces; their disregard for the law, public opinion and common sense – had softened, just enough for her to want them to be pleased with what they were paying so much for. Rose was hoping that, if they were happy with their portrait, they would invite others who could afford such luxury to come and admire it, with the possibility of further commissions.

Rose Yi could never lose her instinct for the need to 'make a living'. Furthermore, she had enjoyed the whole process of invading the intimate privacy of people whose lives were so different from her own; and in creating something that was spectacular which, despite all its faults, gave her a thrill every time she stood back from it.

"Can we fix a date for the unveiling? I can't wait for this to be in its proper place over the fireplace in our long gallery." Hermione was truly thrilled by what she was seeing.

"Yes of course!" Said Rose. "You are right – it should be soon. I'm sure you know that the CPRE is trying to get the permission for Lantrelland development to be rescinded: they're applying to the High Court but I suspect nothing will happen until nearly Christmas, so the sooner we do it, the further from 'troubled times' we shall be."

"I'd like to keep the two things completely separate. There's no need for you and *me* to be hostile. I think we understand each other's position and respect it, don't we?" Hermione looked for reassurance.

"I think we do," said Rose, as sincerely as she could.

She still couldn't dismiss the enmity she felt to people like the Olver-Blythes and felt guilty for benefiting from their wealth in accepting their commission. To make her feel less two-faced, Peter had tried to defend artists through the ages: "since when did great art *not* have patrons – whether it was the church, the aristocracy or the commercially successful? It has kept top professional artists afloat and enabled them to take on apprentices – teach classes and allow 'the people' to create their own paintings, sculpture and music too, come to that!"

"Have you got your diary?" Hermione was already diving into her handbag.

"It's on the desk," said Rose, hoping that her client had not noticed her hesitation

They agreed that a Saturday would be good – more of their friends and family would be able to attend. Hermione said that she hoped Rose would invite her family too.

"It will feel a bit like a wedding! Or the launch of an ocean liner – except I shan't be cracking a bottle of bubbly over it! I'm so excited – it really is a most wonderful painting. I'm going to invite art correspondents from all over the place – as well as our friends from around the county."

Rose blanched a little at the thought of critics looking for angles that they could get their teeth into. Even if they liked her work, some of them would have to say something deleterious – to give their readers something to talk about.

"So how about the twenty-sixth? It's no-one's birthday or anything, is it?"

"It seems to be free – and it gives us a few weeks to get things done," said Rose. "I'll have to get it out through the French windows, on to the quay and by boat over to the fish market." She was laughing. "I've been wondering how to do it, having woken up in the middle of the night realising it won't go through the door into the Warren. We built the frame and stretched the canvas more or less where you see the picture now, without thinking how we would move it out."

"Art thieves just roll paintings up, don't they?" Asked Hermione.

"Yes – but no thank you! It must cause some cracking if the paint's dry and I'd hate to do something like that. I've had a word with the harbour-master and he's assured me we can do it at high tide, with one of the larger fishing boats. We'll make a feature of it – tell the TV people and they can film it, ready for the launch day report. It will make a better story."

"What a good idea! And it will be lovely for us to have on record: we could have a video running on a monitor somewhere at Carnhill, to add to the attractions. A little section about 'the history of the latest portrait'; I can see it in my mind's eye. I don't know about unloading it at Lantrelland, though. There's no quay there, yet!"

"Thank goodness!" said Rose without thinking but hastily trying to cover up her lack of tact by saying: "Anyway we've arranged for a van to take it from there."

"You'll have to add that to our 'postage and packing'!" Said Hermione.

"Don't worry – we shall!"

§

Sebastian had arranged not to be far from Pelynt this week – or next. The twins were due and he wanted to be on hand to give what support he could to help Emily through the ordeal. He wasn't sure about being present for the birth itself: neither was Emily.

"I don't really want you to see me like that," she said; "all blood and gore. I'd rather maintain my image of glamour and decorum. Perhaps I'm old-fashioned but if you want to see what birth is like, go and see lambs being born – it's a messy and primitive business. Much nicer next day when they're gambling in the sunshine. I know I'm not being politically correct but there are times when I'd prefer my menfolk to go and play snooker or Tweet each other."

Sebastian was, therefore, working from home; helping to make sure Emily was keeping her feet up and being on call for her needs, including lunch and other snacks.

"Come and talk to me!" She commanded from the sitting room: he had left the study door open; partly to hear the music Emily was playing for the twins; and partly as her guardian and slave.

"I've been thinking," she said, when Sebastian sat beside her on the sofa, holding her hand.

"Oh dear! Does that mean we have to move house? Or not have children after all?"

"Don't be so bloody disrespectful!" She pinched his finger.

"Ouch! That hurts! But I forgive you: here, pinch the other one." He leaned over and kissed her tenderly. To him she looked fantastic and he still couldn't believe how lucky he was to have met and married her. Certainly, they had both had their 'moments', with doors slammed and tears shed but despite all the differences in their backgrounds and characters they had grown together comfortably and firmly with many occasions for laughter and enjoyment. Even at this late stage of pregnancy their sex life was alive and well, despite Emily's distended burden. She had remembered what Zhang Li had told her many years before, when talking about the Sukuma people in Tanzania.

During holidays with her parents in Africa she had always been able to ask about any subject without embarrassment. The formality of Zhang Li's own childhood in Shenyang had left her ignorant of so many human things that she was determined her own child should not have to endure any of the shocks that she herself had experienced, growing up. It had been soon after Emily's first menstruation and they had been discussing reproduction, sex and all the implications. Watching a heavily pregnant woman walk past their home on the research station, a basket of cassava balanced on her head and a baby slung on her back, Emily had asked:

"And when she and her husband go to bed tonight, will they have sex? Or even want to?"

"I asked Elisia, my Sukuma friend, about that," said Zhang Li. "Apparently their tradition is that parental sex is good for the developing baby! We reasoned that it keeps the man interested and prevents him straying – so it *is* good for the baby in the long run!"

Mother and daughter had laughed at the guiles of 'man management' but Emily had never forgotten it – to Sebastian's relief and pleasure. They had devised various ways and positions to avoid discomfort while being able to express affection and enjoy physical connection. Emily had also ensured that she and Sebastian could talk about such things, although at first he had found this difficult. They sought complete frankness with each other – while respecting each other's sensitivities.

"I don't want to move house or even furniture but I do want to talk about our work. I know I'm going to be pretty busy when these two are delivered – and I may go all mumsy for a while, but I've had lots of time to think, just sitting here and I wanted to tell you about it."

"I've been missing our chats too," said Sebastian. "The place is buzzing with ideas and I think our plans are beginning to work. The volunteer experts seem to be enjoying their sessions; and our advisory board is coming up with good advice."

"So far, so good!" Said Emily. "Our original objectives are still OK; people are finding them reasonable and positive."

"You are right. Our using encouragement and dissemination of positive news is better than trying to scare the pants off everyone. It seems to be working and I like the way we've been promoting renewables as a positive alternative to destructive stuff like fracking for shale gas. The trouble is it's so cheap! The Americans are talking about it 'taking the pressure off oil' – cracking the rocks underground to release all that lovely fossil gas and raking in the money!"

"And causing earth tremors! But renewables seem to take so long to pay their way."

"It makes me think," said Sebastian, "that we *have* to be able to offer the commercial people much more 'ready-to-use' technology for renewables. They don't want to spend their time on prototypes and safety checks. Perhaps we should be devoting more attention to research and development?"

"The big oil companies say they're doing that already! And I'm sure they are!"

"So what *do* we have to offer them that's good for business?" said Sebastian.

"So good that they're prepared to pay us for it! We need a bit of drama," said Emily.

"We've *got* drama all around us but it's not being recognised. Here in Europe we've been having droughts and record temperatures; thousands in Africa and Asia are trying to get past our borders; half our population will die young because of obesity and alcoholism – and what are our politicians talking about? Each other's impropriety! What makes the headlines? Some poor referee who didn't see the ball cross the line!"

"You're right – we've got to spice up our message. We've got to 'edit in' the truly important events and happenings. If Mother Nature makes a statement – it's up to us to report it in such a way as to make it heard!"

"If she has already made it dramatic enough, like that awful tsunami in 2004! Sebastian – I'm really enjoying our pow-wow but I think Mother Nature is beginning to send *me* a message. Something's going on down here!" Emily patted her stretched abdomen; she screwed her eyes up. "Ow! That's definitely what I imagine is the beginning of labour. Shall we phone the midwife?"

CHAPTER 29

"I had such an exciting time with Sebastian at their Plan B office," Miss Weeks was telling Peter and Rose. "I'm absolutely full of it! What has just reminded me are those hedges in the background of this magnificent painting. It was so kind of you to invite me to see it; and what's all this you have discovered about our two families, Peter?"

"Slow down, Miss Weeks! First, I must tell you our big news? Emily's had twin boys!"

"Good Gracious! Boys? Well I never! How marvellous! Are they all well?"

"Yes, thank you; and they will all be home at Pelynt in just a day or two."

"Did Emily have any difficulties?"

"Considering what large babies she produced, I'm glad to say no," replied Rose. "It was quite a short labour and straight-forward."

"How much did they weigh?"

"Six and a half pounds!"

"Gracious! And their names?"

"Petroc and Arthur!"

"Oh!" Miss Weeks looked shocked but tried to cover her surprise. "Very Cornish – but 'Arthur' is so unusual these days, isn't it?"

"That was our response!" Peter and Rose both laughed. Peter went on: "We've come to the conclusion that it's a grandparent's privilege to find grandchildren's names odd when they first hear them. I ought to take Petroc as a compliment, though, didn't I? The Cornish version of my name: and Arthur was royal blood, wasn't he? It's about time that name came back: at least they didn't call him Cecil, Cedric or Brian – although those names will soon start popping up again. Their previous owners have mostly died off by now."

"You are right – some names seem to jump generations – I remember when there were only ancient Emilys and Roses. Now they're all young! Have they given them other names, too?"

"Not yet: they were talking about letting the boys choose some for themselves when they are twelve years old – something to look forward to and think about!"

"What a good idea – it will give them hours of fun. Emily and Sebastian are so creative, aren't they? I was telling you that Sebastian spent nearly a whole morning explaining their 'Plan B' organisation to me. I came away feeling quite inspired. It seems such a right thing to be doing with their lottery win. Such a huge sum of money could easily destroy people, couldn't it? You can imagine – luxury yachts and too much of everything!"

"That's what we thought," said Rosie, "but they're very much 'down to earth'."

"Sebastian impressed on me that Plan B couldn't simply come up with new solutions to global problems – but will campaign against what he called 'today's big sin' of over-consumption. I'd never thought of it that way before but I see what he means. We all want too much of everything!"

"That's why we're against the Lantrelland development – even though we can see it would bring benefits to local people and a lot of fun to the rich. Plan B challenges the idea that humanity must be addicted to 'growth' – more, more and *more* for *me*, now! More for *all* of us who can afford it!"

"I must say I've often wondered about that, too," said Miss Weeks. "How can we go on building roads and filling them with cars indefinitely; or crowding the sky with aeroplanes?"

"Especially if it's all based on fossil energy, which is bound to run out," added Rose.

"Although it looks as if we shall kill ourselves off before *that* happens".

"I suppose it depends on what you mean by 'growth'. I've always thought it meant 'getting better at things' – certainly once I'd reached my five feet four! It would be so much better if we could improve the quality of everything instead of just quantity," said Miss Weeks. "Find more interesting things to do – make things last longer, look better and be more comfortable – learn new skills and arts so that the world could be more beautiful and fulfilling; but of course you'd have to first make sure people had enough to eat and wear: and be healthy without fear of war and crime. There's so much we can all do *without* 'growth'.

"I suppose all that would be classified as 'growth' too," said Rose.

"Well it's not as though we couldn't make a living, improving the quality of life," said Peter. "People have livelihoods from computer games as well as music, films, books and art; and of course there's all kinds of sport, too. Criminals won't want to stop their activities, either. There will still be plenty of work for policemen and barristers."

"I think I must have chosen one of the right careers, then," said Rose. "As long as my paints don't exhaust the last natural pigments!"

"We've almost forgotten this beautiful picture!" Miss Weeks turned to look at the painting that took up so much space in the studio. "It really is giving me such pleasure. There's so much to see – including those hedges. When we've got a minute I'd like to say my piece about them."

"I'd love to hear what you have to say. Are they wrong?"

"Oh not at all, my dear Rosie! They are a faithful depiction of the way hedges are these days – but I'm sad they're not more like they used to be when I was a girl! They were so important to us all then, on the farm."

"Perhaps you can tell us over lunch – I'm starving and I'm sure Peter is. You will join us, won't you, Miss Weeks?"

"Yes please: you always make me feel like family!"

"Well perhaps you are," Peter added. "We can talk about that too!"

§

Sebastian was not finding things so rewarding. The Lantrelland project was going ahead despite anything Plan B could do to prevent it. Hugh Olver-Blythe, invigorated by the birth of his heir, was reaping the benefits of his successful fund-raising and elaborate preparation. Within a few weeks his company had created tens of jobs in East Cornwall for skilled and unskilled people, lifting them out of depressing redundancy. Calm autumn weather had favoured the surveying and placement of the seabed foundations for the new headland and harbour wall with its tidal generator, soon to rise above the waves. Two more coasters had been chartered to carry the granite from Polruan; heavy lorries were grinding their way down the back roads from Bodmin Moor – causing problems to the 'off-season' tourists who took their holidays after the schools had gone back. Nothing Sebastian tried touched those who had the power to save Lantrelland Bay. Appeals 'would be considered'; injunctions would 'be referred to a higher court in due course'; protests were ignored.

The media was feasting on 'exciting new initiatives in East Cornwall' that would 'create extensive economic activity and offer a deprived area great hope for the future.' Central Government was facing an election soon and this was the kind of news Members of Parliament needed to give them any hope of retaining their seats. Rational planning, conservation, rural tranquillity; natural habitat and orderly change seemed to be blindly ignored. Hugh's public relations team made much of the establishment of the marine reserve and fresh sources of renewable energy while developers were queuing up with proposals for yet more tidal and wave power generators where Atlantic rollers released so much of their power.

At home, Sebastian wasn't getting enough sleep. Emily had gone into 'automatic mother' mode – basking in all-consuming love and attention for these two little boys. All she wanted was to be with them, hold them, feed them at her breast and feel them close against her. Contentment enveloped her though she was aware she was taking Sebastian for granted – promising herself it was only while the babies were so small. He would understand and she would make it up to him. Indeed, she made every effort to include him in her little circle of adoration – giving him one child to hold while she changed the other; talking to him and suggesting what he might do for lunch; listening to his endless frustration over work.

It took Rose's intervention to help Sebastian get his wife back.

"Emily – you really must do your exercises," she said, visiting the nursery at the Pelynt barn conversion. "I hardly dare say it but you are not getting your waistline back as soon as I'd like!"

"Mum! I'm feeding two hungry boys! I need loads to eat and drink and it's not for ever."

"I know all that but what does the midwife say?"

"The same as you," admitted Emily. "I know I've got to get a grip but I've been enjoying all this so much: like a kind of dream. I hadn't realised what it would be like. Nothing else seems to matter."

"But it does, Emily. Poor Sebastian is looking like a ghost! He's frazzled, trying to work and keep you supplied. It's time you started to make these gorgeous babies a little less dependent on your entire attention."

"So what am I supposed to do, Mum? Go off and let them holler?"

"No of course not! But you can easily afford a nanny; and there's a woman down the road who's well qualified to do the job. Her own kids are at university and she's desperate for a job. She could live in for most of the week and you could start going out and about again – get some fresh air and give Seb a hand. He's having a rotten time at work."

"Has he been lobbying you?" Emily looked defensive.

"Certainly not but I've got eyes in my head. The poor man's fading away!"

"You're right – I know you are really; give me the lady's phone number and I'll give her a call."

"Promise?"

"Yes; and, Mum, what's that ring? I haven't seen that one before – *and* it's on your ring finger. What's that all about?"

"I was wondering when you were going to notice! You've been so besotted with Petroc and Arthur. I decided to wait until you noticed it. You've always been good at finding rings."

"Don't tell me you're engaged? At your age!"

"What do you mean 'my age'?"

"Well – you know what I mean. It *is* Peter, isn't it?"

"Who else? Ed Puckey?"

"Hardly! But I thought you two had just a 'working relationship' – and not the easiest of those."

"It was at first but the whole thing crept up on me. Peter is such a charming man. I'd never thought about him 'in that way' but he turned out to be such a great pupil on the course; and then we started going out together – and he's been around a lot, this year. I realised he's not nearly as 'old' as I thought! To tell you the truth, I'm nutty about him!"

"Mum! You're not sleeping with him?"

"Why shouldn't I? In fact, I've got something to tell you that I haven't even told him, yet."

"Oh NO!"

"Oh yes! That's partly why I came up here this morning. I went to see the doctor, having had several positive DIY tests. I wanted to tell you first – you being special."

§

"Before I start preaching about Cornish hedges – you *must* tell me the family thing." Barbara Weeks had hardly finished her soup. "I can't wait! Are we related? Is it through your side, Rosie – your father's family? I can't believe it's through Zhang Li's! That would be going back a *very* long time!"

"You and I may indeed be related, Miss Weeks! It's on my side of the family," said Peter, having ordered the wine as they

368

sat in a restaurant next to the fish market. "We're the Cornish ones. Rose's father was an incomer here – from London, when his artist parents came down to escape the rat race in the fifties. The strange thing is, that our connections are all linked with Lantrelland and Carnhill. Even stranger was Emily finding that ring – now her engagement ring – in the Glebe Field!"

"So the twin boys are *my* family too? How lovely! I'm their ready-made great great aunt or something!"

"More like a fifth cousin, probably," said Peter, "but related, yes. I've told Emily and she's delighted. She says you've always *felt* like family. Another strange thing is that the difficult relationship between our family and the Olver-Blythes has been there in the background for many decades. That ring might well be the one that Emily Tregrove hurled over the wall in the summer of 1819. Rose and I have been researching parish records and found that she died on July 29th that year."

"We knew that, of course," said Miss Weeks; "from all the old family papers and diaries: but now I know who to pass them on to. I was worried they might not find a home after I've gone on my way. That's such a relief! You knew she was only seventeen when she died – so tragic; because of Hugh's great great grandfather, Hugh Olver: he jilted her. Didn't I tell you the story, Rosie? Perhaps I only told Emily. It was a sordid business. She died officially of pneumonia but I believe she had no will to live. It was terribly sad."

"Well," said Peter; "I expect you know that Emily's older sister Elspeth married your ancestor Henry Weeks."

"Yes indeed! He was my umpteen greats grandfather."

"Perhaps you *didn't* know that they had a daughter called Tamsyn who eloped with – guess who – Gawen *Trenleven* – my great great grandfather!"

"How extraordinary! She must have been quite a girl! I didn't know that. Are you sure?"

"As sure as I can be. I've done quite a lot of research on the web and in various archives. They ran off to London and got married as soon as they could – but never returned to Cornwall.

Now, two of us have come back and put down roots again! As Dame Edna Everidge would say – 'spooky', isn't it!"

"Another fine woman: my favourite Australian! It certainly is – extraordinary how things go round and round? I wonder whether we have some in-born homing device?"

"I rather doubt it," said Peter. "I think it's just chance – luck – or whatever you want to call it.

"Well – we've all had a good dose of that recently. What with the young ones winning all that money; you two meeting – and me finding long-lost family. We've saved The Glebe at least; although I don't know how life is going to change when a new resort rises out of the water at Lantrelland Bay."

"Which it *is* doing," said Rosie. "We went for a walk along the cliff path last night and you can actually see the waves breaking over the new headland. It's reached the 'reef' level, with great blocks of granite well above the surface; they will soon be putting in piling so that the whole thing can be concreted together. One thing that looks very different is the calm water on the Polperris side of the new foundations – it's quite eerie – so different from before."

"But there must still be an enormous amount of work to do!" said Miss Weeks.

"It's a huge project and must be costing the earth!" agreed Peter.

"In more ways than one!" said Rose. "Just think what that money could be doing elsewhere; but from what I hear, Plan B is never going to win this one, is it?"

"I fear not! We are all going to have to live with it," said Peter.

"So 'big money' is going to have it's own way – again!"

"I'm afraid so – but at least our young ones are adding weight to projects that might help save the planet."

"I'll drink to that," said Miss Weeks, holding out her glass. "Dear me – I'm quite tipsy already; but it's been a delightful evening and like the Olver-Blythes or not, I'm looking forward to the unveiling of this wonderful painting of yours, Rosie dear – or can I say Cousin Rose?"

"That sounds right," said Rose. "Genealogy is far too complicated for my little brain," but I'd love us to be cousins. We *feel* like cousins; and as you say, we all have a stake in the twins. However, now we're all nicely mellow – you might have noticed I haven't had any wine, Cousin Barbara. Perhaps I should tell you about some news about Peter and me. For a start, we're getting married!"

§

"There are urgent gale warnings for Thames, Dover, Wight, Portland, Plymouth, Fitzroy and Sole. A deep depression is moving North with winds, mostly South Westerly, of force eleven, Violent Storm, expected in the next twenty four hours."

"Damn! That means they won't be able to get the portrait across the harbour – it could get blown all over the place," said Hugh, switching off the radio. "That's a hell of a wind!"

"They'll be putting down those barriers across Polperris Harbour, for sure," said Hermione.

"They'll have to wait until the weather's better."

"A good job we've still got a bit of time before the big day. I'm just finishing the invitations. Your PR people have given me the list for the media and will post out our card with the press release. We can send them out to the investors from here."

"You're doing a great job with the Carnhill office," said Hugh. "I'm so impressed."

"Well I've been enjoying it; getting geared up for more visitors and everything's running to schedule, I think."

"So far – although I don't like the sound of that storm. It's coming just when we're most vulnerable. All those blocks of granite are still 'loose' at present. Not concreted together. Clive assures me that his consultants aren't worried and that the risk of 'once-in-a-century weather' is very low. I shall have to leave in a few minutes to pick him up from the train. Is his room ready?"

"Of course!" Hermione said, proudly. "Even with a hot water bottle in place to take off the chill."

"I shouldn't have doubted it! I'm glad he will be here, with this storm coming up. He can reassure me about his calculations. I have a sinking feeling our work could get trashed."

"I'm sure it won't. He and his team know what they're doing. We've left enough time to pick a calm day for moving the painting. I'm more concerned about *that* being in place for the unveiling," said Hermione. "Now I'd better go and see how young Hughie's getting on. Nanny says he's teething and getting quite stroppy."

"He was all right when I went to say good night," said Hugh.

Hermione was pleased; he still hadn't dared ask her to confirm the child's parentage but the two Hughs were beginning to be friends. Hugh Senior lapped it up when the staff pointed out family likenesses but she thought it wouldn't do him any harm to have just that niggle of doubt in the background. Hugh's attention to her had been much closer recently and for the first time for years they were enjoying each other's company both during the day and after bedtime. Hermione had begun taking the pill for the first time in her marriage.

§

There was a parallel situation at the barn conversion in Pelynt.

"I'm back on the pill," Emily told Sebastian.

"Oh good! I hadn't like to say anything but you look so fabulous again – with your neat little waist and delicious bum … " Sebastian began.

"Hey! Hang on! What *is* all this?" Emily was laughing as she brushed her shining hair, seated at her dressing table. "All I said was I'm back on the pill. It wasn't 'I fancy you madly'!"

"That's a great pity because now we've had three whole nights good sleep I hardly feel sleepy."

"Have you closed all the shutters? There's a horrible storm forecast. Listen to the wind!"

Both Emily and Sebastian had a 'thing' about shutters and while making the last few alterations to their barn conversion had added sturdy shutters, each with a heart-shaped opening about the size of a large fist, to let in some light. Their house was exposed to a south-west wind; and gusts made such a bang against the window during gales that having the shutters closed made the young couple feel safer, softening the sudden shocks.

"I'd be terrified if a window actually broke," said Emily. "It would be like having a wild beast loose in the house."

"I have closed all the shutters, bolted the door, checked that the boys are nicely asleep and that the intercom's on; I've shut their door so they can't hear us being noisy."

"Why? Are you going to beat me up?" Emily shook her hairbrush at him. "You dare! And incidentally – I *do* fancy you madly! It must be my hormones clicking back into gear.

Her breast milk had recently proved insufficient for the hungry twins and Sebastian had been preparing and delivering bottles to the voracious pair as she weaned them from herself. Emily was less tired – even if Sebastian wasn't – but between them, they had persuaded Arthur and Petroc to get used to a routine that gave everyone time to catch up on normal life. Emily had been doing her exercises; Sebastian learned how to sleep with his head under one pillow on his 'night off' and was feeling more lively.

This particular night he had come home to find a special supper, the new nanny-cum-baby sitter engaging the twins in hilarious games in the nursery, each of them bouncing in his fun seat. Emily wanted time to get things ready and for the boys to be healthily tired by bedtime. She and Sebastian had enjoyed an uninterrupted meal before seeing off the nanny and putting the boys to bed.

"I wondered what you had in mind," said Sebastian; "and I'm glad it's just what I've had in mind for some time."

"You men are just animals! No sympathy for the poor new mother – her body wrecked and distorted – having to act as a mobile milk bar and being hungry all the time."

"But that was ages ago! You look brand new, now! Am I allowed to give you a once over? I'll tell you if I find a stretch mark." He went across behind her and kissed the side of her neck that was not hidden by the heavy hair. "Mmm – you smell so good!"

Emily looked up into the mirror, seeing their image.

"You haven't got your pyjamas on! It's not that warm is it?"

"It's certainly not cold – this weather must be coming straight from the Caribbean – and anyway – I'm still warm from the shower."

Emily put her brush down, turned round on the stool and undid the towel around Sebastian's waist, throwing it towards the en-suite bathroom. She put her hands on his bottom and pulled him to her, pressing her face against his flat stomach. After that, one thing led to another and for the next hour, they experimented and celebrated; enjoying once more the touch of their bodies against each other; stroking and caressing until Emily felt confident enough to sit astride him as he lay on his back. She lowered herself slowly and carefully, allowing him to enter her.

"I'd forgotten how nice this was," she murmured. Very gently she continued, half expecting soreness or discomfort but finding none. "Does it feel good for you?"

"Wonderful! Better than ever!" He felt her tighten around him. "Just don't move for a minute – I don't want to lose it!" He fondled her breasts. "And no one would ever know you've been feeding half a rugby team with these – they are just as lovely as ever."

He didn't say any more because Emily needed to kiss him and leaned forward, pressing herself against him, enveloping his head with her hair, her lips passionately seeking his. She broke off to say: "I've been missing you!"

After that she abandoned her caution and they rapidly reached an exhilarating climax before sleeping for an hour until woken by demands coming through on the intercom.

"It's your turn – and I'm waiting, so don't be long," said Emily. "Just listen to that wind. I hope our roof's OK."

Sebastian crossed his fingers and tried to ignore the roaring gale as he went to warm up the bottles for the children. He could not, however, suppress the feelings of fear at the force of the storm. He had never heard anything quite like this before. The boys once more settled he went back to the big double bed where Emily lifted the duvet, welcoming him back to her arms.

"Is the weather as bad as this often?" He asked.

"Not since we moved here," she said. "But I remember storms back at home in Polperris when I thought we were all going to be flattened. Didn't you have storms like this in London?"

"Not that I can remember. I'm sure the wind didn't blow like this in Putney!"

"Come here, I'll protect you," said Emily; and they both lost interest in the wrath of Mother Nature as she tried to tear their house down.

§

The noise was terrifying even inside the house at Carnhill. Hugh suggested that Hermione take Baby Hugh, along with his nanny, down to the kitchen, at the back of the house where it was warm from the Aga and the noise less loud. He and Clive decided to get dressed:

"I've got to go and see what's happening to our headland," Hugh told his colleague. "I can't bear not knowing. I'll take my

375

hunting lamp: it's got a terrific beam; I should be able to pick out our granite blocks."

"I'll come with you: I've got my wet gear," said Clive.

The two men, in souwesters and oilskins, told the women where they were going and promised to be back soon.

"For goodness sake be careful," were Hermione's last words to Hugh as he went out through the back door, into the maelstrom of dark air, flying twigs and leaves. Both men had to lean forward and fight their way down the valley towards the boiling sea.

CHAPTER 30

"I never did tell Sebastian or Emily about Cornish hedges," Barbara Weeks told Zhang Li and Charles Johnson. Rose's parents, recently arrived from South America, were strolling with the old lady across The Glebe Field. Her old pony and its donkey companion trailed along behind, hoping for the odd peppermint. She pointed to the stone walls topped with turf and wildflowers; "Seeing these hedges has reminded me."

"What about them?" Asked Charles. "They look much the same as usual and you'd never know they'd just been through a hurricane."

"That just my point: it's because they have all been trimmed so tightly by a tractor and hedge cutter. When we were young, hedges only looked like this once every few years, didn't they – after they had been cut down and re-built by hand? I remember on our farm, just over there – not so exposed to the wind, several of the fields would have had quite large trees growing along the tops of the hedges. We used to let them grow up – just trimming the sides of the earth banks with sickles. It took nearly all the early summer on odd days. Men would go 'hedge paring' whenever the other work had been caught up."

"I remember seeing them do that," said Charles. "It made the sides of the hedges look so neat."

"Well, during the winter, when a hedge grown up tall, we used to take a crop of wood from the top, lay the young saplings flat and take turf from the bottom of the hedge to repair any damage the sheep and bullocks might have made over the previous few years. The wood we cut down would be used for fencing stakes, logs for the fire and faggots for the bread oven, made from the twiggy bits. We really 'harvested the hedgerows', carting the wood away with a wagon and horses."

"So why did that stop?" Zhang Li asked. "It sounds like a good thing to do."

"Oil – cheap fuel: that's my conclusion," said Miss Weeks. "It used to take two or three men at least a week to harvest just two hundred yards of hedge. You only did part of the farm each year – it took so long and was expensive in labour. When hedge-trimmers came in, you could just go over all the hedges each year and nothing grew high except the odd oak or ash tree we were encouraged to leave. Hedges were harvested for one last time and that was it! After that, a contractor trimmed the whole place every year. Men and horses weren't needed any more – not for the hedges or many of the other jobs on a farm. Thousands of people lost their jobs; Cornwall changed – just look around you – how many hedges have got clumps of hazel, blackthorn or beech growing on the top – with wild roses or other nice nesting sites for birds? The countryside looks as though it's been shaved!"

"This field looks the same as I always remember it," said Charles.

"That's because we're so near the sea – the salty wind always kept the plants down except for a few leaning bushes, like those by the churchyard. I'm talking about the hedges inland."

"The church looks all right – nothing changed! Was it damaged in the hurricane?" Two weeks had passed since the devastating storm and tragedy,

"It did lose a few slates but that's been repaired. My old cottage suffered more – I had to have a tarpaulin tied over the roof for a few days to stop the rain coming in."

"It must have been awful! Terrifying!" Zhang Li tried to visualise the night of the great storm. "We've been through a few storms in our time but nothing like *that*, from what Rosie has been telling us. I'm glad we arrived after it was all over!"

"I was so frightened I came down from my room and sat under the stairs until it calmed down a bit. I was there for hours with the wind truly screaming. It felt like the end of the world."

"Which it was, of course, for poor Hugh Olver-Blythe. They still haven't found his body, have they?"

"Not yet: poor Hermione; it must be terrible for her."

"Whatever was Hugh doing, down on the rocks?"

"He and his architect from London were checking to see that the headland they'd been building was still in one piece. They had spent a fortune on shipping granite blocks and it was ready to be concreted in place. Clive Goodman said the sea had gone mad – it was white: boiling! A huge wave came and swept Hugh into the sea. Clive himself was so lucky – he had stayed a few yards higher on the cliff. He dashed back to Carnhill to raise the alarm, only to find the telephones weren't working: his mobile couldn't get through, either. He had to drive inland and even that was like trying to escape from a maze – lanes were blocked by fallen trees. It took hours before he finally alerted the coastguards."

"I suppose there was nothing *they* could do;" said Charles.

"Nothing at all! The next day the sea was still so rough only the rescue helicopter and the lifeboat were able to come out – and they searched for hours. Poor Hermione was standing on the cliffs, watching and weeping. In the end I went down to bring her back. She was distraught. It was so awful – I brought her here. When she finally stopped crying it all came out: she told me how fanatical he had been about the project; although it had saved their marriage: that, and having the baby. They had been happy together for the first time – just for a few months. Now she had lost him and she couldn't bear it."

"You'd never know it had all happened – looking around from here, would you?" Zhang Li shaded her eyes against the autumn sun. "It's really quite chilly: shall we walk on down to the bay? I'd like to see what's left of this famous new headland."

"Didn't Rosie tell you? There's nothing. The whole thing was flattened by the waves. I'm sure the bottom of the sea is scattered with all that granite. You can't see anything above the water. The divers looking for the body say that hardly any of the great blocks are even resting one on top of another – the power of the sea was so phenomenal it treated them like pebbles, rolling them backwards and forward. I suspect Hugh's body might have been crushed and destroyed – they might never find it."

"How frightful!" Said Charles passing through the kissing gate out of The Glebe Field. He gave the still hopeful pony a last quick stroke on the nose before following the two women towards the bay.

"My goodness – I don't remember this road. It's new isn't it?" Said Charles. The path had ended abruptly as they emerged on to new tarmac.

"It was going to be the main road into the new village and marina," said Miss Weeks. "I suspect it will be the only memorial to the project – you know they've gone bust, don't you?"

"Peter Trenleven was telling me. He says a lot of people in the City caught a nasty cold, that night," said Charles.

"Poor Hermione," said Zhang Li. "She's the one I feel sorry for."

§

Plan B's board were discussing strategy.

"We don't have to worry about getting the planning permission overturned," said Sebastian. "It will take years before anyone can raise enough money to start again; and the permission will have lapsed by then. I don't think there will be any threat for a long time."

"It will have put a blight on anything that resembles Lantrelland," said Sarah Harrington. "Investors don't like taking that kind of haircut."

"Did you have anything like that when you were in Zurich?" asked Emily.

"There was a lot of hopping about when Lehman's Bank went down – but you could say that was a man-made disaster: not an act of God like this one."

"I'm not sure 'God' had much to do with this," said Hilary. "I think Mother Nature was just putting on a little event to show humans she couldn't be pushed too far. It's one of the messages we were trying to get across at the Eden Project – climate change

380

can have devastating consequences. That hurricane was 'man-made', if the climatologists are right."

"So what should we be doing, regarding the Lantrelland project?" Asked Emily, now back at work three mornings a week.

"I think we should continue supporting the parts that we always like – the marine reserve and the wind turbines," said Hilary.

"Wouldn't they have been blown away too?" Sebastian asked. "Couldn't it happen again?"

"Well – the Eddystone lighthouse is still standing," said Emily, "and modern turbines are designed to cope with 'once-in-a-century' weather."

"Not so sure about the cables to the shore, though," said Hilary, "with all those blocks crashing about."

"I would have thought the rocks are settled on the bottom by now," said Sebastian. "They can't have done the marine reserve much good, though, smashing up the coral. That will take years to grow again. I think our policy can be to encourage using wind turbines to define the boundary of the reserve, can't it?"

"Agreed," said Hilary. "I remember Tim Smit saying that in Cornwall there are about two hundred thousand households each spending at least a thousand pounds a year on energy. How much of that money stays in the county – or even in the region? He said if the Cornish co-operated in renewables the county could be self-supporting for energy. We've got wind, waves, tides, biomass, biogas and even geothermal hot-rocks: all we need is the motivation and a bit of drive."

"And we've got the capital to provide that!"

"Let's see what we can do, then!" The board was unanimous.

"What else could we be supporting? The interest on our capital is mounting up, now things are picking up on the stock market," said Sebastian.

"On the political side, I think we should follow Lester Brown's advice in trying to get 'the market to tell the truth'. At present we don't put a full cost on using fossil fuels: none of us pays the total price for all the damage it's doing – if we had to, we'd soon change our ways!"

"I read somewhere that even the Republicans in the USA might agree with that," commented Sarah. "If they cut income tax and charged it on fuel instead it would boost economic growth, reduce traffic congestion, make safer roads and lower the risk of more global warming – without making the government run out of money! I think it was one of George Dubya's advisors – a Gregory Mankiw, who said it was the closest thing to a free lunch that economics had to offer."

"We could offer a scholarship for someone to produce evidence and publicise the idea of 'Mother Earth's own bank account' – which we've all been plundering for so long: she needs to collect her debts. We're all going to have to take an ecological haircut!" Emily spoke with enthusiasm.

"Being even more practical I really like what Computer Aid International's doing," said Hilary. "By last year they had donated two hundred thousand recyclable computers to schools, hospitals and charities in Africa and South America. I just read about it in *Appropriate Technology*. We could certainly offer to pay the freight, and more training for technicians who are setting them up for use."

"Good idea! Let's approach them," agreed Sebastian. "I read that, too! In the same issue there was something about cassava making a comeback. Zhang Li pointed it out to me. She said it was what Charles and she had been advocating for years! It's a much safer crop to grow than maize or other grains that depend on rainfall for success. A scientist at CIAT, the tropical farming research centre in Colombia was saying that cassava 'deals with almost anything the climate throws at it!' He said there's no other staple crop out there with the same level of toughness. It was quite inspiring!"

"Cassava's not much fun to eat, though, is it?"

"Granny says it depends on how you cook it," said Emily. "And it's better than nothing to eat if all the other crops have failed. She says there are still lots of improvements that can be made by the plant breeders – like making it more pest resistant. They've already found out how to make it richer in vitamins."

"I wonder how we can help give that a boost?" said Hilary. "I've never tried it, though, have you?"

"I bet you have! You've eaten tapioca, haven't you?"

"Yes – I love it! Straight out of the tin!"

"Well that's cassava – after a bit of processing. It doesn't have to be in a tin either – you can still buy it dry and mix it with milk and spices."

"I know that really: I'm just lazy!"

"We could offer some study trips to CIAT for agricultural ministry people and scientists, couldn't we?"

"As long as they don't get kidnapped when they get there!" Sebastian warned. "We'd have to check out the risks. Has anyone else got any bright suggestions?"

"There's a book just coming out we might like to publicise. It's called something like *'Much ado about mutton'* by Bob Kennard, who I met once," said Hilary. "He was doing a BBC report at the Eden Project. From what I hear it's a mixture of history, photography and cookery, with all kinds of stories about drovers, shepherds and how sheep change grass into meat and wool. With people looking for new dishes and Cornish hill farmers looking for new markets it comes within our remit."

"I like that idea," said Sebastian, making another note. "Anything else?"

"As you know, my grandmother's home on retirement leave," said Emily; "and she was telling me she met several Madagascan post-graduate students who were looking for work experience on renewable energy projects in Western Europe. She was asking whether Plan B offered scholarships for that kind of thing. We do, don't we?"

§

"Come in, Rose. Please excuse all the mess: the builders are still clearing up the damage to the roof; it has meant replacing the ceilings in several rooms." Hermione had not lost her poise; her smile was welcoming, although Rose saw how thin her face was and how tired her eyes.

"I'm so glad you could come. Let's go into the drawing room. It's comparatively peaceful in there and Nanny's keeping Hughie busy. We've got an hour before she goes home." They made their way through the spacious hallway into a richly comfortable sitting room.

Hermione moved the fire-guard and put another log on the glowing embers.

"It's surprisingly warm in here," remarked Rose, "even though it's so big."

"Yes – we have installed under-floor heating and a heat-pump to collect warmth from underground: very green! The fire is just for a focal point. Do sit down, Rose: I'm so glad you have been able to come; I've been missing our chats, especially now."

"I'm so sorry: what you must have been through!"

"Thank goodness I have the baby. He doesn't let us dwell too much on things. You know they still haven't found Hugh? They called off the search some time ago: now it's nearly Christmas."

"That's so sad," said Rose. "What will you be doing?"

"At Christmas? I've invited a few friends to spend a weekend. It's what Hugh would have wanted – not to be dreary. Clive's coming down: he's been so good, making sure I'm all right. In fact that leads me on to say why I've asked you up."

".... the unveiling?"

"It is indeed. Clive and I thought it would give me something positive to remember during the festive season – something good to celebrate – it might take the edge off the sad memories every December. The painting looks so wonderful, don't you think? Hugh looks so well; and so handsome – at his very best."

"Even though I say it as shouldn't – you look good too! I think I caught you at your best, too, didn't I?

"I'm so glad I got you to paint us before we got any older. It led to so many good things for Hugh and me – especially Hughie. It was the happiest few months of our marriage. A good job we met when we did! Do you like it, where it is in the Long Gallery?"

I do," said Rose. "My only concern is the fireplace underneath it."

"Don't worry: it's a mock fireplace – we heat the long gallery the same way as this room – and no one's going to sit around the fire there. Did you bring your diary?"

§

"Have you heard the news?" Sebastian stuck his head around the door of the kitchen early one morning. Emily was sitting, spooning cereal into the twins in high chairs each side of her. It was mercifully quiet as they enjoyed their breakfast.

"No – what is it? I haven't had the radio on."

"They've found a man's body at Talland."

"Is it Hugh?"

"It can't be identified; you're not eating your breakfast, are you?"

"No: why?"

"The body has no head. They can't even use dental records. It will have to be DNA testing."

"Comparing it with the baby?"

"Yes, I suppose so;" Sebastian seemed surprised. "I hadn't thought of that. He doesn't have any other close living relatives, does he?"

"I don't think so; I hope it's positive," said Emily.

"It's unlikely to be anyone else – no one's been reported missing."

"I'm sure it must be him – but I've often wondered whether the baby was his – after all that time with no children. I think Mum feels the same, although she's never said so in so many words. If they *are* father and son it will stop any gossip."

Who else might the father be? Someone from the golf club?"

"Or that architect, Clive Goodman. He's been coming down pretty often, I hear; but it's a good job someone's been taking an interest in the poor woman. Mum says she's been under the most terrible strain – with the company going bust as well as losing her husband. One good thing: Hugh had increased his life-insurance policy as soon as the baby was born, just in case anything happened to him – he was so keen to keep the family name at Carnhill."

"Did your Mum tell you that, too?"

"Yes – she's been to see Hermione several times lately, getting ready for the big unveiling."

"Hermione must be a tough nut! It's still not long since he disappeared."

"She is. Mum says Hermione is planning the event as a launch for next season's tourism on the estate. She's gone ahead with a new car park; and even a souvenir shop – saying it's what Hugh always wanted. She's also admitted that the unveiling will make everyone remember the reports on Hugh's tragic death and help boost visitor numbers – appealing to the ghoulish side of people. Finding a body will bring it all back yet again."

"I wonder what will happen if the DNA doesn't match?"

§

"Are you sure you could be happy, living here?" Charles and Zhang Li are strolling back along the cliff path towards Polperris. "Je, utaweza kukaa hapa kwa furaha?" He spoke in their language of courtship. She replied in the same:

"Kwa nini siwezi? Why not? We've been happy enough living everywhere else; and we had better start getting used to speaking to each other in English – otherwise mine will never improve."

Charles took Zhang Li's hand as the path broadened out, nearing the shelter. "Let's sit in here for a bit and look at the sea: I never get tired of it!."

"I feel embarrassed, talking to you in English – as though we were out to tea with a load of Brits," said Charles. Our mixture of Swahili and Sukuma is much more comfortable – although sometimes it does remind me how you used to refuse to speak to me."

"Well in those days you represented the British – I thought you were a running dog of the Americans; and I was a red hot Party member – but things have changed. China now owns a big chunk of American debt and they need to do business with each other. I think it's much more healthy, don't you?"

"I do," said Charles, "but the challenge for both of them is keeping Mother Earth fit to live on! I'm just thankful people are beginning to get the message."

"Emily and Sebastian have certainly begun to make a difference locally – and we can give them a good few contacts further afield. This Plan B is such a good idea: it's the kind of thing we used to dream about in the sixties!"

"Funny that Rosie has only now got interested!"

"Well she did have Emily to look after; and make a living."

"What do you think about her getting married to Peter Trenleven?" Charles still needed convincing.

"I like him! I like both of the Trenlevens – or should I say *all* of them, especially those lovely twins! All males, though! Perhaps Rosie will produce the first female and break the pattern!" Zhang Li took a cautious glance at Charles. "Why are you limping?"

"It's my knee! All these steps!"

"Well you'd better get it fixed – I'm not carrying you around on my back!"

"Thanks for your loving sympathy; but it was a bit of a shock hearing that Rosie's expecting another child, wasn't it? And Peter's old enough to be her father!"

387

"Thank goodness we Chinese have more respect for the old: he's a lot fitter than you – they're like a young couple together and she doesn't get all her own way!"

"It takes a bit of getting used to – having a son-in-law who's a famous barrister *and* the father of your grand-daughter's husband! I feel we're being taken over by the Cornish!"

"And the Cornish think they've been taken over by the Chinese – we Li's have strong genes – we all look the same and if we don't smile they say we're inscrutable! So come on: stop speaking to me in languages no one around here knows and try to teach me some more English?"

"It always makes me want to giggle – hearing you speak English with an African accent."

"Well *you* should have taught me before – instead of leaving it to my African friends."

"Oh yes! My fault again – but if you really want to, here goes: please correct the grammar in the following sentence: 'Dear Mrs Olver-Blythe, we am delighted to accept your kind invitation to Carnhill on December 12th for the unveiling of the new portrait painted by our daughter.'"

"You had better make sure we don't have to go viewing houses on that day. We shall have to find somewhere to rent if we don't hurry up: Rosie and Peter are going to need all the space they can get before long."

"Do you think she will keep going with her painting and the courses? What with the baby and all?" Charles had reverted to Swahili.

"I think she will. Peter will want to: his work is amazingly good, don't you think?"

"It is: and she's dropping out of politics – that will free up some time."

"It did for me, didn't it?" Zhang Li took Charles' arm and gave it a squeeze. "I'm glad I became a wishy-washy liberal; no one holds it against me when I visit China. I don't talk about it."

CHAPTER 31

Hermione and Clive had been celebrating Clive's divorce decree, which had just come through when the letter from the laboratory arrived.

"Clive, it *was* Hugh's body they found." She burst into tears as she passed him the letter. He put a comforting arm around her, saying nothing until her sobs subsided.

"At least you *know* for sure, now," said Clive; "he can have a proper funeral."

"You won't mind if I bury him here at Carnhill?"

"No: why should I? He's part of your life and I don't feel any competition with him. We always got on well and worked together as a team. You and I have nothing to hide – or nothing that can't be hidden easily."

"Don't you believe it! Everyone will know by now that we're more than business acquaintances. The staff will have picked it up even before we thought about it!" They both smiled despite the sadness of the moment.

"At least the DNA result will stop any tittle-tattle that my baby had anything to do with you! Someone was bound to have suggested it. You're the only other man I've been seen with."

"I don't care, do you? We are all right like this, aren't we? I work in London but we can spend time together there or here, can't we? I get on fine with little Hughie and he seems to like me."

"You're very good with him and yes, he gets excited when I tell him you are coming down; and he misses you when you're not here."

"Will you register him for a decent school?"

"Of course! Shall I be able to afford Eton?" Hermione asked.

"Just about, if you make a success of Carnhill. He might be bright enough to be a scholar, anyway."

"You never know: his father was no fool!"

"And nor are you!" Clive kissed her.

Hermione had known as soon as the body was found it was Hugh – just as she had known for certain that the child was his. Having scientific confirmation that she was right allowed life to continue without the doubts and suspicion that the media seemed to enjoy. It took the pressure off her – and Clive. Until recently their relationship had been entirely professional. Their mutual affection and its consummation had only emerged during the long weeks after the events that had destroyed not only Hugh but his controversial plans.

The change had happened late one night when, after long hours of dealing with correspondence from angry investors, a comforting hug had turned into a passionate embrace.

"One thing *does* worry me – won't the people who did the DNA testing have simply announced the result to the police and coast-guards?" said Clive.

"I had already thought of that," said Hermione. "I was quite sure it was Hugh they found. No one else was missing: so I had a word with one or two people and asked for the result to be withheld until we had everyone together at the unveiling. I said I wanted the press to get the story direct from me and not from anyone else who might want to put a different spin on things. They fixed it with the pathologist in Plymouth, who agreed, since we're so near the event."

"Hermione – is there *anything* your networking can't achieve? Do I detect, too, that you might have thought of bringing an element of drama into the unveiling? It makes a much more poignant story for the tabloids as well as the serious press."

Hermione didn't answer but gave Clive a quick smile and went over to pour more coffee. Her newly acquired business acumen had not missed this possibility.

"Do you think they've become an item?" Emily asked Sebastian as they drove back towards Pelynt after a meeting with Hermione and Clive.

"I wouldn't be surprised: they certainly looked very comfortable together. He's been coming down to Carnhill even more often than he did before their project got washed away."

"It's good that she's got someone to give her some support," said Emily. "Hugh can't have been much fun to live with – and then to die like that: she's been through a terrible time. I used to wonder whether she and Clive were having an affair before Hugh died."

"I wouldn't have blamed them. Dad said he'd heard all kinds of things about Hugh in London 'on business'."

"You don't think we're rubbing salt into her wounds, do you, offering to take on the wind turbines and marine reserve"?

"I don't think so," said Sebastian thoughtfully. "She's no softy and she and Hugh must have lost a packet when the sea flattened their new headland. Hermione told your mother as much, didn't she?"

"She did – yes. She said she had even considered selling Carnhill to pay off some of the debts: Hugh was gambling a lot on that marina. I think Clive must be stepping in with some capital and from what they were saying they want to make Carnhill a bigger and better tourist attraction. It's had a massive amount of publicity during the past year and everyone will have heard of it. What they need now are more attractions locally; things to look at when they're here."

"Like the marine park and wind farm."

"Exactly; and if we step in to help it will show we're not crowing over their losses but are as good as our word – backing positive projects as well as opposing bad ones."

"I think we'll need to get some assurances that the marina idea doesn't make a come-back, don't you?" Sebastian stopped the car as they came to the main road, before turning north towards home.

"Absolutely! I don't think that will be difficult, though. The bankers and investors aren't going to want to risk another hurricane – especially with the worries about climate change."

"Well no one seems to be able to estimate what the risks are any more. The weather-men got it wrong again, didn't they?"

"It was a woman who got the blame, this time, actually!"

"She was let down by her own side! Mother Nature had promised a violent storm at force eleven, and then produced this hurricane. I was looking it up on Wikipedia – it says the waves can be nearly fifty feet high! No wonder Hugh Olver-Blythe was washed away."

"Do you think that body will turn out to be his?"

"I think it's very likely."

"I try not to think about it," Emily shuddered. "I keep wondering whether a head will be washed up too. It's so grizzly. Poor Hermione – she must be wondering – I'd be haunted that something gruesome could still happen."

"I thought she looked a little less strained this time."

"I did too. Perhaps it was Clive being there."

"Will you put the boys in the bath while I take the baby-sitter home? And try to keep the water in bath this time, will you, Sebastian."

§

"Ladies and gentlemen, welcome to Carnhill. I hope you enjoyed the journey from Paddington." Clive Goodman spoke with confidence, every inch the host to an English country house.

The long gallery at Carnhill was crowded, this sunny December Friday. Photographers and television cameras had set up in advantageous positions to capture the new painting and those who would speak about its creation and melodrama that would always be associated with its proud subjects. The scenery outside was recognisable in the painting despite its late autumn colouring: a glistening path across the sea being cut off from the pale sky at the horizon, visible between the steep descents of the cliffs into wooded valleys; in the foreground, the east wing of Carnhill and its grey slate roof. Climbing roses were still in bloom on the sunny walls, as in the painting.

The visitors had arrived by luxury coach from the station to be welcomed with a glass of Bucks Fizz before drifting over to take coffee and wander around with their Carnhill brochures, soaking up the atmosphere and affluence of the warm and comfortable mansion. They had now taken their places in the rows of ornate chairs set out facing the painting, which was subtly lit, allowing it dominate the whole gallery with its rich colours and sharp detail.

"Someone mentioned that it's not often that art critics and news reporters attend the same press conference, so some of you may not have met before – although I'm sure you've been able to put faces to names. We are honoured to welcome so many familiar representatives of the national media – and I'm most grateful to you all for making such an early start this morning. The 'unveiling' of the painting is not going to take long and afterwards, Mrs Olver-Blythe invites you to go through there;" he pointed, "to the dining-room, where you will find a buffet lunch. Then at four o'clock, after interviews and filming, the coach will take you back, *not* to Liskeard, where you arrived, but to Plymouth so you can catch the late afternoon express that should get you home at a sensible time."

There was a general murmuring of approval.

"One further thing, ladies and gentlemen," said Clive, raising his voice. "We've also set the Morning Room up with tables and chairs, telephone and high-speed internet connections so that you can file your stories and reports – so please feel free to make full use of these facilities. First of all, as we indicated in our additional invitation a couple of days ago to the news reporters, Mrs Olver-Blythe has an announcement regarding the sad death of her husband, Hugh. This has been a tragic time for her, as you know; and she has had to bear the brunt, not only of the death of her husband but also the destruction of one of the boldest enterprises of the past decade, by exceptional weather that laid waste to so many of our dreams. As you can see, the lady in the painting is here in person. The artist, Rose Yi Johnson, whom you will be able to meet, later, is also with us. Ladies and gentlemen, I introduce Mrs Hermione Olver-Blythe."

Clive stepped aside and made way for Hermione in front of the cluster of microphones. Her back was as straight as in the painting, her chin held high but she looked distinctly thinner in the face. Instead of country clothes she now wore a close-fitting navy-blue dress and string of natural pearls, her hair with its customary headband, showing her broad forehead and fine features.

"Thank you, Clive; and welcome to all of you," she began, before clearing her throat. She fought off feelings of panic. Only now did the reality of the situation hit her. Until this moment the preparations for today's event had filled her mind, pushing the tragedy into the background. Now in the silence and dazzling television lights, everyone was waiting to hear what she had to tell them – the thought of which she had been avoiding since that fateful night. She forced herself to get a grip: she was damned if she were going to cry but she could not prevent a tear escaping to make its way down her cheek before she caught it with the back of her hand as discreetly as she could. Not before the image was caught by the cameras, to appear in the papers the next day with headlines such as 'weeping widow's moment of truth'.

"We called this small ceremony an unveiling – but as you can see, the painting is not covered – because I can't bear *not* to see it: I'm sure you can understand why."

She turned to look up at the portrait before continuing:

"I won't keep you waiting for the news that I've just received. You can probably remember the night of the great storm as vividly as I do. We had *expected* a storm but not of that ferocity. Local people say they've never experienced anything like it and as you know the damage it caused was unprecedented. That was the night I lost my husband – washed from the cliffs at Lantrelland. Incidentally, if you want to see for yourselves that he had not been acting unwisely, standing where he was, we can take you down there after lunch to the actual spot. The weather should still be fine this afternoon, if the forecasters have it right this time. You will see how safe it must have seemed – high above the waves breaking on the rocks. Our good friend Clive Goodman here, the architect and business partner to my late husband, might easily have suffered the same fate because he too was about to descend that last few yards to stand next to Hugh. "As you also know, Hugh has been missing for many weeks; and only recently were human remains washed up at Talland. We have been waiting for the results of tests comparing the DNA of the body, with that of his closest relative, our son Hugh.. Today I can announce that … ," and at this point, Hermione's voice became less clear as she forced herself to continue, " … they show that the body was indeed that of the father of our little boy. My husband Hugh has finally made his way back to the shore and we shall be holding the funeral next week."

At this, her resolve to remain strong left her and she broke down unashamedly in tears. No one moved and even the most hardened newsmen felt their eyes well up, seeing this brave woman struggle to regain her composure – which she soon did.

"I'm so sorry: it's still very recent and although in many ways it's a relief, knowing where he is – even though ….. ". She could not continue: it would have meant filling in details that everyone present already knew about the body that had been washed up.

At this, Clive stood up, took her arm and guided her back to her seat, before returning to the microphones.

"Mrs Olver-Blythe has agreed to answer questions, and I'm sure you won't mind giving her a little time to collect her thoughts before she does so. I think you will agree she has been very courageous to speak personally about these things but she has been determined that you should hear it from herself and no-one else. In the meantime, perhaps you have some questions you would like to ask me?"

He did not need to mention rumours that Hugh had in fact thrown himself into the sea on seeing the destruction of all his dreams. Hermione had been determined that these should be scotched and that she was the best one to do it. Clive allowed a pause in proceedings while the members of the media made

395

notes and spoke to each other in low voices. After a minute or two the sound of people shifting in their chairs and turning pages in notebooks signalled the end of this interval. Several hands were raised and the press conference moved on.

§

Hermione's bold management of the occasion achieved the results she sought. By addressing the press in person and agreeing to give a succession of exclusive interviews she had ensured she was extensively quoted that Friday evening and the next day. The stories and pictures also made the Sunday papers.

She had known she was taking a risk by inviting not only Rose Johnson to attend, escorted by Peter Trenleven, but also Emily and Sebastian; although she had grown to trust all of them. What she did not know was how much the visiting journalists already knew about previous encounters and the battles for planning permission. It didn't take long for the reporters to work out that the artist was also the local councillor with whom the Olver-Blythes had crossed swords over The Glebe; and that she had had the backing of the well-known barrister who was here in person. It also gave them the opportunity to delve into the motivations of Hugh and Hermione in recruiting Rose to undertake such a sensitive commission. Hermione explained that she had long admired Miss Johnson's work: she was local, living in Polperris: Hermione liked her as a person and had been prepared to by-pass the problem between them.

"And yes, of course, I hoped that we might be able to influence her during our sittings," she admitted to one of the journalists during an interview. "I think we would both agree that we have now become friends," she added.

Over lunch, the word also got round that the artist's daughter and her husband were the ones who had won the record lottery jackpot and the young couple were not slow in responding to questions. They took the opportunity of promoting the aims and objects of Plan B. Such was the interest in this aspect of events that Clive sensibly opened another room to allow interested reporters and feature writers uninterrupted access to the lucky winners who were now apparently going to give their backing to Mrs Olver-Blythe.

Was it true that Plan B had been actively opposed to Lantrelland developments? Yes it was, said Sebastian, who proceeded to give reasons why conservationists and ecologists had been so vociferous in their condemnation of the originally proposed changes to the Cornish coast.

"Is it true that Plan B is no longer working to make sure that these plans are never revived?" Asked a reporter.

"No," said Sebastian. "We believe that the project is 'dead in the water' – only too literally – and we shall remain vigilant but as I said earlier, Plan B sets out not only to fight inappropriate development but mainly to promote projects that can help repair damage already done to the planet on which we all depend. We want to lend weight to devising ways for humans to make a living that will hold good for generations to come. In this instance, we believe that the concept of a marine reserve is exactly what is needed to help restore fish stocks and biodiversity along this part of the coast. Installing wind turbines along the boundary of the reserve not only shows fishermen where it is, but also contributes to Cornwall being self-sufficient in its energy requirements."

"Will Plan B be investing in the company that the late Mr Olver-Blythe set up to include such developments?"

"No, we shall not," said Emily, "although we are setting up a new company that includes both Mrs Olver-Blythe and the architect Clive Goodman on the board. The electricity generated will 'come ashore' on the enlarged Carnhill Estate and it is hoped to build up tourist links with the boat-owners in Polperris. They will be able to offer extended trips to the reserve, perhaps with glass-bottomed boats; and visits to Carnhill with its gardens and other attractions. We have commissioned a mobile jetty that can be anchored unobtrusively in Lantrelland bay during the tourist season so that visitors can come ashore. Mrs Olver-Blythe will be buying several electric minibuses to collect them from there."

The press also wanted to know about Peter Trenleven's presence. One asked:

"What about the church field that brought Mr Trenleven back to his ancestral county? He has told us today that he is retiring from the courts and moving to Polperris. Can you bring us up to date with his connection with The Glebe and his present intentions?"

"I think you will have to put that question to my father himself," said Sebastian, smiling.

"Is it true that there is now a close connection between him and your mother-in-law?" Someone was fishing for the gossip column of one of the Sundays.

"That's something else you might like to raise with my father. I couldn't possibly comment – but the question was asked about the Glebe Field. It now belongs to the National Trust and the present tenant, Miss Barbara Weeks, will continue to rent it for her livestock. She has agreed to guide groups around, two afternoons a week from June to September, showing them the rare plants and insects that have prospered there for centuries. When you have finished with us I'm sure you will be able to meet Miss Weeks over tea."

"We reported last year that you and your husband had decided to devote most of your two hundred million pound lottery win on setting up this Plan B organisation. You were talking about global projects but seem to have scaled everything down. What has brought this change of heart?"

Emily looked at Sebastian who invited her to answer.

"I think it was because we quickly discovered that although to us, the win was amazing and fantastic, in terms of 'saving the world' it was mere pea-nuts! Once we found out the kind of sums that people like the Gates were donating – we decided we must do what all 'little people' have to do: think globally and act closer to home – and for us, Cornwall is home!"

"Does that mean you have abandoned your original plans to help poorer countries?"

"Not at all. We shall be making financial investments in what we consider to be constructive ideas while at the same time giving those ideas maximum publicity."

"Can you give us some examples?"

"One that we've been discussing on the way here is run by a lady called Eunice Makenga in her store in Kenya. We read about it only recently. She sells seeds, fertilisers and other farm supplies. During the recent prolonged droughts, many farmers in East Africa have been left without anything to plant when the rains did come, so she has been buying seeds of traditional crops that are more resistant to dry conditions from a commercial farm at Nakuru. She's selling them in small 'trial packs' that the local people can afford. It will help them get started again. We would like to help both the lady who runs the farm at Nakuru, Janey Leakey – one of the famous archaeologist's family – and Mrs Makenga – to expand the project; and perhaps bring groups from other countries to visit, to see the scheme working. We shall also offer facility trips for reporters and TV crews to go to Kenya to follow up the story."

"And what will Plan B be opposing – now that Lantrelland Village and Marina are no longer on the scene?" Asked a news reporter, looking for leads.

"We are shocked and outraged that the government is apparently condoning the practice of 'fracking' in this country," said Sebastian. "Drilling down into bedrock, pumping water down under high pressure to crack the rocks and releasing 'natural' gas in huge quantities. It's already been found to cause minor earthquakes, which nobody wants – and worse than that, it's going to increase the release of carbon dioxide into the atmosphere, which we all know is helping to change the climate. To us it's unbelievably stupid and we are prepared to spend money on making sure that the public know and understand exactly what the consequences of fracking are."

"But surely that's politics!" Said the reporter.

"So are most things when there's any argument about them," quipped Emily. "That's why we're not registering Plan B as a charity: we want the freedom to be able make 'political' statements and take part in campaigns that we feel are in a good cause but we're not attached to any particular party."

"There's a note here on today's press release about one of Plan B's mottos which claims 'Ignorance is unforgivable: it's not bliss'. Would you like to elucidate?"

"Yes, I would," said Emily. "It's not a new concept: tax collectors and traffic police always remind us that 'ignorance is no defence', but more positively I believe that women have always known that knowledge gives you advantage – I won't say 'power' because historically, in our case, we often haven't had much of that. We share information as we go about our daily life. Men call it 'gossiping' and their own, 'intelligence' and employ spies to gather it. 'Gossip' proves very effective, locally and we believe that sharing useful information could be equally beneficial globally so Plan B is keeping a dossier of 'interesting things' – bits of news and research that we think more people should know about – to catch the attention of the public, politicians and academics."

"Can you give us some examples?" asked a TV researcher.

"We can," replied Sebastian. "We learned not long ago that meat consumption in China is double that in the United States of America. In fact, more than a quarter of all the meat produced in the world is now eaten in China. Their favourite is pork and half the world population of pigs are in China! The Americans still eat much more beef than the Chinese – it's more expensive to produce and the Chinese don't have so much available grassland for the cattle."

"If you'll pardon my asking," asked the researcher, "why is that useful information?"

"If you have anything to do with the food or farming industry, you will know that trends in global supply and demand are very important when it comes to making your own plans."

"Something else we're trying to remind people about is that globally, some four hundred million people are depending on over-pumped water for their food," added Emily. "Boreholes and wells are having to be made deeper and deeper and it simply can't go on."

This produced another flurry of questions and it was not long before Emily had to call for one last question. She pointed to an older lady who was indicating she had something to ask.

"Do you really think that Plan B will be able to make any difference to the great pattern of things?"

Sebastian and Emily looked at each other and smiled. Emily urged him to go first.

"With a bit of luck, yes," he said; "and we seem to be a very lucky couple, so far." He turned to Emily.

"I certainly hope we can contribute to making a difference – starting here at home – because we have two little boys who would like to have the same chances as we've had."

"We know others expecting children who feel the same," added Emily.

EPILOGUE

February 2014

"It's so cold! The kind of weather I remember from childhood in China! How can you get *married* at this time of year?" Zhang Li was tired and irritable as Rose drove her back towards Polperris after yet another disappointing visit to look at a bungalow on the outskirts of Looe.

"Mum – haven't you noticed? I'm beginning to show."

"To show what?"

"That I'm not as slim as I used to be – I have a bigger belly!"

"That's what happens at your age. It happened to me. I was working in the West Indies and I put it down to eating too much sweet fruit."

Rose thought it best to pull over at the next parking spot, which had a panoramic view of Talland Bay and the winter-green valleys leading down to it.

"Why are you stopping?" Zhang Li opened her bag, looking for a tissue to mop up her second cold since Christmas. "I'm not crying: I'm only blowing my nose." She was not in a good mood.

"Mum, I think it's better if I'm not driving while I tell you something. I don't want to take risks."

"Risks? What do you mean?"

"I might not be able to concentrate on my driving while I'm telling you something important."

"Why, what happened?" Zhang Li was beginning to lose patience.

"Mum; I'm really surprised you haven't realised why I'm putting on weight. I'm pregnant. That's why I'm getting married in February – before it becomes too obvious. I don't want wedding photos with me leaning over backwards to balance a huge bump."

There was a silence as Zhang Li took in the news. She wasn't as stoical as she used to be. After years of tolerating the

402

frustrations of working in developing economies, having to hold her tongue, she felt she deserved to be able to speak her mind while enjoying the smoother running of a sophisticated European country. She frowned and pursed her lips.

"Rose Johnson, what are you saying?"

"I'm pregnant, Mum! And Peter's the father – and we're getting married. You've always wanted me to get married, haven't you? Well it's happening; and in a few weeks I'll be able to tell you whether I'm having a boy or a girl."

Zhang Li was astounded. It was not something she had expected to hear after all these years.

"But what about Emily? Does she know? What did she say?"

"She laughed and hugged me! And do you know what she said?"

"Of course not!"

"She said she'd always wanted a little brother or sister – and asked why I'd waited so long. And then she tried to work out what the relationship would be between her twins and Peter! We finished up in hysterics – even after we'd try to draw up a family tree. It was so complicated! But she's thrilled to bits about having a sibling."

"What's a sibling?" Zhang Li's English didn't yet stretch to such words. She had insisted Rose spoke to her in English. For clarity Rose temporarily defied her mother and switched to Swahili the language of her childhood home.

"It's a brother or sister. Peter is going to be your son-in-law; my new baby will be your grandson or grand-daughter; and the aunt or uncle of the twins, your great grand-children."

"Speak in English, please." Zhang Li was now grumpy. "I wish you had told me before. You are too old for babies – over forty! Who else knows?"

"Well, Emily and Sebastian; Peter, of course; the doctor and the midwife. I haven't told anyone else but it will soon be obvious, that's why we're making the arrangements with the Registry Office."

"But why didn't you tell me?"

"Because I wanted to be sure before I said anything. I didn't want you to be disappointed if I lost it or anything." Rose took her mother's hand and kissed it. "You'll be thrilled to have another baby to make a fuss of."

The thought of having three little children in the family certainly appealed to Zhang Li. Even at the recent Christmas celebrations in Polperris she had enjoyed the position of matriarch, not having to busy herself in the kitchen but being given one baby or the other to hold and love. It had been good to experience family members making sure she was warm enough. It wasn't something she had known before. She liked Peter: he was so polite and charming like his son; and he had made extra efforts to help her feel at home. During the unveiling and maelstrom of media coverage it was he who had made sure she wasn't left out of things. He had explained what was going on and introduced her to some of his acquaintances, telling them of her recent work with UNESCO and other United Nations special agencies.

"I think Looe is too far away," she said, changing the subject abruptly. "I want to live in Polperris, so I can walk round to your place. I didn't like that bungalow, either."

Rose decided, with relief, that her mother had accepted the surprise announcement and started the car up, and resuming their short journey home. She took the hint and dropped the subject of weddings and babies.

"Well there's one little cottage in the Warren, a couple of doors up from the Shell House but there isn't much garden and it could be a bit noisy in summer," she said.

"I don't mind noise," said Zhang Li. "I'm used to it; and a few pots will be plenty for us. Your father's arthritis isn't getting any better: he likes a boat better than a garden, anyway. It's not that house with the garden wall right on the harbour, is it? He's always been dreaming of living there so he can step out of the boat on to his own lawn."

"It is! But it's expensive."

"I don't care – we've all got plenty of money now, haven't we?"

404

Later, when Zhang Li had gone out with Charles to buy a newspaper Rose brought Peter up to date with the news.

"She's all right about it, then?" said Peter. "She didn't say anything when she came in."

"She wouldn't; she expects you to tell her yourself – as a respectful son-in-law to be. Anyway, she will have wanted to tell Dad, first."

"I'm not sure you'll want them living quite as close as that, though, will you? If they like the cottage. I'm sure your Dad will love it: we'd be able to wave to them across the water: it's only a minute down the road."

"I was wondering; but just think. I'm going to be so busy this next year or two, what with the baby and all those commissions that are coming in; and you'll have to help with the courses, if we want to keep them going. It will be a godsend, having a babysitter so close; and someone to help host events in the gallery. She and Dad are experts at entertaining: they've done it all round the world."

"So much for my retirement!"

"You haven't got time to retire! You're about to become a Daddy again – and you're getting a recycled young wife and I want you in good order so you'd better delay this 'getting old' business."

§

"If I had said, two years ago, that we'd both finish up living in Cornwall, married and starting new families, what would you have thought, Dad?" Sebastian and his father had decided it was 'time for a walk' and having reached the shelter at the beginning of the cliff path were catching their breath, looking back at Polperris, a haze of wood smoke from the occasional bonfire hanging in the protecting valley. The air was hardly moving and pale sunlight gave the whole village pastel shades of colour.

"Or that you would be a multi-millionaire running a global action group while I painted landscapes and helped out at art classes – quite ridiculous. I'd have said you were going dotty." Peter turned to head westwards on the path. Sebastian followed, laughing.

"What happened, then?"

"It depends when you want to begin," said Peter. "I suppose you could say that it was in about 1145 when someone began building the church at Lantrelland. Every generation or two since then has had to replace its roof. Fund raising has always created problems and we got caught up with the latest repercussions of laying that first foundation stone."

"I'd love to be able to read a history of all the previous restorations, wouldn't you?" said Sebastian, increasing his pace a little to keep well within hearing distance as his father strode ahead.

"Our chapter would make quite good reading," replied his father. "I expect St Gluvias had several benefactors along the way but I doubt whether they included many lottery winners, although fortunes were still made by luck as well as conquest!"

"Funny how our name helped pull us back to Cornwall, though, isn't it?"

"Did it?"

"Yes – Harry said that was one of the reasons you sent me down here – my Cornish name would look good, fighting to save The Glebe."

"Did he? That sounds like Harry being Harry but of course he was right. Shall we pop in an say hello to Miss Weeks? We might get a cup of tea."

"Good idea, Dad! We can take another look at the Glebe at the same time."

"I can tell her about Rosie's latest scan – she'll be very pleased. I expect she'll volunteer to be a godmother, especially now we know it's going to be a girl."

"Are you going to have any time to paint? What with Rosie getting all these commissions *and* having the baby. You'll finish up as a house-husband!"

"I think we shall be able to afford 'day-time cover' that will give us quite a few hours to paint – but if necessary I'll be the one who's on hand for teething and the school run. It will be such a pleasure not having to go to court!"

"I wonder if my new sister will look like all the other Johnson women?"

"Have to wait and see!"

"Mm".

§

"Shall I mention my theory that the Chinese might be distant relatives of Bushmen?" Zhang Li was gathering her thoughts for the forthcoming lecture.

"Why not," said Charles. "It's a good yarn and who knows, it might be possible. People are such amazing creatures. If my ancestors came from the Rift Valley in East Africa and finished up in Northern Germany, then Western France and finally Cornwall, yours might have turned right and finished up in Shenyang!"

"And now look where we've finished up! I've been captured by a Western Imperialist and brought to a fishing village in Cornwall."

"It was your idea!" Charles laughed.

"No it wasn't: it was you, wanting a boat again."

"It was that daughter of ours. She'll never want to leave Polperris. She's not like us, always wanting to be at the next place."

"Well this is her home, isn't it? Poor child – we didn't let her settle anywhere really, did we?"

"Emily's the same. She never really liked living in London. She's got quite a Cornish accent.

"Will you go then?" Charles looked up from *Yachting Monthly* – what he called his 'favourite comic'.

"Of course!" said Zhang Li. "It is a great honour and there are still people around who I went to school with. I'd love to show them that the new generation in China appreciate the work I've done. Some of them gave me a hard time when my father was so unfairly disgraced. He was right, though and they were wrong: because of him and what he taught me I've had a very successful career."

"Do you want me to come too?"

"Of course! Don't you want to?"

"I do, Zhang Li! I would love to see where you were born and grew up; and the university at Shenyang. I shall be very proud of you. What have they asked you to talk about?"

"Prehistoric wall paintings in Africa."

"Your favourite subject!"

"Yes – and I've already thought of a good title: 'Twenty thousand years of African Culture' then I can include all my latest work, too."

"Does it really go back that far?" Charles asked.

"Bushmen paintings in uKhahlamba, South Africa, certainly do," she said. "Then there are those we know about in Tanzania."

"Without which I would never have met you!" Charles put an affectionate arm around an unresisting Zhang Li and kissed her on the cheek. "Are you sure you want to be seen with a 'foreign devil' husband?"

"It's not like that now! You will be treated nicely, don't worry!"

"As long as I don't have to sit on the stage while you give your lecture."

"You won't – but you will have to be there when I get made a visiting professor! I want people to know we can live anywhere and marry anyone we like!"

"You've got it all planned out already – and the letter's only just come!"

"Why not? We only live once!"

"We're not sure of that, either," challenged Charles. "What about all those spirits: and reincarnation?"

"We'll find *that* out in due course!"

THE END

About the author:

Award-winning writer and journalist George Macpherson was educated at St Paul's School, London and Seale Hayne Agricultural College (now the University of Plymouth).

He worked for the United Nations' International Labour Organisation in Africa as a technical advisor on appropriate technology before joining BBC World Service as a producer, later becoming Programme Organiser of the Swahili Service.

Leaving BBC staff to become editor of a monthly farming magazine, he continued his broadcasting on a freelance basis before going fully independent, starting his own daily rural news service on the internet for the Farming Online website. He continued presenting and producing farming and wildlife, medical and musical programmes for BBC World Service, BBC Five Live and BBC Radio Four before moving with his wife Jane, to France to write novels, learn the cello at the local music conservatoire and join in amateur musical events in the Dordogne. This is his fourth novel published as an e-book.

While in UK George was a Fellow of the Royal Society of Arts; Fellow of the Royal Agricultural Society; and an Honorary Associate of the British Veterinary Association.

2452814R00222

Printed in Great Britain
by Amazon.co.uk, Ltd.,
Marston Gate.